Carolina Crossing

Cape Fear Legacy, Volume 2

Kit Hawthorne

Published by Kit Hawthorne, 2024.

CAROLINA CROSSING

First edition. February 20, 2024.

Copyright © 2024 Kit Hawthorne.

ISBN: 979-8224865703

Written by Kit Hawthorne.

This book is dedicated to everyone who's ever fought to defend home and liberty, who's been outgunned, outmanned, disheartened, and despised, but held on anyway, because it was the right thing to do.

Chapter One

North Carolina, 1780.

Fergus Shaw peered through his spyglass at a jagged heap of fire-blasted stone. It might have been an ancient cairn on a Scottish heath, but the battered mantelpiece and charred timbers showed it to be the chimney of a burned house, with a birds' nest tucked in a hollow between stones, and pine seedlings springing from the old cellar. A block or so behind the house loomed the hollow hulk of a church, with sunlight shining through the fallen roof, and brambles spilling out of windows and doors in a riot of spring green. More pine seedlings stood in the streets of what had once been the thriving port city of Brunswick Town. Farther back still, the pine forest rose somber and dark, stretching away from the western banks of the river called Fear.

He lowered the spyglass, and the scene shrank to a miniature ruin far away across the broad expanse of water. The sun shone warm on his shoulders, penetrating the thin linen of his best summer frock coat. Beside him, his sister Catalyn fanned herself.

"You shouldn't have come," he told her. "You're still not strong enough."

She'd grown thin and pale since the baby came. Fergus had heard Tavish, his brother-in-law, all but order her to take to her bed and rest. But Catalyn had only laughed and said the work wouldn't do itself, and no one could argue with that. With only an occasional small vessel able to slip out of port for a quick trip to the French West Indies and back, the supply of goods in town was meager at best, and there was no money to buy any of it anyhow, because they couldn't sell their own wares either. The demand for tar, pitch, and turpentine, the Shaw family's livelihood before the war, had all but dried up. Everyone had to work harder than ever to keep food on the table and clothes on their backs. And now here they were, about to take in someone even worse off than themselves.

Not that Fergus grudged Miss Melina Bryant a place in his father's house. Taking her in was no more than common decency—and Patriots must help one another, now more than ever. As Mr. Franklin had said, *We must, indeed, all hang together, or most assuredly we shall hang separately.*

"I had to come, brother," Catalyn said. "'Twould hardly be seemly for you to meet Miss Bryant by yourself and drive her back to the farm across twelve miles of lonely road."

"Nay, but I could have brought Nessa or Morna instead."

"I'm the eldest daughter of the house. 'Tis right that I be the one to welcome Miss Bryant."

"You mean you wanted to keep an eye on me. Make sure my manners aren't lacking."

A hint of a smile curled the corners of Catalyn's mouth. "Aye, well, you do tend to gawp. You're an excellent young man, Fergus, but conversation is not your strong suit. Have the passengers finished boarding the ferry yet?"

He pointed the spyglass across the river toward the southern edge of Brunswick Town and adjusted the depth until the ferry dock came into focus. "Aye. They've just started crossing."

A murmur of relief ran through the small crowd at the river's eastern shore—Patriots from Wilmington and the surrounding countryside who'd risen before dawn to drive to the ferry and meet the refugees from war-torn Charlestown. Even the best dressed among the townsfolk looked threadbare, out at the elbows and down at the heels. Four years of war and blockade had taken their toll.

Through the glass, he saw passengers and baggage filling every inch of the flat-bottomed, shallow-draft ferryboat. Two upright posts stood along one side of the boat, with a stout rope passing through holes in their tops, like a single thread running through a pair of needles. The rope's ends were fastened one at each shoreline. The ferryman pulled on the rope, hand over hand, moving himself and the boat along the rope, and drawing the ferry across the river.

"What a shame that Sir Henry wouldn't let the refugees travel by ship," Catalyn said. "'Twould have been so much quicker and easier. I don't understand what he was thinking."

"I do. 'Twas a senseless act of petty tyranny. He did it because he could."

"I suppose. Poor Miss Bryant. Six weeks of siege warfare, then an overland journey in summertime, with the British army at large in the countryside, plundering and...insulting the inhabitants."

Fergus didn't answer. They'd all heard the stories of how the British Legion's marauding dragoons treated the property, and the wives, of Patriot soldiers in South Carolina. Nothing like that had happened close to home, at least not yet. In fact, for most of the war, the British had left North Carolina alone.

Four years earlier, in seventy-six, Loyalists had raised a large force around Cross Creek with the goal of sweeping down the Cape Fear River to Wilmington, the province's most important port. The British had believed North Carolina was ripe for conquest and, once taken, would act as a springboard for vanquishing the rest of the southern colonies.

They'd been wrong. Fergus had been among the Patriot soldiers who'd beaten the Loyalists at Moore's Creek Bridge, along with his father and brother-in-law. The British had left North Carolina and not come back.

But they'd looked southward again once France entered the war on America's side. Still convinced that the southern colonies were hotbeds of Loyalism eager to return to royal rule, the British had launched offensives against Georgia and South Carolina. Savannah had fallen late in seventy-eight, and Charlestown a year and a half after. British raiding parties spread from the capital into the South Carolina Lowcountry: stealing horses, plundering provisions, burning houses. Now they were moving into the mountainous backcountry of both Carolinas. No one doubted they'd try to take Wilmington soon.

The ferry was close enough now for Fergus to see faces. Women and children, mostly, and a few boys and old men, but no men of soldiering age. They looked draggled and weary—all but one. A girl, standing near the bow, shoulders back and head high. She was slender and shapely, leaning forward with an air of open eagerness, like a ship's figurehead.

The ferry reached the dock and was made fast, and the passengers began to disembark. Most of them knew their Wilmington hosts and went straight to them, but Fergus and Catalyn had never laid eyes on Miss Bryant. They knew only her age, which was twenty, a year younger than Fergus.

The crowd thinned, leaving only one unclaimed passenger—the figurehead girl.

She was smaller than she'd looked, with hair of rich, vibrant gold, piled high in coiled masses beneath an improbable hat whose plumes seemed to leap. Her features were fine-boned—delicate, even—but with a set to the chin that made Fergus think of an Arabian saddle horse.

And her clothing! Fergus was no expert on women's apparel, but this young woman's gown had a great many parts: panels and ruffles and laces, and ruching, if ruching was the name of that crinkled stuff around the edges. A very fine gown indeed, far finer than the one Catalyn had on—finer even than Catalyn's best gown, that she'd worn to her wedding.

The girl swept the dock with a quick, searching glance, then approached Catalyn with a smile.

"Miss Shaw, I presume?"

If Catalyn was as shocked as Fergus, she gave no sign. "I am Mrs. MacGregor, Mr. Shaw's married daughter," she said. "This is my brother Fergus. And you must be Miss Bryant."

Fergus could not agree. Nay, this spirited, vivid, befeathered, beribboned creature must *not* be Melina Bryant, the war-starved refugee he'd pitied from his heart only moments ago.

"Indeed I am. Delighted to make your acquaintance, Mrs. MacGregor, Mr. Shaw."

The ladies curtseyed, Miss Bryant dipping so low that Fergus could see deep into the creamy bosom above her gown's low neckline. As Catalyn rose, she cleared her throat at Fergus, and he realized he was standing stiff as a shingle, and gawping like a country oaf.

He took off his hat, bowed, and muttered a quick "How d'you do, Miss Bryant?"

She shrugged and said something he couldn't understand.

"I beg your pardon?"

Amusement flickered in her eyes—hazel eyes flecked with green and gold, haughty eyes beneath high-arched brows. "The phrase is French, Mr. Shaw. It means I'm as well as can be expected, which at present is not very well at all."

Fergus felt his cheeks flush. He'd had a little Latin from Reverend Tate's school in town, but no French. He ought to have at least recognized it, for his mother was French herself and had sometimes read aloud from her French Bible, but he'd never wished to study it, nor felt the lack of his knowledge until now. He didn't like being made to feel its lack. And he didn't like Melina Bryant, would never like her, didn't want to like her.

"How was your journey, Miss Bryant?" asked Catalyn.

"Abominable! Mile after mile of rutted roads through uncivilized country. Bad food and public inns, and not even a girl to do my hair. Nothing to see from the Cooper River to Georgetown but marsh grass, oaks, palmettos, and pines, with an occasional rice or indigo plantation. And the heat was so oppressive, I was simply gasping for air. The Long Bay was a change for the better. Such a lonely stretch of coastline! The road was good—hard fine sand packed with seashells, right alongside the Atlantic—and the ocean breeze cooled the air wonderfully. But then I thought what a terrible spot it would be to meet highwaymen, for there's absolutely no place to take shelter. On the other hand, if desperate men *did* try to waylay us, we'd see them coming from miles off. So I scoured the horizon for horsemen, and imagined how I'd fight, and that passed the time better than anything. I was almost disappointed when we reached Withers Swash without meeting so much as a single brigand. Then we crossed the Little River into North Carolina. We stayed last night at the plantation at York, and early this morning set off for the ferry. And here we are."

She smiled at Fergus, looking as if she were secretly laughing at him behind those gold-flecked eyes.

"I'll get your luggage," he said.

"'Tisn't much," said Miss Bryant. "I've only the one valise, the little red one over there. We weren't allowed to bring more. My trunks will follow later by wagon."

The red valise was not what Fergus would have called *little*, but he loaded it without comment, then silently helped Catalyn and Miss Bryant into the carriage before climbing into the box seat. It was a relief to put his back to Miss Bryant, because now he couldn't be expected to contribute to the conversation.

"'Tis ever so good of you all to take me in, Mrs. MacGregor," said Miss Bryant.

"Not at all," Catalyn replied. "We're family, are we not?"

"That's right. Fifth cousins, is it?"

"Sixth. Our fathers are fifth cousins."

This family relationship had only recently come to light. Five months earlier, in January, the Wilmington militia had gone to Charlestown in anticipation of a British invasion. Father, Fergus, and Tavish kept their terms of militia service staggered, so there'd always be at least two men at home. This time it had been Father's turn. He'd gone to work erecting breastworks, and one night, in a Charlestown tavern, he'd met Mr. Bryant. When Father gave his name, Mr. Bryant said that his mother was a Shaw, and after much comparison of family trees, they'd learned that they were kin, descended from two brothers from the Scottish lowlands. One brother had gone to County Down in Ulster Plantation, the other to Barbados.

By evening's end, Father and Mr. Bryant were friends. Besides being fifth cousins, they were both widowers, eldest sons, irrationally afraid of grub worms, and exactly the same age, even sharing a birthday.

Father's militia duties didn't leave much leisure for social calls, but he did see Mr. Bryant once more before the end of his enlistment period in March. By then the entrenchments were finished, and the British had their siege works well underway, with a few artillery pieces already pointed at the city and a flotilla lying in wait outside Charlestown Harbor.

After Father's return, Tavish set off with another group of militiamen to reinforce the beleaguered city, carrying with him a letter from Father to Mr. Bryant. That force never arrived. They received word on the road that the siege was over. Charlestown had fallen to the British.

It was a sickening blow, the worst Patriot defeat yet in a war that had brought many defeats. The Patriot army wasn't granted the honors of war, but was marched out of the city without colors and without arms. More than five thousand troops surrendered unconditionally, including nearly three thousand Continentals from Virginia and the Carolinas. Four hundred cannon, five thousand muskets, three Continental warships, assorted smaller vessels—the toll went on and on, through livestock and property, powder and munitions, and the lists of the dead.

By the first of June, Tavish was back home—with Father's letter still in his pocket. Two days later, Father received a letter from Mr. Bryant, written from a prison ship in Charlestown harbor. Melina, his only child, was alone now, in a city ruled by martial law. Would Mr. Shaw be so good as to receive her into his home, and then send her on to other friends in Newport or Boston, where Mr. Bryant would join her as soon as he could gain his freedom?

Father had read the letter aloud to the family, then set it down on the dining table and said, "Well." No one had asked or wondered what answer he'd give. Of course they'd take her in. Times were lean, but the Shaws were far from destitute. Mr. Bryant was a Patriot and a kinsman. He'd entrusted Father with his daughter's care, and Father would not fail him.

Now, as Fergus drove Melina Bryant home and listened to her lively stream of chatter, he couldn't escape a sense of unreality. Was this the poor fugitive who was to receive his family's charity? She sounded like a giddy girl on her way to a ball.

"What a charming road this is, with the zigzag fences and the fruit trees so heavy laden! How far is it to your father's estate, Mrs. MacGregor?"

"I'm afraid we've a long drive ahead of us, a good three hours. But my sister Nessa will have dinner ready, and then perhaps you'd like to go upstairs and rest before supper."

"Indeed I would. 'Twill be so luxurious to stretch out on a real bed in a private home, and not have to hurry away in the morning. Tell me, what was that sad wreck of a town where I boarded the ferry?"

"That was Brunswick Town," Catalyn replied. "It used to be quite a prosperous little place. Heavy-draft vessels would stop there to let off some of their cargo before continuing to Wilmington. The British razed it in seventy-six and it hasn't been rebuilt. The ferry used to do a brisk business but 'tis hardly used at all anymore."

"What a shame. I saw the ruins of a fine building near the riverbank. It looked like two stories, with the remains of good stables and coach houses and a fine orchard. It reminded me of Trailing Oaks."

"That was Bellfont," Catalyn said. "One of the governors built it years ago. 'Twas a very grand house indeed, before the British burned it down."

So the governor's mansion reminded Miss Bryant of home? What would she say, how would she look, when she saw Father's *estate*, and the bedroom she must share with Nessa and Morna? Fergus didn't want to know, couldn't bear to watch. But he couldn't always be away from Miss Bryant. She'd be there for dinner, and supper, and breakfast tomorrow, on and on until Father could manage to get her onto a ship bound for Newport or Boston.

The Haulover Road had never seemed so long.

BY THE TIME THEY REACHED the home track, Fergus's temples were throbbing from Miss Bryant's trilling laughter and French phrases. Near the cookhouse, his brother Rory—twelve years old, with gangly limbs and a mop of dark hair—came running to take the reins. Fergus halted at the dooryard gate and helped Miss Bryant and Catalyn out of the carriage. As he unloaded the red valise, he steeled himself for Miss Bryant's reaction to the plain house with its unpainted riven siding.

But she wasn't looking at the house. She was watching Father as he approached along the orchard footpath, dressed in his work clothes, with his canvas tool bag slung over his shoulder.

"Is that your hired man?" she asked.

Fergus had to get away, now, before he said something he'd regret. Rory stood holding the reins, ready to take charge of the carriage and Boudicca. Fergus shoved the red valise into his little brother's arms, climbed back into the box seat, took back the reins, and drove to the carriage house himself.

The smell of horse and leather and neatsfoot oil calmed him instantly. He took off his frock coat, loosed his neck stock, and turned up his cuffs, then unhitched Boudicca and gave her a brisk rubdown. While she ate her oats, he wiped the harness and leathers and hung them on their racks.

The work was finished too soon. Fergus didn't want to join the others, didn't want to hear what fresh outrages Miss Bryant was visiting on his family.

Perhaps this would be a good time to give the carriage a thorough cleaning.

With a bristle brush he cleaned sand and grit from the underside and wheels, then wiped down the body with a soft rag. He worked slowly, lovingly, losing all sense of time, until he heard footsteps.

"I'll be along presently," he said without turning.

"Very well, but you'd better hurry if you want anything to eat other than oats and bran mash."

It was Miss Bryant's voice.

"Nessa sent me to call you in to dinner," she said. "Well, she told Morna to do it, but I said I'd go. My, aren't you a careful horseman?"

Fergus didn't answer. He ran his rag into the carriage's grooves to remove all traces of dirt. Maybe if he ignored her, she'd go away.

Then he heard her walking toward Boudicca's stall. He turned to warn her off, but saw her moving slowly and quietly. Boudicca pricked her ears forward in calm interest and sniffed the visitor. Miss Bryant gave her a good scratching under the mane and murmured to her in a low, loving tone.

Well, she knew how to approach a horse, at least.

"I saw the geldings in the paddock," Miss Bryant said. "Handsome fellows. Are they brothers?"

"Aye. The grullo is Hector, and the black is Bran."

"And what is this lady's name?"

"Boudicca."

"After the Celtic queen?"

Fergus glanced up. "Aye. Not many know that."

"Well, I may be a bit more distant from my Celtic roots than your family, but I do read. I know about Hector too, and Bran the Blessed. All very martial names."

"True. Bran's two years old now, and he's getting martial training."

"Cavalry?"

"Light infantry. He'll carry me and my gear to battle and home again. Not as demanding as cavalry work, but he must learn not to bolt at the sound of gunfire. 'Twill be a boon to me to have him trained. Soldiers who provide their own mounts and weapons are allowed a shorter enlistment period."

There was no need to elaborate. Everyone knew about the shortages plaguing the Patriot forces—of horses, men, arms, gunpowder, and money. Fergus was tired of hearing and talking about it. How the Patriots had managed to hold out as long as they had was a marvel.

Miss Bryant laid her cheek against Boudicca's and curved her arm under the horse's neck. "The British brought horses with them from New York to the South last December—enough for the Light Dragoons, the Jaegers, and the mounted portion of the Legion. The voyage was rough, and not many of the horses reached the shore alive. Perhaps they drowned in the holds of sinking ships, or had their legs broken in rough seas, or were blown so far off course that their food and water ran out. Perhaps all three."

Fergus laid his rag aside. Miss Bryant's face was closed and still, her lashes casting a fringed shadow on her cheeks, as she combed her fingers through Boudicca's mane. "Do you know, Mr. Shaw," she said, "there were over a hundred and fifty Americans killed in the Charlestown siege—soldiers and civilians—and around a hundred British. But it is the horses that haunt me. I think of them being led onto those New York transports, trusting and obedient, never to see green grass or open sky again."

"I think of it too," said Fergus. "Of the use and misuse we make of beasts in war, I mean. I sometimes wonder if 'tis wrong of me to train Bran as my infantry mount, knowing what harm could come to him. But if I don't, and we lose the war, what's to happen to him, or to me and my family? Nay, we must do all we can to win as quickly as possible, and poor Bran must do his part."

Miss Bryant sighed. "You needn't justify it to me, Mr. Shaw. I know the hard choices we must all make in time of war."

"How did the British replace the mounts they lost in the voyage?" Fergus asked.

"Stole as many as they found on farms and plantations, and then—you've heard of Banastre Tarleton's Legion? They attacked the American cavalry and militiamen who were guarding the upper reaches of the Cooper, north of the city. Fifteen Americans killed, eighteen wounded, sixty-three taken prisoner—and ninety-eight fine American horses driven off. Good cavalry mounts, probably better than those the British had lost on the voyage. And with the American cavalry neutralized, the British were free to plunder the lands east of the Cooper, raping and despoiling. Aye, Mr. Shaw, I said rape. That's the proper word for it. You needn't look shocked. I detest polite figures of speech. There's no sense using a teaspoon to do a spade's work."

Fergus didn't know what to say. He knew the ugly things men did in war, but he couldn't realize them in his heart. He didn't like to think how thin was the veneer of civilization, or how easily it could be peeled back.

"'Tis a shame about the lost cavalry mounts," he said at last.

"Aye, shame is the right word for it. 'Twas the militia's fault."

"How so?"

She shrugged. "It is always the militia's fault. They were present, therefore they failed."

"But we cannot be sure how the Patriots were disposed, or their attackers."

"I beg your pardon, we can be perfectly sure. An alarum was raised, the militia fled, confusion ensued, and the British won the day. The militia disappoint whenever they are relied upon. That is the one thing they can be depended upon to do."

"Ten to one they were wretchedly armed," Fergus said sharply, "with no powder in their muskets, or no muskets at all. Sometimes all they have is homemade axes and broadswords."

Miss Bryant made a scoffing sound. "I'm sick of hearing excuses for the militia. The truth is they've performed miserably time and again. They simply cannot hold their ground when fired upon."

"Hold their ground when..." Fergus stood. "Miss Bryant, have *you* ever been fired upon? Have you stood shoulder to shoulder with other men, facing a wall of soldiers a hundred times better armed and better trained than you'll ever be? Have you seen the clouds of smoke, and heard the gunfire and the cries of men falling around you, while awaiting your own order to fire? How well do you think you'd hold *your* ground in such a case?"

"'Tis immaterial how well I could do so. *I* am not a militiaman. Is it hard, to maintain discipline while firing and being fired upon? I daresay, but that is the militia's job. And they've failed at it, over and over, like your own Wilmington militia last year at Brier Creek. Their failure is what made the British invasion of South Carolina possible. They turned tail and fled—all the way back to North Carolina, by some accounts."

"Some fled, aye. Others were sliced open by British bayonets, or drowned in the swamps. I wasn't there, but two friends of mine were killed in the battle. The men were badly led and badly supplied. General Ashe had chosen a death trap of a camp site, with its back to the creek and no escape route—"

"Badly led, badly supplied, badly situated. So say all who fail to deliver what is required of them. The truth of the matter is, militia units are inadequate for major engagements. They do well enough for fatigue details, but they're worthless under fire."

Anger rose hot in Fergus's chest and face, and his voice shook as he said, "One of those fatigue details, Miss Bryant, was the construction of breastworks to defend your city, and one of the worthless men doing it was my father."

The light suddenly dimmed. Fergus turned and saw his fourteen-year-old sister, Morna, standing in the doorway, blocking the incoming sunshine. Her eyes were round with shock.

"Catalyn says to tell you both to come to dinner," she said in a small voice, then hurried away, her red ringlets fluttering behind her.

Miss Bryant gave Fergus one last lofty look, then followed Morna out like a schooner carrying full sail.

BY THE TIME HE REACHED the house, Fergus was his own master again, with his waistcoat neatly buttoned and his face composed. Lachlan met him at the door, crawling on all fours with his legs held straight to keep his knees from catching on his baby frock. He grabbed Fergus's ankles, pulled himself up, and grinned with all six of his teeth. Fergus swung his nephew high into the air, making him squeal with laughter.

His sister Nessa met him in the passage. She was a tall girl of eighteen with an easy smile and shining masses of red-brown hair.

"There you are," she said. "I was beginning to think you'd been waylaid by pirates."

"In a forest?" Fergus replied.

She gave him a mischievous smile. "War is hard on everyone. Pirates are having to go farther inland for new recruits."

Fergus followed her into the dining hall and handed Lachlan to Tavish, who settled Lachlan into his high chair at the corner beside Catalyn. Tavish was shorter than Fergus, with dark hair that was always springing free from its queue in front. He and Fergus had always been good friends.

By now, the others had taken their seats: Catalyn and Tavish at Father's right and left; Nessa, as mistress of the table, at its upper end; and Rory and Morna at her right and left. Miss Bryant's place was next to Catalyn's, facing the last empty seat—Fergus's seat.

"But surely we are missing one, Mr. Shaw," said Miss Bryant. "I know my father said you had three daughters and three sons."

Fergus froze. So did everyone else.

"He was not mistaken," Father said with level calm.

Miss Bryant glanced around the table and dropped the subject.

Father said grace, and he and Nessa began serving.

"We often eat dinner and supper together," Nessa told Miss Bryant. "With food so scarce, 'tis easier to pool our resources than for Catalyn and Tavish to eat alone in their own house."

Catalyn gave Nessa a pointed look. From years of experience, Fergus was an expert interpreter of Catalyn's looks. This one meant that it wasn't polite to speak of food shortages in front of a house guest.

"You must show me your house after dinner, Mrs. MacGregor," said Miss Bryant. "I wasn't aware it was nearby."

"But you must have seen it when you arrived," said Tavish. "The little cabin just northwest of the big house. You would have passed it on your way to the carriage house."

He and Catalyn were fiercely proud of their cabin, but on an estate like Trailing Oaks, a dwelling of that size would probably house the slaves.

"Ah, of course," said Miss Bryant brightly. "How silly of me."

"Did you see much of Wilmington this morning, Miss Bryant?" asked Nessa.

"Nay. Only a few blocks of bad road, with some scattered houses and gardens."

Father chuckled. "Then ye saw most of it. Ye'll see the remainder, such as it is, tomorrow when we go to church."

"Church?" said Miss Bryant. "But tomorrow isn't a holiday."

"'Tis the Sabbath," said Father. "And on the Sabbath, we go to church."

"I see," said Miss Bryant. "Pray, how long are the services?"

"It varies, depending on who's bringing the sermon, but generally, three hours for morning and four in the afternoon."

"Morning and afternoon? There must scarcely be time to come home in between!"

"We dinnae come home in between. We stay in town and eat our dinner on the grounds."

Miss Bryant sat back, visibly stunned.

Rory's grey eyes peered soberly at her. "Don't you go to church in Charlestown, Miss Bryant?" he asked.

"Aye, but not every Sunday."

"I thought your father was a Churchman," said Morna.

"He is. But that only means he's on the vestry board, in charge of collecting taxes and such."

"Taxes?" Rory repeated, looking scandalized.

"Miss Bryant adheres to the Church of England," said Father, "which collects taxes for the support of its minister and the upkeep of its property."

"But surely not anymore," said Nessa. "Not since the war."

"Aye, same as ever," said Miss Bryant. "How else could we pay our way?"

"The same way we poor dissenters do," said Fergus. "With voluntary donations."

Catalyn gave him a look.

"It must have been dreadful for you, Miss Bryant, living in a city under siege," she said.

Miss Bryant lifted her chin with a hard smile. "Nay, 'twas fascinating. Papa took me to look at the fortifications. Many of the first families watched, ladies included. The British dug one of their approach trenches in a straight line, not the zigzag that Vauban says to use."

"That who says to use?" asked Rory.

"Sébastien Le Prestre de Vauban," said Miss Bryant, the French name pouring effortlessly from her lips. "He was a Marshal of France in the last century, and a brilliant military engineer. His treatise on siegecraft and fortification is considered the authoritative work on the subject."

"Then why didn't the British do what he said?"

"Because the British engineers didn't think the Americans deserved the compliment of the zigzag approach. I'm afraid the British have a low opinion of us and our abilities. In the case of the approach trench we caused them to regret their carelessness."

The "we" grated on Fergus. It wasn't as if Miss Bryant herself had been among the artillerists firing solid shot down the straight trenches into the British work parties.

"Did you watch the British fleet sail into the harbor?" Nessa asked.

"Aye, from the sea wall. 'Twas the twentieth of March. The moon was full, and the spring flood tide was in effect."

"Och, ye maritime people and your tides," Tavish said. "I cannae understand tides at all. They are an occult mystery, and those who plot tide charts are sorcerers."

"Nay, tides make perfect sense when you take into account the varying gravitational forces of the moon and sun and the effects of local conditions. The spring flood tide happens in conjunction with the full moon and vernal equinox. The sun and the moon work together, producing the highest tide of all. That's how the British admiral managed to get the British warships past the Bar, which would have been impossible if the American commodore had done his job. Charlestown, you must understand, has many natural defenses: mud flats and marshes, tidal creeks, and swamps. But its greatest defense is the Bar."

She pushed her plate toward the middle of the table and used her fork to shape some of her mashed Jerusalem artichokes into a triangle. "The city of Charlestown is on a peninsula—like this. The peninsula is flanked by two rivers, the Ashley and the Cooper, here and here." She indicated the bare areas on either side of the triangle, then lightly pressed the tines of her fork onto the tip of the triangle at right angles, forming a grid. "These will do for the streets. Then over here—but no, first we must have a compass rose." She drew a jeweled pin from her hair. A curl came loose. She tossed it back and laid the pin beside her plate, pointing it toward her side of the table. "There. That way is north. Now, east of the Cooper is the mainland, with the parishes of St. Thomas and Christ Church." She pulled the small platter of scalloped tomatoes alongside her plate, close to the table's edge on Catalyn's side. "And all along the coast of South Carolina and Georgia, we have the sea islands,

James, Johns, Edisto, and ever so many others, but we need only concern our-selves with James, south and west of the city"—she dragged a large platter of fish cutlets closer to her plate—"and Sullivan's, off the southern coast of Christ Church parish. Here, this will be Sullivan's Island." She laid a biscuit on the tablecloth near the small platter.

She looked around at everyone. "Now, the thing that makes Sullivan's Is-land special is Fort Moultrie, though I'm afraid its glory is long past. Let's see...what shall we use for..."

Rory handed her the salt cellar.

"Aha! Thank you, my good sir," she said, and pressed the salt cellar onto the biscuit.

"So, back in seventy-six, the British tried for the first time to take Charlestown. General Lee, who'd come from New York to supervise the city's defense, didn't like Fort Moultrie. In fact, he had said it ought to be abandoned. But the Charlestonians wouldn't listen. The fort had been made of palmetto logs, and you know how spongy they are. When the British fleet"—she placed a small dish of pickled peppers close to the biscuit—"fired on the fort, the palmetto didn't splinter or shatter. The shot just sank in. Some of the balls even bounced off the walls! Meanwhile, the American guns at the fort pounded the British warships. One of their frigates ran aground and had to be destroyed. The British hurried back onto their remaining ships and sailed out of the harbor as fast as they could." Miss Bryant drew the pick-led peppers away in retreat.

"Did you see the battle?" asked Catalyn.

"Aye. I was sixteen years old. 'Twas a glorious day for Charlestown. But I'm afraid the victory made us prideful. This latest siege was different. The British weren't trying to take Fort Moultrie—they had only to sail past it. And that is what they should never have been able to do, because of the Bar."

She reached over, snatched Fergus's biscuit off his plate, tore it into pieces, and arranged the pieces in a row running across the table from Catalyn's place to Tavish's. "The Bar is a long sandbank from Sullivan's Island to Lighthouse Island. In some spots the water is but three feet deep, and ships must sail through the channels to keep from running aground. The best channel is the Ship Channel, here at the south end. The American fleet at Charlestown was much smaller than the British fleet, of course, but the

Americans had the defensive position. We had three of the great Continental frigates, a sloop of war, and more. The harbor should have been defensible. But Commodore Whipple was too lily-livered and indecisive to make proper use of his resources. He bungled our naval operations from start to finish. I have no use for Commodore Whipple."

"What did he do that was so bad?" asked Morna.

"Nothing. He did nothing. General Lincoln told him to station his ships in Five Fathom Hole, where they could fire broadsides into the British warships as the warships tried to cross, but the commodore was afraid his own ships might be damaged in the attempt. Can you imagine? Why were the ships there, if not to protect the city? He hemmed and hawed, and consulted with pilots, and sounded the channels, and conferred with his captains, and wrote letters, and when at last the spring flood tide came, the British fleet sailed through the Ship Channel with no trouble at all." The pickled peppers passed between the pieces of biscuit.

"Where were the American ships?" asked Tavish.

"Lying under the guns of Fort Moultrie, snug as you please, where they could do no good at all. The British fleet were far out of the fort's range in Five Fathom Hole, precisely where General Lincoln had hoped the American fleet would make their stand."

Father shook his head in disgust.

"Then what?" asked Morna.

"Well, once the British fleet passed the Bar, they had to wait for *another* flood tide to get them past Fort Moultrie. They got it two weeks later, along with as fair a wind as they could ask. They sailed past the fort's guns, and received some pretty smart fire, and suffered some men and boys killed, but not enough to stop them making the passage. All the British vessels reached Fort Johnson on James Island without much damage." The pickled peppers sailed to the fish platter.

"Meanwhile, the British army had not been idle. Back in February, General Clinton had landed his troops on the sea islands"—she tapped the fish platter with her fork—"and made their way toward Charlestown by land, stealing cattle and horses, for they'd lost most of their own in the passage from New York. Trailing Oaks was hard hit, as we later learned. The British made free with my father's stables and herds."

"Your father was wise to move the two of ye into town when he did," said Father. "Those who remained in the countryside were ill used by the foraging parties, I've heard."

"So I've heard as well," Miss Bryant said. "And yet it seems craven somehow, leaving Trailing Oaks defenseless, at the mercy of the depredating bands of a foreign army. Well, so the British advanced on the city. It must have been miserable for them, mucking about in brush and marshes all that wretched wet winter. I hope it was. But they made it through, across Johns and James Islands, and then to the mainland. Nine days after the British fleet crossed the Bar, the Hessians and Jaegers crossed the Ashley, and the American riflemen could only watch, because they hadn't the numbers to oppose them. Our militia had disappointed us again. But we had other reinforcements on the way, Continentals from Virginia. How the church bells did peal, the day they landed at Gadsden's Wharf! It cheered us all to see such fine figures of soldiers—real veterans, whose regiments had fought in all the major campaigns—taking their places on the lines with the other defenders."

A smile lit her face, and for a moment Fergus actually wished he could be a splendid Virginian Continental in a fine uniform, and have Melina Bryant look at him that way.

"Well," Miss Bryant said, "once the enemy crossed the Ashley, it was a matter of building entrenchments, and strengthening fortifications, and adding batteries, and hauling guns and stores, and finally firing on one another. The enemy did not confine their fire to the lines. We had houses burned to the ground, and townspeople killed. Some people stayed home, cowering under furniture, but what was the sense in that? A man and woman were killed in bed together by one stray shot, and two horses in a yard by another. So I determined to go about my business same as always, and if a cannonball finds me, says I, then so be it. Papa approved my spirit, and I never took any harm."

"I think I would do the same," said Nessa. "At least I hope I would. But I cannot blame those who feared, especially those with children."

"Aye, entire families were fleeing the city by now, for the Cooper River was still open then. The Cooper was our last hope, our only opening for supplies, and reinforcements, and escape for the garrison if it came to that—which some had the gall to say was the wisest course, once it became clear that no further aid could reach us in time."

"It would indeed have been wisdom," Father said coolly. "The city itself could hold little real value to the enemy. Ports are not so precious, and the British already controlled several. Holding territory is meaningless if the enemy's army escapes and is free to strike again from somewhere else."

"Mr. Shaw, you disappoint me. You would have had the garrison slink out and leave the city to the mercy of a conquering army?"

"Och! Come, Miss Bryant. We're speaking of British regiments, not Alaric and his Visigoths, stripping bare the city of Rome. King George, whatever his faults, wants loyal subjects, not a crushed, demoralized people. His soldiers are not going to be given license to run roughshod over the populace."

Miss Bryant raised her chin. "Is that so? Perhaps you have not heard of the behavior of Tarleton's Legion toward the country folk of South Carolina, particularly the wives of Patriot soldiers who were away fighting."

"Certainly I've heard of it. But those were the actions of soldiers in the field, where supervision is more difficult, not in an occupied city."

Miss Bryant made a derisive sound. "Of course. Men will be men. 'Tis the perennial excuse."

Father's hand froze on its way to his mouth with a piece of biscuit. He laid it down. "Excuse? Miss Bryant, I said no word of excuse, nor do I now. Whether the culprits were caught afterwards, court martialed, whipped, shot, hanged, I cannae tell. But can ye tell me what good it did for the garrison to hold out to the end of the siege? The British have your city now, all the same, and those brave, splendid Virginians ye cheered for so heartily not two months past, and the Continentals from North and South Carolina, will all rot in prison. The Patriot army in the South is well-nigh eliminated, all for want of a little prudence and forethought."

"Nay," said Tavish. "The Virginians will surely be exchanged for Burgoyne's prisoners taken at Saratoga."

Father shook his head. "I hope ye're right, lad, but I'll believe it when I see it."

"What about the siege?" asked Rory, pointing at the city of Charlestown as represented by Miss Bryant's Jerusalem artichokes. "What happened next?"

Miss Bryant looked down at her plate. Clearly, the spark had gone out of the tale. For all her spirited beginning, the siege of Charlestown was a foregone conclusion. But she gave a good finish. She told about the loss of the Patriots' final post on the Cooper River, which ended all hope of help, escape, or supply—sealing the city's doom. And of the fall of Fort Moultrie—no more than a symbolic defeat by that time, but heartbreaking nonetheless. And of the final surrender—the garrison marching out with colors cased, the dawning amazement in the enemy's faces as they saw the Patriots' scant numbers, gaunt figures, tattered clothing, and bare feet.

She drew her plate back and returned the platters to their places.

"When was your father taken prisoner, Miss Bryant?" asked Father.

"Not until the second week. The barracks had been filled by then, so new prisoners were loaded onto ships."

"I was puzzled to hear he was confined in a ship's hold. A most harsh and unusual punishment for a private citizen, especially one of his standing, and with no military office."

"Aye, 'twas mostly Continentals placed on board the ships. Almost all the local men, whether militia leaders or known Patriots who hadn't fought, simply gave their parole and were allowed their freedom. The few who were confined at all were mostly sent to St. Augustine, where I expect they'll be treated as gentlemen. But I'm afraid Papa did not behave in a prudent or gentlemanlike manner when Sir Henry Clinton asked for his parole."

"What did he do?" asked Rory.

"Well, he was still resentful over the plundering of Trailing Oaks by Tarleton's Legion. He sent the general a handsomely wrapped parcel of horse manure with an enclosed note which read: *Please find herein a Token of my Esteem for the honorable General, Sir Henry Clinton, and his officers, and a vouchsafe for my parole. If my horses have not provided a sufficiency of this Delicacy for your Dining Pleasure, I shall be happy to provide more.*"

Father cleared his throat. "Ah. That does explain it."

"Aye, and there's more. After receiving the package, General Clinton sent some of his officers to bring my father to him in person, and as Papa was being led from the house he called out, *What now? The general has already taken my horses and my servants without compensation, and yet he will demand still*

*more! I have naught left to give but my reason and my manhood, and as all the
city is aware, the general would not know how to use either."*

This time Father chuckled. "Imprudent indeed, but I admire the spirit he
showed."

"I feel exactly the same, sir. 'Twas galling to see so many Patriot fire-
brands, like Middleton and Gadsden, pledge allegiance to the Crown, after
all their fine words about death and liberty. But I cannot deny that Papa was
quite drunk when he sent the parcel of horse manure, and drunker still at the
time of his arrest."

"I'd have done as he did," said Rory. "Refused to give parole, I mean. They
couldn't make me take their oath."

"Dinnae be too quick to condemn Mr. Gadsden and the others," said Father. "With the British in control of the city, a man's livelihood and the welfare of his family might well depend on his response."

"I agree with Rory," said Tavish. "The heart and the profession should be
as one."

"Ye're not wrong," said Father. "But every man has his breaking point.
Let us hope and pray we're none of us ever put to the test as Mr. Bryant and
Mr. Gadsden were."

"I wish I could have seen the siege, with all the engines and artillery," said
Rory. "Or gone with Knox to fetch Fort Ticonderoga's cannon over the Al-
leghenies. I hope all the best adventures won't be over before I enlist."

"'Twill be four years before you're old enough," Catalyn said. "The war
will be long over by then."

"You can't know that," Rory replied. "People were saying in seventy-five
that it would be over in a few months, and five years later there's no end in
sight. I think I'll join the Continentals and be an artilleryman. They have to
understand mathematics and chemistry."

"Their fine education doesna stop them being blown to bits by their
own cannon, or stuffed into prison ships like the Continentals taken at
Charlestown," Father said sharply. "Dinnae be a fool, Rory."

Rory scowled down at his plate.

Fergus knew why Father was cross—because he was afraid. But Rory
could be contrary. Bearing down on him might push him away.

Let it drop, Fergus thought. He couldn't lose another brother.

Miss Bryant spoke up. "Do you like machines, Master Rory?"

"Aye. I'm terribly clever with them."

"Rory!" said Nessa and Catalyn together.

"What? I am. Everyone's always saying so. I'm a naturalist, too."

"You're an insufferable little braggart, is what you are," said Nessa.

"'Tisn't being a braggart if 'tis true. If Miss Bryant had asked about my penmanship, I'd have owned 'tis very poor."

"I see you have a bold and agile mind, Master Rory, and a forthright way of expressing yourself," said Miss Bryant. "One day there will be far better uses than war for the minds of enterprising men—and women, I hope and believe—in this nation of ours. Have you heard of the American Philosophical Society? Many of our leading Patriots are members, including General Washington and Benjamin Franklin. The Society has a plan to make a canal to connect the Chesapeake Bay to the Delaware River. It would reduce the water route between Philadelphia and Baltimore by three hundred miles. Imagine that!"

"What's so hard about making a canal?" asked Morna. "Why not just dig straight through and be done with it?"

"Nay," said Rory. "They'd have to make locks, to keep the water from running away to the lowest level."

"That's right," said Miss Bryant. "There's matter enough in the scheme to require all the talents of a gifted mind. Perhaps you'll work on it one day, or find the Northwest Passage."

Rory smiled. "Perhaps I shall."

By the time dinner ended, the tension was gone. Father smiled at Rory and said, "Come, lad. Back to the orchard."

Catalyn took Lachlan home, and Tavish went to see to the stock. Fergus knew he must join his brother-in-law soon, but he lingered until Nessa and Morna started washing up, and Miss Bryant headed upstairs for her afternoon rest. He followed her to the central passage.

"Miss Bryant!"

She paused on the stairway, her chin over her shoulder, her gaze high and haughty. She had the advantage of a few steps' height over him now, and the loftiness of her carriage made more of it than it was. The jeweled pin in her hair gave off a rich golden-brown flash.

"I wish to thank you for your attention to my brother just now," Fergus said. "It was kindly done."

"I wasn't being kind. I attended to him because I like him."

"Of course. But—well, he does love an audience, and he talks a great deal."

"So what if he does? He's a smart, lively boy with a good deal to say, and he says it well. He has high mettle and good action."

"You needn't speak of him as if he's a racehorse, and you needn't take offense."

"And you needn't make apologies for a bright, charming, well-spoken little lad whom you ought to be proud to call your brother. I like him. If I didn't, I wouldn't pretend to."

Nay, she would not. She didn't hesitate to show her dislike of anything or anyone—not cowardly commodores, or worthless militiamen, or Fergus himself. She was the most insufferable young woman he'd ever met.

And yet...

A strange wild longing bloomed hot in his face and chest. He wanted to close the distance between them, across the passage and up that bit of stairway, and pull that topaz pin out of those tawny curls.

Instead, he walked out the front door and shut it hard behind him.

Chapter Two

The horse Bran walked with perfect fluid ease, as if he had no rider, as if he and the man on his back were one creature. Energy of motion flowed from the muscles that rolled beneath the gleaming black coat, slipping into the calves and thighs of young Mr. Shaw. Melina's own muscles tightened and relaxed in sympathy with each rippling movement. She knew what strength and skill it took to appear so still in the saddle.

She rode in the open carriage with Nessa, Morna, Catalyn, Rory, and Lachlan. The elder Mr. Shaw drove while the young men rode horseback, Mr. MacGregor on Hector and the younger Mr. Shaw on Bran. With her back-facing seat, Melina had an excellent view of both riders. Mr. MacGregor was a fine horseman as well, but it was not to him that her eyes were drawn.

Yesterday she'd thought young Mr. Shaw poorly turned out in his plain linen frock coat and waistcoat. Today he wore the identical outfit, evidently his Sunday best. The simple garments fit his long slender body to perfection, and their somber black and grey suited his stark coloring of pale skin and dark hair and eyes.

In Charlestown she'd had many admirers, young men from fine families with considerable estates, some of them quite handsome, and all adept at banter and flattery. Fergus Shaw was quiet, except when he was insulting her, and though neat and respectable and good to look at, he appeared more like an artisan or a mechanic than a gentleman—like one of Christopher Gadsden's Sons of Liberty that formed his artillery company, but without the deferential air. He clearly didn't think much of her. And yet she couldn't help but believe there was good sense and intelligence behind those closed features, and a good opinion worth having. She couldn't stop thinking about him, or take her eyes off him whenever he was near.

"Look at that stand of pines," she said. "There's not an oak among them. How very upright and exclusive they seem, refusing to associate with other trees."

"Aye, those are the longleaf," said Rory. "They're what we make the turpentine from."

"Of course, the turpentine! You must tell me all about it. I want to hear every detail."

This was rash, she knew, for Rory did love to talk, but she needed the distraction. She locked her gaze on him, but it was Fergus's face she saw in her mind's eye: the high, martial brow with its deep widow's peak; the long, jutting chin, decidedly cleft; the black eyes with their penetrating stare. A hard, austere face, that would have done well for a Scottish covenanter from the last century.

She'd seen him smile only once, when Catalyn's baby had met him at the door—a broad, boyish smile that lit and softened his whole countenance.

She willed herself to pay attention to Rory's detailed account of naval stores and their manufacture, but instead of pine resin and kilns, she thought only of Fergus Shaw, holding his infant nephew, or cleaning the carriage in his shirt sleeves, or watching her with haughty black eyes.

CHURCH WAS A STRANGE affair. The services were held in the courthouse, a large block of a building in the center of a crossroads. Occasionally some of the congregants lapsed into a foreign tongue, something with rolling vowels and consonants shaped far back in the throat—Gaelic, she supposed. It added to the air of unreality as the service dragged on and on and on. She kept thinking they'd reached the end, only to find they were starting another prayer or reading.

At long last the final amen was said. They all filed quietly out, men on one side, women on the other, and down the steps of the courthouse to the grassy common. After some exchange of war news, the various families spread their blankets on the grass and took their dinners from their baskets.

The noon meal was no festive picnic. All was conducted with quiet Sabbath solemnity. Melina ate her food, then rose and smiled brightly at Mr. Shaw.

"With your permission, sir, I'd like to take a turn about the green."

"Afternoon services will start soon," he said.

"I'll be quick. Please, sir, I feel as if I've been sitting for years, with one carriage ride after another, and miles of countryside passing by but never a chance to stretch my limbs. I'm sure the exercise will do me a world of good. I promise to be back before the service starts."

"Very well."

She headed east on a muddy street amended by plank walkways and lined with scattered houses and gardens. At the end of the block, the street dwindled to a road and climbed up a slight slope to a building that might have been another church, situated as it was near a burial ground. Melina quickened her pace. Burial grounds were always interesting.

The church building—if indeed it was a church building—was a plain gabled structure of no great size, without steeple or belfry. Melina reached the burial ground and walked slowly from one sandstone marker to the next: a pair of DeRossetts, man and wife, or perhaps mother and son; a whole family of Skillings; a Baby Jones. And suddenly she was looking down at the name Isabeau Shaw.

She'd known, of course, that Mr. Shaw was a widower, like Papa, but the etched letters struck her hard. The death date on the stone was 1768. Fergus would have been ten years old.

She had no clear memory of her own mother, who had died bringing forth a stillborn son when Melina was hardly older than Lachlan. But she remembered the rush and tension of that day, the anguished screams from behind the closed bedroom door, Papa's frantic pacing in the hall—and then the long, dreary, heavy silence of the days that followed.

She looked for a stone for the other Shaw boy, but saw none. The loss must be a recent one, for Mr. Shaw had told Papa only five months earlier, in January, that he had three daughters and three sons. How had the other boy died, and where? And how old would he have been? There did seem to be a gap between Nessa and Morna to allow for a boy around sixteen, old enough for militia service. Did he lie in a hasty grave far from home? She remembered what she'd said to Fergus about the worthlessness of militia forces and felt a little sick.

"Pardon me, madam, but are you lost?"

A tall man approached her—a man with powdered hair, silk stockings, and a silk frock coat over an embroidered waistcoat.

"Forgive me," he said in a rich, cultured voice. "You must think me impertinent. But I've been observing you for some time, wondering if you were lost, and if I ought to offer my poor unsolicited services. Just now, you appeared truly unwell, and I could no longer keep silent, impertinent or not."

She smiled. "Not unwell, and not lost," she said. "Only...only perplexed as to the organizing principles of this city's design."

He laughed. "Aye, 'tis a regular hodge-podge of architecture, the poor hovels cheek by jowl with the grand mansions, and all manner of piazzas and balconies spilling into the street in defiance of good sense and rational city ordinance. But first things first. Let me be no more a stranger to you. My name is Richard Severn."

"How do you do, Mr. Severn? I am Melina Bryant."

Mr. Severn swept off his hat and made a reverence elegant enough to grace a Charlestown parlor. He looked to be around twenty-five, with a broad, well-formed face, clear blue eyes, and a firm mouth. She made a deep curtsey and raised her eyes to find his gaze fixed on her with unmistakable pleasure.

"I am delighted to make your acquaintance, Miss Bryant. You are a visitor to Wilmington, then?"

"Aye, I've come only yesterday, from Charlestown."

"Charlestown! A most charming city. Fairer than Boston, New York, and Philadelphia combined, and now happily restored to royal rule."

Melina's stomach sank. Mr. Severn's smile became stiff, and he said, "Ah. I see we are on opposite sides of the conflict."

"My father is a Patriot," Melina said. "He sent me here after Charlestown fell."

Why had she not said that both of them were Patriots, her father and herself? She never scrupled to make known any political opinion of hers, or any opinion at all. It was craven to submit so meekly, simply because she was starved for interaction with someone of her own condition and class. She could almost see Fergus Shaw in her mind's eye, scorning her weakness, despising her.

But no. She would not spoil the moment by thinking of Fergus Shaw. If she'd sold her principles for a fleeting pleasure, she might as well get the most of it.

"Very prudent of him, no doubt," said Mr. Severn. "I myself have many friends in and around Charlestown. Perhaps you can tell me how they've fared during the recent upheaval."

He named the families he knew, and she gave him reports of them. They had considerable mutual acquaintance, of both Patriot and Loyalist bend, and had probably come near meeting more than once. When she said that her father's estate was called Trailing Oaks, he said that he knew it, had ridden past it many times, and had heard the property praised. Reading between the lines, she gathered that his own family's estate was considerable.

"May I inquire where you are staying?" he asked.

"A little outside of town, with the Archibald Shaw family."

A chill entered his tone. "Ah. You are friends of theirs?"

"Very distant relations, evidently, though I never saw any of them before yesterday. Mr. Shaw met my father while the Wilmington militia was in Charlestown. Papa's mother was a Shaw, and between the two of them they deduced that they were fifth cousins, and born on the same day of the same year. Is not that not remarkable?"

"Astonishing."

The chill had not thawed. "Are you acquainted with the Shaws?" she asked.

"Nay, we move in very different circles, as you can imagine, partisan politics being what they are. Still, I believe they are generally accounted a respectable family."

But...

"Mr. Severn, there is something you are not telling me. Is there some objection to be made to the Shaws?"

"Not to the Shaws themselves, no. Only to the unfortunate son-in-law."

"Mr. MacGregor? How so? He seems a sensible, well-spoken sort of man, and all the family appear to look on him as one of themselves."

"I daresay. Nay, I should not speak. If your father believed the Shaws to be a suitable family with which to place his daughter, 'tis not my place to say otherwise."

"But Papa is barely acquainted with Mr. Shaw, and never met the rest of the family at all. Mr. Severn, please speak frankly. If you know something against Mr. MacGregor, I'm sure my father would want you to tell me."

"Hmm. Perhaps you are right. Perhaps it is my duty. Your father surely would not have sent you, had he but known, to a household which harbors a murderer."

Melina drew back. "Murderer? Mr. Severn, there must be some mistake."

"I assure you, there is none. Mr. MacGregor was jailed for the crime, and nearly hanged, but escaped the charge somehow."

Mr. MacGregor, a murderer! "I—I did not know," Melina said at last.

"You can hardly be blamed for your ignorance, madam. And as you say, the Shaws appear to be a perfectly decent and reputable family in all other respects, though I cannot agree with their politics, or their religion."

Melina sighed. "Aye. They are so very Presbyterian."

"Do you disapprove of Presbyterians?"

"Presbyterians appear to be rather above my approval or disapproval, a very lofty set."

"I take it you are of the Church of England yourself?"

"I am."

"Then perhaps some Sunday morning you will join us for services at Saint James, if your guardian will permit you. I should be happy to arrange a proper introduction."

She thanked him, though it seemed unlikely that Mr. Shaw would consent. In fact, she had an uneasy suspicion that he wouldn't approve with her acquaintance with Mr. Severn at all. It wasn't exactly proper, meeting a man in a burial ground with no formal introduction by a third party.

But she pushed the thought down. She'd had little enough amusement over the past months, and she enjoyed Mr. Severn's company.

"Why do the Presbyterians meet in the courthouse?" she asked. "Have they no church building?"

"Nay, for they are Dissenters, and only the Church of England may own real estate in North Carolina."

"Really? 'Tis not so in South Carolina. The Presbyterians in Charlestown have their own building—aye, and the Baptists, and the Huguenots, and the Jews."

"It cannot have escaped your notice that there are many differences between North and South Carolina. 'Tis difficult to believe they once belonged to the same colony, is it not?"

"Difficult? Well-nigh impossible!"

He offered his arm and began to lead her about the burial ground.

"The composition of both Carolinas was never very promising," he said. "Too many religious extremists—Quakers, Palatines, Huguenots, Presbyterians—as well as the sort of restive and masterless men who are always ill at ease in orderly society, all wanting to live in an isolated and freakish manner, unaccountable to their betters. By the time the Lords Proprietors received their charter, it was too late to impose any sort of decent social directive, as the settlers had their democratic systems in place. A pity."

Melina didn't reply. From what she'd heard, the Lords Proprietors' scheme was in fact a feudal system, complete with titled noblemen and medieval serfs. She couldn't mourn its failure.

"North Carolina in particular," Mr. Severn continued, "at least in infancy, was largely peopled not by enterprising venturers from Britain, but by the poorer sort of failed farmers filtering down from Virginia and Pennsylvania, seeking better or cheaper land. And this, I daresay, is how one might best define the difference between the two colonies. North Carolina is a land of small farms, ten to twenty acres generally, and usually few or no slaves to work them. South Carolina was built on a grander scale—modeled after Barbados, the most British of the Caribbean Islands, with its rich plantations and cultured lifestyle."

He gestured to the unadorned little building she'd noted earlier. "You see how plain is our own church building of Saint James—very different from Saint Michael's in Charlestown, with its grand steeple shining white in the sun, the first sight to be seen from the harbor, welcoming travelers back from the sea."

Melina nodded. "The American army blackened the steeple of Saint Michael's, so the British fleet couldn't use it as a landmark in crossing the Bar. They destroyed the beacon and lighthouse, too. It seems foolish to mind it, when so many worse things happened in town and country, but it pained me to see that black steeple sticking up in the sky."

"I do not think it foolish to mourn any defacement of property. And you are right, many terrible things were done to your city, and to the bodies of men, all on account of a few cents' taxes, and the inconsequential wording of some acts of Parliament. I wonder if those who brought on this effusion of blood still believe the sacrifice worthwhile."

Melina didn't know what to say. What was wrong with her? Why was she being such a coward?

"I am distressing you," said Mr. Severn.

"Nay! 'Tis a comfort to hear Charlestown spoken of by someone who knows it and loves it as I do. I wasn't expecting things here to be so different."

"You must miss your city very much."

"I do. But this is where my father sent me, and I've got to make the best of it until I may return."

"You are very wise. I hope your time will not pass unpleasantly."

Something in his brilliant blue eyes made her cheeks grow warm. Before she could reply, a sharp voice cut through the moment.

"Miss Bryant!"

Fergus Shaw, as rigid and somber and Presbyterian as ever, stalked up the burial ground slope.

"Come away at once," he said. "Afternoon service is about to begin."

Mr. Severn gave Fergus an impeccable bow. "Pray do not blame Miss Bryant, Mr. Shaw. The fault is mine for detaining her in conversation."

Fergus didn't even look at him. He held out his arm to Melina.

"Miss Bryant, come."

Melina wished a fresh grave would open up and swallow her. As calmly as she could, she bade Mr. Severn a good afternoon, then swept past Fergus, ignoring his arm.

He fell in beside her. She walked as fast as she could, but his long legs easily matched her pace.

"What do you mean by talking to that man in the burial ground? Have you no sense of decency or propriety?"

"I have far more of both than you have, Mr. Shaw. Mr. Severn introduced himself, and his behavior was perfectly courteous, unlike yours."

"Unlike mine! Whatever can you mean?"

"The way you cut him just now. 'Twas barbarously uncivil, even for you."

"Miss Bryant, you are a stranger here, so I will make allowances as far as I justly can. That man, Richard Severn, is a Tory."

"I know that. He told me himself. But that was no excuse for you to snub someone so clearly your superior."

Fergus stopped dead. Melina went on a few steps more before turning to look at him. His face had gone white to the lips. "Explain what you mean, madam."

"Only that he is clearly a man of considerable property. 'Twas generous of him to bow to you. He'd have been well within the bounds of decorum to merely nod."

"I see. Mr. Severn is a man of considerable property, and I am only a poor planter's son. In your mind, *that* makes him my superior."

"Don't be obtuse. You know what I mean."

"Aye, I'm afraid I do."

He walked on, so briskly that Melina had to struggle to keep up.

"You make no answer," she said.

"Indeed, I do not trust myself to speak. And if you possess even a shred of civility, you will not speak another word to me this day."

"Nothing would make me happier," said Melina.

They walked in silence the rest of the way. Mr. Shaw waited at the top of the courthouse steps, calm but glowering. Everyone else had gone inside. Silently he motioned Fergus and Melina through the door.

An afternoon of unremitted Presbyterianism was the last thing Melina wanted, but there was no help for it. She felt cheated. Her meeting with Mr. Severn should have cheered her through the latter service, but Fergus had spoiled the memory of it.

The flush of anger passed, leaving a dreary fatigue. The service wore on and on. How could the Shaws and MacGregors stand it? Even Lachlan bore up better than she, and he was scarcely one year old. Catalyn kept him entertained with small toys, but he also crawled and toddled around his mother and his aunts, or napped in Catalyn's arms.

Finally it ended. Mr. Shaw fetched the carriage from the livery stable, the young men fetched their saddle horses, and they all rode home. Melina felt sore inside. From her back-facing seat, she watched the town dwindle away, swallowed up by those infernal pines, miles and miles of them, each as upright and unyielding as a Scottish Presbyterian. She used to love the countryside, loved riding and walking in the wooded acres around her father's plantation, with the cozy knowledge of the house to come back to, and hot water for her wash, and chests and armoires full of fresh shifts and gowns, and soft slippers, and her own bedchamber with its feather bed and finely carved woodwork and silk curtains and silver hairbrush and all the other luxuries that she'd never thought to value before she'd lost them.

Upon reaching the Shaw home, the young men rode directly to the carriage house. Mr. Shaw stopped the carriage at the dooryard and let the passengers out, then Rory took the reins and led the carriage away. Catalyn carried Lachlan to the cabin, and Nessa and Morna went through the dooryard gate. Melina started to follow them, but Mr. Shaw stepped in front of her.

"Hold up, if ye please, Miss Bryant. I'd like a word with ye before ye go within."

Melina swallowed hard.

"I expressly told ye not to wander too far today, and ye agreed to return in time for afternoon service. Instead, ye vanished out of sight, and I had to send my son to fetch ye back with moments to spare. Where were ye?"

"I—I met a gentleman in the burial ground at Saint James. We spoke of Charlestown, and I lost track of time."

"What is the gentleman's name?"

"Richard Severn."

"Were ye previously acquainted with him?"

"Nay."

"And did ye believe that in giving ye leave to take a turn about the green, I had also granted ye permission to consort with unknown gentlemen in burial grounds?"

Melina dropped her gaze. "Nay. I knew I was doing wrong."

"I see. Well, Miss Bryant, I imagine ye were accustomed to a different mode of life in Charlestown. But your father entrusted ye to my care, and that is a sacred charge. While ye live under my roof, ye will do as I say. I am not a hard man, Miss Bryant, but I will be obeyed. Do I make myself clear?"

Melina nodded. She didn't trust herself to speak. Her eyes were already full to the brim.

Mr. Shaw passed through the gate. Melina didn't follow him. The moment his back was to her, the tears spilled over.

She couldn't go inside like this. She ran blindly toward the back of the house and collided with someone at the corner.

"Why, Miss Bryant. Whatever is the matter?"

It was Nessa, the eighteen-year-old sister, looking down at Melina with a frank, friendly gaze.

Melina couldn't answer. She was crying hard now.

Nessa took her hand, led her to the cookhouse, and seated her on a wooden bench.

"There," she said, shutting the door. "Now, you sit here while I get a cold supper together, and cry all you like, and we'll talk when you're ready."

It was a relief to give herself over to her tears. Nessa paid no attention to her but went about her own business, filling a basket with bread, cheese, and fruit.

Finally the storm of weeping passed. Melina drew a deep shuddering breath, then let it out.

Nessa sat beside her on the bench. "Now, tell me what troubles you, Miss Bryant."

"Oh, will you please call me Melina? 'Twill make me feel a little less homesick."

"Are you so very homesick, Melina?"

"Terribly. 'Tisn't that I'm ungrateful, but things are so different here, and I'm worried about Papa. Prison ships are full of sickness, and he's not a young man. Your father's very good to take me in, but I've made him angry. I wandered off today and met a man—a Loyalist, Mr. Richard Severn—in the churchyard at Saint James—and I was gone longer than I should have been, and your brother was sent to fetch me back. 'Twas unseemly—I know that—but we were talking of Charlestown, and I let the time slip away. Your father was kind, but stern, and it was all so dreadful that I don't know how I'll get through this evening, much less tomorrow."

Nessa smiled. "Don't fret, Miss Bryant—Melina. Father doesn't dwell overlong on such things. He'll let it go, and tomorrow will be a fresh day."

"Truly?"

"Truly."

Melina took another deep breath. "Thank you, Miss Shaw. You've comforted me so much."

"Call me Nessa. We're all your friends here—family, even—and we all look on you quite as one of us. Don't forget that."

Melina doubted Fergus would agree, but she managed a tremulous smile.

"Is there anything else I can do for you before we go in?" Nessa asked.

"Actually...there is something I wanted to ask, about Mr. MacGregor. Is it true that he killed a man?"

The change in Nessa's face was frightening, like a storm cloud covering the sun all at once. "Who told you that? Your Mr. Severn?"

"Aye," Melina said meekly.

"What exactly did he say?"

"That Mr. MacGregor had committed a murder, and that he was caught and jailed and about to be hanged, but escaped the charge somehow."

After a long silence, Nessa said, "My sister's husband did kill a man—a man who was trying to rob him. He acted in self-defense. But he ran away afterward, and that looked black against him. And he had no friends or kin at the time. If he'd been tried, most likely he'd have hanged, because the law comes down hardest on the poor and friendless."

"What happened to prevent his trial?" Melina asked.

"War. The district was making a regiment of minutemen, and Tavish was given his freedom in exchange for service. He fought with the minutemen at Moore's Creek Bridge, along with Fergus and my father—though Father was a militiaman, not a minuteman. And after the minutemen were disbanded and turned back into militia, Tavish went on serving, and has continued to take his turn in the rotation faithfully ever since."

"Did your sister know? About—the killing?"

"Not at first. She was half off her head when she found out. She actually went to visit him in jail with a chisel and a pry bar hidden beneath her petticoats, and a scheme for the two of them to run away to the backcountry."

"Nay! You cannot be serious!"

"I am. You wouldn't think it to look at her, but Catalyn is as fierce as a minx when anything threatens one of us. When she's roused she has the worst temper of us all."

Melina thought of all the tender words and glances she'd seen pass between Catalyn and Tavish. It made her ache inside to think of loving and being loved like that. But she said only, "The worst temper of you all? Worse than your eldest brother? Nay, that I cannot believe."

Nessa chuckled. "I understand why you say that. But Fergus is the steadiest, kindest, most patient and even-tempered lad I've ever known. Anyone who knows him well would agree. Tavish loves him like a brother. And that's been good for Fergus, especially since..."

Now Nessa's eyes welled up. She must be thinking of her other brother who was lost. Melina squeezed her hand.

"I believe we're going to be good friends," Nessa said.

"I know we are! I do thank you, Nessa. You've been most kind."

"You're heartily welcome, though I wish I could do more. I'm sorry about your papa. I can only imagine what I would feel in your place. And I'm sorry you're homesick, though I suppose you could hardly be otherwise. Just remember that you're not friendless. Father looks grim, but he's the dearest man in the world. Now, help me get the supper things ready. I daresay you're worn out. You'll feel better once you've got some food in you and another good night's sleep."

Melina hoped so. With what she had planned for tomorrow, she'd need all the shoring up she could get.

Chapter Three

Coming down the stairway the next morning, Fergus met Miss Bryant on her way up. She was dressed in a worn gown of faded linen gown, the likes of which he couldn't imagine her owning. She passed him without a glance, her chin uptilted at a haughty angle, her skirts brushing against him.

In the dining hall, Nessa and Morna were laying breakfast for six on the table.

"What on earth is Miss Bryant wearing this morning?" Fergus asked them. "It looks like an old dishrag one of her servants might use to polish the silver. I should never have guessed that she owned such a gown."

Morna made an affronted sound and shook her red curls back from her face. "Indeed, she does not own it. 'Tis mine."

"Yours?"

"Aye, my old everyday gown that you've seen me wear a thousand times. We're doing a wash today, and all of Miss Bryant's own gowns need laundering or airing, so I lent her one of mine. She is such a little thing, and Nessa is so tall, that mine are a better fit. Old dishrag, indeed!"

"I didn't mean...I say nothing against the gown itself," Fergus sputtered. "'Twould do very well for either of you."

Nessa and Morna both exclaimed at that, and Fergus tried again. "Nay, that's not what I...I'm simply amazed that she would deign to put it on, such a fine lady as herself."

"You make *fine lady* sound like an insult," said Nessa. "And what did you expect her to do on wash day, traipse about house and grounds in nothing but her shift?"

Fergus's face grew warm.

"Perhaps you'd better go and see to your chores, brother," Nessa said.

He went back to the central passage, where he again met Miss Bryant. This time, she was coming down the stairs with her arms full of gowns and shifts. A wave of confusion washed over him. He hurried outside, stumbling over his feet.

He stood against the closed door, breathing deeply. The dooryard was already set up in its wash-day arrangement, with cauldron, copper, washing bats, and tables. The scent of lye stung his nostrils. Before long Miss Bryant's shifts would be swirling about in the copper with his shirts.

He shook his head hard. What was the matter with him? It wasn't as if he cared for Miss Bryant. She vexed him, infuriated him, and ever since her arrival, his thoughts and feelings had been all in a jumble. He could hardly wait for Miss Bryant to be on her way to Rhode Island or some such outlandish place and leave him in peace.

By the time the family sat down to breakfast, Fergus had himself in reasonable order. For a wonder, the meal passed quietly, without any strange questions or outbursts from Miss Bryant.

Father downed the last of his coffee and got to his feet. "Rory, get Boudicca saddled. I'll ride her to town and leave Hector for the work cart."

"What will you do in town?" asked Morna.

"Visit ship's masters and owners to see about getting Miss Bryant to Newport. There's little chance she'll be able to sail out of the Cape Fear itself, but the port's best nautical minds will surely come up with a plan. It may be best to travel overland to Ocracoke Inlet and set sail from there. Last I heard, the British were not watching it as closely as they ought. And if that's not feasible, I'll figure out something else."

"You can save yourself the trouble, Mr. Shaw," said Miss Bryant. "I'm not going to Newport."

Everyone turned and stared at her. She looked straight at Father, with her shoulders back, her chin high, and her hands clasped before her on the table.

"Not going to Newport?" said Father. "What d'ye mean?"

"Precisely what I say. I'm not going. I don't like being as far from my father as I am now, but with things as they are in Charlestown, I couldn't remain there, and Wilmington is really the next best place. Once the Patriots retake Charlestown and reopen the ports, I'll be able to return by ship and reach my father quickly."

"And how long d'ye think all this will take, this recapturing of Charlestown and reopening of the ports? These are no trifling feats, miss."

"All the more reason for me to stay close by. Papa is not a young man, and prison ships are not healthful environments. He will need tender nursing after he is released. Once I'm able, I intend to go to him immediately—instantly."

"And what about his own wishes? Are they to count for nothing? He wanted his only child safe in Newport. Be reasonable, Miss Bryant. Take stock of the times. The war has moved to the South. General Washington may sit on his haunches and stare at New York, but 'tis a stalemate up there. This is the real theatre now. With Charlestown fallen, the British will be setting their sights on Wilmington, the last good port city in the South. What you spoke of two nights ago at this very table—the siege of your city, the plundering of the farms in the countryside—that's all coming here. That's what your father wanted ye well away from."

"I know what the prospects are, and I know what my father wanted. But this is what *I* want, and I shall have it. I refuse to be transported from province to province like a barrel of rice. I shall stay here until the war is ended."

A shocked silence followed. But the worst shock was yet to come.

"Naturally, I am aware that my continuance here will not be without expense," Miss Bryant said. "But once Papa regains his property, I assure you, he will reimburse you handsomely for my upkeep. And not in worthless Continental or state currency, but in hard specie."

All at once the dining hall seemed to darken and shrink and sag, growing shabbier before Fergus's eyes. Nessa dropped her gaze to her plate, face aflame.

Father's voice was thick with strain. "Money isna the issue, Miss Bryant. Your father entrusted ye to my care, and he made his wishes plain. Ye're going to Newport if I have to carry ye onboard an outgoing ship or carriage myself."

Miss Bryant swallowed hard. "I'm sorry to go against you in this, Mr. Shaw. But I believe I've made myself plain. And if you do attempt to carry me aboard, I will fight you every inch, tooth and claw."

Another, longer silence fell. Rory looked troubled, and Morna's bottom lip trembled.

Father stood and walked out of the dining hall, and out of the house. The sound of the front door closing behind him shuddered through Fergus like a blow.

Miss Bryant turned to Nessa and smiled. "There! That went rather better than I expected."

The light, arch remark was too much. Fergus turned on Miss Bryant and said, "You shallow, flippant creature. You want to stay, so stay you shall, and what others might want or need is of no consequence at all. Is this all a lark for you, visiting your rustic cousins on their humble estate? You offered my father money. Money! You might as well scrape the mud off your shoes onto his frock coat."

Miss Bryant looked down at her clasped hands. A flush of color appeared on her cheeks. Fergus didn't care. He wanted her to feel how wrong she was.

"Fergus, that was unkind," said Nessa.

He made a scoffing sound, then followed his father out of the house.

DURING THE SUMMER MONTHS the thin, pungent, oily resin of the longleaf pines ran freely from careful cuts pressed into the bark of the trees and was gathered in boxes carved from the living wood. Later, when temperatures cooled, the resin thickened and was not so pure or so easy to harvest, and once frost came, it would cease flowing altogether. By then, the makers of naval stores would be concentrating on heating pine wood in kilns, to turn into tar and pitch, and the resin would have long since been distilled into precious turpentine.

In the past, Father had sold most of his naval stores to British shipyards. Now that market was closed, and with the British Navy patrolling the coast, North Carolina's shipping trade was all but cut off, slowing local demand for naval stores. Turpentine would keep, so Father didn't cease production altogether, but he thought it wise to diversify. So he'd placed Tavish, who'd spent most of his life as a Virginia stockman, in charge of the farm's livestock, and assigned Fergus to help him. At the height of its productivity, the Shaw turpentine orchard had boasted four workers: Father and Fergus; Alan, a neighbor; and Liam. Now only Father and Rory tended the trees.

Tavish and Fergus were branding new calves today. Many of the Shaws' neighbors also kept cattle, though on a smaller scale, and the lack of fences meant a co-mingling of stock. Cattlemen identified their beasts with ear notches, but Tavish expected the Shaw herd to become superior animals and wanted to make ownership doubly sure, so every June, the new calves received a mark of "AS" on the rump.

After breakfast they penned the calves, then made a final pass through them while waiting for the branding irons to heat. Tavish hovered possessively over his especial glory, a pair of twin bull calves with identical markings.

"Aren't they a handsome pair?" he said. "They'll make a fine team of oxen one day, perfectly matched in size and strength."

He'd said the same thing at least a dozen times in the past four months, but Fergus couldn't grudge him his pride. Twins of any sort were rare in cattle, and this had been a long and tricky birth on a raw winter's night, but Tavish had sorted out the tangle of hooves and hocks and delivered the two bulls healthy and sound, with their mother none the worse for wear.

Aye, let him gloat. They were honest farmers, all of them, beholden to no man, and they needed no coin from the hand of some spoiled chit of a girl.

"Is something troubling ye, brother?" asked Tavish. "Ye look as if a cloud shadow just passed over your face."

"Aye. Miss Bryant gave another...performance...at breakfast this morning."

"Miss Bryant! I had a notion she might be at the back of it. Tell me."

Fergus told him. Tavish listened without interruption.

"Your father's a rare man," Tavish said. "I love him like my own blood. He's treated me like a son, suffered loss and reproach for my sake, and welcomed me into his household with a generosity that has no reserve, and I dinnae forget it. Miss Bryant doesna ken him yet. 'Twould have grieved me as it did you, seeing him defied in his own house, at his own table, by someone who owed him, if not the reverence of one who kens him as we do, then at the least respect due to an elder and a host. And whether intentionally or not, she did it in the most insulting way possible, by presuming on his hospitality, and then offering him coin for room and board—and he a Scot, no less."

"That is precisely what I thought, only I could never have put it into those words if I'd had ten years to try. I wish I had you always about with me, brother, to explain what I mean. 'Twould save me a world of trouble."

Tavish gave him a broad, knowing smile. "Miss Bryant strikes sparks from ye, that's plain to see," he said. "Like flint and steel. Horseshoes and cobblestones. She's very pretty, too."

"What's that got to do anything?" Fergus asked stiffly. "We were talking about my father, and that impudent girl's shameful treatment of him."

Tavish brushed this off with a wave of his hand. "Your father will do very well. By dinnertime today he'll have drafted a speech that shows him to be lord of his domain, and puts Miss Bryant very much in her place, while still allowing her to remain here exactly as she wishes. Come, Fergus. Her delivery may have been faulty, but ye cannae blame the lass for wanting to remain close to her imprisoned father."

"She acted willfully and inconsiderately. She's shallow and spoiled and impulsive."

"Willful and inconsiderate, aye. Impulsive, certainly. Spoiled, perhaps. But shallow? Nay, not truly, only inexperienced with anything outside a rather narrow mode of life. Do her justice, Fergus. Surely ye can see some good in the lass."

Fergus considered. "Well, she's certainly got a sharp mind, and a clear, forcible way of expressing herself. And she's friendly to children, and horses and dogs. But every time I see something to admire in her, she follows it up with some fresh annoyance."

"Like a burr in the saddle," Tavish said with a sidewise look. "A stone in the shoe."

"Aye, which is just another way of saying she irritates me. And how is that cause for you to look so slyly at me, sir? Is that how you fell in love with my sister, by quarreling with her all the time?"

"Nay, ye ken I didna. But love doesna run the same course with all men. I'm a turbulent soul, and Catalyn is peace and rest to me. But you, sir, are inclined to be staid. Ye'll end up with a feisty, spirited sort of woman, mark my words."

"Is that so? And who do you think you are, the Brahan Seer?"

Tavish shrugged. "Mock all ye like. I ken what I ken. Now let's get these youngsters branded before the sun gets any higher. The irons are ready."

They led the calves one by one into the branding cradle and held the hot iron to their rumps. Each calf gave a bellow of surprise, then was immediately turned out into the pasture, where he ran a few steps, stopped, and settled down to graze.

The twin bull calves were branded last of all. Tavish stood watching them a long while, his foot braced against the bottom rail of the fence. Fergus sat beside him on the top rail.

"What vision do you behold now, O Brahan Seer?" Fergus asked. "Two bull calves fitted with a wee yoke, eating bits of carrot from your hand?"

Tavish scowled and pushed him off the fence.

WHEN FERGUS AND TAVISH came in for dinner, fresh-washed linen covered the dooryard with scarcely an inch to spare, shining white beneath the midday sun. The aroma of cleanliness filled Fergus's lungs.

No shadow of the morning's unpleasantness darkened the meal. Miss Bryant didn't say anything startling, and Father was himself again.

"A traveler from Salisbury passed the orchard today and left some news," Father said. "The appointment is official. General Gates is now in command of the Southern Department."

No one was surprised. After the fall of Charlestown, there'd been lots of talk over who would replace General Lincoln. Gates had been a popular favorite, though it was said that Washington preferred General Greene.

"The Hero of Saratoga!" said Rory. "Now things will take a turn for the better."

But Father looked grim. "'Tis a slight to General Washington, not letting him choose his own commanders. If Greene's the man he wants, Greene's the man he should have."

"Well, for that matter, there are many who say Gates should have replaced Washington long ago," said Tavish. "Perhaps they're right. I speak no evil of the man himself—I'm sure I shouldna have done half so well in his place—but perhaps Washington is no longer fit for the job."

"He's had his failures, aye, but he's been poorly supplied from the start, and a lesser commander would have failed worse and sooner," Father replied. "And 'tis perfectly possible to lose many battles and yet win the war. That could happen here, especially now that France is in. If we endure long enough, the war may become too expensive for King George to maintain."

"Aye," said Nessa archly, "and who's responsible for France coming in, Father?"

"She's right," said Tavish. "Saratoga was the victory that convinced France that our cause was worth supporting, and Gates was the general who won it."

"Gates was lucky," said Father. "General Burgoyne was inexperienced and ill supplied. Cornwallis is older and craftier, and Gates will find him a shrewd foe."

Privately Fergus agreed with Tavish and Nessa and Rory. Gates was the man for the job.

Miss Bryant spoke up. "I must agree with Mr. Shaw. All this praise of the Hero of Saratoga bodes ill with me. I fear the general may have been promoted beyond his desserts."

Tavish smiled slyly at Fergus. Do her justice, he'd said, and Fergus did. She meant what she said, of that he was sure. She wouldn't pretend to agree with Father merely to get in his good graces.

"Whenever General Gates reaches North Carolina, he'll find a large army ready," Tavish said. "General Caswell has North Carolina militiamen waiting in Cross Creek, and Baron de Kalb is on his way south with the Maryland and Delaware Continentals."

"Aye, the famed Marylanders," Miss Bryant said drily. "They were supposed to come to us at Charlestown but were held up for lack of provisions and supplies."

"I'm sorry for Charlestown's sake that they didn't reach the city in time," said Nessa. "But think how grand 'twill be when they join forces with Gates and Caswell. The British haven't made much headway in the backcountry, in spite of taking Charlestown. With such a large army, we'll soon drive them out of the South."

The room went dark. Nessa hurried to the window.

"Thunderclouds on wash day! And the sky so clear this morning. Morna, leave the dishes for now, and we'll move the wash indoors."

"I'll help," said Catalyn. "Between the three of us, we ought to be able to manage."

"Nay, not only the three of ye," said Father. He fixed Miss Bryant with a hard stare. "Earlier today, Miss Bryant, ye told me plainly that ye intend to remain in my house. I suppose a young lady of your station is used to being obeyed. But this farm is my domain, lass, and if ye're to remain here, ye'll do it not as a fine lady expecting to be waited on, but as a daughter of the house. We have no servants, and we all work for most of every day, and ye shall work as one of us. Ye offered me money for your upkeep, and because ye're a virtual stranger to me, I shall overlook the insult this once, but never do it again. One mouth to feed is two hands to work, and ye'll pay your way not by coin, but by the sweat of your brow."

Miss Bryant smiled. "I know what you're doing, Mr. Shaw. You mean to make me so sick of work that I'll practically fly to Newport. You are a sly one, sir."

"Not at all. If ye do change your mind and decide ye'd prefer a life in Newport to that of a middling farmer's daughter, then ye're welcome to leave at any time, assuming transportation can be arranged, and I'll be happy to assist ye with securing passage. But if ye stay under my terms, we'll both be the gainers."

"Very well. I accept your challenge, Mr. Shaw. You'll find I'm made of stern stuff."

"I'm happy to hear it. Ye'll begin by helping with the wash this afternoon, and continue by helping my daughters the rest of the day. Whenever Nessa is up and working, so should ye be."

He turned to Nessa. "Dinnae go easy on her, daughter. 'Twill take time for her to learn to do the work well, but any unskilled laborer can haul water or firewood. I'll be checking her hands for wear, and if I find she's been slack, she'll end by tapping the pines with Rory and me, or tending stock with Tavish and Fergus."

The thought of Miss Bryant as his partner in work made Fergus's mind go blank with shock. He shot Nessa a pleading look.

"I think Miss Bryant and I shall get on very well together," Nessa said.

THE CALVES HAD STAYED close to the pen following the morning's branding, so getting the stock under cover promised to be a quick job. Tavish saw to it alone, while Fergus went with Father and Rory to the turpentine orchard to help dip out whatever resin had collected before rain and debris could fill the boxes. Father was glad to reach the orchard ahead of the storm, but as they drove back and still no rain fell, Fergus wondered aloud if they ought to have bothered.

"Nay, listen to that thunder," said Father. "Rain or no rain, I want none of us out in the open."

They unhitched the work cart under the tar shed. Father and Rory stayed to move barrels while Fergus led Hector to the carriage house.

Nessa came running to meet him along the track. "Is Miss Bryant with you?"

"Nay, I am not concealing her in my pocket," he said.

"Well, in the tar shed, then," said Nessa impatiently. "Did she go with you to the orchard?"

"Why would she—" he began, and let out a groan. "How long has she been missing?"

"I don't know! We were all in and out of the house, setting things to dry in all the different rooms. I wasn't exactly keeping an eye on her. And suddenly she just wasn't there. And I thought, since she seemed so interested in turpentine, that perhaps she got bored with laundry and wandered off to help in the orchard after all."

"She's probably upstairs with her feet propped on a cushion," said Fergus.

"You don't think that's the first place I looked? I've searched the house and dooryard thoroughly, and the cookhouse, and the garden. What will Father say?"

"He can hardly blame you," Fergus said. "And there aren't many places on the farm where a fine lady could go to take her ease."

"Nay, but there are plenty of places where she could wander off and get herself killed."

A peal of thunder shook the ground.

"Go back to the house," said Fergus. "I'll put Hector away, then saddle Bran and go look for her."

HE OPENED THE DOOR to Hector's stall and froze in his tracks. Miss Bryant sat in the far corner, curled up tight with her arms over her head, rocking back and forth.

There was no mistaking the faded linen gown, or the bright gold hair, but other than that she couldn't have borne less resemblance to the proud, arch creature who'd matched wills with his father hours earlier. She looked shrunken, broken. Suddenly Fergus felt sick with fear.

"Miss Bryant! Are you hurt?"

She didn't answer.

Fergus secured Hector to a ring, then came inside the stall and knelt beside her. He could see no injury. Perhaps a blow to the head? He laid a soft, fearful hand on her shoulder.

She jerked away from him with a cry. Her eyes had a wild look, like those of a panicked horse.

"Don't be frightened, Miss Bryant. 'Tis only I, Fergus."

He didn't know why he used his Christian name. Nothing about her so far had invited intimacy.

"Fergus," she said in a faint, distant voice. "Fergus Shaw. Am I here, truly, on your father's farm in North Carolina?"

"Aye, of course you are," he said.

"I know you'll think me foolish—I am foolish—but I can never trust myself to be sure. That's why I had to hide. I couldn't let your sisters see me this way."

"What way?"

Thunder crashed overhead, and Miss Bryant buried her face in Fergus's waistcoat. He looked down at her, too shocked to move, then slowly put his arms around her. He could feel her shaking against him.

"Thunder? You're afraid of thunder?"

She spoke into his chest. "Not thunder. The cannonade."

Everything came clear. "The cannonade at Charlestown. You hear the thunder, and it feels as if you're back there with the British artillery firing on the city, and the Patriots' cannon firing on the enemy. You know 'tis all over, but you cannot believe it."

"Aye. 'Tis foolish, I know, but I can't stop. I can't stop!"

"'Tisn't foolish at all. Some memories are simply too strong for us to contain, and they break out at times. I've heard of soldiers who cannot abide the sound of gunfire after they go home, or even a slamming door."

"Does it ever end?"

"It gets better, I'm told."

Thunder crashed again, louder than ever. She cowered against him, and he held her tight. He could feel her breath going in and out, hard and fast beneath her stays.

"Why does it happen?" she asked, her voice muffled against his waistcoat. "What does it mean? I can smell the sulfur from the guns, Fergus. How is that possible? Am I weak in the head?"

"Miss Bryant, you're the last woman in the world I'd call weak in the head. Hard and stubborn your head may be, but sound as a nut. You've only borne more than you should ever have had to."

He picked up a handful of clean, bright straw and eased away from her just enough to hold it to her face. "Smell this. Feel it. Hear it crinkle. Touch the boards of the stall. Feel the grain of the wood. This is real."

She did as he said. Her breathing slowed, and he felt some of the tension go out of her as she rested her head against him once more and shut her eyes.

Minutes passed in silence. He was just beginning to wonder if she'd fallen asleep when she finally spoke.

"I remember the day I woke to find the first British gun pointed at the city. At first they fired mostly at the galleys or the lines—not the town itself, except for a few stray shots. We fell into a foolish sense of security then, but they were only waiting to get their batteries in place on Charlestown Neck. Then the real bombardment started. It went from ten in the morning until midnight. The guns on Hampstead Hill fired hot shot, and it burned some houses in Ansonborough. We started the day bravely enough—going about our business, visiting one another, or looking at the defenses, just as we'd done all along, as if none of it could hurt us—but we were all cowering in our cellars before it was through. Some women and children were killed. Everyone said how horrible that was. But why should we think it worse for a woman or a child than for a grown man? Why is it any more fitting for a man to have his head or half his ribcage torn off by an iron ball?"

"I don't know. Perhaps because 'tis men who make war, and women and children ought to have no part in it."

"But 'tisn't even all men who make war, just a powerful few. Most of those who fight and die are only following orders."

"True enough. The field soldiers do the worst work for the lowest pay and die in the greatest numbers while having the least to say about any of it. It doesn't seem fair. But what's to be done? When my home is threatened, whatever the cause, I must defend it."

She opened her gold-flecked eyes and gazed up at him. "That's just it. Home ought to be safe. It ought not to be allowed for foreign armies to come and destroy people's homes. Charlestown was our city, and it was old and proud and beautiful. What did King George mean by sending his dragoons and foot regiments and hired Hessians to hem it in and starve it out and smash it with iron balls? Why couldn't he leave us alone?"

Her voice had risen. Now she shut her eyes again and covered her ears with her hands. "That horrid cannonade! It went on all day every day and made me hate everyone. I knew the soldiers in the line were suffering far more than I, but I didn't care. The cease fires only made it worse—lovely and peaceful while they lasted, like the first cool weather in fall, but the barrage always started again, louder than ever after the silence. I lost track of how many times they ceased fire, discussed terms, and fired again. I couldn't trust the silence. And it was all so senseless by then. They'd already beaten us. What use was there in holding out for favorable terms? I was glad when Lincoln surrendered, because I thought now the quiet would last. But I was wrong."

She let out a shuddering breath.

"The British ordered the Americans to turn in their weapons and ammunition at the magazine. Some of the muskets were loaded, and one of them touched off a powder keg. I was outside when it happened, reveling in the quiet and the fresh, clean air. Suddenly there was a boom so deep, it sounded like it split the earth. A cloud of vapor rose up, filled with ramrods, bayonets, gun barrels, musket balls, and chunks of masonry. There was fire in the streets—people wailing—burning bodies—limbs hanging from buildings—"

She rocked back and forth again. Fergus was wrung with sympathy. He wished he could say something to ease her distress, but what could words do?

"One man was flung against a church steeple. His body left an imprint. The explosion killed more people than the siege itself—and it was all so senseless and stupid and wrong. We were supposed to be safe now. We'd surrendered. There was nothing left to give. 'Twasn't fair!"

Thunder roared, shaking the stall. Miss Bryant hid her face against Fergus's chest again and wept. He put his arms around her and let her.

The rain began to fall, hard at first, then gently. After a while the thunder receded, and Miss Bryant's sobs subsided.

"Tell me about something that isn't war," she said.

"Like what?"

"I don't know. Something pleasant. I can't remember pleasant things right now."

Fergus's mind was blank. He'd never been clever or good with words, the way Tavish and Rory were. It was real things that he loved, not fancies.

"I'll tell you about the happiest time I can remember," he said. "'Twas before the war, when my brothers and I would build rafts out of casks of tar and turpentine and sail them down the river to port. Sometimes there wasn't a soul to be seen, nor any shore in sight—just herons and gulls, and sometimes alligators. We'd strip to the waist, peel off our stockings, and let the sun soak into our skin. Rory would talk about all the plants and animals and the river currents, and Liam liked to pretend we were sailors. I just listened, or thought my own thoughts, or went to sleep to the sound of the running water."

"You must miss Liam."

Her voice was strangely gentle. He'd never heard her speak that way before.

"Aye, I do."

"How did he die?"

"Die? Liam didn't die. He went to sea."

She drew back far enough to look him in the face, her mouth open in an O of astonishment. Then she laughed. He laughed too, pleased that he'd managed to drive out the fear, at least for the moment.

"Forgive me for assuming," said Miss Bryant. "The way you all talked about him, or didn't talk about him, I thought he was dead."

"I can see why you'd think that. 'Tis mostly on Father's account that we don't speak of him. Liam left on bad terms. Father didn't want him to go to sea—he wanted him in the militia, taking his turn with the rest of us. At least that way he'd be home nine months out of twelve, working on the farm. But Liam wanted to go to sea. And one night, he just left. Went aboard a merchant vessel bound for the West Indies. We couldn't trace him farther, and we only learned that much after Father turned the port upside-down making inquiries. He might actually *be* dead, for all we know. That's another reason Father didn't want him to go. A life at sea is so uncertain, constantly moving from vessel to vessel and port to port. Men and boys die of sickness and accident and combat, or get taken prisoner, or go down with their ships, and sometimes their families never learn what became of them. But Liam always dreamed of far-off adventure. I never did. I always loved home best. When the stock is taken care of and the resin is flowing well and all is as it should be, I feel rich as a lord. With good streams, good grass, strong stock, and the foaling and calving going off well, and plenty of wood in the woodbox, what more is there to ask?"

She smiled at him. "I believe you're very like your father, though you don't look like him."

"I look like my mother. Liam looks like my father."

"Your father is such an unexpected person. I was amazed to find him so young a man, quite in his prime. I actually took him for a hired man at first. He scarcely looks a day over thirty—and yet he's precisely the same age as my father. But my father isn't much like your father. He drinks and eats too much, stays out too late at taverns, and gambles too much on horse races—or he did. When I think of him now, confined on a prison ship, with foul air and foul food—I don't know how he'll bear the strain."

Fergus struggled to find something to say that was both comforting and truthful. But before the silence could grow very long, Melina ended it herself.

"Well, he will bear it, because he must. And I'll go to him and take care of him, and look after Trailing Oaks. I'm his only child—all the son he'll ever have, as he likes to say. We've been everything to each other, ever since we lost my mother and baby brother. Whatever must be done to save Trailing Oaks, and Papa, I'll do."

"I believe you," said Fergus.

By now, the rainfall had subsided to a gentle drizzle and the thunder to a distant rumble. He could smell the sweetness of straw and rain-washed earth, and something else, perhaps lavender, from Miss Bryant's hair.

It didn't seem possible that he was lying here in Hector's stall with Miss Bryant in his arms. He must get her to the house and make some excuse for her absence—they'd both been gone far too long already—but he wanted to stay here forever.

Chapter Four

Melina dressed in the grey light of some hour the likes of which had never seen her rise at Trailing Oaks, but was evidently a normal waking time for working persons in the Shaw household. While Nessa laced her stays for her, she watched her face in the glass. It looked strange and wan.

If nothing else, the hour was suited to sober reflection. Melina had never been one to avoid painful truth. By the time the June sun brought a hint of color through the window, she had her resolve—and she looked like Melina Bryant again, though clad in a plain linen gown with her hair simply dressed for a day of honest toil.

On a whim, she added a silken hair ribbon she'd brought from Charlestown.

She met Fergus Shaw in the central passage, just as she had on the previous morning. He smiled at her, and there was genuine warmth in his voice when he bade her good morning. He'd been so kind and gentle to her in the carriage shed yesterday, holding her in his arms and speaking words of comfort and reassurance. She wanted to know him better.

But there was no future for her with the son of a middling planter of no great wealth. And the sooner she made that clear, the better.

"Good morning, Mr. Shaw," she replied. Then—quickly, before she could change her mind—she went on, "I must thank you for your indulgence yesterday, and also beg your pardon. I cannot think what came over me. I can only suppose that the fatigues of the past month must have overwhelmed me at last and led me to a degree of familiarity that our acquaintance did not justify. I pray you will forgive the liberty. It shall not be repeated."

She'd chosen the words carefully and gone over them until she knew them by heart, and the delivery had come off perfectly. She knew what she was about. By the time she'd reached her twentieth birthday she'd already refused five marriage proposals. The tone she'd used then served equally well now.

Fergus stood a moment, eyes wide and stunned. Then his face closed off.

"There is no need to apologize, madam," he said. "No one could have supposed you to have been sincere."

He tried to make a haughty exit but spoiled the effect by tripping in the passage.

Once he'd gone, Melina let herself droop on the banister. For a moment she wished she hadn't spoken. She'd certainly had no qualms back home about stringing along men she had no intention of accepting. But good, clean, decent Fergus Shaw deserved better than that. He was in a category all his own.

AFTER BREAKFAST, MELINA and Nessa held a council of war.

"Just what sort of work must be done to manage a household?" Melina asked. "Cooking? Cleaning? Knitting? Polishing silver? I've heard the terms, but I've no skills whatsoever. Perhaps I should try several tasks to see if I have a natural affinity for any."

Nessa laughed. "Natural affinity plays little part, I assure you. With time and repetition, you'll learn it all, as everyone does. We ought to work in the garden this morning before it gets too hot, and this afternoon Morna and I have some mending to do. I'll start you on some plain sewing then."

"Aye, sewing! I'm familiar with needles–I've done a bit of fancy work. In the meantime, to the garden!"

Telling weed from sprout wasn't difficult, once Melina knew what to look for, and it was satisfying to pull the taproots from the sandy soil. Dougie, the black-and-white dog, kept them company, and by the time the sun grew high in the sky, Nessa said it was time to get dinner ready.

Sewing was another matter. Twenty minutes in, Melina wished never to see or touch another needle again. Her back ached, her fingers smarted with needle-pricks, and her mind was in a snarl. How could Nessa and Morna go on as they did? How did they not scream and weep and hurl the hussif across the room? They were chatting pleasantly, quite at their ease. How did they make the needle mind them and go where they wished? Their projects looked vastly more complex than hers, a mere straight seam on a man's new shirt. They were mending garments already made, worming their way into tiny seams crossed and puckered by other seams, and shrunken by many washings. Melina would have gone mad over such a task. She might go mad yet. Why must people wear textile clothing? Why not make do with furs and large leaves, or live in a tropical climate?

The afternoon wore on. Melina stuck to her task with deadly determination. Her honor was at stake. She would prove herself an exemplary worker to Mr. Shaw or perish in the attempt.

But her mind kept wandering to Fergus. He hadn't so much as looked at her over breakfast or dinner—difficult, as they sat opposite each other at table. Was it really only yesterday that she had clung to him in the horse stall and felt his arms strong and protective around her? She had poured out her heart to him, sharing fears she had never spoken aloud to anyone, and it had felt perfectly safe and natural.

She wondered suddenly if the pile of creamy linen in her lap was destined to be a shirt of his, then stabbed hard at the seam and pricked her finger.

Nessa heard her quick gasp of pain.

"Would you like to take a quick walk in the woods, Melina? Sewing is so tiring to the back muscles, and you are not used to it."

Melina was already on her feet. "How kind you are, Nessa. You're right—my back and shoulders ache horribly. I'm sure a walk in the woods will refresh me."

And give me a chance to train my thoughts on something other than your brother.

"'Tis coolest along the banks of the streams," said Morna. "Just head toward the river, and you're sure to find one. They'll be high after the rain, so take care."

"And don't stay away long," said Nessa, no doubt thinking of yesterday's prolonged absence.

"No, indeed! I'll be back within a quarter of an hour."

West of the house, the land sloped gently toward the river. Melina drew deep breaths of pine-scented air. Sunlight filtered greenly through the thin canopy of wide-spaced pines as straight as lances.

She thought of the two live oaks that guarded the gate at home—ancient, heavy-limbed trees, wider than they were tall, with dense crowns that met overhead and covered the ground with inky shade. By now, the British might have cut them down, and burned the house, like that ruined mansion at Brunswick Town. She knew they'd raided the stables at Trailing Oaks. It made her throat ache to think of Rogue and Asher and the others carrying Banastre Tarleton's dragoons into the noise and smoke of battle, into the paths of slashing sabers and whizzing musket balls.

Small pools of rainwater glinted in the hollows between tree roots, but the sandy paths were firm, and she was wearing a stout pair of Morna's boots. Not a wisp of cloud showed in the sky that had roared with thunder yesterday, taking her back to the siege in defiance of sense and reason.

For a long time she'd wondered if these episodes of hers were a sign of madness. But Fergus said they were not, and that they would diminish over time, and she believed him. There was no falsehood in Fergus. He was fearlessly himself through and through, as true as steel. Having felt the full force of his disapproval, she could not doubt the sincerity of his tenderness. She'd felt it in his warm solidity, seen it in the brilliance of his dark eyes in his sober face.

She halted in her tracks.

"Stop it," she said aloud. "Stop it at once."

She couldn't allow herself to brood over the perfections of a man she could never marry. Marriage was for alliances, for advantageous joining of property, either landed or mercantile. She'd been taught that since she was old enough to know what marriage was, and she intended to do her duty. Trailing Oaks depended on her. There were no other children to inherit.

She walked on, faster now. She must push down this feeling she had for Fergus Shaw until it went away. Fancies were temporary. Land was forever.

She came to a rain-swollen stream and turned to follow its bank. The air was cooler here and smelled sweet. Overhead, grey fox squirrels with black faces and wee white muzzles scampered among the curving pine boughs. A black-and-white woodpecker beat a brisk tattoo against a trunk. Fallen pine cones longer than her foot lay among the needle litter. Clumps of luscious-looking berries hung from dense bushes and vines, and wedges of fungus grew in a stair-step column up a tree. ·

She stopped.

What business had a black cocked hat and a grey waistcoat to be lying on a huckleberry bush near the bank of the stream? Or stockings and shoes, or a man's linen shirt, or a pair of breeches?

Belated understanding broke over her. With a rough gasp, she jerked backwards, stumbled, lurched forward, fell headlong—

And saw Fergus Shaw bathing in the stream.

He stood with his back to her, water up to his waist, hands resting on its surface. His wet hair, loosed from its braid, formed a gleaming black triangle between his shoulder blades. At the sound of Melina's fall he turned. His profile was like something carved from marble by a Greek master, its high martial brow and jutting chin stark and clear against the dark green water. Then he turned back, unconcerned, and walked deeper into the stream, the separate muscles of his back moving smoothly in a rippling, articulated sequence beneath the skin. He hadn't seen her, but it had been a near thing.

Melina let out a silent sigh of relief. Then, with a jolt of horror, she realized she was spying on a man at his bath—a man not merely naked in his shirt, but actually "from nature." She thought again of Greek statues, and her face grew hot. The water offered some concealment now, but at any moment he might come striding up the bank and find her basely hiding in the wiregrass, peering at him.

She must get away, now, as quickly and quietly as possible.

She crawled backwards on her elbows and knees, not caring how much noise she made or how dirty she got or how the berry vines tore at her skin. Once clear of the bank, she got to her feet and hurried back to the house, where she sewed doggedly for the rest of the afternoon.

IT SEEMED A PERVERSE chance that she of all people was sent to call Fergus in to supper. Her afternoon's walk had failed spectacularly. Rather than driving out the memory of Fergus in the carriage house, it had added the memory of Fergus in the stream.

But she would manage. She would bid him to come to supper, and that would be all.

She found him outside a small shed west of the dooryard, a musket in his hand. Beside him, a stump held gun-cleaning equipment.

The stockings she'd last seen draped over a berry bush were now stretched over shapely calves and slender ankles. Her eye followed the line upward, along the lean curve in the back of the thigh and the fuller curve above that. The sleeves of his shirt were rolled up to the elbows, and his hair, which she'd last seen loose, was neatly braided and tied with a plain black ribbon.

He pulled out the ramrod and dropped it down the barrel. Bracing one foot against the stump, he laid the musket across his thigh, put the lock on half-cock, and unfastened it with a turnscrew. He eased the lock back, then carefully wrapped it and the lock screw in a cloth and set them on the stump. He picked up a stick that had been whittled to a point and shoved it into the vent hole. Standing the piece on its stock again, he wrapped a rag around the muzzle's end and held it as he poured steaming water from a tin cup down the bore. Then he rested the gun carefully against the shed wall. While it soaked, he wiped the lock clean with a damp rag and dried it on his shirt.

Without looking up, he said, "If you're going to watch, you might as well make yourself useful and hand me that bit of fixing wax."

She started guiltily at the sound of his voice but quickly recovered. "As a matter of fact, I've been quite useful today," she said, picking up the chunk of wax and the cloth it rested on. "You can ask your sisters. I weeded the tomatoes, and I sewed a very ugly seam."

He held out his hand, and she gave him the wax and cloth.

"Congratulations," he said, still not looking up.

The musket was a fowling piece from a few decades back. Fergus rubbed the wax all over the lock with his long, lean hands, smearing it against the metal in a thin coat and releasing the scent of tallow and beeswax. His face had a look of serene stillness, and all his movements were careful and precise, without the slightest suggestion of haste. He removed the flint from the cock's jaws, sharpened it with a piece of horn, and returned it to its place. Then he laid the lock on its cloth on the stump again, turned the musket upside-down, and pulled the stick out of the vent hole, allowing the water to run out the bore. He leaned the musket against the wall again to let it fully drain while he cut a patch from a piece of cotton cloth. Flipping the musket right-side up, he laid the patch over the muzzle, drove it into the bore with the ramrod, twisted the ramrod a few turns, and pulled it out.

Melina looked at the patch. "You're a most careful and conscientious gunman, Mr. Shaw. There's not a speck of powder on that cloth."

"Aye," he said as he ran another patch through. "I always clean it well before I put it away, and I go over it afresh before muster."

"Muster?"

"Aye, 'tis my turn. I told you how Father and Tavish and I stagger our enlistment periods so there's always a man on the farm."

"When do you leave?"

"Tomorrow morning."

"Oh. I see."

She felt strangely off balance. "Well, I warrant you'll have the cleanest musket in the Wilmington militia forces."

Smiling, he rubbed a final patch over the fixing wax and ran it down the bore, twisting the ramrod thoroughly. "That's something, anyhow. I only hope they'll have powder enough for us all."

"Where will you go?"

"The rendezvous point is at Cross Creek. After that, I hope we'll join Gates and de Kalb and do something decisive at last—though whether we'll meet either of them in Cross Creek, or elsewhere, or at all, there's no telling. Perhaps we'll get word on the road, perhaps not."

She watched him wipe all around the vent hole and top of the barrel with a damp cloth, followed by the waxy cloth. She felt a hollow sense of disappointment at the thought of his absence.

Nonsense. His leaving will be the best thing in the world for us both.

He picked up the lock, put it on half-cock, and fitted it to the musket's mortise. She handed him the turnkey before he could reach for it.

"You seem to know your way around a musket," he said.

"Papa taught me. He took me hunting sometimes in the woods around Trailing Oaks."

"Are you a good shot?"

"Aye, they used to call me Deadeye Bryant."

He looked up sharply from turning the lock screw, saw that she was teasing, and laughed. She'd never heard him laugh before.

"Do be careful, Mr. Shaw."

The words sounded more anxious than she'd intended.

"I thank you for your concern, Miss Bryant, but there's no reason to worry. Most likely I'll do nothing more than wander around the backcountry until my term expires."

The final word struck her oddly. She imagined him facing the enemy with his shining-clean musket with no shot or powder in it, a lead ball tearing through his shirt and piercing his heart. All at once she wanted to lay her hand to his chest, to feel the heat of his skin and the rhythm of his breathing through the thin linen.

She untied the ribbon from her hair and pressed it into his hand. "Here. Take this. Let it remind you that there are people at home who are thinking of you, and praying for you, and waiting for your return."

As soon as the words were out, they sounded overwrought and foolish. Who did she think she was, a medieval lady bestowing a favor on a knight? How could she be so absurd? And just when things had gotten so courteous and comfortable between them, too!

Something in his face eased, and his dark eyes grew bright. "Thank you, Miss Bryant. I'll put it in my lucky hat."

He took a buff-colored hat from a peg and tucked the ribbon inside the cockade. It was not his everyday hat that she'd seen him wear before. A scorched furrow marked the crown from front to back.

"A British musket ball did that," he said. "'Twas my first battle, at Moore's Creek Bridge, where, as you may recall, the militia forces acquitted themselves rather well."

Melina did recall. "How old were you then?" she asked.

"Seventeen."

A mere stripling. She'd been sixteen herself, with her head full of silken gowns and dances and theatre-going, and the war had seemed very far away. And yet if that gallant force of a thousand untried minutemen and militiamen had not done its duty in a cold North Carolina swamp, the British might well have overwhelmed both Carolinas, and all the South, in a matter of months.

A bag of coarse linen lay on the stump. Melina put the turnkey, fixing wax, and other supplies in the bag.

"There," Fergus said, pulling the lock back to make sure it was fully functional. "That ought to pass muster. Lock, stock, and barrel. And powder, eventually, I hope."

Chapter Five

Fergus couldn't stop looking at the trees. He'd never seen so many different kinds all in one place. At home, longleafs dominated the woods. There were other trees—oaks and cypresses and different types of pine—but the longleafs were the great guardians, straight and tall with limbs held high above the understory, filtering a diffuse haze of sunlight through their needles, and casting a thin shade. Here at Deep River, hardwoods and evergreens were evenly matched, with oaks, maples, alders, elms, and hickories growing alongside pines and firs. Together they formed a thick canopy, beneath which flourished a tangled riot of every imaginable shade of green. Vines crawled along the riverbank, and ferns sprang from every crevice. An occasional rustle in the leaves hinted at snakes.

He waded out to where the river moved fastest and filled his pail. The water was neither cold nor swift in the middle of July, but the current stirring about his legs refreshed him. Bits of leaf and soil eddied past, on their way south and east, where they would join the waters of the Haw, then receive those of the Black, before flowing to Cape Fear, and home.

Making his way back to shore, he saw one of the Continentals pick a wild muscadine grape from a lush overhead vine and give it a speculative look. The man was broad in build, with a snub nose and loose-fitting breeches held up by a belt that had clearly been tightened in recent weeks.

Another man—lean and spare, with a shrewd brown face and a hunting shirt that had seen better days—said something that looked like a warning, but the first man popped the small green grape into his mouth anyway and began to chew. Immediately his expression soured, and he spat the grape out in disgust. Fergus's jaw tightened in sympathy. The fruit wouldn't ripen for another month at least, but he couldn't blame the man for trying.

He'd been shocked at his first sight of the famed Maryland and Delaware Continentals when they'd joined Caswell's militia forces at Deep River yesterday. The elite regiments of seasoned veterans from the north were grim and martial enough in bearing, but as ragged and emaciated as if they'd marched all the way from Philadelphia without a decent meal or a change of clothing.

The snub-nosed man picked up a stick and struck wrathfully at the grapevine. Instantly a long brown snake dropped out of the overhead leaves onto the man's head and shoulders.

He let out a shriek and turned into a mass of writhing limbs and expletives. The snake did its own share of writhing. The lean man leaped clear to a safe distance.

It took only a few seconds for the snake to slither to the ground.

"Kill it!" said the snub-nosed man. "Shoot it!"

The lean man took the pistol from his belt.

By now, Fergus had reached them. "Nay, save your powder. 'Tis naught but a harmless brown water snake."

"The villain attacked me!" said the first man.

"He only fell on you, after you knocked him from the grapevine. He's more frightened than you are."

"I wouldn't bet on that," said the second man, but he put the pistol back, and the snake disappeared into the herbage.

Deprived of vengeance on the snake, the snub-nosed man rounded on Fergus. "This is the most infernal country I ever saw! I've been half drowned in a muddy canal at Gowanus Heights and had the ends of my toes froze off at Valley Forge, but never in all my soldiering days did I see such a wretched place as this, with its swarms of flying insects, and hordes of snakes, and smothering heat with no relief to be found day or night. I'm drove near out of my wits by a thing called a tick, like a whopping great flea that bites down and never lets go, not even after its body's shorn clean off its head. We've marched for days at a time without setting eyes on a human habitation—and with never a morsel of food fit to eat."

Fergus drew himself up stiffly. "I assure you, sir, that North Carolina is as civilized as any state in the Union. If you were a guest at my father's table, you'd find no cause to complain of the fare."

"Then I wish I was at his board this minute, for I'd eat out his whole larder at a sitting, and then start in on the fodder in the barn. I haven't had a square meal since I don't know when, and your state's been awful stingy with the grub. All we've had is lean stringy beef and green fruit for weeks on end. Any more of this and I'll fall to eating grass like Nebuchadnezzar."

"What can you expect?" Fergus retorted. "This part of the state is Loyalist country, and we've months to go before harvest. The few Patriots here have little enough for themselves and the militia."

The snub-nosed man's mouth flattened. "You speak as if we're a band of wayfarers begging for bread. The only reason we're here at all is to save your province from being overrun by the British, and we came a long way to do it."

"You're not the first men to march across state lines to defend a place far from home," said Fergus. "The Continentals of North Carolina spilled their blood at Brandywine and Germantown and were taken prisoner at Charlestown. So if my state seems reluctant to give anything more to the Continental Congress or the Continental Line, it is not without cause."

The lean man in the hunting shirt held his hands up peaceably. "Gentlemen, please! Our nation is a young one, and as soldiers in this war I fear we are fated to be poorly provisioned. We all have legitimate grievances, but our quarrel is not with each other."

Fergus bowed to him. "You're right, sir. Allow me to welcome you to North Carolina. I am Private Fergus Shaw, Wilmington District Militia."

The lean man bowed back. "Corporal John Reynolds, Second Maryland Brigade. My friend is Private William Carson of the Delaware Regiment."

"At your service," Carson muttered.

Reynolds swept his arm toward a shady spot beneath a hickory tree. "I'm happy to meet you, Shaw. Fresh faces and voices and stories are welcome diversions. Step into my parlor, gentlemen."

Fergus set down his pail and sat in the shade with Reynolds while Carson inspected the thick clusters of green nuts growing on the tree's lower limbs.

"I wouldn't try it if I were you," Fergus said. "They aren't ripe yet."

"I was looking for snakes," Carson said huffily. Satisfied at last, he dropped to the ground with a sigh.

Reynolds leaned his back against the hickory's trunk. "So, you're a local man, Shaw. What can you tell us about the enemy's disposition here?"

"'Tis none too secure," Fergus replied. "They still have Charlestown, but they've failed to take the backcountry. They're close to losing the outpost at Ninety-Six, and Lord Rawdon holds the crossroads at Camden by a thread. The militia's harassment has kept them from making lasting gains. And we've had solid victories at Ramsour's mill and Williamson's plantation."

He didn't even attempt to keep the pride out of his voice. Ever since the fall of Charlestown, militia was all the Carolinas had left, and they'd not been idle.

"And did you fight in any of those engagements?" Reynolds asked.

Fergus deflated a little. "Nay. My brigade has seen no action since Cross Creek, early in the war. But that will change soon. General Gates will arrive any day now to take command of us all. Then we can move on Camden. Camden is key. Once the British lose it, they lose all hope of ever controlling the backcountry. We'll drive them out of Charlestown and out of the South for good."

"Let us hope that the Hero of Saratoga lives up to his reputation," said Reynolds.

"Of that I have no doubt," said Fergus. "Tell me about Baron de Kalb. He seems a stouthearted and sensible gentleman."

Carson spoke up, having at last found something he could praise. "Aye, he is that, and more. He's every inch a warrior, French nobleman or no."

"The baron is Bavarian, not French," said Reynolds, "and peasant-born."

"He reminds me of my father," Fergus said.

"Ah, your father," said Carson. "Him of the ample larder. Does he wear a gold-embroidered waistcoat like de Kalb?"

Fergus smiled. "Nay. He looks nothing like the baron. But they have something alike in manner and countenance, something noble and patient and stern."

"I'll be the judge of that," Carson said. "Your father owes me a meal, Shaw. You promised me. Didn't he, Reynolds?"

"I don't believe he—"

"There, see? Reynolds is my witness. You promised me a meal at your father's house, and when this war is over, I'm going to claim it."

Carson lay on his back and folded his hands over his chest. "Perhaps I'll stay on as a permanent house guest. I'll be a regular gentleman of leisure, and make as much trouble as I can."

Fergus didn't reply. He pulled a knife from his belt and brought it down swiftly, its long blade slicing into the earth inches from Carson's face.

Carson jumped up, sputtering curses. "What's the matter with you, Shaw? I was only joking."

In response, Fergus picked up the body of the snake whose head he had just severed. It was a good three feet in length, thick and muscular, and still wriggling.

Carson's face blanched beneath his tan. He shuddered and let out a low groan.

"I thought you weren't afraid of a harmless brown water snake, Shaw," said Reynolds.

"I'm not," said Fergus. "This is a cottonmouth, and its bite would have ruined Carson's day."

He covered the head with a rock to prevent the venomous fangs from pricking anyone.

"I don't think I like your parlor much, Reynolds," said Carson.

Still gripping the squirming snake, Fergus got to his feet and picked up his water bucket. "Then come to mine, both of you. You say you're tired of lean stringy beef, Carson. Here's your chance to try a different meat."

"THAT WAS THE BEST GRUB I've had since somewhere in Philadelphia," said Carson.

They were sitting around the remains of a fire in the militia camp—Carson, Reynolds, Fergus, and Jack Stewart, the only one of Fergus's messmates who'd cared to share a meal of roasted snake.

Stewart was only eighteen, a shopkeeper's son from Wilmington who'd never yet fired his musket in battle. In his eyes, even Fergus seemed a seasoned veteran. He listened, spellbound, as Reynolds and Carson told how they'd fought their way through Brooklyn and Valley Forge, and marched from Philadelphia hungry and barefoot, carrying stores and munitions on their backs. Two thousand of them had set out, but desertion and camp fever had thinned their numbers. Carson had buried a brother somewhere in Virginia.

That trail of hasty ill-marked graves horrified Fergus far more than the Marylanders' tales of open battle. It was one thing to die like a man, facing the enemy with your musket discharged. It was another to spill your bowels in a bloody flux without ever firing a shot.

The conversation turned to home. Reynolds was a farmer, with a wife and son, and a baby daughter he'd never seen. Carson was a shoemaker and a bachelor.

"War is no time for love," said Carson. "My brother was newly married, poor devil. How about you, Shaw? Have you a wife or sweetheart at home?"

"Neither," said Fergus.

"What about the girl who gave you the hair ribbon you keep in your hat?" asked Stewart.

Fergus shrugged. "A distant relation from South Carolina. My father took her in after Charlestown fell. She's nothing to me."

"But you take her hair ribbon out at night and hold it in your hand," said Stewart. "You keep it close to you until reveille, when you stick it back in your hat. I've seen you."

"Oho!" said Carson. "What do you say to that, Shaw?"

Fergus poked the fire to hide his flaming cheeks, mentally cursing the sharp-eyed Stewart and his own weakness. Melina Bryant was a beautiful woman, aye, and it had been sweet, holding her in his arms in the carriage shed. But she'd lost no time putting him in his place the next morning.

"She's a rich man's daughter," he said at last. "She could never care for a plain planter's son, as she herself made abundantly clear."

"And yet she gave you her hair ribbon," said Reynolds.

"She's a vain, flighty creature," said Fergus. "She probably gives away a hair ribbon every week."

And yet there'd been something in her eyes that day, as she'd watched him clean his musket, that he couldn't forget.

TWO MORE DAYS PASSED, and still General Gates did not come. Provisions were low. Heat weighted Fergus down like a woolen blanket. Insects rasped and rattled, bit and stung.

All this he could have borne well enough if only he'd had a meaningful task. But so far in this muster period, he'd done nothing but march and wait, wasting time and energy that could have been spent at home, tending stock or mending fence. He longed for his own bed, his favorite chair in the parlor, the stream where he liked to bathe. They were as clear-cut as crystal in his memory—and so was Melina Bryant, with her wide-spaced hazel eyes and fine-boned face.

He was desperate for orders, for something to do. Finally, his chance came.

Katydids and crickets called across the twilit woods as Fergus hurried to the Continentals' camp to tell his friends the news. He found Reynolds writing a letter, and Carson nursing a flask of rum.

"We're leaving," he told them.

Reynolds turned sharply, and Carson sat bolt upright.

"What?" asked Carson. "When? We haven't been told. Has Gates sent word?"

Fergus held up his hands. "Nay, 'tis only the North Carolinians who are leaving. General Caswell is taking us west to meet some other militia units under General Rutherford."

Carson slumped back with a sigh, and Reynolds laid down his quill.

"General Gates won't like that," said Reynolds. "He'll expect to find Caswell waiting when he arrives."

"Don't mind Reynolds, Shaw," said Carson. "He's just nettled that you get to leave this place while we have to stay. So am I."

Fergus tried to keep his excitement from showing too plainly, but he knew he wasn't succeeding. He hoped the move westward would mean better forage for the horses. Bran had carried him so willingly, and it grieved Fergus to see how lean he'd grown.

"I'm sorry to leave you two," he said, honestly enough. "But we'll see each other again, at Camden or on the way there."

"We'll miss you, Shaw, and your cooking," said Reynolds. "Think of us the next time you roast a snake."

"I'll do better than that," Fergus replied. "We're to thresh some wheat before we go, enough for ourselves and for you. When I see you next, you'll be fat and sleek."

CASWELL'S FORCE CROSSED the Yadkin and headed to the confluence of the Rocky and Pee Dee rivers. Rutherford had already crossed to the other side of the Pee Dee. He and Caswell moved down the river together on opposite sides. Divided foraging parties meant more food for the troops.

A week after they crossed into South Carolina, the Continental Army joined Caswell's militia at their camp. General Gates had come at last to take command.

Reynolds and Carson had not grown fat and sleek. They looked even thinner and more careworn than before, and Fergus said so.

Carson swore.

"We've been on reduced rations," Reynolds told Fergus. "Green corn, green peaches, and scrawny cattle driven out from the swamps. No bread. The officers are using hair powder to thicken their soup."

"What about all the grain we left you?" asked Fergus.

"Long gone," said Carson. "And General Gates didn't see a kernel of the lot that was sent to him. The Virginian militia got to it first."

"Your General Caswell is out of favor with the Commander in Chief, Shaw," said Reynolds. "Gates reached Deep River the day after you left and was none too pleased to find the North Carolina militia gone. He's been lambasting Caswell for stripping the countryside bare along the way to Camden."

"We did no such thing," said Fergus. "Caswell purposely took us on a different route from yours so as not to exhaust the land."

"Talking of routes," said Carson, with a sidewise glance at Reynolds.

Reynolds groaned and shook his head.

"What is it?" asked Fergus.

"There was some difference of opinion over the way we ought to come," said Reynolds. "Our own Colonel Williams favored a more westward route. He said it would lead through country more fertile, and friendlier to Patriots."

"True enough," said Fergus.

"Well, Gates wouldn't hear of it," said Carson, "He chose a direct southward course, on a forced march through worn-out land inhabited by Tories. He was determined to get his men moved in the shortest time possible, even if it meant marching them half to death."

"He must have had his reasons," Fergus said slowly.

"He's trying to prove himself worthy to replace Washington," said Reynolds. "All the naysayers are calling Washington indecisive and slow—so Gates must be the opposite. Every move he's made since taking command in the South has been swift and bold to the point of recklessness."

"You should have seen the transfer of command ceremony, Shaw," said Carson. "All pomp and nonsense. Gates called us his Grand Army and marked the occasion with a thirteen-gun salute—and all of us panting with heat and slapping at insects, and wanting nothing more than some decent grub and a long rest."

The bitter words shook Fergus's confidence, but he said only, "The important thing is that we're together now. We outnumber Rawdon's force at Camden. We'll drive the British out of the South, and end the war before the close of the year."

"Just now, I don't care," said Carson. "After that forced march from Deep River, all I want is to put up my feet and rest."

He was not allowed to. The combined army continued to march southward for six grueling days.

They rested for two days at a plantation called Clermont, a well-tended place situated on smooth swells of rolling ground, with a grist mill along the creek. The sight of the neat, comfortable house and sturdy log barn made Fergus ache for his own home, his family—and Melina. What was she doing now? Did she ever think about that day in the carriage shed? Did she spare a prayer for him now and then? *Do be careful, Mr. Shaw,* she'd said, right before giving him the hair ribbon that was still tucked into his hat. Had her concern been genuine? Or had she forgotten all about him?

As he turned Bran out to graze, he said, "Eat up, my lad. You'll be munching grass at Camden ere long."

LATE IN THE AFTERNOON on the fifteenth of August, Fergus and Stewart met Reynolds and Carson at the Continentals' camp for a brief visit. After weeks of thinking and planning, the Grand Army had finally reached striking distance of Camden.

"'Twill almost be too easy," said young Stewart. "Our army's more than twice the size of Rawdon's."

Carson frowned. "More than twice? Says who?"

"General Gates," Fergus replied. "He says there are seven thousand of us, now that we're all joined up."

"Well, it don't sound right to me. What do you think, Reynolds?"

Reynolds shook his head. "By my reckoning, we have thirty-six hundred at most."

Stewart gave Fergus an anxious glance.

"We're still the superior force," Fergus said stoutly. "Rawdon has only two thousand."

"Numbers alone do not an engagement win," said Reynolds. "Our army is large, but also unwieldy and hodge-podge. Our troops have never once drilled together. How are we to march in the dark on an enemy, and keep to formations, and follow commands? Moreover, the bulk of our force is militia, raw and untried—no offense, gentlemen," he added, with a nod to Fergus and Stewart.

"I don't see why we have to march tonight at all," Carson grumbled. "We'd do better to wait here a few days."

"Aye," Reynolds agreed. "We could gather provisions, renew our strength, add to our numbers, cut off the enemy's supply convoys, and seize their magazines. The mere fact of our being here is a thorn in the British side. Time is on our side, not theirs. Haste can only hurt us."

He pressed his lips together. "I'm tired and hungry, and sick of my fate depending on the rivalries and shortsightedness and dyspepsia of other men. I have a baby daughter I've never laid eyes on, and crops in the field with no one to tend to them but a twelve-year-old son and a wife worn down with work and care. I just want to go home."

No one spoke. They all wanted to go home, but saying so only made things worse. For a moment, Fergus's longing for Melina swelled into a physical ache.

"You'll feel better once we reach Camden, Reynolds," said Stewart, in a clumsy attempt at comfort.

Fergus pulled himself together. "Aye, and better still once we take it. One more day, and the thing will be done. Years from now, Stewart and I will visit you two up north. You, Carson, will make me a bespoke pair of shoes—I'll be a prosperous planter who can afford luxuries, and Stewart will be running his father's shop. We'll all go to Reynolds's farm and see his crops, and talk about the battle at Camden, and how it was the turning point that drove the British out of the South."

Carson nearly choked up.

"If you come see me in Dover, Shaw, I'll make you the finest pair of shoes you ever saw. Better yet, I'll get some young workman to do it while you and I, and young Stewart here, go and have a pint together at the Golden Fleece."

Reynolds only smiled faintly and said, "You two had best get back to your own mess now. Word is we're to have some special treat prior to our forced march to the camp at Saunders Creek."

"Spirits?" asked Carson, perking up. "I thought they hadn't arrived in camp yet."

"Perhaps we intercepted some from the British," Fergus said, getting to his feet. "Farewell, friends. I'll look for you at Saunders Creek if I have a chance, and if not, I'll see you in Camden."

Back at their own camp, Fergus and Stewart were disappointed to learn that the spirits had not arrived after all. As fortification for the night's march, each man was given a full gill of molasses, which seemed more fitting as a remedy for sluggish bowels than as a treat for men about to march into battle. But after weeks of gnawing hunger, he wasn't about to turn it away. He poured the thick black liquid over his cornmeal mush, stirred the two into a sticky sweet sludge, and ate.

THEY MARCHED IN PROFOUND silence, passing through a wide-spaced forest of longleaf pines, over wiregrass already flattened by the passage of many feet. A full moon shone ahead. Fergus felt strange and solemn at being part of something so large and momentous and...grand. So what if General Gates had overestimated their numbers? This was still a Grand Army, and Fergus was proud to be part of it.

The baggage train followed somewhere in the rear of the column. Bran was there, pulling a wagon. Fergus didn't like leaving his horse in the care of strangers, but he'd been given no choice in the matter.

As he marched, his musket made a reassuring thump at his back. The cleanest musket in the Wilmington militia, Melina had called it. It was clean now, and his cartridge belt was full. All he needed was the chance to prove himself, and soon he would have it. The Grand Army would drive the British out of Camden, and Cornwallis would be forced to give up Charlestown. Melina's city, and her father, would be freed.

Beside him, Stewart suddenly bent double, then broke ranks. Fergus wondered, but didn't speak. General Gates had ordered strict silence for the march.

A few minutes later Stewart came back, looking wan. Soon after, another man fell out. Another followed, and another. Then Fergus felt an uncomfortable rumbling sensation in his own bowels. He tried to wait—surely they must reach Saunders Creek soon—but discomfort turned to urgency, and he hurried out of the ranks to find a convenient ditch.

His relief was only temporary. A few minutes after rejoining the column, he fell out again. By the third time, his martial spirit was ebbing low. He forced himself to think of Lexington and Concord, of British outrages at Charlestown and the surrounding countryside. They'd killed and plundered there, and stolen Melina's horses. And they would do it all again at his own home if they weren't stopped.

So he told himself. But all he could care about was the stabbing pain in his belly, and all he wanted was a hospitable bush to hide in until he'd evacuated the last traces of last night's molasses and cornmeal mush. A treat? They'd have been better off going hungry.

The moon was high overhead and shining bright as day when musket fire shattered the nighttime stillness.

The men halted. Not being in the vanguard, Fergus couldn't see what was happening, but he could hear hoofbeats.

"We must have encountered an enemy patrol," Stewart whispered.

But the exchange of fire had gone on too long. It sounded like a very hot fire indeed.

Gunfire continued through half an hour or so, followed by a sudden silence that pressed on the ears, as if both sides had ceased firing at the same instant. Then the men were marched a mile back down the road and ordered to lie on their arms until daybreak.

"I don't like this place as a field of battle," Fergus said.

He and Stewart were stretched out on the wiregrass beneath the stars, resting and waiting. With dawn only a few hours away, and the enemy encamped only a mile off, sleep was out of the question.

"Why not?" asked Stewart. "The road is firm, and the land is smooth and level."

"It only looks that way. This country is full of morasses and swamps. Our numbers won't do us any good if we can't flank the enemy and come around his rear. We'll be forced to go head-to-head, with our reserves stuck behind us."

"Then we'll mow straight through them, and be in Camden in time for supper."

Fergus didn't reply. It was too late to change anything, even if he could. The die was cast, and he ought not to sap Stewart's courage on the eve—nay, the morning—of his first battle.

"Let's rest while we can, Stewart," he said at last. "Dawn can't be far off."

IN THE GREY LIGHT BEFORE sunrise, the American battle lines formed up. To the right of the road was the Second Maryland Brigade, with the Delaware Regiment to the right of them. On the road's left were the three brigades of North Carolina militia, then the Virginia militia, some light infantry on the far left, and French cavalry behind them. The First Maryland stood in reserve behind the main line.

Fergus knew all this from charts, but there was a world of difference between seeing labeled blocks on a piece of parchment and standing in a line of men with a musket in his hand.

Reynolds was with the Second Maryland and Carson with the Delaware. They were somewhere in the line of men across the road, two hundred yards or less away, but they might as well be across the world. He knew the men of his own brigade, but the rest were strangers.

Straddling the road itself, between the Second Maryland and the North Carolina militia, were three six-pounder guns. There were two more between the Second Maryland and the Delaware. The rest were with the First Maryland.

Fergus's shirt stuck to his back. Already the air felt hot and humid without a breath of wind. He could feel the last seconds ticking away. This was the moment he'd been yearning for, the moment of action, but now that it was here, he wished himself back at Deep River, roasting snake meat over a fire, or anywhere but here.

A dark smudge like black smoke crawled up the road from the creek where the British forces had passed the night. As soon as the column drew close enough to reveal the outlines of individual men, the American artillerists on the road opened fire. The blasts tore through the morning stillness, firing grapeshot into the column. Fergus heard the cries of men and saw bodies fall, but the gaps closed and the column kept coming, deploying from column to line about two hundred yards from the American position. By now, British uniforms showed scarlet in the first rays of the rising sun. The line kept unfolding, stretching out to both sides in a wall of red. Cannon muzzles flashed, and the stench of powder mingled with the scent of pine.

The enemy regiments formed up. Fergus knew the commanders by reputation, but not by sight. He couldn't tell which regiment was which, though he could see by the preponderance of uniforms that the enemy had far more regulars than his own side. But there could be no mistaking the dragoons on horseback, still in column along the road, or their slim, youthful commander in his green jacket.

Fergus's mouth went dry. He was seeing Tarleton, and his Legion, with his own eyes.

He heard Stewart's quick intake of breath beside him, and his whispered, "Is that Bloody Ban?"

Fergus nodded. Out of the corner of his eye he saw Stewart's face turned toward his, with an almost pleading expression, but he kept his own gaze locked ahead. Tarleton was strikingly handsome, almost girlish in the face. All the stories Fergus ever heard about Bloody Ban, raping women and cutting men to bits after they'd cried for quarter, swirled through his mind.

The waiting was over. The battle had begun.

Chapter Six

Melina was spreading berries on a drying rack when Morna's slender shadow cut across the late August sun.

"Fergus is home."

Melina's heart leaped within her, but she kept her voice calm. "So soon? His enlistment wasn't supposed to end for another month yet. Did your father get word from town?"

"Fergus isn't in town. He's here on the farm, now. And...there's something wrong with him."

Melina let the berries fall from her hand and lifted her head. Morna stood braced and stiff in her worn linen gown, her flushed face surrounded by damp red curls. She looked small and young and frightened.

"Is he hurt?" Melina asked.

"I suppose he must be, but I don't see any wound on him. He acts like he's had a knock to the head. Father's in the orchard, Nessa's still in town, and Catalyn is in the cabin with Lachlan. Melina, I don't know what to do. He came with me up the west track as far as the tar shed, but he stopped there, and I can't get him to the house."

Melina got to her feet and wiped her hands on her apron.

"Take me to him."

Morna led the way, plainly relieved to share responsibility with someone else, even a flighty houseguest from Charlestown.

Standing in the shade of the tar shed was a horse, with the bones of his shoulders and hips showing sharp through a dull dark coat, eating grass as fast as he could. With a nasty jolt, Melina recognized Bran. He had no saddle. His driving reins had been knotted for riding.

Beside him was a man.

Melina stopped short. Fergus was even more changed than Bran. He wore no frock coat, and his waistcoat hung open at the sides, showing a filthy shirt. All his garments hung loosely on him. His head was bowed, his face shaded by a buff-colored hat—his lucky hat, now grimy and battered—atop unbound, tangled hair. He stood stock-still, as if frozen to the spot, his musket in his hand.

A knot of dread formed in Melina's stomach. She wasn't ready for this. For a moment she considered sending Morna to fetch Catalyn, but Lachlan was fussy and fretful with a summer cold. She made herself walk on.

"Welcome home, Fergus. We didn't expect you back for some weeks yet. What news?"

Fergus raised his head. His face was blackened with powder or dirt or both. Only the crinkle lines around his eyes and mouth showed pale. His cheekbones stood sharp through the skin above several days' growth of beard, and his bloodshot eyes were sunken beneath heavy lids.

"Where is my father?" he asked. His voice sounded harsh and rough, as if he hadn't used it for a while.

"In the turpentine orchard. Morna, go fetch him."

"Nay!"

The word was almost a snarl. Melina and Morna exchanged frightened glances, and Morna's eyes filled with tears.

"I can't see him," Fergus said. "Not yet."

"Why?" asked Melina. "Fergus, what has happened?"

Fergus looked at Morna, then at Melina. She read the mute plea in his eyes, and in that moment fear and helplessness vanished. Someone else seemed to take over, someone cool and collected who knew what to do.

In a voice she didn't recognize, she said, "Morna, take Bran to the carriage house. He's half-starved, and too much grass all at once might hurt him. Find Tavish, he'll know what to do. Then go to the house and fetch your brother some fresh linen, a clean pair of breeches, some soap and towels and ointments, razor, glass—anything he might need. Take them to the carriage shed and leave them there."

Morna took Bran by the bridle and led him away.

"All right, 'tis just the two of us now," Melina said. "What is it that you have to say?"

Fergus only stared at her. Now that he had her alone, he seemed reluctant to begin.

"Did you make the rendezvous with Caswell in Cross Creek?" Melina prompted him.

"Aye."

"Then what? Did the militia forces join General Gates's army?"

He made a sound in his throat that might have been a laugh, or a sob.

"Fergus, please. You're frightening me."

His sharp gaze cut through her. "You should be frightened. The army was annihilated. The Patriots are finished in the South. The entire Continental Line was wiped out at one go. There's nothing left to stand against Cornwallis but some scattered militia units, and you know how reliable they are."

So. The blow had fallen at last. Melina had long feared it, even while pretending to believe it could never come. The war was lost.

But there was no time to grieve. She took the musket from Fergus's hand, checked to make sure it was unloaded, and laid it by. Then she took his arm and tried to lead him away, but he stood firmly rooted.

"I cannot speak to my father," he said. "I cannot see him."

"I'm not taking you to your father. You're going to have a wash."

Still he didn't move. His dark eyes were like burned holes in his face. "Did you hear what I said? The Continental Line is destroyed."

"I heard you. And I said you're going to have a wash. You look as if water hadn't touched you in weeks. Your linen is a disgrace."

He let himself be led then, all the way to the stream where she'd seen him bathe, that day that now felt like a lifetime ago.

"There," she said with forced cheerfulness. "We've had a rain only yesterday, so the water is fresh and plentiful."

He didn't reply. He stood still, staring across at the far bank with unseeing eyes.

A fresh wave of fear rose in her throat. Had his mind been broken beyond repair? Timidly she reached up and removed his hat.

"So off with your clothes, then," she said brightly, "and down into the stream, and you'll have a lovely bath and feel good as new."

"I'm not an imbecile," he said in a fully rational tone. "I'll strip myself as soon you go away."

Her cheeks flushed hot. "Oh! Of course. Very well. I'll go and see if Morna's brought your clean linen and things. I'll bring them here, and leave them on this blackjack bush for you, and give you your privacy."

"All right."

As she turned to go, he seized her wrist.

"But don't go far," he said. "Wait for me, after you bring the clothes and things. You're the only one I can..." He swallowed hard. "Wait for me," he said again.

"I will," she said, wrung with sympathy. "I'll come right back and stay close by while you have your wash."

She was halfway to the carriage shed before she realized she was still holding the hat, Fergus's lucky hat, with the musket ball graze across the top. Something was stuffed inside the fold—her own hair ribbon, tattered and creased.

Tears spilled over before she knew they were welling up, and her breath caught in great gasping sobs. She pressed the hat to her chest with both arms, shaking all over.

Then she dug her nails into her palms and forced herself to take long, slow breaths. There was no time to fall apart. Fergus needed her.

Morna was waiting for her outside the carriage shed with a bundle of clothing.

"What's the matter with my brother?" she asked in a quavering voice. "What's happened to him?"

"I don't know, but I'm going to find out. Go to the house and wait, dear."

Morna blinked rapidly. "I'm sick of war. I hate what it's done to everything."

Melina laid a hand to Morna's cheek. "He's alive, Morna. Hold fast to that. We'll sort the rest out later."

She took the fresh clothing to the blackjack bush, then waited in the woods until she heard Fergus calling her name. She found him in a shady spot near the bank of the stream, lying on his side, propped on one elbow, on the clean wiregrass. His soiled clothing lay in a neat pile nearby, so saturated with grime that she wondered whether it ought to be burned rather than laundered.

The beard was gone, and his skin, cleansed of dirt and black powder, now showed cuts and bruises. His sleeves were rolled up, and his shirt was open at the neck, revealing sinewy forearms and a lean chest. His hair, still damp, hung loose around his shoulders, mostly free from tangles now. He hadn't put on shoes or stockings, and with his feet and calves bare to the summer breeze he almost looked like something out of a tranquil bucolic painting, except for the dark eyes burning in his face.

She seated herself beside him.

"I must give an account of myself," he said without looking at her. "I owe that much to my father. I want to tell the whole tale through to you, tell it properly from start to finish, and then never speak of it again. You have a good mind, Melina. You understand battle, and you don't flinch from the truth. You can remember what I tell you and pass it on to my father. Will you do that for me?"

"Aye, of course."

He took a deep breath, let it out, and began.

The Patriot forces, he said, had united on August seventh, at Lynches Creek between Cheraw and Camden. General Gates called them his Grand Army—Fergus looked nauseated as he repeated the words. They were a large force, but not as large as Gates thought—North Carolina militia, the Continentals from Maryland and Delaware, Armand's Legion, and some militia units from Virginia. The plan was to attack Rawdon's forces at Camden. Camden was key, the British link to Ninety-Six and the backcountry, and their entry point for invading North Carolina. If they lost Camden, they'd have to abandon the interior of South Carolina—Georgia, too—and couldn't hold Savannah and Charlestown much longer. Their Southern Strategy would fail, and the war would end.

"I was a fool," Fergus said. "So quick to trust the Hero of Saratoga. The signs were there all along, and I wouldn't see. Gates was an incompetent commander, arrogant to his subordinates and inconsiderate of his men, but I made excuse for him—even when he marched the troops to the point of exhaustion on half rations for eight days in a row. I thought he must know what he was doing, or he'd not have won at Saratoga. Now I see he was only lucky then. Father understood that. So did you."

Melina didn't trust her voice to answer. She wished she'd been wrong.

"We met the British on the road to Camden," Fergus said. "Rawdon and Cornwallis had set out to attack us at the same time we'd left to attack them. We were somewhere over three thousand by then, and by all accounts Cornwallis's force was not quite two thousand. But ours were mostly militiamen, and theirs were mostly regulars. And we were fighting on ground better suited to them than to us. But we were not doomed from the start. Had we been led better, or had any of a multitude of things gone differently, we might have won."

The cords in his jaw and throat stood out taut through the skin. Melina ached to take his hand, but knew she couldn't. Tenderness would break him now. He could have none of it until his tale was told.

"We formed up just before dawn the next day," he went on. "The North Carolinians were placed on the front line, between the Continentals and the Virginia militia, so I got to see the whole sorry fiasco. As soon as the lines were drawn up, everything fell apart. Gates ordered the Virginia militia to advance first. The Volunteers of Ireland let out a war cry and charged them with bayonets. And the Virginians—the Virginians fled, dropping their weapons without firing a shot. So did most of the North Carolinians. 'Twas like a contagion of panic spreading through the whole mass of them, quick as lightning. I felt it myself. There was a Wilmington boy beside me, Jack Stewart, eighteen years old. He dropped his musket and ran like a hare. I nearly ran after him. Do you know what stopped me?"

"Nay."

"You did. Everything you'd ever said about militia—their cowardice and stupidity—along with everything *I'd* said about how any militiaman would be glad to stand his ground if only he had powder in his musket. This was my chance, maybe my last chance. So I fired."

Melina's throat felt hot and choked. She'd never dreamed that Fergus would take her careless words to heart so.

"I don't know how long I stayed there, firing and reloading," he went on. "I checked my cartridge box later and found eight cartridges missing. The morning was still—not a breath of wind—and the smoke hung so thick I could barely see a yard ahead. With most of the militia gone, the First Maryland Brigade moved up to take their place in the right wing. De Kalb led a bayonet charge, and I even heard a victory cheer from our side at one point.

But it didn't last. The First Marylanders got driven back, and Tarleton's cavalry poured through the gap, then fanned out to attack us from the rear."

He turned and looked at her. "I saw him, Melina. I saw Bloody Ban. He's young, not much older than I am. He charged through the ranks in his green coat, slicing through men with his saber—"

His face twisted, his fist closed on the sand, and for a moment Melina thought he would be sick, but he swallowed hard and went on. "General Gist finally took what was left of the Marylanders and ordered a retreat. I went with them. I saw de Kalb, already cut up by bayonets, kill a British soldier as he fell. The Redcoats started stripping him of his gold-embroidered waistcoat before he was even dead. We fled through the swamps, where the Legion cavalry couldn't follow. They were cutting down militiamen along the road, hacking at them with sabers as they ran. Our baggage wagons were parked a hundred yards or so beyond the bridge. Some of Armand's dragoons were plundering the Maryland officers' baggage. Dead men still warm on the road around them, and our own soldiers stealing, stuffing their pockets with gold coins and passing around gin bottles, and laughing!"

He shut his eyes, gathered himself, and said, "I found Bran. He'd been unhitched from his wagon, and one of Armand's dragoons was leading him away. I clubbed the man on the head with my musket stock, swung onto Bran's back, and rode off." He took a deep shuddering breath and let it out. "And that was the end of the battle of Camden, at least for me."

"Where did you go?"

"I didn't have a destination in mind. I just headed north. I met men along the way, and we'd exchange news and sometimes travel together. But the journey was hard, and it was Loyalist country. The locals were quick to pick off stragglers on the road. It was safer to travel alone through the woods. Eventually I ended up in Charlotte Town. General Caswell was there, and Colonel Williams of the Marylanders, but not General Gates. I don't know what became of him. The best that can be said of him—and believe me, I heard it said often—is that he rode remarkably well for a man of his age, and got himself away from the battlefield early and quickly. As fast as he was riding, he might have made it all the way to Philadelphia by nightfall."

The bitterness in his voice stung her. It wasn't right, it was horribly wrong, for Fergus to sound that way, after he'd gone off so hopeful and trusting to do his duty.

"I know how easy it is to find fault after the fact," he said. "And in all fairness, not everything that went wrong was Gates's fault. For my part, I can forgive his miscalculations and errors in judgment. But I can never forgive him for fleeing the field. With him gone, there was no one to order the Marylanders to retreat. They kept getting beaten back, and reforming, and fighting again, until there was almost nothing left of them, and General Gist took matters into his own hands. Had they retreated in time, the Continental Line would not be in ruins. But Gates wasn't there to give the order, and they wouldn't run."

A long silence passed. Melina wished she knew what to say or do to give him comfort.

"There was talk of regrouping in Charlotte Town," Fergus said at last. "But what was the point? What more had I to give, and what hope was left for our cause? There was nothing for me to do but go home and see to the safety of my own kin. So I did—and here I am."

A breeze off the stream stirred the dried strands of hair around his face. "I suppose I should go to the house now," he said. His voice sounded flat and dreary.

"There's no rush," Melina replied

"I shouldn't be a coward about it. If it's got to be done, better sooner than later. But I dread facing them all. Is that horrible of me?"

"Not at all. I know this was not the homecoming you hoped for."

He made a scoffing sound. "Nay, it is not. I thought I would return a conquering hero. I thought we would take back Charlestown, and your father would be freed."

"I know all about the folly of false hope," she said. "I thought Charlestown would never be taken to begin with, remember? We were wrong, that's all. 'Tis nothing to be ashamed of."

He pushed himself up on one arm and turned toward her. His sunken eyes were calmer now.

"Thank you," he said simply.

He had a nasty purple bruise on his cheekbone, and a half-healed scrape along his jaw—that lean, square jaw that had haunted her memory ever since their first meeting. A leaf fragment was caught in his hair. She disentangled it gently. Then, moved by an irresistible impulse, she took his face between her hands and kissed him on the forehead.

She lingered a moment with her lips against his skin before drawing back. He held still, his weight resting on one elbow, his head bowed.

Then he lifted his face to hers, plunged his hand roughly into her hair, and kissed her hard on the mouth.

A tremor of shock shot through her, followed by a flood of wild joy. She put her arms around him and felt the lean muscles of his back beneath her hands. Her coiled hair came loose and spilled over her shoulders.

It was over almost before it started. Fergus turned loose of her as if she'd scalded him, stumbled to his feet, and put a good yard of space between them.

"Leave me," he said, the words clipped and curt, his back to her. "I'm no fit company for you or anyone else."

She struggled to catch her breath. "I'm sorry," she said. "'Twas my fault. I shouldn't have—"

He pressed his hands to his head as if to shut out the sound of her voice. "Don't apologize. Just go."

His voice was sharp and hard. Stung, Melina retorted, "Give me half a moment to find my hairpins, if you please."

He turned, his face showing confusion and shame, and made a half-hearted move as if to help.

"Nay, I'll do it," she said.

Her hands shook so that she could hardly twist her hair up and pin it in place. A cramped, embarrassed silence filled the air.

She finished at last and got to her feet. She scarcely had the strength to stand, with her swimming head, pounding heart, and limbs that had turned to jelly. Without looking at Fergus, she said, "I'll find your father and tell him you're home."

"Will you tell him about the battle?"

"Of course."

"Thank you," he said again. "You have been a better friend to me than I deserve."

It hurt her to hear how humble and contrite he sounded. He had taken a liberty, but she didn't feel insulted. She wanted him to do it again. Every atom of her being longed to take him in her arms and never let go.

"I'll gather my things and meet you at the house," Fergus said. "And I will be myself again."

Melina turned her back on him and hurried away to the turpentine orchard.

MR. SHAW LISTENED WITHOUT interruption to the whole tale—or at least to what Melina chose to relate of it.

"So that's that," he said. "The Continental Line is broken. But what of Fergus himself? How is he?"

"Battered and malnourished, but uninjured—on the outside, anyway. He's rather more battered on the inside. He wants to master himself, but—well, he's doing his best."

Mr. Shaw frowned and didn't answer. Some distance away, Rory was collecting resin from a tree, and clearly trying to listen to their conversation.

"Rory, lad, we're done for the day," called Mr. Shaw. "Gather what's in the buckets, and we'll take the work cart to the tar shed. Your brother Fergus has come home."

Mr. Shaw wiped his hands on his grimy smock and picked up his work bag. He moved without haste, and a casual observer might have thought him untroubled. But then he cast his gaze around one last time, and Melina caught the look of helplessness in his eyes.

She took his arm. He laid his hand over hers and gave it a squeeze.

DESPITE WHAT HE'D SAID, Fergus was not himself again, and Melina wondered if he ever would be. He'd always been quiet, but there was something beneath his silence now that hadn't been there before. She saw him flinch at sudden noises and grow stiff whenever anyone touched him. She'd even seen his hand fly to the knife at his belt once, when the front door slammed. But he ate what that was set before him, let his sisters fuss over him, and gave no cause for alarm.

No one questioned him about the battle or said anything about the war at all. They spoke only of home matters—how much turpentine had been gathered in the orchard, how the chicken with the twisted foot kept laying double-yolked eggs. It was as if the destruction of the Grand Army had never happened.

Fergus asked after Melina's father, and she was able to give him a good report. Papa had written to her several times from the prison ship—short, cheerful letters full of hope that he would be released soon. He'd scolded her for refusing to go to Rhode Island, but not very hard, and she knew he was secretly pleased that she'd chosen to stay close to him, and proud of the spirit she'd shown.

Catalyn had brought Lachlan to the main house, and Tavish had joined them from the barn. Lachlan was fussy from his summer cold, and his fretful cries dampened the mood. Nessa and Melina had to carry the conversation between them. Tavish and Mr. Shaw said little, but they looked troubled. Catalyn was preoccupied with trying to comfort Lachlan, and Morna kept smiling too brightly, her eyes glassy, as if she couldn't rid herself of the vision of how Fergus had appeared when she'd first seen him. Rory, usually such a chatterbox, couldn't seem to find anything to say.

"You ought to sleep well tonight," Nessa told Fergus, "back in your own bed, with plenty of good food in you."

Melina wasn't so sure. She'd been amazed, when she first came to the Shaw house, to learn that there were only three bedrooms upstairs, and that she was expected to share one of them with Nessa and Morna. She still wasn't used to it.

"Nay, there's no need to crowd Rory," said Fergus. "I'll bed down in the hay loft. I'm used to sleeping outdoors now."

Nessa looked scandalized. "You'll do no such thing! Not while I'm alive and mistress of this house. Hay loft, indeed! You've a fine mattress upstairs beneath a solid roof, and you're going to sleep there if I have to tuck you in myself."

Fergus opened his mouth and shut it again. He looked trapped, and no wonder. After a grisly battle, followed by days spent fleeing for his life in hostile Loyalist territory, in constant fear for his life, surely the last thing he needed or wanted was to sleep in a confined space with a small defenseless brother.

"Nay, Fergus should certainly sleep in the hay loft," Melina said. "Change is stressful to the body, even when it is for the better. A sudden change in air, besides the change in diet, would be most unhealthful. He must acclimate himself slowly."

"How is it a change of air?" Nessa protested. "We keep the windows open every summer night."

"But a house has residual vapors which are never fully purged, even by a thorough airing," said Melina.

Nessa mulled this over. "Very well. If you're sure."

While Nessa and Morna were washing the supper dishes, Melina carried Fergus's bed linens to the carriage shed. The sun had set by now, and the heat was abating.

Fergus was waiting for her in the hay loft. She pushed the bundle of linens up to him, then climbed the steps. As soon as she stepped onto the loft floor, he launched into what was clearly a prepared speech.

"I must apologize, Miss Bryant, for my earlier behavior. You must think me the worst sort of scoundrel for repaying your kindness with such...treatment." His face grew red. "I can offer no excuse. I can only say how sorry I am."

But Melina was prepared, too. "Please say no more, Mr. Shaw. What happened between us today was bound to happen at some point. Two young persons, temperamental opposites, and not unattractive, living in the same household—it was inevitable that sparks should fly. Now that it is past us, we are free to be excellent friends, as I hope we shall."

He stared at her a long moment, his face giving nothing away. Finally he said, "Miss Bryant, have you ever visited County Cork in Ireland?"

"Why do you ask?"

"Because I think you must have kissed the blarney stone. I have never seen your equal for making errant nonsense sound like well-reasoned truth."

Her cheeks grew warm, and in spite of her supposed gift of blarney, she could think of nothing to say.

"A psychological inevitability," Fergus echoed. "Almost as good as residual vapors. You certainly have a gift. Let us call it tact."

Melina pulled herself together. "So. You see through me, and I see through you. What are we to do about it?"

"I think that we shall be friends," Fergus said. "Excellent friends, as you said."

"Good," said Melina. "I might not always have shown it, Mr. Shaw, but I do hold you in the highest esteem."

"You have shown it. And again, I thank you."

He was still clutching the bundle of linens. She stepped over to take it from him, but he didn't let go. Their hands touched, and for a moment Melina was in danger of undoing all her tact and kissing him again. Why was he so tall, so grave, so utterly desirable?

"I can make my own bed," he said.

Reluctantly, she let go and stepped back. "Very well."

There was nothing left for her to do, but she didn't want to go.

"I'm glad you're home, Fergus," she said at last.

"So am I." His gaze darkened. "But I wonder how long home will be safe from Cornwallis. With the Continental Line destroyed, he's sure to turn to Wilmington soon."

She'd had the same thought herself. But rather than fear, she felt a fierce pride. Fergus wouldn't, or couldn't, speak of the war to his family, but he could to her.

"Don't think of that now," she said. "Just rest."

She didn't rest very well herself that night. When she did sleep, her dreams were troubled—not with recollections of the shelling of Charlestown, but with the memory of a stolen kiss by the bank of the stream.

Chapter Seven

A twig snapped in the woods to Fergus's right. He ducked behind the wagon, heart pounding, and reached for his weapon.

But there was no musket hanging at his back, and no enemy firing at him—only a deer stepping daintily over the pine needles. And this was not the road leading from Camden, whose woods were full of British regulars and South Carolinian Tories, but the familiar road to Wilmington.

Fergus straightened up and took a deep breath, pushing down the nausea of fear, and stole a glance at Tavish, who was still walking calmly ahead, driving the ox that pulled the wagon. Either he hadn't noticed Fergus's lapse, or he was pretending he hadn't. A full month had passed since Fergus's return from the disastrous battle at Camden, and he was still seeing enemies behind every tree.

They were taking a load of grain to sell to the commissary in town. With the market for naval supplies almost dried up by the war, the Shaws had had to find other sources of income.

"I hope the army gives us a decent price for our crop today," Tavish said.

Fergus shrugged. "The price is only numbers, and the numbers don't matter as long as they keep paying us in worthless Continental currency instead of good coin."

Tavish considered this. "Well, if they give us enough paper notes, we could always use them as bedding for the horses."

"We'll not be paid in Continental notes any longer if the British take the town," said Fergus.

"Aye," Tavish said wryly, "for we'll not be paid at all."

An agony of suspense hung over the early autumn. With Camden under British control and the Continental Army destroyed, Cornwallis was sure to invade either Wilmington or Cross Creek soon. Then North Carolina would fall to the British, as South Carolina and Georgia had. It was inevitable.

In spite of the gloomy prospects, Father, that dourest of Scotsmen, had kept his head.

"We'll all keep getting up in the morning, doing our work, and going to bed at night, and enjoying our blessings," he'd said. "We're not destitute, and we have each other. And the war isna over. There's time yet for the tide to turn."

Just hearing him say it in his unflustered way had made everyone feel better. And as the days passed with no invasion, hope raised its head. The victory at Camden had cost the British dearly in troops and supplies. The delay helped the Patriots more than the British, and the longer Cornwallis waited, the less secure his hold in the South became. In the South Carolina backcountry, small bands of Patriot militiamen nipped away at the enemy, and in Georgia, a daring insurrection had come close to wresting control from the British altogether.

The revival of hope put Fergus on edge. After Camden, he'd made up his mind that the war was lost, but now he wasn't so sure. It was exhausting. He would rather know the worst at once and be done with it. He couldn't bear to go through that crushing disappointment all over again.

The town appeared shrunken and shabby in Fergus's eyes. People in worn clothing went quietly about their business, making scant purchases from half-empty shops that had few goods to offer. Fergus and Tavish joined a queue of farmers waiting to sell their crops to the commissary officer. Supposedly the food was needed to feed the army, but there was no regular army in the South now. Fergus hadn't forgotten the gnawing hunger of the summer weeks he'd spent with the militia. He wanted to turn the cart around and go home, and keep the grain for his own family and stock, and let Washington's army fend for itself, as he had done, for whatever time was left to them before the war was lost.

But he stayed in the queue with Tavish, and turned over the load to the commissary officer, and received some worthless paper in exchange.

They were leading the empty wagon away when they were hailed by a red-haired man with a bluff, honest face, dressed in a threadbare suit.

"Mr. MacGregor! Mr. Shaw! Good day to you."

"Mr. Stratten!" Tavish replied. "How d'ye do, sir?"

"Tolerably well. How does your little son?"

Tavish's smile faltered. "About the same. We hope he will regain his strength when cooler weather comes. Have ye been selling your crop?"

"Aye, and with the profit I made, I can just afford a single dram of whisky. Will you join me at the pub, gentlemen?"

Fergus didn't want to go. The prospect of whisky was appealing enough, however little he and Tavish could afford such luxuries right now. But the talk was sure to be of war, and he was sick of hearing it.

Before he could speak, Tavish accepted for both of them, and they went.

Leithan Stratten owned the shipwright's business in which Tavish had once served as apprentice. He also owned some farmland inherited from his mother, one of the Highland Scots of the colony that had settled in Cross Creek some forty years earlier.

As soon as they'd taken their seats and been served, Tavish asked, "What news from upriver, Mr. Stratten? Any sign of Cornwallis's army?"

Mr. Stratten smiled. "Nay, for Cornwallis has surprised us all, and hit Charlotte Town instead."

"Charlotte Town?" said Tavish. "A crossroads village of some twenty homes and a courthouse?"

"Aye. No doubt he expected a meek surrender or an easy victory, but the Patriot militia knew he was coming and put up an organized defense. Cornwallis took the village, but not without effort, and not without cost."

Fergus stared into his glass, trying not to listen while Mr. Stratten told of Patriot riflemen sniping at the enemy from protected positions behind stone walls and houses.

But when Stratten spoke of Captain Graham's mounted infantry, Fergus paid attention. He had wanted to serve in mounted infantry himself, and had trained Bran accordingly, but Gates had put all the horses to work pulling wagons in the supply train. The value of mounted infantry was in its mobility—as with Graham's men, who had gathered in the woods north of town and fired on the enemy from there. The British returned fire but hit only trees, and Graham's men got away on horseback.

There it was, the stir of hope deep in Fergus's chest, like a tender seedling pushing its way through the earth. With Gates out of power, the militia was free to work independently, led by junior officers, like Graham, familiar with the area. They could gather quickly in small units, fight, and get away, back to their homes and their crops, rather than wasting time coordinating with one another into huge ungainly forces. Fergus might have his chance yet. He might even serve under Graham himself.

"'Twas bravely done," said Tavish. "I hope we'll hear more of this Captain Graham."

Stratten shook his head. "Not in this life, we won't. Graham's dead, shot three times and slashed with a saber."

The seedling of hope withered, and Fergus hunched over his drink again.

"But Patriot casualties were light overall," Stratten went on. "And our forces retreated in good order, ready to harass the British another day."

Tavish sipped his whisky. "That's a shame about Graham. We can't afford to lose any more good officers. We're already without senior leadership. General Caswell is ill—and even if he recovers, he's unlikely to be returned to command, after being blamed for the loss at Camden."

"Aye," said Stratten. "'Tis the same old story, with the regular army despising the militia. Every failure needs a scapegoat."

Fergus spoke at last. "Caswell may not have been a brilliant commander, but he looked after his men. He'll not be easily replaced, nor will Rutherford."

He'd never served under General Rutherford, the leader of the Salisbury District Brigade, which had traveled south with Caswell's force, one on either side of the river. But he'd briefly seen him in action at Camden, and heard him praised afterward by his surviving men.

"We'll get Rutherford back in a prisoner exchange," Mr. Stratten said.

"Rutherford is dead," said Fergus. "I saw him struck down at Camden, by a saber wound to the head."

"Well, he didn't die of it. He was captured and is being held in Florida."

"What news from the west?" Tavish asked. "Has Cornwallis taken action to subdue the backcountry?"

"Aye," said Mr. Stratten. "Major Patrick Ferguson is heading that way with the American Volunteers—provincial troops—and Loyalist militia from the Carolinas. 'Tis a large force, and growing larger as it goes. Ferguson put out the word that if the Patriots in the west don't surrender their arms and swear allegiance to the King, he'll march over the Blue Ridge, hang their leaders, and lay waste to their homes and fields by fire and sword."

"Rash words," said Tavish. "The mountain men do not intimidate easily."

"True," Mr. Stratten replied. "I wouldn't be surprised if they decided to take the fight to him. If they do, 'twill be a mighty clash."

"And what can ye tell us of Cross Creek, Mr. Stratten?" Tavish asked. "How are the people disposed there toward the Patriot cause?"

"None too favorably, though the Patriots still hold sway. The Loyalists may have been subdued by the battle at Moore's Creek, but they haven't given up, and they'll be ready to take their revenge if ever the balance of power shifts."

"The same could be said here," said Fergus. "From where I sit now, I can see five men who would make life a torment for local Patriots if ever Wilmington fell to the British."

A grim silence fell. The three men finished their whisky and left the pub.

Just outside the door, they met a middle-aged woman with a round, pleasant face.

"Why, Mr. MacGregor!" she said. "Good afternoon to you, sir. How do you do?"

"Mrs. Kellam!" Tavish replied. "I'm glad to see you. How are your chickens?"

"Tolerably well, I'm happy to say. I still have one of those Dominickers that you rescued from the tempest, and strange to say, she's my best layer. How does your good wife, and your little lad?"

They chatted a while, Mrs. Kellam giving news of other townsfolk whom Tavish had helped or worked alongside during the hurricane of seventy-five.

"Is it always like this with him?" Mr. Stratten asked Fergus, after Mrs. Kellam had gone.

"Aye," Fergus replied. "That hurricane made my brother-in-law a popular figure in the town. He saved a boy from drowning, and rescued Mrs. Kellam's chickens, and helped a hog that was caught in a tree. His admirers are everywhere."

No sooner were the words spoken than a spare, shabby figure across the street caught Fergus's eye. A grey wig, with three sausage curls on each side, perched askew above a face with a strangely deflated look, as if it had once been plump and full but had shrunk, like the body inside the threadbare greatcoat. Leaning on a cane, the man crossed the street and hobbled toward them as fast as he could. His small, flat eyes were fixed like gimlets on Tavish. With a sickening lurch, Fergus recognized Gordon Currie, former shipwright, Tavish's former master—and Mr. Stratten's father.

"Well," Fergus amended, "*almost* everywhere."

"Tavish MacGregor!" Currie spat out. "Look at ye, strutting about town as if ye hadna killed a man with your bare hands. Ye should've been strung up for your crime—and ye would've, if not for those foul rebels taking ye into their ranks. But ye'll not escape the King's justice forever. Ye'll hang yet, when Cornwallis takes the South."

Mr. Stratten stiffened at Fergus's side. "Justice? How dare you even speak the word, and to Mr. MacGregor of all people? He saved your wretched life, and after you'd knocked him on the head with a maul and left him for dead!"

Mr. Currie turned his poisonous gaze on Mr. Stratten.

"Shut your mouth, thief! Ye're no better than he is, robbing me of my property!"

"I? Rob you?" said Mr. Stratten, his voice rising. "You're the thief, you old reprobate! You stole that property from my mother, and treated her vilely!"

"Your mother," said Mr. Currie, the words dripping with contempt, "was an illiterate Highland hussy. I dinnae ken whose son ye are, but ye're none of mine."

Mr. Stratten's face flushed a dusky red, and he raised his walking stick. Before he could strike, Fergus and Tavish grabbed his arms and dragged him away. Mr. Currie followed them, hurling abuse at their backs for a good half block before they outpaced him.

By then Mr. Stratten had stopped struggling. They turned a corner and released him. He drew himself up and straightened his clothing.

"How I abhor that man," he said. "He's rotten to the core. I would to God he were not my father."

"Everyone knows him for a bully and a thief," Fergus said. "He's lost his business and his position in the community. He can do no more harm."

"Nay, that viper still has teeth," said Tavish. "He'll do mischief yet if he can find the means."

"BUT I DON'T UNDERSTAND," said Melina. "How is it possible that such a man is at liberty? How has Mr. Currie not been locked up for his crimes?"

She and Fergus were sitting together on the bank of the stream, with a basket of cornbread cakes on the ground between them, and the midmorning sun warm on their backs. She was wearing one of Morna's old gowns and had her golden hair pinned back in a workmanlike knot at the nape of her neck.

"In the eyes of the law, his crimes have been redressed," Fergus replied. "He beat Tavish within an inch of his life—and Tavish was released from his employ. He cheated his wife of her property—and it was restored to her son and heir."

"But that isn't all he did. He beat Tavish repeatedly, and his own wife as well. Why was nothing done then?"

"You know why. The law allows a man some discretion in how he chooses to discipline his own apprentice...and other members of his household."

"A great deal of discretion, evidently."

"I don't say I agree with it. I speak of what is, not what ought to be. And there is some recourse available, for apprentices and for wives, if the beating is severe enough and the judge is sympathetic."

"That isn't fair."

"Nay, it is not. Treating people as property is never fair."

She looked at him.

"*We hold these truths to be self-evident,*" he began.

"*...that all men are created equal,*" Melina added.

They finished together, "*...that they are endowed by their Creator with certain unalienable Rights, that among these are Life, Liberty and the pursuit of Happiness.*"

Melina sighed. "I never hear those words without great uneasiness. It made Papa uneasy, as well. I've heard the issue argued around our table over and over among him and his friends, with never a solution to be found. Papa inherited his slaves from his own father. He always tried to treat them kindly and justly—so far as kindness and justice are possible in an institution fundamentally unkind and unjust. But what more could he do? If they were all given their liberty, what would they do, where would they go? Who would hire them? They'd be competing for work with white men who would not take well to the competition. Would not bloodshed be inevitable in such a case?"

"I don't see how it could be avoided," Fergus agreed. "And in North Carolina, freeing slaves is against the law in any event, unless they perform some great service to the state. My family has never owned a slave, and I'm glad of that. But many other families do, and the more years pass, the more firmly entrenched the institution becomes."

"Aye. 'Tis a thorny problem—and the longer 'tis put off, the worse it grows, and the harder to solve."

Fergus picked up a cornbread cake. "These cakes are perfect. Delicately crisp on the outside and mealy-moist within. Did you really make them yourself?"

"From start to finish. I began early in case I burned them and had to bury them behind the garden and try again."

Of all the changes Fergus had found at home since his return, the most striking was the change in Melina. She was as quick-witted and high-spirited as ever, but she'd grown surprisingly competent in her work on the farm. She still made mistakes, but she brought an eager energy to her tasks and cheered everyone with her enthusiasm. It was hard to believe that she'd been with them only four months. Only the day before, he'd heard Nessa say, "Melina has become one of us now. How will we ever get along without her?" The words had hit him hard. He did not want to think of the time when he must get along without Melina.

When he'd finished eating the cornbread cake, Melina urged him to have another.

"Aren't they needed for dinner?" Fergus asked.

"Nay, I'll make more. You finish this batch."

"I've already eaten two."

"So? I thought you said you liked them. Were you lying?"

"Nay, but—"

"Then eat another. You're still too thin, Fergus. You want feeding, and plenty of it."

"But you're stuffing me like a sausage," he protested. "I can't keep eating this way."

"You can and you will. You've got a long way to go before you need worry about losing that genteel figure of yours. I don't like those hollows beneath your eyes, or the way your waistcoat hangs on you."

He enjoyed being scolded by her, and teasing her in turn. Ever since he'd come home from Camden, there had been an ease and familiarity between them that was far more comfortable than what he'd felt for her at first. They were like brother and sister now. Almost, at least. Some of the time.

He'd never thanked her for looking after him that day, not properly. She'd taken charge of him with a brisk matter-of-factness that was exactly what he needed. The memory of the battle had clung to him like a foul crust until he'd peeled off his filthy clothes and stepped into the water. He'd started to feel his way into his own skin again, there in his own familiar stream, with the long overhanging branch that dipped close to the water, and the black-jack bush on the high bank—the very bank where they were sitting now.

He turned and looked at her. That delicacy of features, that graceful lift of her head—she was so small and finely wrought, but strong as steel, and with unexpected depths.

She must have felt his gaze, because she turned toward him. "What is it?" she asked.

"The day I came back from Camden," he said, "you brought me here to bathe."

"You were very much in need of a wash."

"Aye. But you brought me here, to this exact spot, where I always bathe. You even laid my fresh linen on the blackjack bush, the way I always do. Surely that was a strange thing to happen purely by chance."

Her smile vanished, and a rush of color flooded her face.

"I—I saw you here," she said. "One afternoon before you went away."

"You saw me bathing?"

"Only by the most freakish accident! I went for a walk and happened upon you. I certainly didn't expect to find—I don't make a habit of spying on gentlemen at their baths! Anyway, I didn't see—that is—The water was dark."

Fergus felt his own face grow warm. He didn't know what to say or where to look. All at once he knew that he'd been fooling himself. His feelings for Melina weren't brotherly in the slightest. And what of her feelings for him? Why was she so flustered? She was not one to waste regret over a minor accident. It would be more like her to have told him right away about seeming him in the stream, and make a jest of it. Could it be, was it possible, that she cared for him as well?

She picked up the basket of cornbread cakes and hurried away, leaving him with much to think about.

WHEN THE FAMILY WENT to town for church that Sunday, they learned the latest news from the backcountry. Major Ferguson—the one Mr. Stratten had spoken of, who'd threatened to hang the Patriot leaders and burn their homes and fields—was dead, and his force was shattered. Patriot regiments from the backcountry, along with some Georgians and Virginians and one regiment from the South Carolina coast, had followed him to Kings Mountain, a spur of the Blue Ridge. They'd ridden all night in the rain to catch the enemy by surprise. The mountain was bare on top, but the slopes were wooded, which favored the attackers. They advanced from tree to tree, firing on an enemy who had no cover. Before long, the Tories were raising white flags. But the only quarter they got was Tarleton's quarter, which was to say, no quarter at all.

Ferguson himself was shot from his horse. His foot caught in the stirrup, and he was dragged to the Patriot side. When an officer approached for his surrender, Ferguson shot the man. The Patriots fired back, and by the time the smoke had cleared, Ferguson had eight musket holes in him and both his arms broken. The Patriots then stripped his body, used it as a latrine, wrapped it in an old oxhide, and buried it.

The backcountry Patriots had won a tremendous victory—perhaps the greatest southern victory to date. But Fergus was sickened by the thought of Patriots firing on men who'd surrendered—on fellow countrymen, no less. It was all American troops on both sides. Major Ferguson was the only combatant present who had ever set foot in England.

Of all the mischief the British had done in the South, the worst of it was turning the conflict into a civil war. It had started after the fall of Charlestown, when General Clinton had urged the defeated Patriots to swear allegiance to the Crown and join the Loyalist militia. Those who refused were treated as enemies and rebels. Overall, his hard stance had backfired. Americans who wished to remain neutral resented being forced to pick a side, and many who might have been content to stay at home chose to fight for liberty. But others gave in to the British, turning on their own neighbors and families. And plenty on both sides took advantage of the enmity to further personal feuds or enrich themselves at the expense of their fellow countrymen.

As they filed inside the courthouse for church, Fergus thought of the Loyalists he knew in Wilmington. Some were men he liked and respected. Many families—the Hoopers, the Maclaines—were divided in loyalty. Every time he saw them, he pitied them from his heart, and thanked God that his own family had been spared that grief, at least. Their only rupture had been Liam's going to sea—and Liam, at least, was fighting on the Patriot side. Fergus couldn't bear to imagine his brother taking up arms against himself and Tavish and Father.

He could barely concentrate on the church service that day, but he did his best. He prayed for Lachlan, still not recovered from his lingering illness. He prayed for all the household. For Melina's father. For Liam.

On the carriage ride home, they all talked over the Patriot victory at Kings Mountain. They were a smaller party than usual, for Tavish and Catalyn had stayed home with Lachlan. The carriage looked strangely empty, and Fergus missed Tavish in his accustomed place, riding Hector to his right. His mind wandered until he was brought up short when Father asked,

"Miss Bryant, how you would like to start attending Saint James Church?"

Fergus had his eye on Melina when the words were spoken. She was in a back-facing seat, which gave him an excellent view of her—a fact he had long appreciated on the rides to and from town. Now he saw her eyes go wide and her mouth drop open.

She turned around to look at Father. "Mr. Shaw! Can you be serious?"

"I can, and I am."

"Why, I hardly know what to say! I thought you were afraid to let such a frivolous creature as myself out of your sight in town."

"I was, at first," he said candidly. "But ye've been with us four months now, and shown yourself to be a good, steady, reliable girl. Catalyn tells me ye dinnae even nod off during Elder Stewart's prayers anymore, and that's a test of fortitude for anyone. As such, I believe ye may be trusted to behave yourself with all decorum at a church service of your own preference."

"My dear Mr. Shaw! You overwhelm me."

Just for a moment, Fergus thought she might say that she preferred, after all, to keep attending Presbyterian services with the family. But then she said, "I accept your kind offer, and thank you most heartily."

Fergus didn't say another word the rest of the way home. As Melina chattered happily about next Sunday, a darkness grew inside him, a swell of emotion that he didn't want to name.

Father stopped the carriage at the dooryard gate. Fergus dismounted and went to help the women down, as usual. He didn't return Melina's bright smile.

He was silent all through supper. Anger and dread made a leaden weight inside him. Melina tried to draw him out with her teasing, but he didn't respond, and after a while she gave up, looking puzzled and hurt. He knew he was being beastly, but he didn't care. He kept it up all that week, until Saturday night.

He lay on his sheets over the sweet-smelling hay, watching the dying moon through the loft window. Two months after coming home, he still slept in the carriage shed. The solitude was restful. These days his thoughts and feelings were too big for the house to contain.

Tomorrow was the day. In a matter of hours, the family would ride to town for church. Melina would go to Saint James, and turn her charm and wit on the parishioners there. How they would admire her! Anyone would admire her. She was a beautiful and intelligent woman. And no doubt she would find much to admire in them.

For the thousandth time, he thought of the day when she'd fed him cornbread cakes by the bank of the stream, and he'd learned of how she'd accidentally seen him bathing there. Was it mere feminine modesty that had made her flush and stammer? Or something more?

And even if she did feel something for him beyond sisterly regard, what did it matter? She would never marry a man of his limited means.

He rolled over with a sigh. The straw seemed strangely lumpy tonight. He'd been trying to beat his bed, and his thoughts, into submission for about an hour now.

The carriage house door opened. Firm footsteps sounded below, followed by a knocking at the base of the loft steps.

"May I come up?"

It was Father's voice, at once gruff and deferential, asking permission to enter the loft of his own carriage house.

Fergus didn't want company, but he couldn't very well refuse.

"I'll come down," he called. He pulled on his breeches and climbed down the ladder.

The combined scents of leather, hay, neatsfoot oil, and clean horse rose to meet him. Bran, nearly restored to his proper weight, rested in the stall where Fergus had once held Melina in his arms, and the carriage stood exactly as it had the first day of her coming, when they'd talked of horses and war. Everywhere he looked was some reminder of her, as if he needed any. She was in his thoughts constantly now.

Father got right to it. "For the past week, ye've been going about mute as a fish, glowering at everyone who comes near ye. What's troubling ye, lad? Is it this talk of the doings at Kings Mountain?"

"Does it have to be anything in particular?" Fergus hedged.

"Aye, for ye it does. Ye've never been one for moods and caprices. When ye're dejected, ye have reason to be."

Fergus couldn't argue with that. He opened his mouth, shut it, and finally burst out, "Why did you give Miss Bryant permission to go the Church of England?"

Father blinked. "That's what this is about? Lad, why on earth should it matter one whit to ye where Miss Bryant chooses to worship?"

"It matters a great deal! The Crown has used the Church of England against our people for centuries, trying to force us and all dissenters to conform to their strictures. They've spilled blood over it. You know that better than I do."

"Aye," Father said. "But the point of religious liberty is for each man to have the freedom to choose according to his conscience, not for everyone to be Presbyterian. Why do ye care if Miss Bryant makes use of that freedom to attend Saint James?"

"Because once she's with her own sort of people again, she won't belong to us."

The words sounded foolish and childish in his own ears.

"Her own sort of people?" Father repeated. "All men are created equal by God. That's self-evident."

"Aye, but once created, we sort ourselves as quickly as we can, and keep to our separate stations. It may not be right, but 'tis what men do."

"Usually. Not always. And Fergus, lad, what makes ye think Miss Bryant *belongs* to us in any event?"

Fergus felt his face grow warm. "I didn't mean...You mustn't suppose that I have any...matrimonial design on her. I'm not such a fool as that. I know she could never think of me that way...nor do I think that way of her, of course. But I do value her friendship very much."

"As do I. But ye cannae make people stay, lad. They must stay because they want to. Otherwise there's no merit in it. Would ye want her to go to Presbyterian services with us week after week while secretly longing for the order of worship she grew up with and loves? Would ye want to force her to deny her heritage and her faith?"

Fergus sighed. "Nay. I know you're right. 'Twas generous and proper of you to let her go. I'll try to be glad you did."

Father returned to the house, and Fergus climbed back into his loft. There, as he pulled up his blanket against the chill October air, he confessed to himself that he loved Melina, had long loved her. He loved her vibrant spirit, her quick wit, and her kindness that always caught him by surprise. And because he loved her, he ought to want what was best for her, without taking thought for himself. But he ached for her to stay with him always—to belong to him, and him alone—and that must make him a selfish man.

He had not forgotten Melina's first Sunday in Wilmington, and how he had seen her walking in the burial ground with Richard Severn. Even now, the very thought of the man made Fergus's blood boil, though Severn had never done him any harm. Severn had property and wealth, and no doubt he was considered handsome, with his powdered hair and aristocratic features, his silk stockings and embroidered waistcoat. He was everything Fergus was not, would never be. And in a matter of hours, he would be in company with Melina again, hearing her laugh, gazing down into her gold-flecked hazel eyes.

But Severn was a Tory. Melina would never look twice at a Tory. Fergus would be ashamed to have her know that such a thought had even entered his mind. But he couldn't help it.

He tossed on his bed. He prayed, wrestling with God. When sleep finally came, it brought confused dreams of musket fire and swamps, and of Melina leading him gently to his bathing stream, and of Richard Severn riding up on a fine horse and taking her away.

FERGUS HELPED MELINA into the carriage. He'd been stiffly polite to her all week, when he'd spoken to her at all, but now he smiled at her, and she smiled back with forgiving eagerness.

Catalyn and Tavish joined them this morning, along with Lachlan, who'd improved wonderfully over the past week. As they rode to town, Fergus watched his nephew squirming and jabbering in Catalyn's arms and thanked God for the baby's restored health.

Morning service seemed longer than usual that day. Melina joined the family for the noon meal, but they ate indoors and spoke only of the war. Fergus had to wait for the ride home to hear what he really wanted to know.

Melina was charmed, absolutely charmed, with Saint James Church and the people in it. They were so very attentive to her, she said.

"There were a great many Loyalists, of course, but quite a few Patriots as well. There was one vestryman with his hands all swelled up with gout—"

"Cornelius Harnett," said Father. "He served in the Continental Congress, and led the Sons of Liberty years ago."

"Aye, he was part of the Stamp Act crowd that terrified me when I was a little girl," Catalyn added.

"He and Colonel Ashe led the Patriot militia forces that burned Fort Johnston," Fergus said. "And he was one of two North Carolinians excepted by name from Sir Henry Clinton's proclamation of general amnesty in seventy-six."

"Correct," said Father. "So ye see, Miss Bryant, Mr. Harnett is a very notorious Patriot, and well worth your acquaintance."

"Good for him. Oh! And I saw a beautiful painting in the church, of Christ in his crown of thorns. Someone said it had been salvaged from a Spanish ship after a battle."

"Before my time," said Father. "Captain Johnstone could tell ye all about it, if he were here. I understand he has many of the salvaged effects from the Spanish ship in his home."

"Aye, and he's still got cannon mounted along the stone fence around his house," Tavish added. "To defend against the Spanish, he says."

"Who is this Captain Johnstone?" asked Melina. "Why have I not met him?"

"He's an old sea captain of the best sort," said Fergus. "But he's gone away. Fitted up as a privateer just after the war began."

"He was very good to Tavish," Catalyn said. "Lachlan is named for him."

"Papa used to have sea captains visit our home," said Melina. "Such colorful men they were, with such fascinating stories to tell."

She spoke of them, and of British officers who'd been her father's guests during the late French war, and of other Wilmingtonians she'd met at Saint James. No mention was made of Richard Severn.

Fergus was glad to see her happy and vivacious, so comfortable and content in his family's company. She seemed to belong with them more than ever now. He felt as if a heavy weight had been lifted from his shoulders.

Friendship was not all that he wanted from her, but it was all he had, and all he was likely to get. He must content himself with it, and not ruin it by vainly reaching for more.

Chapter Eight

"Mr. Shaw, do let me bring Dougie into the carriage," Melina said, craning around to face the box seat.

Mr. Shaw sat straight on his perch without turning. "He's a dog. He can walk."

"But he isn't walking. He's having to trot hard to keep up with the horses, and he's tired. See how his tongue lolls."

"He's panting to cool himself. That's what dogs do."

"You aren't even looking at him!"

"Miss Bryant, I have seen that dog accompany Fergus and Tavish while they manage the stock. With all his loops, circles, and switchbacks, he easily walks six miles for every one of theirs, and comes in fresh as a racehorse at the end of the day. 'Twas at your insistence that I agreed to bring him on this trip at all. He is not going to ride in the carriage like one of the family."

"What a thing to say! A dog *is* one of the family."

Mr. Shaw did not reply.

Melina turned to Fergus, riding Bran on the carriage's left. "What do you think, Fergus? Doesn't he look tired?"

Fergus looked at the lanky dog trotting between Bran and Hector. "I think he looks perfectly healthy, and pleased to be having a holiday."

Melina sat back with a huff and folded her arms. "Beastly men."

They'd been traveling south on the Haulover Road for two or three hours now. With the resin flow dried up for the year in the turpentine orchard, most of the garden produce in, cattle and hogs taken to town to supply the army, and calving not due to begin for some weeks, Mr. Shaw had ordered a beach holiday for the family. A string of Patriot victories in the South that fall had given them much to celebrate.

They'd started before sunrise. The chill in the crisp November air brought a tingle to Melina's blood, and the east wind smelled of brine. She grew more excited with each passing mile. She'd felt shut in on the Cape Fear, after living all her life in view of the sea.

Her eyes strayed to Fergus, and she privately compared his seat to that of Richard Severn, who was a bit too self-conscious and vain of his fine tack and expensive saddle horse. Mr. Severn was a fair rider, but not half as good as Fergus, who rode with fluid grace and controlled strength.

She never looked at Richard Severn without comparing him to Fergus—and now that she attended Saint James Church, she saw Mr. Severn every week. He always sought her out after services, and was unfailingly attentive and charming. He'd introduced her to his well-dressed, empty-headed mother. Without being boastful or crass, he'd made plain the extent of his substantial property, which was mostly mercantile rather than landed. He spoke of Charlestown in glowing terms, giving the impression that he would be happy to transfer himself there, and invest in some ships, and form alliances with planters.

Melina was no fool. She knew Mr. Severn was hinting—more than hinting—at the eligibility of a match, and indeed, from the perspective she had been taught, the union would be advantageous for both parties. There was profit to be made in Charlestown just now, with so much valuable property to be bought cheaply—and with Patriots shut out of all official business, the Loyalists were the only ones who could do it. And Richard Severn was precisely the sort of man she had grown up thinking she would one day marry—wealthy, intelligent, an excellent manager, even good to look at. Papa would have approved of him in all things except his being a Loyalist.

But Trailing Oaks didn't need rescuing. British rule in Charlestown wouldn't last. The Patriots would win the war, and Papa's estate would be restored without any help from Richard Severn or his money. Melina Bryant didn't need anyone to condescend to her.

Besides all that, whenever she saw or heard or thought of Mr. Severn, she always came up against his absolute inferiority to Fergus Shaw, an ordinary planter's son of small property and indifferent education.

As they traveled south, with the Cape Fear River on their right, the sea drew ever nearer on their left. After they passed the ferry house, the peninsula narrowed to a point at a strip of water, where the river met the Atlantic. Here they halted.

The land lay low and flat, almost level with the sea, with a few dunes and tussocks of grass.

Fergus pointed to the land across the strip of water. "That's Bald Head Island," he told Melina. "It used to be part of the peninsula, but a hurricane in sixty-one cut it off from the mainland, forming that new inlet there."

Once free of harness and saddle, the horses rolled luxuriously on the sand, twisting and writhing to remove the feel of tack from their backs. Lachlan laughed and laughed at the sight.

Melina had never harvested oysters before. Mr. Shaw gave her a wire basket, a pair of work gloves to protect her hands from the sharp shells, and a short-handled rake with two center prongs, and two end prongs cut off short.

Nessa pointed to a grassy marsh. "That looks like a good spot."

Sure enough, the marsh grass was growing from an oyster bed. Nessa and Morna showed Melina how to use her rake to pick up the clumps of oysters and knock them apart. Any singles with shells three inches across or more went into the basket. Smaller ones were put back in the bed and allowed to grow.

"How delightful this is!" Melina said. "I've eaten oysters countless times at home, but I never even thought about how they were gathered."

Nessa smiled. "'Tis a messy job. I should think you'd be tired of such things by now."

"Nay! It feels vital and real to be laboring with my own hands for my daily bread."

"Well, mind where you step," said Morna. "There are vital crabs in the oyster beds with very real claws."

Melina stood still for a moment and looked around her. The rest of the family was spread out in the marshes, except for Catalyn and Tavish, who kept to the beach with their little son. Tavish was digging a fire pit, and Catalyn was helping Lachlan scoop sand into a small pail.

Nessa and Morna filled their baskets far more quickly than Melina filled hers. She was constantly stopping to consider whether a particular shell was big enough to keep, or squealing at the scuttling crabs, or marveling at how the wet sand sucked at her boots, or exclaiming over the hand-like shape of an old dead shell with several smaller oysters growing out of it like fingers.

Once the baskets were filled, they were brought to the camp site, where the men had prepared a metal grate and filled several pails with fresh water. The oysters, still in their shells, were spread on the grate, one layer at a time, and rinsed of salt and sand. Once clean, they were ready to roast in the firepit.

"'Twill take time for the fire to grow hot enough," said Mr. Shaw. "I'll mind it and call the rest of ye when 'tis ready."

The family dispersed, and Melina found herself paired with Fergus. They sat on the shore together, taking turns looking through Fergus's spyglass at pelicans, herons, and sandpipers, and occasionally checking the horizon for sails. Sometimes, when Fergus wanted to show Melina something in particular, he'd lean his face close to hers and rest his hand on her shoulder.

When Dougie found them sitting on the shore, he brought his toy ball, dropped it at Fergus's feet, and sat on his haunches, eager and expectant. Fergus picked up the ball and threw it in a magnificent arc that sent Dougie hurtling in pursuit. Dougie fetched his ball with single-minded devotion. Melina took a few turns throwing, but she couldn't throw as far or as well as Fergus, and Dougie always gave her a patient look when he brought the ball back to her, so she contented herself with watching instead.

Fergus stopped before Dougie could exhaust himself. "We don't want to wear you out, old fellow," he told Dougie, rubbing the dog's shaggy ruff.

Dougie put his paw on Fergus's ankle, cocked his head, peered into Fergus's face, and whined low in his throat.

Melina put her arms around Dougie. "Oh, you good, clever dog! Never you worry. Fergus will keep your ball safe for you. Now go enjoy your holiday, and sniff at sea oats, and stay away from crabs."

When she turned him loose, she saw Fergus smiling at her.

"What?" she asked.

"Nothing. Only...it surprised me, when you first came to us from Charlestown, to see the way you are with animals. I didn't expect a fine lady to be such a lover of dogs and horses, or know so much about them."

"We always had horses at Trailing Oaks—and grooms to look after them, of course, but Papa wanted me to know how to care for them myself. 'Tis a mistake for a landowner to leave the management of the estate and its affairs entirely to others."

"You had dogs, too?"

"Aye, Papa always had hunting dogs, and I loved them dearly. But for my seventeenth birthday he gave me a dog of my own, a King Charles Spaniel. I called her Ruby. You would not have found her impressive. She wasn't useful. She didn't hunt or herd or sew or keep house. She sat on my lap, and slept on an embroidered cushion, and had her belly rubbed and her pert little ears scratched. She weighed all of seven pounds, and most of it was fur—the loveliest silky red coat you ever saw. She had a plumy tail and a tiny pointed nose and soft, round, liquid-black eyes. And oh, she was clever. She could jump on command, and bow, and beg, and kiss, and roll over, and speak, and stand up on her hind legs, and tell her left paw from her right. I would ask her, *Ruby, what did King Charles say to the Short Parliament?* And she would sit back on her little haunches and hold up her front paws and beg. I'd ask, *Ruby, what did King Charles say to the Long Parliament?* And she'd lie down and put her paws over her ears. 'Twas the most cunning thing you ever saw."

She glanced at Fergus. "I don't mean to make light of the Long Parliament, of course. It was very important. A precursor to the American Revolution, some say."

"What on earth are you talking about?" Fergus asked.

"The English Civil War. Because Ruby is a King Charles Spaniel."

He stared at her a moment, then laughed. "You are the strangest girl I ever knew. Well, Ruby sounds like a dear dog, and with you as her mistress I'm sure she had the best life a dog could have."

Melina's throat suddenly felt thick and sore. She swallowed hard, then said, "She had all that was in my power to give her. I only wish I could be sure she's alive and well now. Nay, I wish I had her with me still, and I'm not ashamed to say so. I know some would think it wicked of me to care so much about a little dog when others have lost life and limb and kin, but I love her dearly, and I cannot believe I am wrong to do so. I cannot believe I could love her as much as I do if God who made her did not love her more."

"I agree," said Fergus. "But I don't understand. Where is Ruby? Why is she not with you? Why did you not bring her from Charlestown?"

"Because we were not allowed to bring more than one trunk apiece."

"But surely one tiny dog—"

"That's what I said! She could have ridden on my lap and made no trouble at all. But the British officer in charge of getting us out of the city said I couldn't take her. I wish I'd known in time to make better arrangements, perhaps left Ruby with the vicar's family, but the carriage was about to leave, and I had to act fast. I gave her to a neighbor who happened to be standing by, a Loyalist woman called Mrs. Parker, who promised to send Ruby to me later. I believed her. But I never heard from her again, though I wrote to her repeatedly. I remember how Ruby looked at me as I handed her over. She was trembling and whining. She could always tell when I was anxious or upset, and the last weeks of the siege had been hard on her. Thunderstorms frightened her, and the cannonade was—well, you know. I told her I'd see her again soon, that Mrs. Parker would take good care of her and send her to me in North Carolina to stay with our cousins, but it wasn't true. I didn't mean to lie to her, but I let her down. I know she's only a dog and couldn't understand, but she trusted me, and I failed her."

The surf and sand turned to a blur, and Melina dabbed at her eyes.

Fergus was silent a long time. Finally he said, "I remember when you first came to us. You were vexed over being allowed only one trunk. I thought it was because of gowns. I misjudged you, Melina. I'm sorry. I didn't know."

She sniffed. "You couldn't know. And I didn't want to say anything about Ruby until I knew she was on her way. Otherwise your father might have told me to leave her in Charlestown."

"Father? Not likely."

"I know that now. But he was a stranger to me then. You all were. If I'd known Mrs. Parker wasn't going to send Ruby to me, I'd never have left her behind."

"I believe you. You'd have unloaded your trunk and let the carriage go to Wilmington without you."

She let out a shaky laugh. "You think me foolish."

"Nay. I think you're valiant."

She felt his gaze on her. "I was so afraid for Ruby during the latter half of the siege. Food was running short, and whole families fled. Many of them abandoned their dogs. We had whole packs of them roaming the streets. The soldiers were ordered to kill any dog they found, but not by shooting it, because they couldn't afford the loss of powder. I was so frightened Ruby would run out of the house and be knifed or strangled before I could reach her."

"I'm sorry you had to live through that. I'm sorry it happened at all. I hope and pray this war will be over soon. Perhaps we're through the worst of it."

"Perhaps we are."

She swept her arm out to the Atlantic. "Perhaps some grand naval battle is being fought at this very moment, deciding the issue. Or perhaps some intrepid smuggler is making it past British warships to Ocracoke Inlet, with Liam on his ship, getting crucial supplies to the Patriots."

Fergus got to his feet. "That's the spirit! We're on holiday, and ought to make the most of it and not let the war cast its shadow over us. Will you join me for a walk in the surf, Miss Bryant?"

"I'd be honored, Mr. Shaw. But I'm afraid 'twould be improper. We have no chaperone."

He threw back his head and laughed.

"Your prudence does you credit, Miss Bryant. I'm afraid we have no elderly matron to act as chaperone. But may I suggest as chaperone my family's long-time friend, Mr. Dougald Black, a gentleman of irreproachable character? I'm sure he could be prevailed upon to accompany us in all decency and propriety."

They both turned to Dougie, who looked back at them with his head cocked and one ear turned inside out.

"Mr. Black's reputation is well known in all the best circles," said Melina. "I gladly accept him as my protector."

Her petticoats were already kilted up. Now she removed her boots and peeled off her stockings. Fergus peeled off his stockings as well, and when he'd finished laying them neatly alongside his shoes he caught Melina staring at his exposed legs.

"What is it?" he asked.

"I'm just glad you have such good calves. And they're even better looking with the stockings off, which is more than some men can say. Some men actually stuff their stockings to get the desired effect."

He laughed again, loudly and heartily, then replied in mock shock, "My dear Miss Bryant, I have never stuffed in my life."

They waded in the surf with Dougie, who adopted a peculiar front-to-back, up-and-down gait that made him look like a porpoise. Fergus followed him farther out, but Melina kept to the ankle-deep water. It was too cold to go deeper, and besides, she liked better to watch the two of them roughhousing together. It was wonderful to see Fergus so happy and relaxed, to watch his strong man's body moving at play in the surf like a child's.

Before long, Fergus was soaked to the skin, and Dougie looked as sleek as a seal—until he shook himself from nose to tail, scattering icy droplets. Melina let out a shriek of protest.

"The water is positively glacial! Bad Mr. Black!"

"'Tis not so very cold once the initial shock wears off," said Fergus. "Wade out, and give it a try."

"Nay, I thank you. I'll keep to the shallows, where the sun warms the water a little."

"You, Miss Bryant, keeping to the shallows? You amaze me."

"Aye, I'm a delicate creature, bred in a balmy southern clime."

"A balmy southern clime! Charlestown is only a hundred and seventy miles southwest of Wilmington. I don't know what that is in latitude, but it cannot be much. Come into the surf with me, Melina. You'd like it. I know you would."

Melina knew she would too, and so she didn't dare. She enjoyed Fergus Shaw far too much—the gravity that made his jokes all the funnier, the way he teased without wounding. He knew things about her that no one else on earth knew, and she knew his secrets as well. She could not, must not, jeopardize their friendship by any unguarded behavior.

His wet shirt clung to him, showing the lean muscularity of his chest and arms.

He glanced down at himself. "What are you looking at? Have I got seaweed stuck to me?"

Melina pulled herself together.

"Nay. I was only thinking how thin you still are since returning home," she said.

It wasn't true, but it was the best she could do.

He looked outraged. "I'll have you know I'm as fit as I ever was. So is Bran. I'll show you."

He put his fingers to his lips and let out a piercing whistle. The horses were near the carriage, where they'd eaten the fodder brought from home. At the sound of his own particular call, Bran's head lifted, his ears perked forward, and he came running, eager as a dog.

Fergus greeted him with tender words and a good scratching along the mane. "Aye, you're a fine strong lad, that you are. But Miss Bryant thinks we're weak and spindly. We'll show her, won't we? How about a nice gallop down the strand to put us both through our paces? You'd like that, wouldn't you?"

"I don't see how you're going to manage that," said Melina. "He isn't wearing a strap of tack."

He gave her a quick smile and took some of Bran's mane in his hand. His long legs swung through the air, and in half an instant he was on Bran's back and galloping down the beach.

Melina stood rooted to the spot, her breath stolen away. She was safe from impropriety here, but oh, the sight of him, all fluid motion and strength and unbounded joy, made her ache inside. She wanted to be riding behind him, her arms around his middle, feeling the tight ridges of muscle beneath the thin wet linen of his shirt; she wanted to press her legs close against his and nest every curve of her body against a corresponding curve in his. They would fit together exquisitely—she knew they would.

And suddenly he was turning and riding back again, his face lowered and set, his black hair streaming behind him like a banner. Melina's heart hammered in her chest and her knees shook. She wasn't ready to look him in the eye, let alone speak to him–he would see straight through her and know.

Bran slowed to a canter, then stopped, and Fergus slid to the ground, his face flushed with triumph. "Well, madam! Do I pass my physical?"

Melina couldn't speak, couldn't breathe, couldn't do anything but stare.

Just then Mr. Shaw called them back to the campsite with an unintelligible shout and a wave of his arm.

"Coming, Father!" Fergus bellowed back.

They started back, returned for their shoes and stockings, and started back again. Bran followed them, his head bobbing up and down as he walked, and Dougie frisked ahead, stopping occasionally to dig in the sand.

Fergus was right. He'd regained the flesh he'd lost over the summer. The hollows around his eyes and the sharpness at his cheekbones had filled out. But ever since his return, there'd been something in his silences that hadn't been there before. Today, the shadow had truly lifted for the first time.

The metal grate was laid over the fire, and the oysters were placed on the grate in small batches, cup-side down, and steamed in their own juices. Once the meat was cooked, the top shell would pop open, and someone would remove the oyster with a pair of long-handled tongs and set it on a clean board covered with an old cloth.

There was a constant bustle, with cooked oysters coming off the fire and raw oysters going on, and sharp empty shells being tossed into a pile, and shucking knives flashing in the firelight. Tavish kept Lachlan safe in his arms and fed him cornbread soaked in oyster liquor, while Catalyn flipped more cornbread cakes in the griddle over the fire and brought Tavish's oysters to him.

Everyone had a preferred method of cooking and eating oysters. Rory liked his practically raw, which the rest of the family found revolting, but Tavish liked his a bit more well done than the rest. Nessa liked to shuck and spear several at one time, put them in a bowl, add butter, and eat them all at once with the work out of the way. Melina admired her efficiency but couldn't imitate it. Once an oyster was shucked and she saw it lying there in the bowl in rich, meaty perfection, she lost her head and ate it at once. Morna fed several to Dougie, and Mr. Shaw pretended to be cross, but Melina knew he didn't really mind.

Mr. Shaw had a very definite system. His movements were precise and methodical and unvarying. With his hand protected by a thick work glove, he'd pick up his oyster, pry off the top shell with his knife, spear the meat, and put it in his mouth while setting the empty shells into his own private heap, where they'd accumulate until he added them to the large pile. He'd follow up the oyster with a bite of cornbread, then a shot of whisky.

He didn't waste a single motion or vary his routine by one whit. And Fergus followed the exact same system. His movements were identical to his father's. He even placed the oyster shells in the same relative spot on his left side. Their physical dissimilarity made the resemblance even more striking. Fergus and Catalyn looked much alike, and were said to take after their mother, but Fergus was very like his father in other ways.

Some oyster liquor spilled on the sand. Dougie sniffed at the spot, dug at it with a hopeful paw, and tried to delicately bite the good-tasting juice with his front teeth.

"Look!" said Melina. "Mr. Black is eating sand!"

Mr. Shaw's brows lifted. "Mr. Black?"

Fergus gave Melina a private smile. "Mr. Dougald Black, Esquire."

Mr. Shaw sighed resignedly. "This dog is rising rapidly in the world. He'll be a town commissioner ere long."

"Aye, and elected to Continental Congress," said Rory.

"Well, he had a lovely romp in the surf with Fergus today," Melina said. "I wish you all could have seen it."

"I'm glad Fergus acquitted himself well in the water," said Mr. Shaw. "I wouldna have predicted it after his first encounter with the ocean."

Fergus let out a groan. "Not this story again, Father. 'Tis as stale as a ship's biscuit."

"Nay, 'tis fresh to me," said Melina. "Do tell, Mr. Shaw."

Mr. Shaw took some more whisky. "He wasna much bigger than young Lachlan there, and excited to be visiting the seaside, or as excited as he ever gets about anything. He was with his mother, walking determinedly out in-to the water in that single-minded way of his, until he got hit by his first wave. Then he halted in his tracks, turned on his heel, and walked straight out again as fast as his fat little legs would take him. I caught him before he could reach the carriage. He looked up at me with those big dark eyes and said, *Go home now.* I picked him up, tossed him over my shoulder, and car-ried him into the surf."

"Did he fight you?" Melina asked.

"Nay. He was a spirited, stubborn little lad, but he understood when a thing was inevitable. And after I plunked him back into the water he soon perceived its virtues. We came here many times when the children were small, Isabeau and I, and I kept bringing them here myself after I lost her."

"How did the other children behave?"

Mr. Shaw leaned back, warming to his topic. "Catalyn loved best to sculpt in the sand. She made the most elaborate castles, ornamented with shells and stones and seaweed, and kept Morna with her. Nessa was Fergus's playmate, always good-natured and adventuresome, and never complained if the games got rough."

"She was the one who made the games rough, more often than not," Fergus put in. Nessa smiled sweetly at him.

Mr. Shaw paused a moment before going on. "Liam, now—he took to the water like a selkie. Sometimes he played with Nessa and Fergus, but more often he kept to himself, riding the waves. Perhaps I should've seen at the time that he'd never be able to keep away from the water for long."

No one spoke. Fergus smiled at Melina, a faint, wistful smile that made her throat hurt. The family had received no word from Liam since his departure. There was no way of knowing where he was, or if he was dead or alive.

"Rory kept to himself a great deal too," Mr. Shaw said briskly. "Always observing things in or out of the water, and keeping up a running monologue about all he saw."

"I did not keep up a running monologue," said Rory, who had only recently outgrown this childhood habit and didn't like to be reminded of it.

"You did so," the rest of the family said in unison.

The fire died down, and Lachlan fell asleep in his father's arms. Catalyn made a snug blanket nest for him in the carriage. Slowly and carefully Tavish got to his feet and carried him to it. Dougie followed. He dug up a slight hollow in the sand beside the carriage and curled up in it with a sigh.

Rory picked up the linen work bag he'd brought from home and went back to combing the beach for interesting shells and artifacts from wrecked ships. He'd already found a fragment of Delft pottery and an old sextant.

Fergus gave Melina a quick glance over his shoulder and walked back toward the shore. She knew he wanted her to follow him, and she did.

When they were clear of the others, he said, "I have something for you. Hold out your hand."

"Is it something horrid?" she asked.

"Nay, not at all."

She held out her hand, and he dropped something into her palm—a tiny sphere no larger than a spring pea, black and softly lustrous.

"I found it in one of my oysters," he said. "Nearly broke my tooth on it. Is it not lovely?"

"Lovely indeed!" said Melina, turning it around with her finger.

Fergus suddenly looked shy. "I know you must have many fine jewels. This one is probably of no great value, but I thought you might like to have it, to remember."

She smiled up at him. "It is the perfect remembrance of a perfect day. Thank you, Fergus."

He smiled back. His hair looked stiff, and she could actually see grains of salt at the temples. His shirt lay open at the neck, exposing a nut-brown chest with a strip of paler skin running along the shirt's V on one side. His forehead was richly brown as well, with a hint of red at his cheekbones and the bridge of his nose.

His hand was clasping hers, though she couldn't remember taking it. He suddenly seemed very near.

They both let go at the exact same moment. Fergus stepped back, and Melina busied herself tying the pearl into a handkerchief, trying to hide the blush that she was certain had risen in her cheeks.

The sun was warmer now, shining out of a clear, bright sky above the ocean's deeper blue. The two of them walked together along the shore for most of the afternoon, then harvested more oysters together before gathering back at the campsite with the others. By now, everyone looked thoroughly disheveled. Hair, salty and windblown, had assumed strange shapes, and clothing was unkempt.

Mr. Shaw built the fire back up, and they all ate again of the delicious meat and cornbread while the sun sank behind the pines west of the river. Lachlan fell asleep again, in Catalyn's arms this time.

When darkness came on in earnest, they sang—sometimes together, sometimes individually. Melina knew airs she'd learned in Charlestown that the others hadn't heard, and Nessa knew a surprising number of Gaelic songs that she'd picked up from an old admirer of Catalyn's. None of them knew Gaelic, so they couldn't say how accurate Nessa's renditions were, but they sounded convincing to Melina.

Morna spread a blanket over the sand and stretched out on her back with her red curls spread around her. "Isn't it lovely to be away from the war, if only for a day? It seems as if we hardly ever stop thinking about it anymore.

Everything we do or say or plan comes back to it somehow or other. I know 'twasn't always so, but I can hardly remember the time before."

"You and Rory have passed too much of your lives so," Mr. Shaw said. "I never truly lived under the shadow of war before this one. The late French war didn't touch us in Wilmington."

"What was the French war like in Charlestown, Miss Bryant?" Nessa asked. "Did it affect the city much?"

"In a way, though of course the actual fighting took place hundreds of miles off. Some of the town's importers and exporters became quite rich—or quite a bit richer, I should say—supplying goods to the troops and materials for the city's fortifications, and buying French vessels taken as prizes. I was only a little girl at the time, but I remember the British naval and army officers who visited our home. Many of them are fighting against us now."

Mr. Shaw banked up the fire to last through the night. Melina could see its glow through the tent she shared with Morna and Nessa. Over the past month or so she'd finally grown used to sharing her sleeping space. It was as if she'd truly become a part of this big, boisterous, affectionate family.

She'd never longed for brothers and sisters, exactly. Her baby brother had died at birth, without a history or a personality or even a name to give substance to his absence. And Papa had kept her too busy for loneliness. From an early age, she'd been his constant companion, learning to ride and hunt and manage the estate. As sole heir, she'd taken her responsibility seriously, and however much Papa might have grieved his lost son in private, he always said how fortunate he was in having so intelligent and capable a daughter.

She thought of him now as she grew comfortably warm under her covers. She'd worried horribly about him over the summer months, when the heat had exacerbated the filth and confinement of his miserable prison. The defeat at Camden had hit her hard. She'd never put the same unlimited confidence in Gates that some did, but she'd still hoped for a Patriot victory, leading to the liberation of Charlestown or at least a prisoner exchange. The shattering of Gates's army meant no release for Papa. It had been the middle of August then, with summer far from over in the South. She'd kept her anxiety to herself, for Fergus's sake and for everyone else's. Everyone was suffering, and everyone knew it. Talking about it didn't change that.

Papa had survived the summer—she had his letters to prove it—and now fall had come, bringing the blessed relief of cool weather, and the victory at Kings Mountain, and a string of other Patriot wins.

Who would have guessed the backcountry militiamen would make such coolheaded and tenacious fighters? Perhaps it was as Fergus had said—the militiamen needed only to be well supplied and well led. And they were operating in smaller groups now, which worked to their advantage. Smaller groups were easier to feed and easier to move—they'd learned that much from Camden.

She fell asleep to the dull roar of the waves.

IN THE MORNING MELINA and Morna took the empty oyster shells back to the bed—*reseeding*, Morna had called it. When they returned, the carriage was loaded and ready for the journey home.

"What a lovely time we've had," Melina said. "Thank you, dear Mr. Shaw, for giving us such a splendid holiday."

"Free food for a large family," he grumbled. "That's all 'twas."

"Aye, and a twenty-five-mile round-trip journey to get it. You can pretend all you like, Mr. Shaw. You don't fool me."

Mr. Shaw ignored this.

Dougie had contrived to cut his foot on an oyster shell and limped around looking very sorry for himself until Mr. Shaw said he could ride home in the carriage.

"Might as well," he said. "No doubt he'll have his own phaeton before long."

Lachlan laughed his infectious gurgle at the sight of the lanky dog sprawled on the carriage floor. Rory complained about the cramped seating and wished openly for his own saddle horse. Mr. Shaw replied that Rory was welcome to buy one if he could produce the funds. Morna said that Nessa was taking more than her fair portion of the seat. Nessa said she was taller and entitled to a larger space.

"What a merry party we are!" said Melina. "We should go on holiday more often."

"Och, daughter," said Mr. Shaw. "I dinnae ken if my spirits could bear the ecstasy."

He often called the other girls *daughter*. As terms of endearment went, it was on the thrifty side, a mere acknowledgment of a filial relationship. But he made the word sound wonderfully tender. Had he meant to call her that, or done so unconsciously? Either way, it gave her a warm feeling inside. She had her own papa, of course, and he had always been all the family she had needed. But it was pleasant to be a part of this other, larger family, if only for a little while.

Chapter Nine

Fergus slammed the front door behind him, shutting out the raw December wind. He and Tavish took off their coats and hung them in the hall. Firelight spilled out from the dining room, along with the tantalizing aromas of dinner. They had just returned from town, where they'd sold some cattle and hogs to the army and tarried long enough to hear the news.

"Well?" asked Melina, setting a stack of cornbread cakes on the table. "Is it good or bad?"

Fergus and Tavish looked at each other. "Good, on the whole," said Tavish as he walked to his place beside Catalyn at the table. "General Gates's successor had finally taken command."

"Excellent!" said Melina. "Four months is more than enough time for Gates to sit at his ease in Hillsborough, sending out dispatches that no one reads."

"We did well enough without any general leadership at all," Fergus said as he took his seat. "The southern forces have performed far better without it than they ever did before. Give me a plucky militia colonel defending his own home any day, and keep your Continental generals."

"At least the Congress had the sense to let General Washington make his own choice this time," said Tavish.

"Aye, and what a choice it was!" said Fergus. "An asthmatic Quaker with a limp."

"I think General Greene's origin is in his favor," said Melina, her eyes sparkling at him from across the table. "He must truly be devoted to the Patriot cause in order to turn away from his pacifist upbringing."

"He isn't qualified," Fergus shot back. "He got all his knowledge of war from books."

"He's no less qualified as a general than Washington is as Commander in Chief. Lack of qualification is what the Continental forces have in common. We're none of us fit for what's required of us, but we do it nevertheless, on pure faith and grit if need be, because we must. No one has proven that better than the backcountry militia these past months, now that they've been allowed to find their own style of fighting."

"On that, at least, we agree. I only hope General Greene has the sense to give the militia forces their head and not try to fit them into the Continental mold."

Then Father said drily, "If the two of ye are quite finished, I'll say grace, and we can eat."

"Please do, Mr. Shaw," said Melina. "Fergus and I understand each other perfectly now."

FERGUS WOKE WITH A start. For a moment he didn't know where he was. He sat there, his face damp with a chill sweat, whipping his head from left and right, until the lines around him fell into place and he recognized his sleeping loft above the carriage shed. In the dim grey light he could see three of the barn cats that had learned to appreciate his warmth, now startled into wakefulness like himself.

He lay back with a sigh, his heart still pounding, his breath fogging the air above his face. He'd been dreaming of Camden, of running through slick wiregrass as cannon fire roared all around him.

He shut his eyes, then opened them. There it was again—a volley of deep, muted booms. It wasn't a dream.

He made his way to the loft window, opened the shutter, and looked out at the cold January morning. The sun hadn't yet risen, and a glitter of frost covered the ground. Past the curve in the track, Tavish was standing in the open door of the cabin, his rumpled shirt hanging to his bare knees. Rory was just opening one of the upstairs windows in the main house, and Melina, wrapped in a shawl, was already looking out the other, her golden hair tumbling over her shoulders in soft waves. Father was away, serving with the militia.

"Is it thunder?" Melina called out.

"Nay," Fergus shouted back. "Too regular."

There it went again, one shot after another in rapid succession. They all looked at each other.

"Could the British be attacking the harbor?" Tavish asked.

"Nay!" said Rory. "It was thirteen discharges. I counted. A *feu de joie*! They're celebrating something in the town!"

Another cascade of fire went off. This time Fergus counted, too. Rory was right.

Over a month had passed since Major General Greene had arrived in South Carolina to take command. Anything might have happened—including final victory over the British.

Fergus reached for his breeches. "I'll saddle Bran and ride to town to get the news," he called.

He returned a little before noon. Melina went out to meet him.

"You certainly took your time about it," she said tartly.

He smiled. "I had to make sure of the details."

"And? What is it? What's happened?"

She was so bright and eager and beautiful. He wanted to take her in his arms, and spin her around, and kiss her perfect mouth. But he only said, "I'll tell everyone at once. Gather the family while I see to Bran."

He took Bran to the carriage house, unsaddled him, rubbed him down, and gave him some oats. The barn cats twined around his ankles as he worked, as if they knew there was reason to celebrate.

He was still a few steps away from the front door when Melina opened it and drew him into the parlor, where the family waited. Catalyn sat near the fire, with Lachlan in her arms and Tavish standing behind her, his hand on her shoulder. Nessa and Morna sat side by side, while Rory paced back and forth, with Dougie at his heels.

"Well?" asked Nessa. "What's the news?"

Fergus took a seat. "Victory in the west," he said, "but not final victory."

He told them how General Greene had sent a force southwest under the command of Daniel Morgan, a frontiersman who'd fought in the late French war. Morgan took his men to Ninety-Six, and Cornwallis sent a thousand British regulars under Colonel Tarleton to intercept him. Morgan chose his battleground well—open meadow, ringed by hardwoods, and hemmed in east and west by creeks and ravines—making it impossible for the enemy to flank the Patriots. He deployed his men in three lines made up mostly of militia, with his best sharpshooters in front, and ordered them to fire three shots and then withdraw to the back. Tarleton thought they were running away and followed to finish them off. He didn't see the Continentals hidden behind a ridge until it was too late. By then the militiamen had reloaded and encircled the enemy.

"Bloody Ban couldn't get his men to obey him," Fergus said. "They fled the field, leaving guns and cartridge boxes behind them. But the cavalry cut off their escape. It could have been a slaughter. Tarleton's men clearly expected no mercy, as they had shown none in the past. But most of the survivors were taken prisoner."

"How many?" asked Tavish.

"Around six hundred."

A stunned silence fell.

"Six hundred British regulars?" Melina said. "Cornwallis will want them back."

"Aye," said Fergus. "Morgan is driving them to the Virginia border to reconnect with Greene, and Cornwallis is on his way to catch them."

"That will be quite a race," said Melina. "The Patriots with a fresh victory hot in their bellies, and the British hell-bent on revenge."

Tavish frowned. "If Cornwallis catches the Patriots before they reach the Dan River, everything Morgan gained will be lost."

"The Patriots will get there first," said Nessa. "They must. Morgan is in familiar territory. All those ridges and waterways on the way to the Dan—the British won't be able to navigate them."

"Aye, and the British will be marching hungry," said Fergus. "They're cut off from their supply centers, and the Patriots captured their baggage train."

Catalyn shut her eyes and pressed her cheek to the top of Lachlan's head. "I almost wish I didn't know. How will we bear the suspense?"

"We'll bear it," said Fergus. "We must."

He caught Melina's eye, then walked out the back door. He stood on the stoop, gazing at the longleaf pines covering the slope that rose behind the house. Every needle showed sharp and clear in the wintry air.

The door opened and shut behind him. Melina had joined him, as he'd known she would. He didn't have to turn. He could feel that it was her.

"There were survivors from Camden with Morgan," he said. "North Carolina militia and Maryland Continentals, fighting together against Tarleton—and winning."

His throat burned, and he swallowed hard. Had Reynolds and Carson been there? Had they escaped the carnage at Camden? He had no way of knowing. He could only hope. And hope didn't seem as foolish as it had a few months ago.

Then Melina took his arm.

He laid his hand over hers, covering it.

"If the Patriots win the race—if Morgan reaches the Dan River first, and joins forces with Greene—"

"I know," Melina said. "It could be the beginning of the end."

He put his arm around her. She nestled against him, and he breathed in the sweet scent of her silky hair. Backcountry militiamen, beating British regulars, led by the most feared and hated British commander. If that could happen, anything could happen—even a middling planter's son winning the heart and hand of a highborn girl.

FOR THREE DAYS, THEY all reveled in Morgan's victory. Then Tavish went to town to get the latest news, and came back looking grim.

Fergus's heart sank like lead. "The British beat Morgan to the Dan?"

"Nay," said Tavish. "At least—I dinnae ken. This news is closer to home. An express has arrived from Charlestown, advance warning from the Patriots there. Major Henry Craig is on his way to Wilmington with an invading force, under orders to take the city for the Crown."

Chapter Ten

The last few stars shone hard and bright in the January sky. Melina's breath fogged in the chill morning air. They'd all gathered behind the house, where the woods rose in a gradual slope to the north. Hector and Bran stood ready, with knapsacks and gear strapped to their saddles.

"We'll meet General Lillington at the Northeast Cape Fear River," Fergus told her. "It curves above the city to the east for about ten miles before turning north. The crossing points are few. It should keep the British out of the interior."

All this sounded good in theory, but depended on the militia's ability to master the crossing points—and that would be far from easy. Once again, the militia was short on ammunition, with fewer than five rounds per man. How could they possibly hold off Craig's force with that?

But Melina only nodded. There was no reason to dwell on the weak points. No doubt Fergus was well aware of them already.

Wilmington wasn't the first southern town to be occupied by the enemy. It was North Carolina's largest city and most important port, and everyone had been expecting the British to take it for the past year. But that didn't stop the shock of the actual fact of a foreign army in their town, walking their streets, quartered in civilian homes.

Melina thought of the Wilmington militiamen, Mr. Shaw among them, struggling to organize a defense on the Northeast Cape Fear—and of General Morgan, still making his way across North Carolina with his British prisoners. Cornwallis had ordered the assault on Wilmington before taking off after Morgan. With Wilmington under British control, Cornwallis would be able to get supplies through Cross Creek and have a secure place to retreat to if necessary.

A few yards off, Lachlan clung to Catalyn and blinked sleepily.

"I dinnae like leaving ye this way, with no men on the place," Tavish told Catalyn. "Craig's bound to send foraging parties to the countryside."

"There isn't any choice," Catalyn replied. "You and Fergus must get out while you can. The town is taken. If you stay, and raiders come, you'll be killed. You can't protect us if you're dead."

"She's right," Melina said to Fergus. "The only way you can do any good is to harass the British from the outside, and keep them contained, without being caught."

She tried to sound convincing, but she didn't want him to go. She wanted to bind him hand and foot and hide him away somewhere close to her until the war ended and the British went away for good.

But the British wouldn't go unless someone made them.

Tavish cupped Lachlan's head in his palm and kissed his brow. Then Catalyn handed Lachlan off to Nessa and took Tavish's hands in hers. Something passed between them, something so raw and urgent that Melina had to turn away. Her gaze fell on Fergus, who was watching her with a look that made her cheeks flush hot.

He held his buff-colored cocked hat in his hands. She ran a finger down the scorched furrow along the crown and felt in the cockade for the ribbon she'd given him. It was still there. Touching the hat was almost like touching him, and the closest she could come just now, with his family standing by.

She thought again of how he'd kissed her that August day after returning from Camden. She wished he would do it again, but he couldn't—not here, not now. Would there be another chance? Would she ever see him again?

"We'll send word as soon as we can," Fergus said.

Melina nodded. They'd arranged for a dead drop inside a hollow tree on a hill—the candle-tree, Fergus called it. Woodpeckers had a nest there.

Tavish pressed Catalyn's hands to his lips, then said, "Rory, ye must take care of Boudicca. She'll be ready to foal in another two months. Keep an eye out for foraging parties. If they come, get on Boudicca and ride her away, hard. We cannae afford to lose her to the British."

"I know," Rory said. He was standing next to Morna. He was as tall as she was now, all ankles and knees and wrists.

"And look after your sisters," Fergus added. "You're the last man on the place."

Rory gave a quick nod. His jaw was set, and the cords in his neck stood out.

The gathering dissolved in a confusion of embraces, last-minute instructions, and messages to Mr. Shaw, whom Fergus and Tavish would be joining soon. In the end, Fergus gave Melina only a sharp parting glance and a press of the hand, and then he was gone.

MELINA SHIVERED IN her cloak as she waited in the queue of wagons and carriages at a checkpoint north of town. Some blocks ahead, a column of dirty black smoke rose into the pale January sky. The woods surrounding the town had been cut down, and now the felled timbers were being built into an abatis along a ridge of high ground between Second and Fourth streets. The sight of the bare stumps, and the tree trunks sharpened into spikes, made her want to cry.

The queue moved forward, and Melina advanced to the checkpoint. A soldier motioned her to stop without looking up from the list in his hand. His frayed red coat was sun-bleached to pink.

"Name?"

"Melina Bryant."

"Place of residence?"

"The Shaw farm."

"Your business in the town?"

"I wish to check the welfare of some friends."

He looked up then and fixed her with a pair of unnaturally blue eyes. "You want to have a good gossip, you mean."

Anger rose hot in Melina's chest, but she lowered her gaze demurely. "You surely cannot blame me, sir. We've all been cramped and confined for ever so long."

"Aye, I'm sure your trials have been many. No balls or trinkets or goods for new gowns."

Melina forced herself to smile—a deep, ingenuous, wide-eyed smile that had served her well in the past. "Don't be too severe upon us women, sir. We must have some pleasures."

"Now that the city has been restored to royal rule, I expect that you and other young ladies shall be introduced to many new pleasures."

Melina felt the smile stiffen on her face. The soldier held her gaze a moment more before making a cursory search of the carriage and waving her through.

The column of smoke grew thicker and darker as she followed Third Street south. Just past Chestnut lay a smoldering heap of charred timbers and ash. Bits of broken plate and folds of cloth showed through the debris, and the blackened chimneys stuck up stark and skeletal in the wreckage—all that remained of the home of Mr. Hooper, signer of the Declaration of Independence. What of Mr. Hooper himself? Had he gotten away, or been caught and hanged by the redcoats?

A block past the smoking ruin, at the corner of Market and Third, the Burgwin house stood proud and immaculate, white paint gleaming, the rails of the full balconies shining crisp in the winter sunshine. The mansion seemed to be gloating, somehow. Red-coated soldiers moved about the grounds. Major Craig must have taken the house for his headquarters.

To the left, British soldiers were carrying pews out the front door of Saint James Church. These soldiers wore the short green coats and black helmets of Tarleton's Legion.

Melina's stomach lurched. For a moment she wished she hadn't come, but she pushed down the weakness. Catalyn hadn't wanted her to take the carriage to Wilmington. A British-occupied town wasn't a safe place for known Patriots, she'd said. But they couldn't all stay on the farm for the duration of the war. Even if they'd been able to do without shopping, and selling stock and produce, they had to get information, sometime and somehow, about the war's progress and the state of the town. And in Melina's opinion, she was the fittest person to do it.

She turned right on Market and drove toward the waterfront. Some sort of pen was being constructed in a hollow between Second and Third—a strange place to keep livestock.

She stopped the carriage at Polly Robertson's house. No one answered her knock, and the curtains in the front room hadn't been drawn.

A slave woman came up the walk next door, carrying a laden basket. Melina hurried to meet her.

"Can you tell me where the Robertsons are?" she asked quietly.

"Mr. Robertson's gone away with the Whig militia," the slave woman answered. "Miz Robertson and the children left town. Lots of Whig ladies did—Miz Hooper, Miz Barnett, Miz Boyd."

"Were there many killed in the capture of the town?"

"Not one. The militia spiked the cannon and got out before the British came. The town surrendered without firing a shot."

An unconditional surrender! Melina writhed inside. But there was nothing more they could have done. If the end result was going to be defeat either way, better a bloodless surrender than a long, deadly siege.

The front door of the house next to the Robinsons' opened, and a tall woman in a silk gown came out.

"Sally, go around back and put your shopping away."

The slave woman gave a quick curtsey to her mistress and hurried away.

The woman stepped to the edge of the high porch and looked down her long nose at Melina.

"Good day, madam," Melina said. "I was just asking your girl about the Robertsons. Miss Polly is a friend of my cousin's."

"The Robertsons ran away to Duplin County," the woman said. "I guess they thought that was a better place to be rebels in, now that the King's justice has been restored in Wilmington. Maybe you should look for them there."

"Perhaps the agents of the King's justice will punish the vandals who destroyed Mr. Hooper's property," Melina said sweetly.

The woman's mouth thinned. "Hooper got off lighter than he deserved. Traitors should be hanged."

Melina gave the woman a radiant smile. "I see. Is that Mrs. Robertson's potted palm I see on your porch, madam?"

The woman stalked back into her house and slammed the door.

Melina returned to the carriage, keeping her steps measured and her head high, but shaking with rage. Traitors, indeed! How could it be treason for citizens to insist on the rights guaranteed to them by their own Constitution? And what was a Constitution *for*, if not to guarantee those rights? The Magna Carta, the Bill of Rights—were they true expressions of God-given liberties, or only suggestions to be followed or discarded at the whim of whatever sovereign happened to be wearing the crown?

A thunder of hoofbeats came up the road. Half a dozen redcoats on horseback rode up to the pen on Market Street. One of the horses had what looked like a sack of meal slung over its back. The soldier in the lead dismounted and cut away the ropes that held it in place. It slid off the horse's back and fell to the dirt road, letting out a scream of pain.

Cheers and jeers rose from some townspeople on the sidewalk. The bundle on the road took the shape of an old man, slight of frame and not tall, in filthy, disheveled clothing.

The soldier who'd cut him down kicked him in the side. "On your feet. Quick, now!"

The man lay in the street, gasping for breath. The soldier took a riding crop from the saddle and whipped him.

The man screamed again. He struggled to comply, but his feet gave way beneath him. The soldiers laughed.

Then Melina saw the hands with their swollen, gouty knuckles beneath tightly stretched, shiny red skin.

"Mr. Harnett!" she whispered.

She could barely recognize the kindly old Patriot she'd met at Saint James Church. He stumbled to his feet at last, and the soldiers drove him toward the rough pen. Surely they didn't mean to keep him there!

But they did. Mr. Harnett staggered into the pen and huddled against a rough-hewn picket.

Another soldier shut the gate behind him and gave a mock bow. "I hope you enjoy your stay, sir. You'll have company soon. We're rounding up all your rebel friends."

Melina turned away, sickened, and shut her eyes.

"Miss Bryant!"

She looked up. Richard Severn stood before her, tall and elegant in a greatcoat of fulled wool with a black velvet collar. He wore a narrow-brimmed hat with a high, tapering crown. It couldn't have been more different from Fergus's worn cocked hat with the scorch mark on top and her hair ribbon nestled in the cockade. She used to know all the latest fashions, but this one was new to her.

Richard looked as handsome as ever, and the tender concern in his eyes made Melina's own eyes fill with tears.

He drew her arm through his and led her away. Already a crowd was gathering at the bull pen, yelling mockery at Mr. Harnett.

"Certain elements of the town are none too friendly toward those of your political persuasion at present," Richard said. "I'm sorry you had to witness such things."

"I'm only sorry for Mr. Harnett," said Melina. "Such an amiable gentleman! 'Tis shameful for his neighbors to treat him so."

"'Tis certainly an uncouth display," Mr. Severn replied.

Melina halted and drew her arm away. Blinking back tears, she gave him a watery smile. "Thank you, Mr. Severn. You've been most kind."

"Please, madam, this is nothing. Let me take you away from here. My carriage is at your disposal."

"That is good of you, but I drove myself to town."

His gaze strayed over her shoulder. "Ah, of course. I recognize Mr. Shaw's rig. You are still staying with his family, then? Are you well provided for?"

"We have all we need, thank you."

"And how is your father? Have you heard from him lately?"

"About a fortnight ago. The cold weather is a welcome change, he says. He always writes cheerfully, but I know how he must suffer."

"As do you, in spite of your brave words."

She bowed her head. She was just about to thank him again for his kindness when he asked, "Are you sure you do not suffer needlessly?"

Melina went cold. "Wh-what do you mean?"

"You know what I mean," he said gently. "If you were to return your allegiance to the Crown, you would be allying yourself to friends who could then exert themselves on your behalf and on your father's. You could secure better treatment for him—perhaps even a release on promise of good conduct. Trailing Oaks, and all your property in Charlestown, would be protected. You might even be able to get clemency for some of your rebel friends."

All at once, Melina's imagination ran wild with images of Papa released from prison, of Trailing Oaks restored to its former glory, of the Shaw Farm protected from further Tory harassment, and of Fergus and the others being spared from hardship and even death. Was it possible? Just how far did Richard's influence extend?

The next moment, she was deeply ashamed of herself for entertaining the thought even for an instant. Her father had chosen to go to a prison ship rather than take the Oath of Allegiance to the Crown. How would he ever hold up his head again if his own daughter gave in to weakness? How would she ever look Fergus in the eye, or any of the Shaws—she, who despised turn-coats and Summer Patriots, and said so, loudly and often?

She raised her head. "It may be that turning my coat would buy some ease in the short term," she said. "But I will abide by my convictions. I know the Patriot cause to be just and right, and I know it will prevail in the end."

"Very well," said Mr. Severn. "We will speak no more of it. Did you come alone to town, Miss Bryant?"

"Aye. I suppose you'll say that was foolish of me."

A smile crinkled the corners of his eyes. "There's no need for me to say it, for you know it as well as I do. But I will say this. Should you ever need anything, anything at all, do not hesitate to let me be of service to you. My home is but one block from here, a stone house with a wisteria vine covering the porch. You know it?"

"I do. Thank you, Mr. Severn. I'm most obliged. And now I really must be returning home."

He walked her to the carriage and helped her up to the box seat. They said their goodbyes, and she drove away.

The Patriots were going to win. She reminded herself of that over and over as the houses of the town began to fall away. She had only to keep faith and wait. The war would end, and Papa would be released, and they would be home again, together. And maybe, just maybe, there would be a place on Trailing Oaks for Fergus. He had no great wealth or property to bring to a marriage, but he was sober and hardworking and capable—unlike so many eligible bachelors who didn't know how to manage an estate properly and would fritter away their fortunes, and hers, in gambling and drink. Surely Papa would see the value of such a son-in-law—especially considering how good the Shaws had been to her, and what devoted Patriots they were.

Aye, victory was close at hand, along with everything else Melina could possibly wish for. She needed no favors from Richard Severn, whose gaze she could feel on her back.

Chapter Eleven

"Och, the pungent aroma of marsh gas," said Tavish. "It perfumes the air of our camp like rotten eggs."

"'Twould perfume it far more in the heat of summer," Father replied. "Be thankful we're here in January and not August."

The militia forces had made their camp on a hill near the Northeast Cape Fear River. The site was protected by a deep marsh along the river's north shore. A narrow causeway ran beside the marsh and ended at the hill. The river was four hundred feet at this site, and passable only by Heron's Bridge. The middle section of the bridge could be raised to allow tall ships to pass—or to shut the enemy out of the Patriot camp.

"I don't mind the smell," said Fergus. "This camp is secure and defensible, and I like it. It reminds me of Moore's Creek Bridge."

"It does have something of the same look and disposition," said Tavish. "Moore's Creek Bridge—our first battle. How long has it been? Four years? Five? I remember it like yesterday."

"There isna much to remember," said Father. "'Twas all over in a few minutes."

"That was the best thing about it, besides the fact that we won," said Fergus.

At Moore's Creek, the Patriot forces had removed planks from the bridge and greased the girders to keep the Tories from crossing and marching into Wilmington. This time, Wilmington was already taken, and the Patriots wanted not to disable a bridge, but to hold it. How they could possibly do that while conserving their precious few rounds of ammunition, Fergus didn't know.

Major Craig had arrived only yesterday in Wilmington. All the militia members remaining in town had withdrawn to join the units—including Father's—that had been called out previously by General Lillington. The combined forces had then secured their stores in camp and made ready to defend Heron's Bridge. So far, Fergus had spent most of his time gazing southward along the road that led ten miles or so to home. He'd also made a rough sketch of the drawbridge mechanism to include in their first packet of letters. Rory would be interested in that. So would Melina.

Melina. Fergus shut his eyes and saw her, looking up at him with her gold-flecked eyes. What would she do, what would she feel, if he died out here, and she never saw him again? Would she shed a few tears and then forget him? He didn't think so. And what if he lived? Was it possible that she could care for him? Could the two of them have a future together?

It did no good to wonder. The thing to do now was to survive—and win.

Somewhere to the west of them, Morgan and Cornwallis were still running their race to the Dan. If Morgan won, it would mean the beginning of the end for the British. But if Cornwallis won, then whatever the militia forces did here at Heron's Bridge would matter little to anyone but themselves.

BRAN'S HOOVES STEPPED quietly across the moonlit forest floor. The woodland grew thicker the farther the patrol moved from the river. Tavish rode to Fergus's left, some yards away. The rest of the horsemen were spread out to his right.

Hours earlier, a mounted lookout had failed to return to camp. He might have deserted for home, or met an accident—or been captured by the enemy. Fergus scanned the woods for a riderless horse. If the lookout had fallen and broken his neck, the location of the camp might still be secure. Otherwise—

A flash of movement about a hundred yards off caught his eye. Fergus halted, signaling to the others.

The form of a horseman emerged from the woods. He wasn't one of theirs. Silently and swiftly, the patrol circled around.

Then a shot rang out, and the patrolman to Fergus's right fell from his saddle without a cry. Suddenly the woods were filled with enemy horsemen and foot soldiers. Shots echoed all around, and smoke filled the air.

Fergus wheeled around and headed north. There was nothing else to do. His patrol was outnumbered. The best they could hope for was to reach camp before the enemy did, and raise the drawbridge.

Camp was a mile away, and the enemy was pressing him hard. Hoofbeats thundered behind him. A shot whistled past, grazing his sleeve. His eyes strained for a glimpse of the river, but it was Melina that he saw, with her hazel eyes and golden hair.

By the time he came in sight of the bridge, more Patriot militiamen were waiting on the south shore with muskets ready, but the gap between the Patriot patrol and the enemy was too narrow to allow them sufficient time to fire. As Fergus clattered onto the bridge, he heard the defenders get off one volley before making their own retreat.

He leaned forward in the saddle, urging Bran on. Moonlit water streaked by on either side. Behind him, the galloping hooves of his pursuers thundered over the bridge's timbers.

Bran gained the north shore. Fergus took cover in some scrub before turning to fire at the enemy soldiers still charging over the bridge. He got in one shot before joining the retreat.

There was no time to raise the drawbridge. The Patriots were fleeing for their lives, leaving their camp and most of their precious provisions behind.

THE NEXT DAY, THE BRITISH captured five American supply ships. Two more ran aground and were burned by their crews. Guns, rice, tobacco, flour, rum, turpentine, and the ships themselves—all lost. A day after that, Craig's men went on another rampage, destroying provisions and burning Patriot plantations.

"We can't hold on," Fergus said, after the militiamen heard the news. "How can we fight without powder or shot?"

"We never had much of either, in any part of the Patriot army," Tavish replied. "I've heard that Mr. Franklin has actually advised General Washington to arm his men with bows and arrows."

"Mr. Franklin is no soldier," said Fergus. "This isn't the Middle Ages, and we can't send archers against muskets and cannon. Without ammunition or stores, we have no chance of dislodging the British from Wilmington."

"We were never going to dislodge them," Father replied. "But we can harass them. We dinnae have much shot in our muskets, but they dinnae ken that. Nip and tuck, and ride away to fight another day. That's all we can do, and for now, 'tis enough."

A fortnight later, an express rider came with news from Virginia. The Patriots had won the race to the Dan.

Chapter Twelve

Pine needles crunched beneath Melina's feet as she made her way through the woods. Ahead, the candle tree showed stark and pale among the red-brown bark of the other longleaf pines. It was a tall, broad tree, notably old even in this forest of ancients, and housed a colony of woodpeckers. The adult birds pecked continually at the tree's trunk, opening small wounds from which a constant stream of resin flowed. The resin hardened in white, waxy-looking rivulets, forming a sticky layer that kept snakes from slithering up and robbing the woodpeckers' nests. A small hollow about four feet from the ground offered an excellent place to stow things—like the bundle of letters, carefully wrapped in oilcloth, that Melina was clutching beneath her cloak.

This was her third time to make the mail exchange since Tavish and Fergus had gone away to join the militia forces outside of the town. Every other Wednesday, she took a bundle of outbound letters to the tree and brought home the bundle that had been left there.

Everyone wrote, and most of the letters were shared, except for those that passed between Tavish and Catalyn. Melina had no excuse to keep Fergus's letters private, but he always managed to include references and jokes that had meaning only for her. He was no great penman—each of his paragraphs was a single rambling sentence, with clauses strung carelessly together by indifferent punctuation—but she loved his letters and read them over and over until she knew them by heart.

Melina stopped in her tracks. A horse was ground-tied near the candle tree, and the corner of a man's cocked hat was visible, just past the edge of the pale trunk.

Then a tall figure in a greatcoat emerged from behind the tree. Melina's heart leaped within her, and she broke into a run.

Next thing she knew, she was in Fergus's arms, and he was holding her tight, with her feet off the ground. He smelled of woodsmoke and bay rum.

"Fergus! What are you doing here?"

"Bringing the mail! What else? I'm free today, with no fatigue details, and no picket duty until tonight. So I thought, why not?"

Had he only happened to get the day free, or had he planned it that way? He knew Melina was the one who made the trip to the dead drop every other Wednesday. Had he wanted to see her?

He set her down, and she held him at arm's length. He looked healthy enough, but older, somehow. There were lines on his face that hadn't been there a few weeks ago.

But all she said was, "You're looking well. Are you getting enough to eat?"

"Aye, we've got pork on the hoof when we need it, and plenty of rice. And you?"

"We've got some old hens to stew, plus all the hens that are still laying, and plenty of cornmeal. And we'll be sowing corn and putting out sweet potato slips before long."

"Good. Come, I mustn't keep you standing. I found you a good dry seat."

He led her to a fallen oak and got her comfortably situated before seating himself beside her.

"You're wearing a sword!" Melina said.

"Aye. I spend so much time on horseback now that I needed a blade."

She imagined Fergus surrounded by the enemy, slashing with his new sword as musket balls flew past him, and then wished she hadn't.

"Now, tell me all the news from home," he said.

There wasn't much to tell, but she made the most of what there was. She'd had another letter from Papa—short and cheerful, like all his letters, and filled with the expectation of a Patriot victory and his own release. Melina had given up needlework for the present and started reading aloud to the family in the evenings. She had started with John Locke and planned to work her way through the Shaw bookcase. Rory had kept up Tavish's training of the young twin steers, and they were shaping into a fine team of oxen. He had also built Boudicca a pen in a grassy hollow near a stream, and fitted the gate with an ingenious locking mechanism of his own design, to discourage horse thieves.

"Next week will be March, so the foal should be born soon," she said. "And Catalyn's baby will—"

She clapped her hand to her mouth. "Oh! Forget you heard that. I didn't say it. You know nothing."

The lines of his face relaxed into a smile. "Catalyn is expecting another baby? How wonderful! How long has she known?"

"I don't know what you're talking about. You must have misheard me."

"Oh, come. I'd have found out soon enough, and you know you can trust *me* not to speak out of turn. When is the baby due?"

"October, she thinks. Tavish doesn't know yet, so keep quiet until he has a chance to read her letter."

A silence fell. Melina knew Fergus was wondering if the fighting would end by October and if Tavish would live to see his second child. She wondered it too, but there was no point in saying so.

"Tell me your news now," Melina said. "What have you heard about the race to the Dan? We heard that Morgan beat the British there, but that's all we know. Is Morgan still with the army?"

"Nay, he went home after joining forces with General Greene. His health is broken, but he made it. The Patriots reached the Dan River twelve hours ahead of the British. Greene is in command now. He's trying to bring in militia units from the southwest. If he succeeds, the British will be surrounded. Victory is in sight, Melina, truly."

"Oh, I can't wait to tell Papa! He'll be so pleased."

"Aye, tell him. I'm sure he'll be released soon, and I look forward to meeting him."

Something about the way Fergus said this made Melina's pulse flutter. Was it possible that he wanted to ask Papa for her hand in marriage?

"Everything feels easier now," he went on. "All this running around the countryside, harassing the British, it actually *means* something. We still can't drive Craig's men out of Wilmington, at least not yet, but we can stick in his side like a thorn and keep him from subduing the whole area. How are things in town?"

"Not as bad as they could be, but bad enough."

She'd already written to him about how the most prominent of the Patriot men had fled before the British arrived, and of the recapture of some of them—including poor Mr. Harnett, who was still being held prisoner in the bull pen, exposed to the harsh cold, and to jeers and abuse from Tories. Now she told him about the departure of the men's wives and children from the town. Major Craig hadn't let them take anything but their clothing. He wouldn't let them use carriages, and once they had a boat ready, he kept them standing for hours waiting before finally allowing them to leave.

Fergus shook his head. "A disgusting abuse of power. It makes my blood boil to think of it. And their husbands and fathers not there to defend them."

"They were right to try to get away. Mr. Hooper would have been hanged if he hadn't escaped. Besides, we women are not defenseless. We're stronger than you think."

He smiled. "I know my sisters are intelligent, capable women, and of course any man would be a fool to underestimate you. What else is Craig doing, besides persecuting women and children? Still sending raiding parties out for cattle?"

"Aye, but so far they haven't hit us. Perhaps they won't."

With the Patriot militia keeping the British from moving beyond the Northeast Cape Fear River, trade was bottled up in town, and prices had tripled. But Melina didn't tell Fergus that. She spoke of nothing that wasn't cheerful, which meant she left out quite a bit. She knew Fergus was doing the same thing.

The shadows lengthened as they talked, and the chill in the air grew. At last, Fergus stood.

"I must go. I've kept you here too long in the cold, and I've told you everything that's in my letter."

She'd told him everything in her letter too, but she would still read and reread his letter once she took it home. She got to her feet, and they exchanged packets.

A silence fell. Melina didn't know how to say goodbye to him. She'd thrown her arms around him before, or else he'd thrown his arms around her—she couldn't remember, exactly. But that had been in the first flush of surprise and delight. She couldn't embrace him again, no matter how much she wanted to.

He didn't seem to know what to say or do either. In the end, he clasped her hand briefly, then got onto Bran's back and rode away. She stood rooted to her spot, watching him until he disappeared.

MELINA SET HER QUILL down on the blotter of the writing desk and looked over the flowing script that already filled half a page. She had so much to tell—about the birth of Boudicca's pretty bay filly, and the big fish Rory had caught, and the sudden growth of the town's population as Tories flocked to Wilmington. It was rumored that the Patriots had retaken Heron's Bridge. She hoped it was true.

She propped her chin on her hand and gazed through the parlor's front window at the pine boughs tossing lightly in the breeze. It was a mild, sweet day, like a foretaste of spring. Everything felt full of promise. They had only to hold on a little longer, and the Patriots would win the war, and the British would leave Wilmington, and all would be right with the world.

She would have to go to Charlestown after Papa was released. He was tough, and in his letters he always made light of his suffering, but he'd been locked in a prison ship for the better part of a year and would need tender care. Once he had his strength back, he would surely want to visit his Shaw cousins, and see the place where Melina had spent so many months, and express his thanks in person.

What would he think of Fergus? That was the question that kept running through her mind. Fergus could hardly be more different in temperament from Papa, and marriage to him would not be considered a brilliant match by her set. But Fergus was an upright and honorable young man. Anyone could see that. Besides, when had Papa ever been able to refuse Melina anything she truly wanted? And she did want Fergus Shaw. She wanted him with all her heart. And although he had never spoken openly of his feelings for her, she did think that he—

"Writing to Fergus again?"

Melina started, and turned to see Nessa, still in gloves and hat, giving her a knowing smile.

"Just a few lines," said Melina. "A postscript, to tell him about Boudicca's foal."

Nessa laid a folded paper on the writing desk. "Perhaps you'll want to add the latest news from Charlestown. I picked this up for you in town just now."

Melina glanced at the address and opened the seal. "Mrs. Elliot! What possible reason could she have to write to me?"

"Is she not a friend?" Nessa asked.

"She was," said Melina, opening the seal. "She and her husband were Patriots, but they chose to remain in Charlestown after it fell to the British, and Mr. Elliot took the Oath of Allegiance to the Crown. Summer Patriots! I have no use for them."

She unfolded the paper and read the opening.

Dear Girl, it is with great heaviness of Heart that I write to inform you—

All the air went out of the room.

"Melina? Are you all right?"

Nessa's voice seemed to come from a great distance. Melina couldn't answer. She held the letter in her hand and stared at the words until the lines of text swam before her eyes.

Chapter Thirteen

Bran's hooves stepped over the damp forest litter as Fergus made his way to the candle tree. Rain had fallen earlier this morning, and the air was sweet with the promise of spring. Winter was losing its hold at last.

He'd finagled another afternoon's liberty in hopes that Melina would come to meet him at the dead drop again. He had told himself that he wouldn't be disappointed if she didn't. It was too much to hope for—but he hoped it anyway.

And there she was, seated on the fallen oak log, waiting for him, earlier than his most sanguine expectation. Her head was bowed, and he couldn't see her face, but he knew her instantly. His heart leaped as he halted Bran and slid out of the saddle.

But there was something dejected about the small cloaked figure with its rounded shoulders.

"Melina?"

She lifted her head to show wet cheeks and eyes shining with tears. A sob tore loose from her throat, and she flew at him.

"Fergus! You came!"

He put his arms around her. She was shaking against him, her face buried in his greatcoat.

"Dear heart, what is it? What's happened?"

Most of her reply was lost, but he caught the words *letter from Charlestown* and *Papa*.

"Oh, Melina!"

Her grief tore at him. His instinct was to act, to fight, to protect, but there was no foe within his reach. All he could do was hold her close and let her cry.

When the storm of tears began to subside, he led her back to the oak, sat her down, and sat beside her. He still had one arm around her, and her head rested on his chest.

"How did you learn of it?" he asked. "Did someone write to you?"

"A neighbor from Charlestown, Mrs. Elliot. She was very kind. She said she and Mr. Elliot would do all they could to see that Papa gets a proper burial, since I can't go there myself. It happened a month ago. All these weeks, I've been thinking about how the war would end soon, and Papa would be freed—and he was already gone."

"Was he ill for long?"

"I don't know. Mrs. Elliot couldn't tell me. He said nothing of illness in his letters. He was always cheerful, expecting to be released any day. And I was stupid enough to believe him—or perhaps it was willful ignorance on my part. How could I have been so heartless? How could I have been happy while my father was living in a stinking ship's hold, away from sunlight and fresh air, slowly dying?"

"He wanted you to believe it. I would have wanted the same in his place. He loved you, Melina, and he was proud of you. Knowing you were safe was his greatest comfort."

She sniffed. "I keep thinking about the day the redcoats came for him. Everyone knew how he'd defied General Clinton, and sent him a parcel of horse manure, and refused to take the Oath of Allegiance to the Crown. It was only a matter of time until he was taken. He'd already told me that I was to go to your family in Wilmington after it happened. He didn't resist the soldiers. He walked out with his head held high, in his best frock coat, and told me calmly that he'd see me soon. I thought he was so splendid and brave. I was proud of him, and sorry for all the girls whose fathers had taken the oath. But he was walking to his death. He'll never go back to Trailing Oaks, or pet his dogs, or sit in his favorite chair. I'll never see him again. He was all the family I had left—and now he's gone."

"Nay, you will see him again, and your mother and brother as well. You know you will. And you mustn't ever say or believe that you're alone. You still have us. We're your family now, Melina."

He dropped a kiss on the top of her golden head. He was taking a great many liberties, but she didn't seem to mind. She nestled closer to him, clung to him.

"You're right—I know you're right. And I'm thankful, truly I am. But...Oh, Fergus! I'm so tired of it all—of waiting and hoping and trying to stay strong."

"I know, dear heart," he murmured. "So am I. But we must wait a little longer. The war will be over soon."

PRIVATE WARD RAISED his glass. "To the enemies of our country. May they have cobweb breeches, a porcupine saddle, a hard-trotting horse, and an eternal journey!"

The other men let out a roar of approval and drank. Fergus smiled at the familiar toast and sipped his whisky.

Ward drained his own glass and set it on the bar. "Another!"

"Nay, we haven't time," Fergus said. "We must hurry if we're to make it back to camp before dark."

"Don't be such an old woman, Shaw. We've been living rough for two months now, and a man can only bear so much. God only knows when we'll have another chance to drink spirits before a roaring fire or even whether we'll live to see the new day. Sandy! Bring another for Shaw as well."

Sandy refilled their glasses, and Ward got to his feet and raised his again.

"To Major Love, on the occasion of his richly deserved promotion!"

A man at a corner table smiled and raised his hand in acknowledgment. The rest of the men cheered and drank, Fergus included. They'd all heard how Major Love liked to amuse himself by riding into Wilmington, shooting British sentinels, and luring dragoons into ambush.

"Your turn, Shaw," said Ward.

Fergus stood and raised his glass. "To Mr. Robert Bryant, a Patriot."

He drank. The others drank also, though they didn't know Robert Bryant from Frederick of Prussia.

Of course, Fergus hadn't known Melina's father either, but he felt as if he had. Robert Bryant hadn't been the most prudent of men, but he was warm-hearted and courageous. He hadn't deserved to die a foul death in the hold of a prison ship.

More toasts followed.

"To General Washington and the American Army!"

"To General Lillington!"

"To the backcountry colonels!"

"To Light Horse Harry!"

"Here's to us, because no one else is likely to!"

"Confusion to the British!"

Then it was Fergus's turn again. "To peace—may we love it enough to fight for it."

Everyone looked more serious after that one.

Ward muttered a curse and dabbed at his eyes, then knocked back his whisky. "Sandy! Another round!"

Fergus knew he ought to protest. General Lillington had sent a group of them to drive off some cattle in order to keep them safe from British foraging parties. But when they'd seen Sandy Rouse's tavern, they'd decided to stop and take some refreshment first.

Fergus hadn't had as much to drink as the others, but he was beginning to feel very comfortable inside. All his aches and pains, sorrows and fears, were melting away in the pleasant warmth of the whisky and the fire.

When the sun set, he again spoke of leaving.

"'Tis too late to start now," said Ward. "We'll get the cattle in the morning."

The next thing Fergus knew, he was waking up beneath a table with his head resting on his saddle. The fire had burned low, and the candles were all out. The room was quiet except for the shifting and breathing of twenty or so men, many of them using their saddles as pillows as well.

The room was too warm, and it stank of liquor and unwashed men. Fergus lurched to his feet and stumbled to the door. It was bolted, and the bolt stuck. He opened a window and stuck his head out just in time.

He emptied his stomach, then lay a moment draped across the windowsill, taking deep breaths of the clean, cool March air. When the spinning in his head had subsided, he climbed out the window and eased it shut it behind him.

Bran was standing patiently with the other horses. When he saw Fergus, he whickered softly. Fergus untied him and led him to the shelter of a scrub oak thicket. With only his horse for company, Fergus lay down in the leaf litter and went back to sleep.

HE WOKE TO GUNFIRE.

He jerked awake, not knowing where he was, a confused memory of Camden clouding his mind. Then he saw the walls of the tavern wavering in swirls of light—torchlight. Red-coated British soldiers guarded the entrance, and a racket of fighting came from within.

Bran snorted uneasily. Fergus got to his feet and gripped the horse's mane.

A man burst through the tavern door with a yell, using his saddle as a shield and slashing with his sword, fighting like a berserker. It was Major Love. He fought his way thirty yards or so before the redcoats bayoneted him.

The door hung crookedly on its hinges in its broken frame, its bolt sticking out uselessly from the splintered wood. From within the tavern, a British soldier kicked it open. Then he frog-marched a spindly young militiaman outside and took him to an officer—a short, broad, muscular man. Fergus had never laid eyes on Major Craig before, but he'd heard him described enough to know him when he saw him.

The young militiaman was quaking and moaning. Fergus knew him, but only a little. His name was Merton, and he was part of the detail that had been sent to drive the cattle. Craig questioned him, but Fergus couldn't hear what he said, or Merton's answer. At the end of it, Craig pulled a pistol from his belt and shot Merton in the head.

The shots and blows from within the tavern had ceased. Someone was screaming horribly, but a blunt thud cut off the sound.

Fergus's heart pounded, and his breath came fast and shallow. He wanted to get on Bran's back and gallop away as fast as he could, but that would be suicide. There was nothing to do but stay hidden and hope he and his horse weren't found.

A short time later, the British departed, leaving a deathly silence. Fergus waited a little longer, then crept out of his hiding place.

The scene inside the tavern was like something out of a nightmare. There were bodies *everywhere*, and the air stank of blood. He made a cursory search for survivors, knowing he would find none.

Someone was coming. Fergus crouched beneath a window and peered over the sill.

A dozen or so men rode up, dressed not in red coats but in ragged shirts and waistcoats like his own. Fergus recognized the intense, hawkish face of Lieutenant Colonel Bloodworth, the blacksmith who'd made his sword.

Fergus walked out with his hands up. All eyes turned to him at once and immediately recognized him as one of their own.

Bloodworth had dismounted and was staring down at the body of Major Love. Fergus joined him. Without looking up, Bloodworth said, "James Love was my friend."

They stood a moment in silence. Then Bloodworth went to work straightening Love's limbs, making the body as seemly as possible. Fergus helped him. Bloodworth tried to shut the eyes, but they stayed open, so he took out a handkerchief and covered the face.

"What happened here?" Bloodworth asked.

Fergus told him. Bloodworth listened without comment or any change in expression.

"We weren't even supposed to be here," Fergus said. "We were supposed to be driving off the cattle, but Ward saw the tavern and—but nay, I'm only shifting blame. We were shirking our duty, and I knew it. I should have made the others leave. Why didn't I make them leave?"

"Never mind that," said Bloodworth, "Some live and some die, and the wherefores of it are more than we can fathom. Guilt is a hole with no bottom. Don't fall into it. Just keep your wits about you and fight like a man, until these butchers are driven out of our country or death takes you. There's nothing else to be done."

Fergus helped Bloodworth and his men bury the dead. He dragged his bloodstained saddle outside to a clean stretch of grass and stood a moment staring stupidly at it. He cleaned it as best he could, but the stench of blood persisted. It was part of the leather now, part of Fergus himself, soaked into his skin, filling his lungs, rimming his fingernails.

He rode back to camp. Bloodworth was right. There was nothing else to be done.

THE PATRIOTS HAD RETAKEN Heron's Bridge and were using it as their base. They still controlled the crossings of the river, which meant the British were unable to strike at the interior of the state. But the Patriots were no nearer to driving the British out of Wilmington than they had been for the past two months. Fergus was sick to death of it all. When would the war end? Would it ever?

For days after the slaughter at the tavern, his head ached, his ears rang, and he couldn't concentrate on anything. Had it really been only four months ago that he'd walked along the shore with Melina, and they'd made their elaborate jokes about Mr. Dougald Black? It felt like something that had happened years ago, when he was a little boy.

He wanted to see her again, wanted to lay his head on her lap and have her smooth his hair away from his face and sing one of the songs she'd sung at the beach that day. But how could he be with her now, after all he'd seen and done? He wasn't the same Fergus Shaw to whom she'd given a hair ribbon before he'd gone away to Camden, or even the one who'd held her in his arms only days earlier as she'd wept for her father.

When the second Wednesday came again, he left early to take the letters to the dead drop, and came away before Melina could meet him there.

Chapter Fourteen

Melina leaned on her hoe and gazed at the neat rows of corn sprouts crossing the loamy soil. The tiny yellow-green leaves were like a promise that all winters must end, and so must all wars. She had only to endure a little longer, and courage would have its reward. The killing would stop, the British would leave, and good times would come again.

The April sun shone warm on her shoulders through her thin linen gown. Nearby, Catalyn pulled the few small weeds from around the young pepper plants. Nessa was thinning the carrots, and Morna had just filled a basket with early greens for their dinner. The four of them had been working in the garden all morning and had their skirts kilted to the knees. Melina's limbs ached, and her back was stiff, but she could keep up with the others now. She was proud of the calluses on her fingers and palms. Calluses meant work, and work meant food—and she was strong enough to do her part.

Three trays of sweet potato slips stood beneath a screen, hardening off to the Carolina sunshine so they'd be ready to plant early in May. Lachlan played in the newly turned soil of the sweet potato patch, digging with a trowel, the wind ruffling his dark curls. Dougie dozed between garden rows. Over in the square pen, Rory was leading the young twin oxen in their small yoke.

A solitary gull glided overhead. Lachlan looked up at it and cried out, "*Ee-oh! Ee-oh!*"

Letting her hoe fall to the ground, Melina swept him into her arms and spun him around. "You darling, clever little man! That's right. The gull says *ee-oh, ee-oh.*"

Lachlan squealed and giggled and waved his trowel.

"He really is a remarkably bright child," said Nessa. "How many animal sounds does he know now, Catalyn?"

"Six," said Catalyn, smiling. "Cat, dog, horse, cow, pig, and gull."

Melina set Lachlan back on the ground, careful not to catch his feet on the skirt of his frock. He plopped down on his bottom and went on digging.

"Isn't gardening wonderful?" Melina asked. "Look at all those dear little corn seedlings, poking their heads up out of the soil just as they're supposed to, only ten days after we planted the kernels. They *want* to grow. All we have to do is plant them, and water them, and cultivate the soil, and pull the weeds, and they'll do the rest."

"All we have to do?" Morna scoffed. "It still adds up to a lot of work, most of it in the heat of summer."

"I know. But isn't it marvelous to think of all the potential for their future selves being locked away inside them?"

The words sounded artificially bright in her own ears. Nessa gave her a worried look.

Six weeks had passed since Melina had learned of her father's death. She'd allowed herself three days to grieve. There wasn't time for more. There was too much work to be done, and she had to keep her spirits up. If she let herself slip into despondency, she might not be able to come back again.

But it was heavy going. She hadn't seen Fergus in over a month now. She'd gone to the candle tree as usual for the past three mail exchanges, only to find the bundle of letters left inside the cleft in the candle tree, with no Fergus waiting for her. He'd made his excuses in his letters each time, saying that he couldn't get leave to stay. It was a bitter disappointment. Melina wanted to see Fergus with her own eyes, hear his voice, touch his skin. She'd heard in town about the slaughter of Patriots at Rouse's Tavern, but no one knew all the names of those who'd been killed, and that first Wednesday when Fergus hadn't shown, she'd feared the worst. But his letter was in the bundle as usual, and he'd made no mention in it of the incident.

His letters had changed. They were shorter than they used to be, and empty of the private jokes and references that used to make Melina smile. It didn't seem possible that they'd been written by the man who'd held her in his arms as she'd wept for her father.

She shut her eyes as images of Papa flashed through her mind: riding his horse, petting his dogs, playing at dice, laughing until he was red in the face. It wasn't right for him to die alone in that stinking ship's hold, while Summer Patriots like Mr. Elliot flourished. And though she despised herself for it, now and then she found herself wishing that Papa had done as they had done, and taken the Oath of Allegiance to the Crown. He wouldn't have had a fine story of brave defiance to tell his grandchildren one day, but at least he'd have lived to see them. Now he was lying in a lonely grave somewhere in Charlestown.

Her breath caught in her throat, her mouth went dry, and her pulse quickened. The panic was coming. It came more than ever these days. She had to get away before it took hold.

She carried her hoe to the garden shed and hung it up, keeping her back to the others, then walked briskly away from the house. Her breath came in quick gasps, and her heart raced like a trapped bird's.

The panic was full-blown now, clawing inside her chest. She wrapped her arms around herself, trying desperately to hold onto reality, focusing on the physical world around her. But the ranks of longleaf pine standing straight and tall across the drive were like soldiers in formation, marching on the house. She wanted Fergus, hungered and thirsted for him—for the feel of his arms around her, and the sound of his voice low and calm in her ear, telling her that everything would be all right. But Fergus wasn't here, and everything wasn't all right.

The news on the war front, as usual, was both good and bad. General Greene had finally met Cornwallis in battle in Guilford County, two hundred miles away in the North Carolina piedmont. Technically the encounter had been a Patriot loss, but only because the Patriots had left the field in British possession. Cornwallis had paid dearly for his win, and everyone said that another such victory would ruin the British army.

Cornwallis had then brought his men to Cross Creek, no doubt hoping to resupply and regroup, but the Patriots had enough advance warning to carry off what they could of food and goods, and burn the rest. After a brief stay in Cross Creek, Cornwallis's force had headed down the Cape Fear River to join Major Craig. The militia had done its best to harass his army and delay its march south, but with only a few rounds of ammunition per man, they had no chance of stopping it. It was now late April, and Cornwallis's army was securely installed in Wilmington. The militia forces were still in the countryside, harassing the enemy as well as they could with next to no ammunition—at least, they had been. They might have all surrendered or been captured by now. Fergus could be dead, for all Melina knew.

She sank onto the hard-packed drive and buried her face in her arms. Something nudged her hand, something cold and wet, and she cried out in alarm.

But it was only Dougie, sitting on his haunches, peering anxiously at her. He was getting some grey in his muzzle and around his eyes.

He laid a rough paw on her arm and whined low in his throat. Melina put her arms around him, and felt his fur, and breathed in his familiar doggy scent. Slowly the panic subsided. When she released Dougie, he lay down beside her, panting and relaxed. She ran her hands over the white sugar sand of the drive and listened to the chorus of songbirds going about their springtime business.

She must go back to the others now, and be twice as merry and vivacious as before so they wouldn't know how weak she'd been. There was nothing else to be done. They all had their burdens to carry.

Dougie lifted his head with a jerk, then got to his feet and let out a single sharp bark. His legs were stiff, his body oddly drawn back. The hair along his back rose.

Melina followed the direction of his gaze. Through the widely spaced trunks of longleaf pines, she saw an ox-drawn wagon on the road, along with several horsemen, heading toward the house. The horsemen's coats were red.

Dougie let loose a barrage of barking, edged with a snarl.

Melina scrambled to her feet and hurried back to the garden. Dougie went with her, backing up slowly, still barking.

"What is it?" Nessa asked.

"A British raiding party is coming," said Melina.

Catalyn picked up Lachlan. He squirmed to get free, but she held him close. Then they all walked together to the drive and waited, as if the redcoated riders were expected visitors and not marauders from an enemy army. They had already done everything they could to protect themselves and their property. Boudicca and her foal were still hidden in their paddock in the woods, and some of the food was hidden also, as much as they'd dared. It wouldn't do to hide all of it. That would only make the raiders angry. Melina silently prayed that they'd would be content to take what was within easy reach and not go searching for the rest.

Rory left the oxen standing in their yoke in the square pen and hurried over. He placed himself in front of Melina and his sisters and stood with his feet firmly planted and his arms held out slightly from his sides, puffing up his chest like a half-fledged rooster trying to protect a flock of huddled hens from a fox. Dougie slunk over to Rory's side.

The soldiers turned in to the drive. Then they dispersed, with some heading to the barn and others to the carriage house. The remaining four kept coming straight ahead. When they reached Melina and the others, they halted and dismounted.

"What's your business here?" Rory asked. His voice had deepened in recent months, but it was still a boy's voice.

One of the redcoats stepped three paces ahead of the others. Melina's stomach lurched as she recognized the full face, rounded chin, and bright blue eyes of the soldier who'd met her at the checkpoint in Wilmington months earlier, when the British had first taken the town.

"What is my business?" he said in a mocking tone. "Only to appropriate that which is rightfully owed to the forces of His Majesty, King George the Third, by all his subjects, loyal or otherwise. Namely, food for the troops, and fodder for the beasts."

To the soldiers behind him, he said, "Search the cookhouse."

"Aye, Lieutenant," they replied, and headed off.

"You won't find anything worth taking," Catalyn said. "This is April—too early for the garden to start producing, and too late for much of last year's crops to remain. We've little enough for ourselves."

The lieutenant looked Catalyn over, letting his gaze linger as he had with Melina at the checkpoint. "I know what month it is, madam. Food is scarce for all right now, and supplying His Majesty's Forces is a patriotic duty which loyal citizens are happy to fulfill. As for the disloyal—well, they may not relish it, but if they're sensible, they know there's no point in resisting. Where are the men of this household?"

"They are away on business," Nessa said. "We expect them back at any moment."

The lieutenant let out a huff of laughter. "Rebel business, you mean. And I don't think you do expect them back—not alive, anyway. But I like your pluck, miss."

The soldiers who'd been sent to the cookhouse returned. Two of them carried sacks. The third, a tall, heavy-featured man, said, "There isn't much flour, Lieutenant, but we found some rice and potatoes, and the cornmeal sack is nearly full."

"Indian corn!" The lieutenant pulled a face. "I cannot understand how the colonists can bear to eat that coarse stuff. 'Tisn't fit for human consumption."

"Shall we leave it, sir?" the tall man asked. He wore a red coat, but his accent sounded North Carolinian.

"And let it nourish the enemies of the Crown? Nay, Sergeant. You know better than that."

The lieutenant drew his sword and slashed the bulging bag with the blade. The cornmeal ran out with a sad hiss. The soldier holding the bag grinned, and when the cornmeal stopped flowing, he strewed the remainder on the ground. Dougie barked at him.

The tall sergeant's heavy features grew heavier still. "There's no need to waste it, sir," he said. "'Twould have done well enough for animal fodder."

"Thank you for that information, Sergeant. I'll keep it in mind."

He had to raise his voice to be heard over Dougie's sharp, strident barks.

"Private Burchett!" the lieutenant shouted. "Silence that dog."

The man holding the empty cornmeal sack dropped it and drew his musket from its sling.

Rory made a dive at Dougie and tried to wrest him away, but Dougie wriggled free. He was a long, lanky, flexible dog, and he wore no collar.

Burchett aimed the musket.

"Please don't shoot him, sir!" said Nessa. "My brother will shut him in the woodshed."

"I can't get a grip on him," Rory said.

Melina seized the empty cornmeal sack and bunched up the fabric between the sack's opening and the cut made by the lieutenant's sword, forming a makeshift noose. Together she and Rory managed to slip this around Dougie's neck. Dougie kept barking as Rory dragged him to the woodshed, but his barks had a hoarse, choked sound now. Lachlan giggled and started to bark also.

The lieutenant gave Lachlan a contemptuous glance. "In England children are taught to speak words," he said. "But these southern colonists are a degenerate lot. The hot sun bakes their brains, making them dim-witted and lazy. In another generation they'll scarcely be human. Oh, I beg your pardon, Sergeant. I was forgetting that you're a North Carolinian yourself."

The sergeant flexed his jaw and said nothing.

"Is that your child?" the lieutenant asked Catalyn.

"Aye," she replied, cupping the back of Lachlan's head in her hand.

"Give me his clothes," said the lieutenant.

A shocked silence followed.

"His what?" Catalyn asked.

The lieutenant made a scoffing sound. "You see what I mean?" he said to his men. "Addle-pated, all of them. Can barely recognize human speech." Turning back to Catalyn, he said loudly and with exaggerated clarity, "His clothes. Take them off and give them to me."

"But why?"

"Because I told you to."

Catalyn's arms tightened around her son. "Please, sir, he's only a little lad. Don't do such a wicked thing."

The lieutenant's bright blue eyes went cold and flat. "Madam, you ought to be grateful. If I had that child's father here, I'd rip his rebel heart out of his chest."

Melina felt sick with helplessness. She hated herself for standing idly by, but there was nothing she could possibly do to fend off a party of armed men, and anything she attempted would only make things worse.

Catalyn set Lachlan on his feet. With shaking fingers she undid the fastenings of his frock.

Lachlan watched her face. "Mama?"

"'Tis all right, darling," she said, but she couldn't keep her voice steady.

Lachlan's bottom lip began to tremble.

Moving with brisk efficiency, Catalyn stripped him to his shift and rolled his shoes and stockings inside his frock. With his bare legs and feet sticking out beneath the bright linen garment, Lachlan looked small and unsure of himself. He clung to his mother's petticoat and whimpered.

Catalyn held out Lachlan's things to the lieutenant. He glanced down at the little bundle in her hand, then turned an eloquent gaze to the shift Lachlan was still wearing.

"You can't mean it, sir," Catalyn said. "You can't possibly mean to steal a baby's shift off his back."

The lieutenant put his head to the side, considering. "Very well. I'll let the boy keep his shift—if you take off that fine gown of yours."

Burchett let out a vulgar jeer. Melina's knees went weak, and she saw Catalyn's face turn sickly white.

The lieutenant lightly ran his fingertips down the worn, faded fabric of Catalyn's bodice. "Colonial fashions are so *outré*, are they not, Burchett?"

"I don't care much about ladies' wearables, Lieutenant," said Burchett. "I'm more of an enthusiast for what's underneath."

Melina hadn't seen Rory return from the woodshed. Now he streamed into her field of vision and charged, ramming his head into the lieutenant's stomach and knocking him off his feet.

Burchett grabbed Catalyn roughly by the arm. She stumbled, and Lachlan, still holding onto her, fell hard on his bottom.

Melina launched herself against Burchett, saying, "Leave her alone!"

Burchett backhanded Melina on the side of the head, sending her sprawling. "You wait your turn!" he said.

Melina landed hard on the packed sand of the drive, scraping the heels of her hands. Her ears rang, and spots swam before her eyes. By the time her vision cleared, the sergeant had pulled Rory off the lieutenant. There was blood on Rory's shirt and on the lieutenant's sword. Lachlan was screaming, and a fresh barrage of barking came from the woodshed.

The lieutenant raised his sword.

"Leave the boy alone, Lieutenant!" said the sergeant. "Let's just take the stores and go."

"You forget your place, Sergeant," the lieutenant said.

"Nay! My place is here, in America, where I've got to go on living after this war is done. I'm not about to be brought up on court martial on account of a lieutenant who hasn't got the self-control of a rutting boar. Either we leave now, or General Cornwallis receives a full report of your activities in the Carolinas, including all the parts you'd rather leave out."

They stared at each other a long moment. Then the lieutenant said, "Burchett, let the woman go."

With a grumble, Burchett pushed Catalyn away. She landed on her knees, picked up her wailing son, and held him tight. Nessa rushed over to Rory. His face was white and set, but his eyes were clear.

In the end, the soldiers took a barrel of ale, the flour, the potatoes, some eggs, and all the salt pork. They wrung the necks of all the hens but took only as many as they could fasten to their saddles.

All this time the twin oxen had been waiting patiently in their little yoke. The sergeant gestured to them now.

"That's a fine yoke of oxen," he said. "The general will be glad to have them."

"Nay, they'd slow us down," said the lieutenant. "And I'm sick of the stink of cattle."

He drew his pistol.

Melina and Morna started screaming, and went on screaming as the lieutenant walked down the length of drive to the square pen. He shot the first ox in the forehead. It went down still in its yoke, forcing the other to its knees. The remaining ox let out a bellow of surprise and fear, which was cut short by a second shot.

Burchett found the trays of sweet potato slips and emptied them, strewing them far and wide. The lieutenant came back from the square pen and rode his horse through the garden and cornfield, tearing and crushing the young plants.

Some of the other soldiers torched the outbuildings. Melina watched the flames climb up the walls as she held tight to Morna, who was weeping freely now, and clinging to her.

When the sergeant passed within a few feet of them, he muttered, "I'm sorry for this."

"What's the use of being sorry?" Melina retorted. "What's the matter with you? Why are you on their side?"

"Because 'tis the side that's going to win," he said simply. "Do you really think a ragtag army of farmers and carpenters and shopkeepers can stop the most powerful fighting force in the world? I've got a family of my own, and a farm not much different from this one. I've got to protect what's mine, miss. You should do the same."

As the raiders were riding away, Melina wanted nothing more than to sit on the ground and weep, but there was too much to be done. Dougie was yelping frantically from within the flame-licked woodshed. Leaving Morna, Melina ran to open the door, but it was already too far gone.

For a moment she stood, stiff with horror. Then Rory rushed past her with the axe and started chopping through the shed's back wall, where the flames hadn't reached yet.

Once free, Dougie ran frantically from one member of the family to the next, barking hoarsely and wagging his tail with all his might. His singed fur smelled of smoke.

The fire in the woodshed had spread to a stack of kindling inside, but there were other, more valuable buildings to save. They smothered the flames as best they could with feed sacks soaked with water from the well. It was awkward, back-breaking labor, and it took time. Again and again Melina carried heavy, sopping-wet sacks past the dead hens and the dead oxen, still lying where they'd fallen, to beat the flames with the sodden fabric. The scene was like a nightmare, but she didn't wake up. Smoke stung her eyes, and sweat ran down her sides. Her back ached, her legs shook, and the muscles in her shoulders and arms screamed in protest.

They saved the carriage house and the cookhouse, but the tar shed was a total loss. They all stood for a moment watching the roof collapse.

"'Tis a good thing you hid the last of the tar and turpentine, Rory," Catalyn said. She was holding Lachlan on her hip. His sobs had subsided to shaky breaths.

"I hadn't thought of that," said Nessa. "The fire would have been much worse if the turpentine barrels had still been here."

Rory stared at the ruin of the shed and didn't answer.

"Come to the house, brother," said Catalyn. "I'll see to your wounds."

"I'm well enough," Rory said shortly. "He didn't hit anything vital. He only cut my arms."

"The cuts still need to be washed and dressed."

"Leave me be."

Nessa grabbed him by the shoulders and made him look at her. "Rory, you couldn't stop them. None of us could. There was nothing else anyone could have done."

"It was my job to protect the place and all of you. I should have stopped them, or—"

"Or what? Died trying? What if you had? Where would we be then? We can't afford to lose you, Rory, and I thank God that we didn't. What happened today could have been far worse."

"'Tis bad enough. And what if they come back? Craig still has the town."

"He can't keep it. He's got to leave sometime. We have only to hold on, and outlast him. The war can't go on forever. The British will lose, and go home, and we'll have our country back. Now go with Catalyn and let her take care of you."

Rory followed Catalyn to the house without further protest.

Nessa looked around. "Looks like we're having stewed hen for supper."

She and Melina filled their arms with chicken carcasses and carried them to the cookhouse while Morna drew more water from the well to scald the birds. Everywhere she turned, she saw signs of destruction. The Shaw farm had been violated, just as Trailing Oaks had been.

Then Melina and Nessa went to the square pen and unfastened the yoke from the dead oxen.

They knelt a moment beside the two strong, patient, gentle creatures that would never pull a plow.

Then Nessa got to her feet. "We'll butcher them after supper," she said. "It's going to be a long night."

Exhaustion hit Melina like a load of bricks. Her limbs felt heavy, and she ached inside. She wanted to crawl into some dark hole and hide there until the war was over.

Ever since the fighting had begun, she'd been telling herself it would end soon, and the Patriots would win. All at once, she knew that she didn't believe that anymore. The war was going to keep on until it destroyed everything and everyone she loved—unless she found a way to salvage and protect what she could.

Chapter Fifteen

Wildflowers carpeted the forest floor, and shrubs bloomed bright in the understory, filling the woods with color and fragrance. Spring had come in all its fullness to North Carolina, and Fergus, riding Bran to the candle tree, breathed deep and drank in the sights.

For more than eight weeks now, he'd been in a fog, dazed and numb, going through the motions of his routine like a sleepwalker. He cooked and ate his scant meals, went on patrol, and cared for Bran. Every other Wednesday, he got up before dawn, took a bundle of letters to the candle tree, and left it there—without lingering in hopes of seeing Melina. Later, after dark, he'd go back and pick up the packet left for him. He took his turn going into Wilmington on horseback to lure British soldiers into ambush. These excursions didn't accomplish much, but they gave him something to do, and every enemy soldier eliminated was some gain. Riding back to camp at a full gallop, expecting every moment for a British musket ball to tear through his flesh, was the closest he came to feeling alive. But no matter how fast he rode, or how many kills he made, he couldn't ride backward in time to prevent the slaughter of Patriots at Rouse's Tavern.

Then, this morning, the fog had lifted. He didn't know why. He'd woken to the stirring of songbirds warming up before their first performance of the day, and knew at once that it was Wednesday, and that he wanted to see Melina, and tell her that he loved her.

Perhaps it was lunacy—nay, it was certainly lunacy—to think she could care for him, much less marry him. So he had told himself again and again. A woman like her, with a vast estate to protect, had to make an advantageous alliance. But then he'd remember a thousand tiny things that, taken all together, said that she did love him. And expecting every day to be his last had put things into perspective. He didn't fear dying, so why should he fear rejection? If Melina didn't love him, he would probably be dead tomorrow anyway, so his pain would be of short duration. And if she did, then it would be something to keep inside him while he was making those perilous runs to town, and ease his last moments on earth.

When he caught a glimpse of a feminine form through a thin screen of early morning mist, his heart caught in a spasm of pure joy. He hadn't been sure that she would be there, waiting for him, after all those weeks when he had failed to wait for her. Had she waited every time, hoping he would come? It didn't seem possible—and yet, there she was.

A leggy rosemallow bush stood nearby, covered with big blossoms of pale pink, deepening to purplish red at their throats. Fergus dismounted and ground-tied Bran. Then he pulled out his knife, cut a few of the rosemallow stalks, and added a handful of yellow larkspur to make a bouquet.

He took off his hat, steeled himself, and walked on.

But he stopped in his tracks when he got a good look at the woman. She was taller than Melina, and her hair was not gold, but russet-brown.

"Nessa?"

She turned to him. He saw her face, and his mouth went dry.

"What is it?" he asked. "What has happened?"

She closed the space between them, took his arm, and led him to the fallen oak trunk where he'd sat with Melina. He let himself be led. He seemed to have lost all his strength.

They sat. Nessa kept hold of his arm.

"A British foraging party came to the farm," she said.

His heart dropped like a stone. "When?"

"Thursday before last."

One day after the last letter exchange. "What did they do?"

"Not as much as they might have. They didn't torch the house, or get to Boudicca or her foal. But they did take all the food they could find, and trampled the garden and cornfield, and set fire to the outbuildings. The tar shed and the woodshed were lost, but we saved the rest. They wrung the necks of the hens and left them lying, all but a few that they carried off. And they shot the oxen. Just shot them dead in their little yoke." Her voice broke, and she made quick dabs at her eyes.

A quaking started inside Fergus, a deep thrumming rage. "Did they lay a hand on any of you?"

She looked down. "They started to—or one of them did, a British lieutenant. Rory tried to stop him. The lieutenant cut him with his sword. He's all right, though—Rory, I mean. And then a Loyalist sergeant made the lieutenant stop, and they went away."

Fergus sat silent, digesting the news. Nessa was right—it might have been worse. But it was bad enough. The attack had the character of a personal insult. The British army was well supplied from Charlestown. They had no real need to commandeer food from locals, and they knew it. Killing more hens than they could take, shooting the oxen rather than driving them off—these men wanted not to supply their own needs, but to punish Patriots.

Images flashed through his mind in no particular order. The wobbly newborn twin calves on the night they were born. His own small self in the cornfield years ago, dropping kernels into the sharp holes made in the soil by Father's hoe. Melina and his sisters hanging wash in the dooryard, singing over the work. Rory as a curious and talkative toddler, as a baby. The house Fergus had lived in all his life, with its comforts and quirks, its own particular history, its modest but solid prosperity—and above all, the security that had always surrounded and infused it. The redcoats had destroyed that.

"Was anyone else hurt?" he asked.

"Nay," said Nessa. "But Melina—"

Nessa's lower lip trembled. Fergus went cold all over.

Part of him had known all along, from the moment he'd seen that it was Nessa waiting for him at the candle tree, that something had happened to Melina, something terrible. Not hurt by the redcoats, Nessa said. Was she ill, then? Desperately ill? Dead? Thirteen days was plenty of time for a fever to carry her off. Why, why had he stayed away all those weeks? Had he missed his last chance to see her?

Nessa raised her head. Her eyes shone with tears. "Oh, Fergus! She's gone over to the Tories."

The words hit him like a blow to the head. They made no sense. He wanted to say that there must be some mistake, that Melina would never turn Tory. Instead, he heard himself say, "When?"

"The Sunday after the raid. We all went to church as usual, Melina to Saint James and the rest of us to the Presbyterian service. And at noon, a Negro servant brought us a message from—from Richard Severn, saying that Melina had returned to her rightful allegiance to the King and would no longer presume upon our hospitality. She would move that afternoon into the home of Mr. Severn's mother. A servant would be sent to the farm to collect her things."

"Impossible," Fergus said. "She would never do it, not voluntarily. He must have carried her off, abducted her."

"That's what I said. I went to Mrs. Severn's house right then and there, and demanded to see Melina. I said I wouldn't leave until I was satisfied that she was there of her own volition. So Melina came downstairs, and..."

Nessa took a shaky breath and let it out. "I'll say this for her—she had the good grace to look ashamed of herself. She didn't try to justify her actions or pretend that she'd truly changed her convictions. She admitted freely that the whole thing was a purely mercenary move to save Trailing Oaks. She apologized for stealing away as she had without saying goodbye—she said it was the only way she could do it at all."

It wasn't possible—and yet it had the ring of truth. The words sounded like the words Melina would use if she'd done such a thing.

"Did she...did she leave any message for Father or...or anyone?" he asked.

"Only a general message to all, thanking us for our hospitality and friendship, wishing she could have repaid them better, and hoping we wouldn't think too harshly of her."

Nothing for Fergus, then. Think harshly of her? If only he could. He knew what Trailing Oaks was to her, and how determined she was to save it. All her life, she'd strived to be all the son her father could ever want, and now that he was gone, she'd do everything in her power to protect his legacy.

Fergus loved his home, too. He wanted to protect his own family. But the best way to do that was to fight for liberty. So he'd been telling himself since the war began. So said his family, and all the other Patriots. It helped, having people on his side who believed as he did. It made the struggles and deprivations bearable. And every time a Patriot turned his coat, taking the Oath of Allegiance, abandoning his principles, selling himself for security and ease, it was like an enemy cannonball blasting through that wall of solidarity. But

Melina's defection was more than a breach in a wall—it was like something being torn from his body.

She'd broken faith—she, Melina Bryant, so brave and splendid and stalwart. She'd valued other things more than the ideals Fergus was fighting for, the ideals they had shared—and she believed the Patriots were going to lose.

"There's more," Nessa said. "I might as well tell you now, because you've got to hear it sometime or other. Oh, Fergus. Melina is engaged to marry that man—Richard Severn. The banns were published this last Sunday."

He got to his feet and walked away, turning his back to his sister. Keeping his voice as even as possible, he said, "No surprise there. Severn is rich and well connected enough, here and in South Carolina, to secure her father's property, if anyone can. But she could hardly expect him to exert himself on her behalf out of mere friendship. She made up her mind to marry him before she left the house Sunday morning."

"I believe that, as well," Nessa said miserably. "And yet I did think…forgive me for saying it, brother, but I did think she truly cared for you."

"Nay. There was never any reason to think that she…that she and I…"

His throat closed off. He shut his eyes and swallowed.

He was still holding the bouquet he'd meant to give Melina. Part of him wanted to fling it away from him, but that wasn't the sort of thing he did. He wasn't the only one who was suffering. His family had lost Melina too, and had their property stolen and debased before their eyes. He ought to be thankful—he was thankful—that they had come through the ordeal as well as they had. They were all he had left.

He went back to Nessa and handed her the bouquet and his bundle of letters. She handed a packet to him—filled, no doubt, with written accounts of everything she'd just told him. He didn't want it, but he took it.

"Take care of yourself, Fergus," Nessa said. "Give Father and Tavish our love."

"I will. Give our love to those at home."

He stowed the packet of letters in his saddlebag. His cocked hat was still tucked under his arm. He reached inside the fold and took out the silk hair ribbon that Melina had given him before he went to Camden. It was creased now and fraying at the ends. The delicate fabric snagged on his rough fingertips.

He let it fall to the forest floor. Then he swung himself into the saddle and rode back to camp. All that remained for him to do was to make the enemy pay for hurting his family, and he would do it.

Chapter Sixteen

Richard's mother owned a dog, a Pomeranian called Sweet Steenie, a beautiful but ill-tempered little creature with a delicately pointed muzzle, a luxurious coat, and a habit of snapping at anyone who came near him. He had for his personal use a small upholstered hut, framed with gilded wood and stuffed with plump velvet cushions. He looked balefully out at Melina and Richard's engagement party from behind the drawn-back silk curtains that framed his arched doorway, fur combed to shining perfection, teeth bared.

It would be easy to say that Sweet Steenie had been spoiled by luxury, but Melina didn't believe it. Ruby used to have plenty of special cushions, blankets, and toys, but she was obedient and sweet-tempered. So was Dougie, who slept on a mound of straw.

But that was a dangerous line of thought. Memories of Ruby's melting-soft eyes and sharp, intelligent face always made Melina's eyes sting with tears, as did recollections of Mr. Dougald Black, with his lanky lope and absurdly long tail.

"What is the matter, my dear? Are you unwell?"

Richard stood before her, holding two glasses of champagne. Melina forced herself to smile. "Nay, I'm perfectly well, only the room is rather warm."

"Aye, summer has come with a vengeance. I cannot alter the weather, but I can offer you this."

He held out a glass. Melina took it and drank. It was good, but she'd lost her taste for champagne. The effervescent bubbles felt frivolous, and she longed for some of the good Madeira that Patriots drank.

"Better?" Richard asked.

"Much better, thank you. How did you manage to get such excellent champagne through the blockade?"

He smiled. "I have my ways. And nothing is too good for my future bride."

He was wearing his hair in the new négligé style, a deceptively careless-looking disordered crop. His coat was made in the latest fashion, double-breasted, cut away above the waist in front, and descending in back to a long tail that reached nearly to the knees. But Melina never looked at him without thinking of Fergus Shaw's severe plainness of dress and simple braid of black hair. The négligé style would look absurd on Fergus—not that he would ever be caught dead in it to begin with.

Richard had caught her staring. "What is it, my dear? Something amiss with my appearance?"

"Not at all. I was only thinking how well you wear the new styles. You are far more fashionable than I. My polonaise was in the very latest style when I had it made, but Miss Talbot gave me to understand how very dated it is now."

"Miss Talbot? But she said your gown was charming."

"She said that to give point to how out of fashion it was."

Richard chuckled. "I cannot fathom the complexities of female communication. But you need not want for clothing. The war may have slowed trade, but there are still ways of obtaining scarce goods, for those with the knowledge and means. I would be happy to have new gowns made for you, as I have told you already."

"Indeed you have, and 'tis most generous and considerate of you, but you know very well that I mustn't allow it. 'Twould not be proper before we are married."

That last word had a bitter taste that all Richard's wealth and good looks could not allay.

The footman admitted a fresh batch of guests, setting off another round of introductions. There were a good many red coats among the newcomers. Cornwallis had left Wilmington months earlier, taking most of his troops with him, but Major Craig and his men were still quartered in the town, along with a detachment of Jaegers and the Royal North Carolina Regiment. The regiment was a provincial corps whose origins reached back to the first

Loyalist troops raised by Governor Martin early in the war. It was possible that some of them had fought against Fergus at Moore's Creek Bridge. But Melina smiled at them all and accepted their well wishes.

"I am glad to meet you, Miss Bryant. I wish you all possible happiness, now and in the future."

"How delightful to meet you at last, Miss Bryant! You must come and visit me soon."

"Your betrothed is a most enchanting creature, Mr. Severn. Please accept my most ardent congratulations and felicitations on your coming nuptials."

And on and on, until one name brought Melina up short.

"My dear," said Richard, "allow me to introduce Mr. Gordon Currie. Mr. Currie, my future bride."

Melina started, thinking she must have misheard, but when she looked into the man's face she knew instinctively that there was no mistake. She saw the cruelty in the small eyes, the set mouth, and the hand that gripped the knob of his cane.

"Miss Bryant," said Mr. Currie, bowing stiffly.

Melina returned a negligent curtsey. "Mr. Currie."

When the crowd of newcomers had dispersed, she asked in a low voice, "Richard, surely that is not *the* Mr. Currie?"

"I suppose he must be, as he is the only Mr. Currie in town."

"The same Mr. Currie who treated Tavish MacGregor so cruelly, and robbed his own wife of her property?"

"My dear, you mustn't be unjust. Remember that you have heard but one side of the tale, which is hardly likely to be impartial."

"Mr. Hooper saw Tavish's injuries and heard his story, and he was convinced."

"A traitor such as Mr. Hooper may not be the best of guides, my dear. Perhaps Mr. Currie could have behaved with greater restraint toward Mr. MacGregor, but the man was his apprentice, after all. As to the property in Cross Creek, 'tis putting a rather fine point on things to say that he stole it from his wife. As her husband, he would naturally own any property she brought into the marriage. Whether he disposed of it in a way that did not suit her, or without consulting her, I do not know. It may be that he acted inconsiderately. Beyond that I cannot accuse him."

"Is he a friend of yours?"

"I would not call him a friend. In truth I do not care for the man. He never had a very attractive personality, and his reduced circumstances have made him grasping and obnoxious in his desire to advance himself. But he has made himself useful to the Loyalist cause, and I find it best to cultivate a civil acquaintance with him."

Melina watched Mr. Currie hobble over to the refreshment table. Frail as he appeared, there was yet a core of toughness in the slight, stooped figure.

How exactly had he made himself useful to the Loyalist cause? Had he had a hand in the raid on the Shaw farm? She knew he resented the Shaws, whose intervention had led to the loss of his apprentice, his business, and his reputation. She could well believe he'd sold out early and hard. There were offices and favors to be given to eager Loyalists, and property to be confiscated from Patriots and bestowed elsewhere. Mr. Currie might even hope to wrest his business, and the remaining land in Cross Creek, back from his Patriot son. Such things had happened in Charlestown, and now they were happening here.

Not to her, though. She'd made her choice in good time, and Trailing Oaks would be saved.

But, oh, what an odious choice it was. It took every ounce of self-mastery she possessed to smile at Richard, and not recoil from the touch of his hand. His manners were as perfect as ever, and of course she was very much in his debt for all he had offered to do for her. If he had acted out of friendship, or common humanity, he would deserve genuine gratitude. But he had acted conditionally—and the condition was herself. It wasn't coercion, exactly, but neither was it strictly honorable. Fergus Shaw would never have proposed such a bargain to a woman, would never dream of such a thing. What must he think of her for accepting it—for more than accepting it, for seeking it out? Did he sympathize with her desire to save Trailing Oaks, or despise her as what she was—a Summer Patriot? And what would he say if he knew the other part of the bargain, of protection for his own home and family?

She hadn't told Nessa about that part, of course. She'd been tempted to, if only to soften the harshness of her betrayal, and show the Shaws that she wasn't being wholly selfish. But she hadn't done what she'd done to earn anyone's gratitude. She'd done it to save what could yet be saved, for herself and the Shaws, and was well aware that she'd sacrificed her honor to do so.

Richard's voice roused her from her thoughts.

"My dear, allow me to present one who is lately come from your own beloved city—Lieutenant Kerwin of the 82nd Regiment of Foot. Lieutenant Kerwin, Miss Bryant."

Melina found herself looking into a rounded, wide-eyed, youthful face—a face she knew, and had hoped never to see again.

His bright blue eyes met hers without a hint of compunction. "How do you do, Miss Bryant? Please accept my best wishes for your future happiness."

He must have forgotten her. He must have assaulted so many people on so many different occasions that he couldn't remember the faces of his victims.

"I must say, I am surprised to hear you offer them, Lieutenant Kerwin. My well-being was certainly no concern of yours when last we met."

The words were out before she knew she was going to say them. Out of the corner of her eye she saw Richard turn and stare at her.

But Lieutenant Kerwin only smiled. "Clearly, circumstances are altered now, Miss Bryant. You have altered them, and I commend you for your prudence."

Her face flushed hot, and her blood pounded in her ears. She must get away before she smashed a fist into that smooth, childlike, repulsive face.

"Excuse me, Richard. I must get some air."

She walked blindly away, stumbling against Sweet Steenie's hut, and hearing him snarl. The room suddenly seemed stifling and full of people—all of them loyal to the government that had authorized the plundering of the Shaw Farm and Trailing Oaks.

At last she reached the door and escaped to a porch. The posts were encircled by the twining woody stems of a wisteria vine. There were no blooms left this late in June, but the vine was thick with leaflets. They hung around the post and over the edge of the roof, stirring lazily in the warm evening breeze.

The porch was scarcely cooler than the house, but here at least the air moved a little, and there was no crowd of Tories stealing the air out of her lungs.

The door opened and closed behind her.

"Melina, my dear, whatever is wrong?"

Without turning, she said, "Richard, that man Kerwin led the raiding party at the Shaw farm. I've told you what was done there. 'Twas he who acted so barbarously, destroying food and crops and livestock, and stealing the clothing off an infant's back. He would have done worse, too, had one of his own company not threatened to expose him."

"I'm sorry you had to endure such an ordeal, my dear. War is an ugly thing."

"I know that. But this man Kerwin is vile. He is not the sort of person you would want as a guest in your home."

Richard paused before replying. "Melina, darling, you are but lately come to the side of justice in this conflict, whereas I have been unwavering in my loyalty to the King. I can say with confidence that I know those of my persuasion better than you do."

"On the contrary, I think you know them far less, for you see them in polite society, on their best behavior. I have seen Lieutenant Kerwin in action, and I tell you that he shot cattle and left them lying, wrung the necks of hens that he did not take, wantonly despoiled the sustenance of a peaceable family, and used his sword on a thirteen-year-old boy."

"Calling the Shaws peaceable is stretching the truth rather thin, is it not? I know as well as you do that the men of the family are with Lillington's rebels at this very moment and have shed the blood of the King's loyal subjects. If they wanted their women to be let alone by the King's army, they should not have chosen the side they did. And boys can bear arms as well as men fully grown."

She spun around and looked him in the eye. "Rory was unarmed, and defending his sister from rape."

Richard made a face as though Melina had said something impolite. "Oh, come, my dear. Surely you don't believe the lieutenant meant to go through with it. 'Twas an empty threat to intimidate you all and ensure that you'd regard the raid with a proper perspective."

"Proper perspective? Pray, which perspective is the proper one?"

"One of gratitude that it hadn't been worse. Try to see the thing rationally, not through a cloud of hysteria."

For a moment Melina couldn't speak—not because she had nothing to say, but because she had far too much. Who was he to lecture her, to tell her that war was ugly? He'd never had *his* property distressed or been in any personal danger at all. He'd never even served in the Loyalist militia. She'd seen far more of war and its effects than he. How could he be so pompous and stupid?

"You weren't there," she said at last. "You didn't see. You may have known Lieutenant Kerwin longer, but I know him better. He is not the sort of person I wish to break bread with."

Abruptly, Richard's tone, and his face, changed. "If you think you can dictate my guest list, Melina, then you forget your place. Lieutenant Kerwin will remain here as long as he wishes, and you will govern yourself and be civil to him. I will allow you a moment to collect your wits. After that, I expect you to return to the party and do your duty."

He turned and left without another word.

Melina stood shocked and mute, staring at the door Richard had shut behind him. Sounds of the party came through the walls—the clink of glassware, the music of a pianoforte, the laughter and chatter of pleasant voices. Tory voices.

She stalked over to the corner of the porch and leaned onto the porch rail, longing for a cool breeze.

To her left, the setting sun cast stark shadows of the pickets surrounding the bull pen, where Patriot prisoners were kept—but not Mr. Harnett, not anymore. He had died late in April, three months after Melina had seen him hauled into town, sick and weak and slung over the back of a horse. Farther west, a prison ship lay moored in the harbor, but Melina never looked that direction if she could help it. She felt desperately sorry for the men on board, wasting away from hunger and disease, just like Papa. Some of them had been captured at the battle of Camden. Fergus might have been among them, if he hadn't gotten away in time.

Only one figure was abroad at this hour—a boy around ten years of age, carrying a large haversack and making his way up the cross street. Idly Melina watched him from behind the thick screen of wisteria leaves. The road passed over an archway of fine masonry work. It looked like a passageway in a cathedral, but she'd been told it was only a storm drain.

The boy left the road and followed the grassy slope down to the tunnel entrance. He glanced around casually, and evidently seeing no one, passed through the archway.

No reason he shouldn't steal away to a shaded underground cavern safe from prying eyes. He might be meeting friends, or seeking solitude. But in that case, why look so furtive about it? Nay, that boy had business there, business that he wanted to keep secret. Patriot business, unless Melina missed her guess.

Well, let him. She certainly wasn't going to tell on him. The actions of one boy were hardly likely to tip the balance anyway. The Patriots were going to lose. She'd made up her mind to that.

She turned to face the door. The thought of going back inside repelled her. She would far rather sneak into the cool shade and solitude of the storm drain as the boy had done. But she had chosen her course, and now she must abide by it. She opened the door and went into the parlor.

A fireplace was centered on the long wall, flanked by mantel shelves beneath windows draped in crimson swags. Two wing chairs stood at identical angles on either side of the fireplace, opposite a camelback Chippendale sofa upholstered in silk damask. A landscape painting hung in the pediment above the fireplace, which was covered by a fire screen of floral tapestry. The millwork's white paint showed bright and crisp against ochre-colored walls.

Some opening bars of music sounded from the pianoforte, and a singer began a song, putting a moratorium on conversation, which was fine with Melina, who didn't want to talk to anyone anyway.

Then she heard the lyrics.

The song was a recent one, written in mockery of the Patriots, with particular attention to General Washington. It was mean-spirited, inane, and far too long. At the end of one verse, two lines that ought to have rhymed did not rhyme, conspicuously. The missed rhyme was an obvious one that turned the line vulgar and crass. Clearly, the song had been altered for polite society, but the knowing smiles and titters of laughter showed that its true meaning was lost on none.

The next song was even worse. It concerned the reduction of Charlestown and was as absurd as it was offensive.

Richard's mother, an empty-headed, overly frilled woman who in all the months Melina had known her had never said a word worth listening to, smiled and wagged her head from side to side in imperfect time to the beat. Richard himself was deeply absorbed in taking a pinch of snuff from an ornate snuffbox. Did he not hear? Did he not remember that his bride-to-be had suffered through the siege that the song was mocking? Or did he not care?

He had asked Melina herself to sing and play, but she'd made excuse, claiming to be too shy to perform before so grand a company. The truth was that she didn't want to. All the songs she knew, she'd sung at New Inlet during the beach holiday, when she'd walked with Fergus in the surf, and seen him gallop bareback along the strand, and made jokes with him about Mr. Dougald Black. Singing those songs here would be a desecration of the best day of her life.

She withdrew into a small alcove, leaned her head against the wall, and wondered how many more hours of this party she would have to endure. She could claim a sudden headache, but that seemed cowardly. She'd made her bed, and now she must lie in it.

The song ended at last. When the polite applause had died down, Melina heard a feminine voice saying, "I'm getting bored with these silly political songs about generals and sieges. I want to travel, and go to concerts, and see plays. Hurry up and win the war, Lieutenant Kerwin, so we can all get on with our lives."

She recognized the voice at once. It belonged to the Miss Talbot who had obliquely insulted Melina's gown.

"Aye, Kerwin," said a gruff male voice. "Hurry up and win the war. You can start by clearing out the rebel militiamen who've been infesting the Northeast Cape Fear for the past five months. What are you waiting for, man? Why don't you round them all up and dispatch them?"

"Because they're hiding in swamps, and refuse to meet us in pitched battle like men," replied the smooth, cultured voice of Lieutenant Kerwin. "Occasionally a rebel will come into town on horseback to lure out our men into an ambush, but that is the extent of their martial spirit."

Melina knew perfectly well why the Patriots were limiting themselves to the few kills they could make through such ambushes. It was because they hadn't enough gunpowder for more. How the British had failed to deduce something so obvious, she couldn't fathom.

"Why do your men let themselves be lured, Lieutenant?" asked Miss Talbot.

"Because we need horses, and the rebels have them. We're picking them off one by one and taking their mounts for ourselves."

Melina felt suddenly sick. She lived in dread of one day seeing Bran or Hector among the horses in the stable yard used by Craig's men and knowing that Fergus or Tavish had been unhorsed and possibly killed. It hadn't happened yet, but that didn't mean it never would. She had no way of knowing whether Fergus was alive or dead at this very moment.

"Have you seen the great party of freed Negroes going about in the town, the Black Pioneers, or whatever they're called?" asked another lady whose voice Melina didn't recognize. "They ran away in seventy-six and came back to Cape Fear with Cornwallis. 'Tis too droll to see them putting on airs to their former masters and mistresses."

"Aye, most diverting," said the gruff gentleman. "The Negroes have gone over to the British in great numbers. Cornwallis is quite exasperated. Once he has them, he must feed them, and there is only so much he can do with them. They're fine for work parties, but one wouldn't want to actually *arm* them. But of course, the main thing is to get them to desert their Whig masters."

A black footman stood well within earshot of this conversation. He wore livery and a white wig—Melina thought his name was Cyrus. She wondered what he thought of the words he could not help but overhear.

It felt strange to see so many slaves at work in the Severn home, and stranger still to remember that the sight had been a familiar and unquestioned one at Trailing Oaks. More and more, Melina found herself thinking how wrong it was for one group of people to do all the work while another reaped all the benefits. Slavery was incompatible with the ideals set forth in the Declaration of Independence, and sooner or later there would have to be an accounting for it.

The entire Severn house looked tawdry and overly fine in Melina's eyes. She had lost her savor for luxurious living. She kept wishing for something to do, something more useful than fancywork, and the habit of early rising had become so deeply ingrained that she was now incapable of sleeping past sunrise.

She missed the Shaws, and their home. She missed the clean, spare beauty of the parlor with its bookcase full of well-read volumes, the wing chairs in need of fresh upholstery, the work table where Morna had taught her to knit, and the front window, framed with plain homespun curtains, through which she used to see Fergus coming in from work.

But none of that could be helped. Duty always had some disagreeable aspect to it, and she was doing her duty now, paying the price for saving Trailing Oaks and the Shaws' home—and possibly their lives.

A round convex mirror with a wide gilt frame hung high on a wall, reflecting light back into the room. Melina looked up into it and saw her own distorted image, trapped in a bizarre miniature backwards world.

"THE MYSTERIOUS SHARPSHOOTER has struck again," said Richard.

It was a hot, still afternoon, some days after the engagement party. Melina wasn't sure how many. Days ran together in this house, with nothing to do and nothing to look forward to. She was sitting with Richard in the front room of his mother's house. Across the passage in the dining hall, Sweet Steenie was growling over his dish of shredded chicken.

The sharpshooter had first struck earlier in the week when some of Major Craig's men were waiting outside Nelson's liquor store for their grog ration. Suddenly a shot rang out, and one of them dropped dead. No one saw the shooter. Before the first man was carried away, a second was hit. The shot seemed to be coming from the direction of the river. The soldiers assembled, and as they marched down the wharf, a third shot was fired into their ranks, after which they broke formation and took cover.

"Was the shooter caught?" Melina asked.

"Nay. He shot another soldier in front of Nelson's today. Then a dragoon rode to the dock to search for the rifleman and was shot off his horse."

"Perhaps the soldiers would do well to stop assembling outside Nelson's liquor store."

Richard gave her a peevish glance. "'Tis no laughing matter."

"I wasn't joking. Has the shooter's hiding place been determined?"

"Nay. The command is utterly bewildered."

"Surely there can be no difficulty. The rifleman can hardly have been treading water. Either he's shooting from on board a ship, or he's concealed somewhere across the river—on Eagles Island, say."

"With all the rice and indigo fields, and the sawmill? Impossible."

"The peninsula at the forks, then. There's plenty of cover at the Point."

Richard shook his head. "The Point is a good four or five hundred yards from the Market wharf. Not even a backcountry rifleman could make such a shot, and no rifle shoots so true."

A memory drifted up of a man Fergus had once mentioned in a letter. An odd man, a sort of Renaissance man—doctor, preacher, blacksmith, wheelwright...gunsmith. A passionate Patriot, inventive and highly intelligent. Could it be...?

Richard was watching her. "What are you thinking about so intently there, my dear?"

Melina came to herself with a start. "Did I look thoughtful? I was only feeling sluggish and stupid. 'Tis this abominable heat."

Bloodworth, that was the man's name. Thomas Bloodworth.

"Aye, July in the South is a sore trial. After we are married, we will spend our summers in Rhode Island and our winters at Trailing Oaks. And speaking of our wedding...isn't it time we set a date, my dear?"

"I've told you, Richard. I can't have new gowns or linens made until some merchant ships make it through, nor can I pay for them until my estate is disentangled."

"And I have told you that I can easily procure the goods for new gowns myself. And until Trailing Oaks is restored we can live here quite comfortably with my mother, in a household amply supplied with sheets and pillowslips."

Melina gave him what she hoped was a winning smile. "I'm already living on charity, Richard. Allow me this one sop to my pride, to enter our marriage with an unencumbered dowry."

It was a flimsy excuse. A lack of dress goods and bed sheets wouldn't stop her from marrying a man she truly loved. The truth was, she didn't trust Richard to make good on his promise to show clemency to the Shaws without an incentive. He would continue to look after Trailing Oaks, because he would consider it his, but once they were married he would have nothing to motivate him to help the Shaws except honor and decency—and Melina wasn't sure how much of those qualities Richard possessed.

"The merchant ships will make it through when the war ends," he said. "And the war will end when the rebels are beaten. If you have any information that might hasten that day, you had better tell me."

She widened her eyes. "I? Oh, come, Richard. I'm no military strategist. What could I possibly know that would be worth passing along?"

"Well, I don't know, my dear. If I knew what it was, I wouldn't be asking. But I sometimes suspect that there's a great deal more inside that pretty head of yours than you let on."

Melina did her best to look as if there were nothing inside her pretty head but gowns and balls. Before the silence could grow too uncomfortable, a sudden rumble of thunder made the thin china cups on the tea table rattle against their saucers.

She was on her feet in an instant, hands shaking, heart slamming against her ribs. Outside the big front window, the light had changed color, and the trees were tossing their tops and showing the undersides of their leaves.

Richard hadn't noticed her reaction. He was on his feet as well and peering out the window. "There wasn't a breath of wind or a cloud in the sky when I drove home not half an hour ago. Now there's a bank of thunderheads massing up in the east. I must go and make sure that Malachi has put the carriage away."

He hurried outside, leaving Melina alone. A few seconds later, the storm struck in a furious lash of wind and rain. A fork of lightning cut through the sky, followed by more thunder, louder and longer than before. Sweet Steenie trotted past as fast as his short legs could carry him and made straight for his little hut.

Thinking that Sweet Steenie had the right idea, Melina headed up the stairs toward her room, but she had scarcely reached the landing when a brilliant flash of lightning blinded her. Thunder cracked almost at the same instant. Tree branches scoured the landing window, and Melina could feel the house shaking all around her.

So she went downstairs instead, all the way down to the cool, dark cellar, where she huddled against some sacks of meal and potatoes, like a woodland animal hiding in an underground den. But there was no place truly safe, no cellar deep enough. The noise and destruction of the cannonade would find her, crush her, bring the house down on top of her in a crash of burning, splintered wood.

"This is no cannonade," she whispered. "Only a thunderstorm. And it will be over soon."

But was it? Would it? She couldn't tell anymore. More than anything, she longed for Fergus to put his arms around her, and murmur comforting words, and help her remember what was real.

How long she stayed there, she couldn't tell. It felt like an age but might have been no more than ten minutes. The storm spent itself at last, leaving her drained and exhausted in her dark corner.

The cellar door opened, and footsteps came down the steps. Melina froze, praying that no one would find her like this, raw and exposed, with her tear-streaked cheeks, mussed hair, and cobweb-covered gown. She kept her eyes shut in a childish hope that no one could see her if she couldn't see them.

She heard a rustling sound, followed by a clink of bottles. Then the footsteps went back up the steps, and the cellar door closed again.

Melina let out a shaky breath. She had to get out. She was in no condition to withstand an interrogation about Patriot secrets. She must find some safe, private spot to collect herself before she saw Richard again.

The cellar windows admitted enough light to show the slanting doors that led outside. Within minutes, Melina had climbed out of the cellar and crossed the stable yard to the street. Then she went down the slope and passed under the stone archway into the storm drain.

It was dim and cool in here. The air smelled of damp stone and waste water, and the ground was wet, but not sodden. Holding her skirts above her ankles, she stepped carefully past broken bottles, china fragments, and leaf mold. The light behind her was sufficient to guide her, and as it faded, another light appeared ahead of her, from around a bend in the stone wall. The tunnel must open onto another street.

Her steps quickened. She would see where the tunnel led, marshal her wits, and make her plan.

But the glow was warmer than sunlight, especially just after a storm, and as it grew it flickered. Melina stopped, listened, and cautiously rounded the bend to see, not another stone archway leading outside, but a torch mounted to the rough stone wall beside a haversack that hung from a stout peg.

Melina waited a moment to make sure she was alone, then crept over to the haversack. It was stuffed full with sundry items, including a knife, a man's much-mended shirt, a bag of cornmeal, and a parcel of letters. She had found a dead drop—another piece of Patriot intelligence for her pretty head.

This was the sort of dilemma she hadn't planned for when she'd decided to defect to the Tories. She'd never expected to be called upon to give up Patriot secrets, because at the time she'd been convinced that the British would win, quickly and by a wide margin. But weeks had passed and turned into months, bringing no end to the war, only a continuation of this stalemate, a fragile balance that might be tipped by the smallest of advantages—like the identity of the Eagles Island sharpshooter, or the location of the Patriots' dead drop, or the truth about their pitiful shortage of ammunition. If Major Craig knew how poorly equipped the militiamen were, he could wipe them out in one swift, ruthless campaign. The interior of North Carolina would fall to the British, the rest of the South would soon follow, and the war would end.

A sound of footsteps came from the darkness ahead.

Another boy, or the same boy she'd seen before, coming to collect the delivery? Nay, this was a man's tread, firm and sure, with wide-spaced steps.

There was no time to get away, and if she ran, she'd be heard. Melina flattened herself into a cavity along the wall and waited.

A shadow approached, huge, hulking, monstrous. She held her breath.

The shape drew closer, shifted, and shrank into that of a young man, slender and tall. The torchlight threw his face into sharp relief, carving deep shadows beneath his cheekbones and in the deep cleft of his long, square chin.

"Fergus!"

She said his name before she could stop herself.

He turned sharply. "Melina!" There was no anger in his face or voice, only astonishment. "What are you doing here?"

It wasn't an easy question to answer. The thunderstorm, the cellar, and Thomas Bloodworth were all jumbled together in her mind.

"Are you hurt?" Fergus asked.

Tears came to her eyes. Even now, his first instinct was to protect.

"Not hurt," she said. "Only frightened by the storm."

The weak, pitiful words were made even weaker and more pitiful by the quaver in her voice. Worse, they called to mind another stormy day, a full year earlier, when she'd hidden like a child in the carriage house, and he'd held her and comforted her.

A painful silence fell. Then Fergus said, "Well, the storm is over now. You should go home."

There was still no anger in him, only this horrible distance.

"Are—are you well?" she asked. "And your family?"

She had no right to ask, but he answered, "Aye, all well."

Another silence.

"I won't tell the Tories about the dead drop," Melina said.

"All right," Fergus said, as if it didn't matter much, and she knew the Patriots wouldn't be using this spot again.

There was nothing more to say, and yet there was everything to say.

"I haven't given away any Patriot secrets," she went on, despising herself for the pleading tone in her voice, but unable to stem the flow of the words. "Richard has asked me, but I haven't told him, and I won't. I didn't want to leave, Fergus, but I had to. It was the only way to—"

"To save Trailing Oaks," Fergus finished. "I know."

She bowed her head. "I suppose you think I'm weak."

"I think you wanted to save your home. I think you always wanted that, more than you wanted anything else. Certainly more than you wanted me."

The words pierced her through. He had never spoken openly of the feeling between them—not until now, when it was too late to act on it.

"Was any of it real?" he asked quietly. "That day in the carriage shed, when you clung to me? The beach holiday at New Inlet? Did you ever care for me at all? Or was it only a game to you?"

"I cared," she whispered. She wanted to add that she still did, that she was fathoms deep in love with him, that she'd left not only to save her home, but to save his, and possibly his life. But he would only say that he didn't want her protection, and despise her for offering it.

His eyes glittered in their pools of shadow. "I loved you," he said softly. "I tried not to, but I couldn't help myself. And for a little while, I actually thought that you—that you and I—that there might be a future for us together, once the war is over."

Melina couldn't speak, couldn't breathe. She ached to go to him, to put her arms around him and never let him go.

But he was already turning away. "Well, I was wrong. It was never going to happen. You were always going to put your money on a winning horse, like Richard Severn. I was only ever fit to pull a plow."

He shouldered the haversack and took the torch from the sconce.

"Goodbye, Melina," he said. Then he turned and walked away.

She stood and watched him, her arms rigid at her sides, her throat choked with tears. What would he do, what would he say, if she ran after him now, and said that she'd been wrong, and asked him to take her away with him?

There was no sense in wondering. The thing was impossible. If she went back to the Patriots now, Richard would find her, and he would make the Shaws suffer. If there was a way out of this trap of her own making, she was going to have to find it for herself.

She kept her eyes on his straight, slender form until it vanished into shadow.

Chapter Seventeen

Fergus didn't tell Father or Tavish about seeing Melina in Wilmington. He informed command that the dead drop in the tunnel had been compromised, and that was the end of the matter. They all had plenty to think about without worrying over Fergus's affairs of the heart.

Most of the talk in the militia camp was of Thomas Bloodworth, the Patriot officer and blacksmith who'd made Fergus's sword and taken charge of burying the dead after the massacre at Rouse's Tavern. Bloodworth had spent a very entertaining week sniping at British soldiers from inside a hollow cypress tree on Eagles Island, using a special rifle of his own creation that could carry a two-ounce ball. It had taken the British six days to trace Bloodworth's location, during which time he'd picked off several enemy combatants at his leisure. By the time the British reached his hollow tree, he'd gotten away. His week's work wasn't a huge victory, but it was inventive and enterprising and lifted everyone's spirits.

And Patriot spirits were in need of lifting just now. A new Tory villain had lately come to Wilmington, a vicious and bloodthirsty militia captain called David Fanning. All spring and summer, Fanning had been wreaking havoc in the backcountry of South Carolina, drawing more and more Tories into his band, and stirring them up against their Patriot neighbors in acts of increasing violence. He'd come to Wilmington to seek a field officer's commission—and the British must have approved of his methods, because they'd promoted him to colonel and presented him with a new sword and a red officer's coat. He'd done mischief enough as a militia captain. Now, with official license from the British army, he would only get worse. Outrages and vengeance, reprisals and counter-reprisals were tearing the country apart.

FERGUS CROUCHED BEHIND the ridge of fresh-turned earth with his musket ready. To his right, Rockfish Creek lay low and sluggish behind its north bank, at its summer ebb. The creek formed part of the border between New Hanover and Duplin Counties, running in a winding easterly course toward the Northeast Cape Fear River. Near the Wilmington-Duplin Road, it turned north for a mile before heading east again. The road crossed the creek just east of this bend before veering northwest.

Days earlier, Major Craig had set out from Wilmington determined to subdue the countryside once and for all. No more paroles would be given—any man who refused to submit to the Crown would lose his property and his life. The few hundred Duplin and New Hanover militiamen waiting behind the ridge with Fergus were all that stood between Craig's force and the country's inhabitants.

The Patriots had gone to work in the August heat, raising an earthen breastwork from the bend in the river to a little past the bend in the road, well within range of the crossing. From here, the Patriots could coolly and methodically pick off the enemy—or would have been able to, if they'd have had enough powder and lead to do so.

It came at last, the tramp of approaching foot soldiers and horsemen. The Patriots took position, aiming at the bridge. Fergus felt neither excitement nor fear, only resignation to an unpleasant task.

The Patriots fired. And the British, no doubt expecting an ambush at the crossing, fired back. Their numbers were about the same, but as usual, the enemy were better armed and better supplied. They quickly set up some three-pound field pieces and started firing solid shot. Beside Fergus, a man went down, flung onto his back with the top of his head gone.

A few rounds each, and the Patriots' shot was spent. There was nothing left to do but retreat, abandoning the Patriots of Duplin County to Major Craig's wrath.

"WHAT A DISGRACEFUL rout," said one of the Duplin men. "And why? Not because of cowardice on our part, but because we hadn't sufficient shot. We'd have won if we'd been properly supplied. General Kenan's been writing to the governor for weeks, begging for powder and lead, but the governor sent none."

"Because he has none to send," Tavish answered shortly. "The governor is only a man. He cannae conjure gunpowder out of thin air."

The Patriots had regrouped at Island Creek, tired and dispirited, and missing over a quarter of their original force.

"Where is Father?" Fergus asked suddenly.

Tavish blanched. "Didna he ride away with ye?"

"I don't know," said Fergus. "I don't remember."

A cold, sick feeling formed in his stomach. He and Tavish stared at each other a moment in speechless horror. Then Tavish clapped Fergus on the shoulder and said with false heartiness, "We'll find him."

They made a thorough search among the regrouped survivors, asking again and again if anyone remembered seeing a lean red-haired man around fifty years of age. No one could give any account of him, whether he was living or dead, captured or free. All the while, the sick feeling in Fergus's stomach grew.

"He may yet come," Tavish said. "His horse may have been lamed on the way."

It wasn't much of a hope. Any man who hadn't gotten away quickly was either captured, wounded, or dead.

CRAIG'S MEN STAYED ten days in Duplin County, burning, looting, and killing. Local Tories joined him, swelling his ranks as the force moved on to New Bern. The Patriot militia could do little more than snipe at the enemy's rear flanks. They did manage to make some kills and take some of the Tories' artillery pieces.

At the battle on the road to Camden, Fergus had fired many rounds into a line of enemy soldiers obscured by smoke and confusion and didn't know whether he'd hit anyone. He knew now. All the battles and skirmishes he'd fought in since Craig took Wilmington were close, small, and personal. Every man he shot might be one who'd hurt his family, plundered his home, or killed his father.

He hadn't realized how much he relied on his father's presence. Archibald Shaw was no great orator, but his steady, cautious, practical optimism had cheered all who knew him. Now, Father was gone, and Fergus was only making the best of a bad job, trying to get it over with and done. But the job didn't end, and Fergus wondered sometimes, in brief glimmers of near panic, what it was doing to him, whether it was making him unfit for the home he was fighting to defend.

And still he kept on. There was nothing more to do.

The plunder and destruction continued. Stories of atrocities piled up—of burnings and lootings, of unarmed men shot dead in front of their wives and children, of a defenseless boy cut down with a broadsword. Not all the atrocities were on the enemy's side. A band of Patriots went on a killing spree, venting their rage on the guilty and the innocent alike, and inflaming the Tories to even greater retaliation. Major Craig returned to Wilmington, claiming that his expedition to subdue the countryside had been a success. But nothing had changed except that there were now many more dead on both sides, with the survivors locked in an ongoing and ever escalating civil war. Fergus began to believe that he would live rough in the woods forever, shooting other men and burying his companions when they fell.

"I'M GOING TO SALISBURY," he told Tavish, one afternoon late in August.

Tavish's face was lean and haggard, marred by bruises and cuts in various stages of healing. He didn't look like Tavish—he looked like some forty-year-old uncle of his who'd been living wild on the frontier. Fergus's own face, seen in the glass when he shaved himself, had more lines than he remembered, and a strange flatness to the eyes.

They had yet to receive any news of what had happened to Father after the battle—whether he'd been hurt, taken prisoner, or killed. The uncertainty made a dark blot in the back of Fergus's mind, where he kept all the things that he couldn't afford to let himself dwell on now.

Tavish nodded. "I knew ye'd want to go, as soon as I heard about Rutherford's new regiment."

Fergus had never served under Rutherford, but he'd seen the general in action at Camden and heard him praised by his men. After being released in a prisoner exchange earlier in the month, he'd gone to the backcountry and immediately called a muster for the fifteenth of September. With General Rutherford free, North Carolina finally had a commander capable of mounting a successful campaign against the British in Wilmington.

"He's setting up a new regiment under Colonel Smith," said Fergus. "Infantry and cavalry together, styled as a legion. You could come, too."

"Nay. I'd rather stay close to home."

Fergus didn't argue. He'd expected as much.

"Do you remember Captain Graham?" he asked. "Leithan Stratten told us about him, that day last fall when we saw him in town. He said Graham had led some mounted infantry at the defense of Charlotte Town. Everyone thought he'd been killed, but he survived. He's a major now, with a command in Colonel Smith's regiment. Perhaps I'll serve under him."

"I hope ye do, brother."

Parting from Tavish felt strange and wrong. They had served together for the entire war.

But Fergus packed his gear and loaded Bran's saddle in resolute calm. He was going to take back his state, or die trying.

Chapter Eighteen

"Come into the parlor with me, my dear. There is something I wish to say to you."

Melina's heart seemed to turn over inside her chest. Richard was smiling, but the smile was a frosty one. Whatever he was about to say couldn't be good, and she wasn't ready for it.

Three months had passed since their engagement party—three exhausting months, in which she'd done her utmost to placate Richard, keeping up the pretense that she intended to marry him, while working furiously behind his back to gain the leverage that would enable her to get away from him and protect herself and the Shaws from his vengeance. Richard held a position of trust with Major Craig and had access to the British war chest—a collection of funds, including hard currency, goods of various sorts, and real estate confiscated from Patriots, all used in the prosecution of the war. Through careful observation, and innocuous-seeming questions put to Richard's mother, his servants, and his Tory friends, Melina had come up with a list of highly suggestive coincidences, in which the confiscation of certain Patriot estates had been followed by the appearance of new luxuries in the Severn household. But it wasn't enough. It wasn't proof.

"Certainly, Richard," she said, keeping her voice calm as she removed her gloves and hat. She had just returned from a round of social calls on people whose company was abhorrent to her, but who always had useful news to pass along.

She followed Richard into the parlor and took a seat. Richard remained standing. Sweet Steenie came out of his ornate upholstered hut and sat on his haunches in front of the doorway, watching them both.

"You have lived as a guest in my mother's home for many months now," said Richard. "She has given you all the attentions proper to a future daughter-in-law. But you have yet to set a date for our wedding, despite my urgings. Whenever I ask, you remind me that your financial affairs are still entangled—and I remind you that there is no need for Trailing Oaks to be entirely sorted out before our wedding can take place. You cannot believe that I will cease working on your behalf after we are married. I almost begin to believe that you regard my mother's house as a sort of roadside lodge for your own personal convenience, and that you do not intend to marry me at all."

It was no more than she had expected. She was only surprised that he hadn't said it sooner—and yet for her purposes, it was still too soon.

But the time had come, whether she was ready or not. She must take the plunge and hope for the best.

"I'm sorry to have given you reason to doubt me, Richard," she said. "But there are affairs other than those of my Charlestown properties which require sorting. Do you remember what you said to me the day I saw you in town right after the British had taken Wilmington?"

He frowned. "That was a long time ago. I cannot recall my exact words."

"I can. You said that if I were to return my allegiance to the Crown, I would be allying myself to friends who could exert themselves on my own and my father's behalf. Friends who could not only protect my property, but secure my father's release."

"You would have done well to take me up on the offer then," Richard said gently. "If you had done so, your father would still be alive today."

This was a low blow, but Melina couldn't let herself react to it now. "You also said that I could get clemency for my Patriot friends," she continued. "It is too late for my father, but there is one who has acted as a father toward me, on whose behalf you can exert yourself if you choose to do so. Archibald Shaw was wounded at the battle of Rockfish Creek. He was taken prisoner and is being held on the *Forbay* in Wilmington Port. I learned this today while paying a call. His family has not been allowed to ransom him or to see to his comforts and upkeep."

"Ransom him?" Richard repeated. "Why should he be ransomed? He is no officer, only a common man at arms of no great fortune, and not valuable enough to be exchanged for any of our own officers."

"But as a prisoner of war—"

"He is not a prisoner of war, my dear. He is a traitor, a criminal. The customs regarding treatment for prisoners of war do not apply to him."

"All of that could as easily be said about my own father, and yet you offered to secure his release."

"Because he *was* your father, and not some fifth cousin of whose existence you were unaware two years ago. Come, my dear. You cannot honestly expect me to wear myself out on behalf of every rebel who is remotely connected to yourself."

"I expect you to honor your word, Richard."

A silence fell. Richard was no longer smiling.

"So," he said. "You propose a quid pro quo. You'll marry me if and when I secure Mr. Shaw's release. Or will you only put me off once again, and hold out for more favors for your rebel friends?"

She was in too deep to turn back. Melina steeled herself, then said, "You're the one who first proposed the quid pro quo. I'm simply reminding you of the terms. Freeing Mr. Shaw would be a demonstration of good faith on your part."

"Good faith? Have I not already shown good faith in untangling your financial affairs?"

"That's no more than self-interest. Once we are married you will consider yourself a joint owner of my Charlestown property."

"Precisely. But what is Archibald Shaw to me, or any of the Shaw family?"

"You said—"

Richard waved a hand. "I say a great many things, my dear. I say *I am your humble servant* to men who are no better than myself, and in many cases a good deal worse. These are polite nothings. Only fools take them seriously."

He picked up his snuffbox and opened it, releasing a pungent aroma of tobacco and cloves. A chill ran down Melina's spine. She had known for some time now that Richard's polished manners were a cover for self-serving pragmatism, but something in his tone filled her with dread. She had a feeling that she was about to see the real Richard Severn for the first time.

"So you lied to me," she said. "You never had any intention of helping my friends."

He froze with his pinch of snuff halfway to his face. He shot her a cold glance, then brought his fingers to his nose and lightly inhaled the powdered tobacco, one nostril at a time. Then he brushed away the excess with a handkerchief and shut the snuffbox with a sharp metallic click.

"I hardly think you're in a position to quibble over the purity of other people's intentions, Melina," he said.

"What do you mean?"

"You know precisely what I mean. You lived among a prominent Patriot family for almost a full year. You know more about the Patriots' dispositions and plans than you let on—certainly more than you have told. What about a demonstration of good faith on your own part? If you truly want this war to end, you'll do everything in your power to hasten that day. Do not let sentiment blind you, my dear. The sooner Lillington's ragtag militia is exterminated from the countryside, the sooner the King's loyal subjects can return to peace and prosperity. But whether sooner or later, the end will come. You made a prudential choice to join the winning side. Now you must follow through, for your own sake. No man, having put his hand to the plow and looking back, is fit for the kingdom of God—or for the kingdom of George the Third."

Melina rose to her feet. "There is nothing to be gained by prolonging this interview. I'm going to my room."

She started to sweep past him. Quick as a snake, he grabbed her by the upper arm. She let out a cry of fear and pain.

"Your room? You have no room. Nothing in this house belongs to you except the gowns and trinkets you managed to carry out of your rebel city after it was taken. Everything else—everything you eat and drink, the pillow you lay your head on at night, the very air you breathe—you owe to me."

She struggled to free herself, but he only tightened his grip. "Let go of me, Richard," she said. "You're hurting me."

"I hurt you because I must. I have the power of life and death over you, my dear. I have offered the carrot, but you have willfully turned your face away from it again and again. Now you must become acquainted with the stick."

He marched her into the central passage, grabbed a ring of keys from a hook beneath the staircase, and dragged her up the stairs. When they reached her room, he flung her inside. She fell to her knees, hitting the side of her head against the dressing table.

"You know what Major Craig has been doing in the countryside," he said from the doorway. "Another few weeks, and this infernal rebellion will be put down for good. Your rebel friends will be shot or hanged, if they haven't been already—or disemboweled and beheaded, like those worthless rebels in Ireland—and their property will go to more deserving persons. Think about that. I give you until tomorrow morning to set a date for our wedding. If you still refuse, then there are other ways of bringing off a marriage."

The door slammed shut, and the key turned in the lock with a vicious click.

Melina's heart was racing, and she was shaking all over. Her head pounded, and her shoulder had been badly wrenched when Richard threw her to the floor. She heard the sound of her own breathing, quick and shallow, and felt the familiar clawing panic inside her chest.

She crawled under the dressing table and covered her head with her arms, but she couldn't hide from the fear and pain. Her breathless sobs were like the panting of a trapped animal.

She tried to marshal her thoughts, to master her emotions. She thought of Fergus holding her in his arms in the carriage shed, grounding her in reality. But Fergus wasn't here, and most likely she would never see him again. Reality had fallen to pieces, time had no meaning anymore, and she was going to die.

At long last—it might have been an hour later—the panic lost its grip, leaving her drained, exhausted, and covered with a cold sweat.

The sun slanted through the window, casting a leafy shadow of an oak bough onto the rug. Melina watched its pattern slowly shift in the mild breeze while she considered her situation. Surely Richard did not intend to—well, force a marriage, like some medieval schemer out of an old legend, intent on acquiring a woman's estate or a favorable alliance by hook or by crook. The whole idea was preposterous—yet here she was, locked in her tower with her wicked captor plotting below.

She wanted nothing more than to get into bed and sleep for a week or so. Instead, she crept out of her hiding place and walked over to the window. Through the screen of oak leaves, she could just glimpse the bull pen where

Patriot prisoners were still being held. Mr. Currie was standing outside it, waving his cane and hurling abuse at those trapped inside.

With a shudder, she turned away and went to her trunk—the same trunk that had traveled with her from Charlestown to the Shaw farm and now here, to Richard's mother's house in Wilmington. She opened it, reached under the layers of winter gowns, and pulled out her oldest petticoat, which was folded into a stiff bundle. With a quick and needless glance over her shoulder to make sure she was alone, she unwrapped the cloth to reveal a packet of letters, written in a clear, spare hand.

And then she did climb into bed, taking the letters with her. She had the contents memorized, but she read them all over anyway. Every line had some private joke or tenderness, so that she was soon laughing through her tears.

She'd had no right to take Fergus's letters away with her when she defected to the Patriots, but she'd done so anyway, hiding them in her petticoat before leaving for church that Sunday morning.

She finished the last letter and laid it aside with the others. Then she picked up her prayer book from her bedside table. She opened it, bending the covers backward to expose a gap between the back cover and the endpaper, and removed a folded paper closely written in her own hand with everything she knew or guessed about Richard's freehandedness with Tory funds. She stared at the columns of words and figures, trying to make something more of them, searching for the connection that would turn them into something she could act on.

With a sigh, she laid her head back against the pillow and shut her eyes.

She woke with a start to hear a key turning in the lock. The shades were drawn, but she knew she had slept for at least an hour. She tried to hide the letters by stuffing them under the pillow, but the door was already opening.

A light from the passageway showed the small, slender form of Peggy, the housemaid—a sweet-faced girl with skin like polished ebony. Melina spread her skirt over the last of the letters as Peggy walked in, carrying a tray.

"Peggy! What are you doing?"

Peggy shut the door with her hip. "Mr. Richard said for me to bring you a cold supper, Miz Melina. Shall I bring it to you over there?"

Well, it looked as if Richard didn't intend to starve her, anyway. Melina smoothed her hair back and tried to settle her nerves.

"Nay, just set it on the dressing table, please."

"Very well, miss. I'll come back later for the tray. Oh, you dropped one of your papers."

"Never mind, Peggy," Melina said quickly. "Leave it."

But Peggy had already knelt and picked it up. She froze with it in her hand, her gaze fixed on its contents. In one sickening instant, Melina knew that Peggy understood exactly what it said and what it meant. Peggy would take the list to Richard, and all hope would be lost.

Peggy looked up at Melina, her eyes round and solemn. In a hushed voice, she said, "What you want, miss, is the book Mr. Richard keeps behind the panel in his office."

"Wh-what do you mean?" asked Melina. "What book?"

"Mr. Richard's ledger—the real ledger, not the one he shows the redcoats. The one that tells where the money and things really go."

Melina's head was swimming. "And...you've seen this ledger?"

"My man Cyrus has. He can read and do figures. His master taught him, the one he had before the Severns back when he was a boy. And Cyrus taught me. Mr. Richard works on the ledger in front of Cyrus, because he don't know Cyrus can read. There's things in there would land Mr. Richard in a heap of trouble if the redcoats found out. Cyrus can get it for you without Mr. Richard knowing."

Melina thought of the quiet black footman who waited on the Severn table, dressed in livery and a white wig, his face impassive as a mask. Apparently the man knew how to keep a secret.

"Why are you telling me this?" she asked. "Why would you help me?"

Peggy smiled. "Slaves see and hear a lot more than most white folks think. There's nothing that happens in this house that we don't find out about sooner or later. Like that bit of paper of yours with all them dates and sums scribbled on it, and that bundle of old letters hid in your trunk. We know you want to put something over on Mr. Richard, Cyrus and me, and we'd like to see that happen. Mr. Richard is a bad man, Miz Melina. He tricked you into coming to him for help. That raid on the Shaw farm, when the redcoats killed their stock and hurt that boy? That was Mr. Richard's doing. He knew it'd make you come to him for help. He really wants that Charlestown property of yours."

Melina dropped back against the pillows. *Richard* had orchestrated the raid? Somehow that had never occurred to her. She had known for many months now that he was a dishonorable and untrustworthy man, but she had never suspected he was as bad as this. And looking at Peggy's pretty young face, she felt certain that Richard's slaves had far more reason to resent him than she ever would.

She must be careful, and not allow any of her actions to blow back on Peggy and Cyrus. It was a good thing that Richard underestimated them even more than he underestimated her.

She patted the bed beside her. "Sit down, Peggy. Before we do anything else, we must make a plan."

IN THE DARK HOURS BETWEEN sunset and moonrise, while Richard was dining at the other side of the house, Melina opened the window of her second-floor room and scaled down the oak tree. Cyrus was attending Richard, and Peggy was waiting on Richard's mother, so they couldn't be suspected of helping her in the event that her disappearance was discovered.

Scaling down the big oak was no easy feat, but she had climbed every tree on Trailing Oaks at some point in her childhood, and her strength and skill did not fail her now.

Keeping to the shadows, she made her way to the home of Archibald Maclaine, an attorney and state legislator whose politics were Patriot, but whose close ties to Tories, including his son-in-law, had kept him out of the Continental Congress. Her business there did not take long. Within an hour, she had climbed back into her room. She was awake the rest of the night, packing her trunk and going over her plan again and again in her mind.

Her stomach was tied in knots all night, but when Peggy brought her breakfast tray, she suddenly found herself ravenous.

"Does Richard suspect anything?" she asked.

Peggy shook her head. "There ain't been no hue or cry over your escape down the tree last night. Mr. Richard spent the evening with some Tory gentlemen, drinking and playing cards. He don't know you were ever out of the house, and he ain't been in his office since yesterday morning, so he don't know the ledger's missing."

Satisfied, Melina attacked her breakfast. Peggy moved calmly around the room, setting things to rights.

What could Melina do to help Peggy and Cyrus? She'd been wracking her brain over that question for hours but hadn't come up with much. For the two of them to try to escape now would be suicide, unless they wanted to defect to the British, which they did not.

"I'm finished eating, Peggy," she said at last. "You can take my tray away now, and have Cyrus tell Richard that I'm ready to talk. But before you go…"

She took five gold sovereigns out of her pocket and pressed them into Peggy's hand. "Keep these on you at all times. Sew them into your shift. And when your chance comes to escape, you take them and run, you and Cyrus—to the frontier, or wherever it seems good to you to go. I wish I could do more for you both. Thank you, dear girl, and thank Cyrus for me too. You'll both have my gratitude, and my prayers, until my dying day."

Peggy's sober face broke into a sweet smile. "Thank you, Miz Melina. We'll be praying for you, too."

Melina gave her a quick hug. Then Peggy slipped the coins into her own pocket, picked up the tray, and took it out of the room. The door shut behind her, and the key turned in the lock with a sharp click.

Alone again. Melina's mouth went dry and her heart raced. Had she forgotten anything? What would Richard say when she told him what she had done? Was there something she didn't know, some important piece of missing information that would make the entire plan collapse?

But when he came into her room with that smirk on his face, the fluttery feeling in her stomach turned into cold resolve. She knew exactly what she had to do and say, and she knew she would succeed.

Richard shut the door and leaned against it, folding his arms across his chest. "Well, my dear? Are you ready to tell what you know about the Patriots' plans, and name the date that will make you my wife?"

"Nay," Melina replied. "I'm not going to marry you, Richard. I'm going to walk out of this house this morning with all my belongings and take a hired coach to the Shaw farm. And you are going to let me, and never contact me again, or cause any harm to the Shaws or myself."

His eyebrows lifted. "Oh? And why would I do such a thing?"

"Because last night, while you were drinking and gambling with your friends, I climbed out of that window and paid a visit to a person in town. I gave that person a sealed packet of information, including a certain book that you used to keep hidden behind a panel in your office."

Richard's smirk melted away, and his face lost its color.

"Aye," Melina said steadily. "I've known about your double-dealing for a long time now. You foolishly left the trick panel ajar one day, and I found your ledger and knew at once what it meant. Your redcoat friends would be very disappointed in you if they knew what you've been doing, Richard—especially Major Craig."

He crossed the floor in two strides and seized her by the shoulders. "You shameless vixen! Where did you take that ledger? Tell me at once, or I'll make you wish you'd never been born!"

"I wouldn't advise that, Richard. You see, the person I gave the packet to doesn't know what's inside. But should I fail to make contact with him by a given day of the month, every month, he has agreed to hand the packet over to Major Craig. In the event of my death, or at my order, it goes out immediately. The British and the Tories will have full evidence of how you've enriched yourself with funds meant for the war effort."

He shook her. "You false, wicked girl! You want to ruin me!"

Melina wrenched herself free from his grip. "On the contrary. I'm perfectly content for you to go on robbing your own side in this war. The more you steal from the British war chest, the better for the Patriots. There is absolutely no need for me to expose you, unless harm comes to me or the Shaws."

It was tempting to add a proviso protecting Cyrus and Peggy. But Richard had no reason to suspect either of them of helping her, and she didn't want to give him one.

She walked over to the door—Richard had neglected to lock it behind him—and opened it wide. "Please ask one of the footmen to carry my trunk and valise downstairs, Richard, and send a messenger to the livery stable. And I think you'll want to send a gift of food to the Shaws, some flour and cornmeal and cured meat, since you were the means of depriving them of their oxen and their garden produce."

Within a quarter of an hour, she was riding in a hired carriage, heading north, taking deep breaths of freedom.

She strained for a first glimpse of the house, peering eagerly between the wide-spaced pine trunks, and when she finally caught sight of the dooryard fence and the warm brown of riven siding, her throat ached, and her eyes blurred. She'd missed the Shaw farm as sorely as she'd ever missed Trailing Oaks.

But this was not a homecoming. It was only a call, a brief visit to explain herself as best she could and leave the foodstuffs from the Severn pantry. She couldn't stay here again, couldn't possibly expect the Shaws to want her after the way she'd left them to join the other side, no matter how impossible it had seemed to her at the time to do anything else. After she'd had her say, she would take the carriage back to Wilmington and find a place to stay. She had jewels enough to pay her room and board, if she could find a household willing to take her. Perhaps the Maclaines could recommend someone.

The carriage rounded the bend in the drive. Fire damage still showed on the carriage house and cookhouse, but the worst of it had been patched over with boards. The remains of the tar shed lay in a heap of ash and charred beams.

This was September, too early for fall color, but the few garden vegetables had gone yellow and brown at the edges. The Shaws had clearly replanted after the raid and salvaged what they could of the damaged plants. A thin stubble in the cornfield showed how meager a harvest had been made there, and weeds were creeping in from the edges, eager to take back the land. In the scanty sweet potato patch, she saw signs of a harvest in progress, with a few undersized red-gold tubers lying on wooden frames to dry in the open air, and others packed in bushel baskets, ready to be taken to the cellar. But no one was there—only a lanky, plume-tailed, black-and-white dog, running from the cabin to the big house and back again, barking nonstop.

Melina stepped out of the carriage. "Dougie!" she called.

The dog stopped in mid-stride, his head jerking up with the ears cocked forward. He saw Melina, gave a strangled yelp, and ran to her.

She bent down to greet him, and he planted his paws on her shoulders, knocking her down. He licked her face and hands while letting out strange frantic cries.

Someone rounded the corner from the cabin. It was Nessa, dressed in her oldest gown with her skirts kilted and smeared with dirt, as if she'd just been digging up sweet potatoes. She stopped in her tracks.

"Melina! What are you doing here?"

There was no hostility in her tone, only shock.

"I haven't come to stay," Melina began. "I only wanted to see you, and explain—"

A bloodcurdling scream cut off her words. Nessa turned an anguished face toward the cabin.

"Is that Catalyn?" Melina asked. "It can't be time for the baby yet, can it?"

"'Tis too early," said Nessa. "But her water broke, and the pains are getting worse."

"What can I do to help?"

Nessa stared at her a moment, clearly torn. Melina's sudden arrival at the farm must have raised a thousand questions in her mind, but this was not the time to ask them. So she said instead, "Well, if you truly mean that...could you take care of Lachlan? He's sleeping upstairs in the big house, but he'll be waking soon and wanting his dinner."

"I'll look after him," said Melina. "I brought food. I'll take it to the cookhouse."

"You...brought food?" Nessa repeated.

Before Melina could explain, another cry pierced the air.

"Go to your sister," she said. "We'll talk later."

Nessa headed back to the cabin without another word.

All this time, Dougie had been standing braced and stiff on his long legs, watching the conversation, knowing there was trouble but unable to understand what it was or do anything about it. Now he looked up at Melina with a question in his eyes.

"Come, Mr. Dougald Black," she said. "We have work to do."

He accompanied her back to the carriage at a businesslike trot. She told the driver to carry her baggage to the house while she took the cornmeal and other foodstuffs to the cookhouse. Then she paid the driver and went through the dooryard and into the house with Dougie at her side.

The moment she walked through the door, the silent house seemed to wrap itself around her, welcoming her back. Everything was exactly as she remembered. She climbed the stairway to the room she had once shared with Nessa and Morna and found Lachlan on the bed, just sitting up from his nap, tousle-headed and sleepy-eyed. He had grown since she'd seen him last. Would he still know her?

He blinked a few times, then smiled, held out his arms, and said, "Mina."

Melina gathered him up in a tight hug. "Oh, Lachlan, you dear little boy! How I've missed you! Did you have a good nap? Let's go downstairs and play, and later on we'll see about your dinner."

No fire had been lit or laid in the parlor fireplace, but the room was warm enough in late September. Lachlan went straight to his box of playthings and pulled them out one after another. Melina helped him stack his wooden blocks, keeping watch through the window for Nessa or Morna. They didn't come. Neither did Rory. He might be working in the turpentine orchard, getting the last of the resin from the trees before cold weather stopped the flow, or tending stock. He'd likely be home soon and wanting his dinner as well.

But none of them came. When the parlor clock struck noon, Melina took Lachlan to the dining hall and fed him cornbread cakes and cheese from the Severn larder. There was no point in making a big dinner when she didn't know who would want it or when.

When he'd finished, Melina took him outside. There was no need to open her trunk and change into an old gown. All her gowns were old now.

The network of vines in the sweet potato patch looked sparser by half than last year, but after what the redcoats had done, any yield was good. The lobed leaves had started turning a rich buttery yellow. Melina had helped to harvest sweet potatoes last year and knew what to do. First she found Lachlan a good spot at a hill that had already been dug. Right away he started playing in the loose sand and jabbering happily to himself. Then Melina took a shovel to a fresh hill. She dug around it gently, starting a few feet out and working in, careful not to slash the underground roots. Once the hill was thoroughly loosened and turned, she rooted through the soil for the tubers, wiped them as clean as possible with her hands, and laid them on the wooden frame to dry.

Every now and then, she heard a cry coming from the cabin, and she prayed.

The sun was on its way down over the horse pasture by the time she'd finished. Her hands were covered with dirt to the wrists, with crescents of sand lodged under the nails. Slowly she got to her feet and stretched her sore limbs and aching back. She felt weary and dazed, but she'd made good progress.

She wished Morna or Nessa would bring her an update. Was it her imagination, or were Catalyn's cries growing fainter? And if they were, was that good or bad?

She brushed the sand off Lachlan and herself, put away the gardening tools, and took him inside, where she washed them both as best she could. Lachlan was more interested in splashing the water in the basin than in cleaning himself, so they both ended up pretty damp. Back in the parlor, she played blocks with him until he started to yawn.

"Where Mama?" he asked.

"Mama is resting," Melina said. "I'll take you upstairs for your afternoon nap, and you'll see her in the morning."

The words sounded eerily familiar, and she suddenly felt certain that they'd been said to her, years ago when she was not much older than Lachlan. But Melina hadn't seen her mother again until she'd been laid out for burial, cold and white, with a blanket-wrapped bundle no bigger than a loaf of bread in the crook of her left arm.

Lachlan stared at her, round-eyed.

"Papa?" he said.

"Papa isn't here."

She reached for him, but he jerked away.

"Want Gwandpapa," he said.

"Grandpapa isn't here either, darling."

"Want Unky Ferg."

A deep stab of longing cut through her chest. She, too, wanted Fergus, had never stopped wanting him, and felt his lack more than ever here in the place where she had first grown to love him.

"Uncle Fergus is away," she said.

Lachlan went through the rest of the family one by one, and each time Melina had to tell him he couldn't see them. His lower lip began to tremble.

"Mama," he said again.

"Lachlan, darling, I can't take you to Mama. You must go to bed now, but you'll see Mama tomorrow."

There it was again, that glib promise. Was it true? Or had she told Lachlan a lie?

He stared at her a moment, his round blue eyes filling with tears. Then he put back his head and wept.

She picked up and carried him to a rocking chair. On and on he wailed, louder than she would have thought possible for one so small. At first she tried to comfort him, but that only seemed to irritate him further, so she let him be and rocked him in silence.

After a long time, Lachlan's cries grew quieter, and the shuddering breaths between them grew longer. The cries turned to whimpers, then sniffles. Lachlan rested against Melina, weary and spent. She felt his breath, shallow and shaky at first, then growing gradually slower and deeper until she knew he was asleep.

She could carry him upstairs now and lay him on the bed, but she kept rocking, relishing the light pressure of his slumbering little body in her lap. Memories of her own brother's birth and her mother's death, long forgotten, flooded her now. She pressed her lips to Lachlan's sweet-scented curls and shut her eyes.

The parlor was steeped in shadow when she woke to find Nessa standing over her.

"Another boy," Nessa said quietly.

She wasn't smiling. Melina whispered, "Is he...?"

"He's well enough, I think, only very thin. He weighs exactly what Lachlan did when he was born, but he's two inches longer. I never saw so thin a baby, but then Catalyn is skin and bones herself, so 'tis to be expected. He seems alert and strong, anyway. Time will tell."

"And Catalyn?"

"Exhausted. The labor itself was straightforward enough, but she hadn't any strength. She seems better now that 'tis over. She's resting now. Morna is with her."

Melina laid her head against the chair's back. A tear slid down her cheek and onto Lachlan's head.

"I'll take Lachlan upstairs," said Nessa. "Then we can talk."

She lifted Lachlan out of Melina's lap. He snuggled down against her shoulder without opening his eyes. Melina sat, drained and limp, listening to the sounds of Nessa's movements upstairs, smiling when she heard the third step give its familiar creak.

Within a few minutes, Nessa came back to the parlor and drew a chair close to the rocker.

"I'm listening," she said.

Melina told her everything, from Richard's first offer of protection for herself and the Shaws, through her decision to accept it and him, and her growing awareness that he was not trustworthy, on to his threats, and ending with her escape from his house and his control.

Nessa listened without comment or question to the end. Then she said, "It sounds to me as if your biggest mistake was trusting him."

Melina sighed. "I made so many mistakes that I can hardly tell which of them was the biggest. Certainly I was a fool not to see through Richard. But I was also wrong to cross over to the enemy at all. I should have had more faith."

"You thought you were helping us and saving your home," Nessa said simply. "You thought it was the only way. I don't know what I would have done in your place. I hope I'm never offered such a choice."

"I never gave up any Patriot secrets," Melina said. "And I never stopped wanting to come back here. But I couldn't—not until I could be sure Richard wouldn't come after me or retaliate against your family."

"I understand," said Nessa.

A silence fell. Then Melina said, "My trunk and valise are in the central passage, near the back door. When you're ready, we'll load it into the carriage, and you can drive me to town. Or if you'd rather keep Boudicca at home and safe from the Tories, I'll walk to town and then hire a carriage to come pick up my things."

"What are you talking about?" Nessa asked.

"I have to find a place to stay," said Melina.

"Don't be stupid," said Nessa. "You'll stay right here. You're one of us now. This is your home."

"But—"

Nessa held up a hand. "There's more work to be done than ever, and fewer people to do it. We need all the able-bodied workers we can get."

Melina nodded. "Thank you," she said.

It didn't seem like enough to say, but she couldn't sort out the words, and anyway her throat was thick and choked. Another, longer silence passed. Then Nessa got to her feet.

"Are you hungry?" she asked. "I need to take something to Morna. Catalyn should have some broth, but there's nothing to make it with."

"I brought a plucked stewing hen from Richard's mother's house," said Melina, "and plenty of onions, and cornmeal and flour and lots of things. I'll help you with supper."

They headed out to the cookhouse together.

"What about Rory?" Melina asked. "When will he be back?"

"Rory's gone," Nessa said shortly. "He joined the militia."

Melina was too stunned to answer. Rory, a soldier? He was barely fourteen years old.

"What about...the others?" she asked.

"Father is being held prisoner on the *Forbay*—but you said you knew that. We haven't been allowed to see him. Tavish is still with Lillington's men. He's well, or was when last we heard from him. He left us a note a fortnight ago, to let us know Rory had reached him safely."

Reached *him*, not *them*. Melina's mouth went dry.

"And Fergus?" she asked, dreading the answer but needing to know.

"Fergus has gone to Salisbury to join Smith's Legion under General Rutherford. They're putting together a large force, one capable of taking back Wilmington—at least that's what we hope."

Melina made a sound somewhere between a gasp and a sob. Nessa gave her a wondering look.

"He's all right, then," Melina said.

"Aye, as far as we know. I'm not sure how often we'll hear from him, now that he's with Smith's Legion. They'll probably be moving around quite a—Melina! What's wrong?"

Melina's breath was coming fast and shallow now, and her hands were shaking. She sank to a bench.

"When you said—I thought he must be—He's truly all right?"

"Aye, perfectly well, and so proud to be in a mounted infantry unit at last, and determined to take back Wilmington for the Patriots." Nessa sat beside her and put an arm around her shoulders. "You were worried about him?"

Melina nodded. "I know I haven't any right, after...after the way I hurt him. But I can't help it. I love him, Nessa. I love him."

Nessa didn't speak, but her silence had comfort and compassion in it, reminding Melina of another time when Nessa had comforted her in the cookhouse—her first Sunday here, after she'd met Richard Severn for the first time, and disgraced herself by walking with him, a known Tory, in the burial ground. Fergus had come to fetch her, and made his displeasure plain, and she had chided him for snubbing Richard—or as she had said, *someone so clearly your superior*. How many times had she cringed over the recollection of those words? How could she have been so blind? Fergus was Richard's superior in every way that mattered, and no property, status, or luxury was worth losing him.

She was crying hard now. Nessa let her weep, as Melina had done with Lachlan. When at last her tears were spent, Melina took out a handkerchief and dried her face.

"I'm sorry," Melina said.

"Nay, don't be. I always suspected you cared for him, but I never imagined..." Nessa gave Melina's shoulder a squeeze. "I'm glad you're back."

"So am I."

A restful silence passed, broken only by a pine warbler's chirruping trill. Then Nessa got to her feet and said briskly, "We'd better start on that chicken if we're going to have any broth for Catalyn. You said you brought onions? How about celery? We still have a few carrots. I'll start on the chicken, and you can make the cornbread."

As they worked, Nessa began to hum a Scottish air. Melina took it up, and soon they were singing together as they used to do.

Once the chicken was simmering, Nessa took Lachlan to see his mother and little brother. He looked owlish and thoughtful when she brought him to the cookhouse afterward.

"Your turn now," Nessa said to Melina. "Catalyn wants to see you."

The one-room cabin was smaller than the Severns' front parlor, but it had an air of comfort and even beauty that the Severn house couldn't touch. The golden-brown pine log walls made the space dark, but it was a warm, friendly darkness, brightened by painted furniture and pieces of blue and white delftware in the dishes dresser. Homespun curtains hung at the windows—one of which looked over the horse paddock. The table and chairs stood at that window. Melina could picture Catalyn and Tavish sitting there together, drinking their coffee.

The exquisite whitework quilt that usually covered the bed had been folded and set on a trunk. Catalyn lay propped with pillows, her dark hair in a thick braid that trailed over one shoulder, a blanket-wrapped bundle in her arms. Nessa was right—Catalyn was too thin.

Morna was pouring boiling water into a pitcher. It gave off a good, clean, herbal aroma. She smiled at Melina.

Catalyn smiled, too, and held out a hand. Melina walked over and took it in hers.

"Nessa told us," Catalyn said simply. "I'm glad you're back, Melina. Thank you for looking after Lachlan today."

"I was glad to do it. He's such a dear little boy. I've missed him. I've missed all of you."

Catalyn pulled back a bit of blanket from the bundle beside her. The new baby's face was red and squashed, and his little fists moved around as if he had no control over them.

"We're calling him Archibald, after Father," Catalyn said.

"Archibald MacGregor," said Nessa. "A fine, strong name for a fine, strong lad."

Her re-entry into the Shaw household was like putting on an old glove. She'd never expected it to be this easy. Her happiness was a gift. It made her light and buoyant, and it dared her to hope that Fergus might forgive her and love her again. There was no way to get word to him now. But if the new regiment did retake Wilmington, then Fergus would come home, and she'd have her chance.

Chapter Nineteen

"Long Swamp, Gum Swamp, Jordan Swamp, Mill Prong Swamp," said William Davis, counting off on his fingers. "Brown Swamp. Big Raft Swamp and Little Raft Swamp. Every day I hear tell of another swamp that we've got to drive the Tories out of. I begin to think the Carolina Lowcountry is nothing but swamps, one after another."

"Nay, there's much more to it than that," said Thomas Tyer, who, like Fergus, was a Brunswick County man. "Isn't there, Shaw?"

"Aye, 'tis a fine country," said Fergus. "Rich sandy soil. Good pasturage, good tillage, good ports. And great open forests of pine."

"Well, I can't say I'm impressed with the bits I've seen of it so far," Davis grumbled, plucking a sprig of bright green duckweed out of a crevice in his saddle. "Give me the backcountry any day. I'm sick of damp and rot and mildew. I haven't been thoroughly dry since we left Salisbury. Any more of this, and I'll have mushrooms growing out of my ears."

Fergus smiled as he ran a hand over Bran's freshly brushed coat, feeling for any remaining twigs or leaves from his dip in swamp water earlier that day. The Patriots had driven several hundred Tories out of Raft Swamp and taken over their encampment here at McPhaul's Mill. Now they were cleaning their gear and spreading it to dry as best it could.

The October night was too overcast for stars, but patches of pearly cloud lit the sky. Around the camp, fallen logs and rotten stumps gave off the blue-green glow of foxfire, and from somewhere deep in the woods came the ripping sound of a bear clawing open some deadwood in search of bark beetles.

Slowly and methodically, Tyer drew his whetstone down the edge of his sword blade. "You're the worst grumbler I ever met, Davis," he said. "Here we are enjoying one victory after another in Smith's Legion, and all you can do is complain about a little moisture. Don't you see? We've broken the enemy's spirit. Only a few weeks more, and we'll sweep down to Wilmington, and none of that Tory scum will dare stand in our way."

Fergus didn't venture an opinion. Camden had cured him of making optimistic predictions, even when prospects were good, as now. But even the most cautious Patriots had to admit that the tide of the war in the South had turned. For nearly three weeks, General Cornwallis and his army had been under siege at Yorktown by the American regulars and their French allies, and the consensus was that the British were losing ground. Meanwhile, in the countryside, the civil war continued its ugly course, fought on both sides by American-born men. The Patriot army that had begun gathering a month ago under General Rutherford had been steadily growing ever since, and now numbered fourteen hundred, including three hundred and fifty horsemen. Slowly and steadily, they were overcoming the remaining pockets of Tory resistance.

Tyer squinted down the edge of his blade a moment, then drew the stone over it again. He was meticulous about his sword to the point of obsession. Fergus had known him and Davis for less than a month, but you learned a lot about a man by spending nearly every hour of every day with him, sleeping out of doors, fighting a common enemy, and never having quite enough to eat. William Davis reminded Fergus of Carson, his friend from Delaware. Carson and Reynolds—had they survived the battle of Camden? Probably not, but Fergus had no way of knowing. He'd asked after them whenever he'd met a survivor from one of their regiments, but no one could say for sure. Maybe it was better not to know.

"Isn't that blade sharp enough yet, Tyer?" Davis asked.

"It got a few new nicks from Tory bones in today's engagement, and a few spots of corrosion from Tory blood," Tyer replied.

"As often as you rub that stone over it, I'm sure it ought to be the sharpest sword in the Patriot army," said Davis.

Tyer smiled faintly as he went on drawing the stone over the blade. "Perhaps so, but it will never be sharp enough for all I want it to do."

The words sent a chill down Fergus's spine. Tyer's father had been hanged by a Tory, and though Fergus didn't know the details, he did know that Tyer cherished his grudge, and in this Tyer was not unique. By this stage in the war, every man in Rutherford's army had some sore grievance or another. The nearer they drew to Wilmington, the hotter their blood ran, and the more difficult they became to control.

Fergus knew how easy it would be to give in to vengeance and take out his anger on every Tory he saw. It was something he fought against daily.

He hadn't written home at all since leaving to join Rutherford, and no letters from home had reached him. Anything could have happened in the weeks since he'd gone away, and he wouldn't know. Was his father still rotting away on a prison ship, or had he died there? Was Tavish still serving in Lillington's militia, or had he been wounded or killed? And what of his sisters and youngest brother at home? Had Tory raiders returned to the farm? Had Catalyn's baby been born?

And then there was Melina. He thought most often of her. Sometimes, without thinking, he'd feel in the fold of his cocked hat for the hair ribbon she'd given him well over a year ago, only to remember that he'd thrown it away.

The summer before last, in the weeks leading up to Camden, the thought of Melina had been a constant presence with him, though he'd had no reason, then, to suppose she could ever care for him. Now, when she was past obtaining, he wanted her more than ever. And if his love had been folly a year ago, it was wickedness now, because he was yearning after another man's wife.

THEY RETURNED THE NEXT day to the site of the battle, combing the swamp to flush any remaining Tories out of hiding. It was tedious, dirty, irksome work, wading waist-deep through black mud, getting scratched by briars and sawgrass. Yesterday's dead lay where they'd fallen, pierced by lead balls or cut down by sabers. The Patriots found no survivors, but they did find a herd of steers, which to Fergus was far more welcome.

News must have spread that the Patriots were scouring the swamps, because the Tories stayed out of them after that. The Patriots moved their camp to the Brown Marsh, which had been Tory territory only a month earlier. Little by little, the Patriots were taking back the country.

A few days later, they mobilized again, ready to move to the outskirts of Wilmington. The time for the long-awaited siege had come at last.

GENERAL RUTHERFORD divided his large army—five thousand strong by now—and sent Colonel Smith along the southwest side of the Cape Fear with a hundred dragoons and two hundred mounted infantrymen. These, he said, should be enough to keep the Tories quiet and cut off British supply routes into Wilmington. The main force, under Rutherford, would cross the Cape Fear at Waddell's Ferry and approach the city from the north, and also cut off supplies from that side. Moving parallel on either side of the river, the two forces would make their way to Wilmington.

"Our value is in the size of our force," Rutherford had told his men. "Our numbers alone are enough to intimidate the British, if we are prudent. We mustn't actually exchange fire with them, because we haven't enough rounds to sustain a pitched battle."

"I do not like this," Tyer said later. "I thought we were done with caution. That is why I answered Rutherford's muster call to begin with, so that I could finally do something of value. But this is only more of the same. This is acting as craven as the British think us. They despise us as cowards because we will not meet them in battle."

"'Tisn't cowardice. 'Tis necessity," Fergus replied. "The general is right. We haven't the powder for a sustained conflict."

"We have our swords."

"But we cannot simply descend on the city in a cavalry charge and cut down Craig's entire force! We must go on intimidating them. As long as they're afraid to engage us, they won't be able to forage. We can starve them out without loss of life."

Tyer gave him an incredulous look. "You say that like it's a good thing. What's wrong with you, Shaw? The enemy raided your home, stole your family's food, and killed your stock. Doesn't that put a fire in your belly? Don't you want to fight, and take your revenge?"

Fergus did want revenge. He knew perfectly well that the raid on the farm was what had pushed Melina over the edge and into the arms of the enemy—into the arms, to be exact, of Richard Severn.

"What I want," he said at last, "is for my country to be free. And the best way to make that happen is to act prudently."

"Well, I for one am sick of waiting," said Tyer. "Our leaders are always telling us to wait and be patient—and all the while the enemy runs roughshod over our homes, spoiling our property, and killing peaceable men like my father. He was hanged like a criminal while I was being patient with Lillington. Every day that his killer lives is a reproach to me."

"I know. But you must be—" Fergus almost said *patient*. "You must be rational," he said instead.

"Is it rational for an army the size of ours to fear a garrison the size of Craig's?"

"Having the larger force doesn't ensure victory. Camden taught me that. I know you hold the Tories in contempt, Tyer, but a British regular is an altogether different foe, and we haven't enough shot to beat them. We must maintain a menacing presence in the countryside without risking an open engagement. That's the only way we can keep the upper hand."

Tyer shook his head and said no more.

COLONEL SMITH'S FORCE met little resistance as it made its way toward Wilmington, and what resistance it found, it dispatched. Patriot forces had the town surrounded now, but some British deserters managed to slip away to the Patriot camp. According to them, Major Craig, desperate for supplies, had sent foraging parties with barges on fresh routes down the Cape Fear. Major Graham went to intercept them with ninety mounted men, mostly from backcountry counties. As one of the few local men in the detachment, Fergus acted as guide.

It was a miserable journey, cold and wet. When they reached Brunswick, Fergus sat in his saddle a moment, rain streaming over him, and gazed at the nub of beach at New Inlet where his family had had their oyster-baking holiday one year ago.

What a perfect day that had been—perfect weather, perfect company, perfect accord. And in all his memories of it, Melina was central—sharing his spyglass to look at seabirds, walking on the beach with him, telling him about her life in Charlestown, and the little dog she'd loved and pampered and been forced to leave behind. Ruby, that was the dog's name. Melina had taught her to do a complicated set of tricks centered on King Charles and the English Civil War, because that was the sort of girl Melina was.

But the holiday was over, and Melina was lost to him forever.

There was no sign of the enemy. The Patriots continued southwestward, moving away from the city now in their effort to cut off Craig's foragers. It was frustrating to come so close only to move away again. More than ever, Fergus wanted the whole wretched business over and done with. Davis found plenty of fresh material for grumbling, in the weather and the delay. Tyer didn't speak at all, but used their few moments of rest to sharpen his sword.

Their detachment traveled deep into Brunswick County, almost all the way to the South Carolina border, before turning north again to join Colonel Smith above Livingston Creek, not far from where General Rutherford was camped.

Fergus was cooking some lean stringy beef the next day when a series of pops went off in quick succession.

Everyone froze. It was small arms fire, coming from some distance away.

"What's happening?" Davis whispered. "Is it a skirmish?"

Another round of fire went off. This time Fergus counted.

"Thirteen rounds," he said. "'Tis no skirmish. 'Tis a *feu de joie*. There's a celebration going on in Rutherford's camp."

The rest of the afternoon passed in a curious blank watchfulness. No one dared to say aloud what they were all thinking—that General Rutherford wouldn't waste powder and shot to celebrate a minor victory.

In the evening, a horseman arrived, fair-haired and blue-eyed, and dressed in a Continental uniform. He looked barely older than Fergus.

"That's Colonel Lee," Fergus heard one of the captains say. "Light Horse Harry himself."

Lee had come to them from Yorktown, after a stop at Rutherford's camp, and brought news. Cornwallis had surrendered almost a month earlier, on the nineteenth of October.

The war was over. The Patriots had won.

FERGUS SAT ASTRIDE Bran, next to Davis on his sorrel gelding, with other horsemen drawn up around them, looking down from a hill on the town of Wilmington. The sun had just risen over the rooftops, casting long shadows and bathing the dockyard in pale rosy light.

The town looked smaller than when Fergus had seen it last. Shabbier, too. The redcoats had formed columns and were marching down to their transport ships. Some civilians stood huddled nearby, apparently waiting their turn to board—Tories, no doubt, anxious to get out of Wilmington now that the tables had turned and their Patriot neighbors had the upper hand.

"They're leaving," Fergus said softly. "After a ten-month occupation, they're actually getting onto their ships and sailing away. All we have to do is go home."

Davis grinned at him. "Speak for yourself. My home is in the hills, and I've still got many miles to ride before I'm there again. But I'm happy for you, Shaw."

He had barely finished speaking when the ground started shaking with a rumble of hooves. A dozen or so dragoons had broken free and were charging down the hill and toward the town.

"What's happening?" asked Davis. "Did the trumpet blow a signal? I didn't hear one."

"There wasn't any given," Fergus said. "Look at the man riding in front. Isn't that Tyer on his bay?"

Davis groaned. "Aye, and Stuart and Collier with him. Hotheads, all."

A pit of dread formed in Fergus's stomach. "Oh, Tyer," he muttered, "what are you going to do?"

A Tory stood in the road, right in the path of the charge. Tyer drew his sword and brought it down, slicing the man's head open in a single vertical blow.

Only one column of British soldiers now remained on the dock, waiting to board. Tyer and the others charged into them, hacking and hewing. A scattering of fire erupted from the broken column. The gun ports on one of the transports swung open, and the artillery pieces slid forward, their muzzles pointed in the direction of the town.

Fergus watched in speechless horror. This couldn't be happening. Not now, with Cornwallis's surrender an accomplished fact, and the enemy trying to depart in peace.

A deep boom shook the air as the ship's cannon fired. Rutherford yelled at his men to hold their position. If the British started killing townsfolk, and the enormous Patriot army got drawn in, this could escalate into a full-scale conflict, ugly and bloody.

It didn't. The remaining Patriot soldiers obeyed the general's command, and the renegade dragoons had already ridden away, leaving the British ships with nowhere to direct their fire. The dead Tory was carried off, and the British regulars reformed their column and boarded the transports, followed by the departing Loyalists. By the time Rutherford marched his men into town, the ships were well on their way down the river.

No more gunfire had been exchanged, but there was brawling enough going on among the townsfolk. Clearly, not all the Tories had chosen to leave with the British, and some of the Patriots were exploiting the transition of power to settle old scores or pursue personal gain. Fergus had seen the same thing happen on both sides more times than he could count. How long would it take for his country to heal? Would it ever?

The blood of Tyer's victim was already soaking into the dry dust of the road. Bran rode past it without spooking. He used to shy away from the scent of blood, but he'd long since grown indifferent to it.

Fergus and Davis were heading east on Market Street when they saw one man beating another with a riding crop. The man who was being beaten had his hands bound behind him. His coat had been cut and dirtied by the crop, but had clearly been a fine one. He knelt in the dust, cowering beneath his captor's blows.

"You there!" Fergus called out. "What are you doing to that man?"

The man with the riding crop didn't even glance up. "Taking him to the bull pen," he said, still striking the other man across the shoulders and head.

"Looks more as if you're trying to beat him to death," said Davis.

"He resisted arrest."

That may have been true, but the prisoner was clearly in no condition to run now. Fergus drew his sword and rode Bran closer. The man with the riding crop backed away. He took in the sight of Fergus, mounted and armed, and lowered the crop.

"What's your name?" Fergus asked him.

"Jasper Wilcox," the man said sullenly. "I've got to take this fellow to the bull pen. That's where Major Craig put all the Patriot leaders when he took over the town. Mr. Harnett, Mr. Ashe—he tossed 'em in and left 'em to rot. Now the Patriots have all been set free, and we're filling the bull pen with Tories instead. Turnabout is fair play, ain't it, Mr. Severn?"

Fergus went cold all over. Was that really Richard Severn cringing on the ground with his hands tied behind his back? The man who had taken Melina away from him?

"Well, Mr. Severn," he said, "what have you got to say for yourself?"

The man spat blood, then lifted his head just enough for Fergus to see his face. His features were bruised and swollen beyond recognition, and he was rather less well turned out than the gentleman who'd walked in the churchyard with Melina her first Sunday in Wilmington. But when he spoke, Fergus knew his voice at once.

"Please," he said. "Please help me. Don't let that man take me away. He'll kill me."

"'Tis no more than he deserves," said Wilcox. "This man used to dine with Craig, and falsely accuse respectable Whig men of all sorts of plots and things. And when those men got thrown into the bull pen or the *Forbay*, and their lands and goods got seized, Craig gave him a share of the take. I know it firsthand, because he did it to my family. I found my mother's silver tea service in his house just now, and a painting that used to hang in my father's study."

"I tell you, I had no hand in seizing any man's goods," Severn babbled. "Those things were given to me by Major Craig."

Wilcox raised the riding crop again.

"Leave him alone," Fergus said to Wilcox. "I'm taking charge of him now. If he's done wrong, he will pay."

Wilcox's gaze strayed to Fergus's sword, and the brace of pistols in his belt. In the absence of uniforms, it was impossible to tell an officer from a common cavalry soldier or mounted infantryman, and this war had made majors and colonels of many a young man.

Wilcox took the end of the long rope that had been tied around Severn's waist, silently handed it to Fergus, and melted away.

"Where is this bull pen Wilcox was speaking of?" asked Davis. "Do you know, Shaw?"

"I never saw it, but I've heard of it. The Tories built it down the street from the Church of England—or what was the Church of England. I suppose they'll have to call it something else now."

At the sound of the name *Shaw*, Severn looked Fergus full in the face for the first time.

"Fergus Shaw," he said in a whisper.

"Richard Severn," Fergus answered. "We meet again. What are you doing still in town? Why didn't you leave on the transports with the others of your stripe?"

"I had property to protect," Severn replied.

"Ill-gotten property, from the sound of it. Is your property worth your life? Or did you think your wealth would protect you?"

Severn didn't answer. He wiped his nose against his shoulder, leaving a smear of blood on his dirty coat.

"Come along, then," Fergus said. "On your feet."

"Where are you taking me?" Severn asked.

"To the bull pen."

Severn bowed his head and hunched his shoulders as if he were being beaten again. "Nay! Don't throw me in there. The rebels will kill me! Let me go home. I've got money—good hard currency, not those worthless Continental notes. I'll pay you to act as my bodyguard and defend my home. Please! Most of my slaves have run away. I have no one."

"No one? What about Mrs. Severn? Where is she?"

"At home, locked in her chamber upstairs."

"You didn't get her away from here? What is wrong with you?"

"She didn't want to go! Besides, she'll be all right. The rebels won't hurt her."

Fergus stared at him in horror. Idiotic man! He had let his greed blind him to the danger, putting Melina in harm's way.

He handed the rope to Davis and said, "Take him to the bull pen. It should be just up this road past Second Street."

"And where are you going?" asked Davis.

"To guard this man's house. From what Wilcox said, it sounds as if it's being plundered."

"Take me with you, Shaw," Severn pleaded. "I won't give any trouble. I'll stay quietly in the house. I'll do whatever you want, if you'll keep me out of the bull pen."

"Stop blathering," said Fergus. "Show some self-respect."

Davis was already leading Severn away. Severn stumbled after him, screaming over his shoulder at Fergus. "I kept my end of the bargain, Shaw! I made sure the raiders didn't go back to your family's farm! I protected you, just as I said I would!"

"Davis, wait!" Fergus called.

Davis halted, and Fergus edged Bran up to Severn.

"What do you mean, you kept your end of the bargain?" he asked.

"The bargain I made with Melina, to protect your family. I kept it. I did what I said I would do."

All at once, Fergus understood. The blood rushed to his face, hot with fury.

"You coerced Melina into accepting your hand by offering to keep the raiders away from my family?"

A look of horror rose in Severn's face. "Sh-she didn't tell you?" he asked.

Of course she didn't tell him. Fergus could see it all now. Having weighed her options and chosen her course, Melina would keep the terms of the bargain to herself, and not ask for anyone's pity or gratitude for the sacrifice she'd made.

And it had been a sacrifice. She'd never loved Richard Severn. That much had been plain all along. She loved him, Fergus—but not as much as she loved her home. She'd given him up to save Trailing Oaks.

Or so he'd thought. But he'd had it all wrong. She'd joined herself to this—this despicable man, this insect—not merely to save Trailing Oaks, but to save *him*. Who knew what she had suffered for the past months, with this man as her husband? And she'd done it, at least in part, for his sake, and his family's.

Davis let out a low whistle. "Ah. So this is the scoundrel who took your girl from you, Shaw?"

He brought his sorrel close alongside Bran so that he and Fergus were nearly face to face. Quietly he said, "What do you want me to do? Leave him with you? Say the word, and he's yours."

Fergus was silent. Even in an orderly transfer of power, there were bound to be some loose ends. It would be the easiest thing in the world for Richard Severn to meet a quick, brutal death, at Fergus's hand or by some other means. Fergus had killed many men by now, and Severn deserved to die as much as any of them, and probably more than most. Fergus could make a widow of Melina, and no one would ever need to know how it had happened.

"Take him to the bull pen, Davis," he said at last. "And make sure that he and the other prisoners come to no harm. I'm going to his house now."

"Are you sure?" Davis asked.

"I'm sure."

He'd never visited the Severn house, but he knew which one it was. When he reached it, he found the front door standing open. Some furniture had already been hauled outside, and a man was backing his way through the doorway carrying one end of what looked like a Chesterfield sofa. An elderly black manservant, dressed in livery, watched in dismay from the porch. Behind him, a fluffy little dog ran back and forth, frantically yipping.

Fergus put a stop to the plundering of the house and sent the looters on their way. When they'd gone, he asked the slave, "Has any harm been done to the house or its inhabitants?"

"Some of the silver was taken off, and some paintings and china," the servant said. "And one of the Tories took Mr. Richard away."

"What of Mrs. Severn? Where is she?"

"Upstairs, sir, locked in her chamber."

"Safe?"

"Aye, sir. None of the looters made it past the first floor."

Fergus helped the man move the furniture back inside the house, then glanced up the staircase. Did he dare to go up to her, and tell her that he knew the truth now, that he understood? He wanted to see her sweet face again, and hold her in his arms, and tell her that he loved her, that he'd never stopped loving her, and never would.

He turned his back to the stairway. Nay, he did not dare. If he saw her now, he would lose all self-mastery. She'd made her bargain—an ill-fated one, but her own. He must honor it, and her. All he could do for her now was to guard the house and keep her from harm.

THE SUN WAS WELL ON its way down before reasonable order had been restored. A dragoon relieved Fergus at his self-appointed post at the Severn home, allowing Fergus to stand in line outside the Burgwin house with the others to receive his share of whatever payment Rutherford saw fit to give to his men. This turned out to be salt, of which the British had left behind a great store. The Patriots' supply wagons were being loaded with it for transport back to Salisbury, a bushel for every man. Since Fergus was already so near home, he took his share right away.

He was just hefting the sack to his shoulder when a familiar voice called his name. He turned to see Tavish, thinner and more ragged than when Fergus had seen him last, but smiling.

"It *is* you!" Tavish said, clasping him by the hand. "Well met, brother! I've been searching for you for hours. No one seemed to know where you were."

"I was guarding the house of...one of the Tories. Some of our men, and the townsfolk, have been overzealous in the flush of victory."

Tavish nodded grimly. "Aye, I've seen plenty of that myself. 'Twill take a long time, I fear, before this land recovers from civil war. But I have good news for you. The prisoners who were being held on the *Forbay* have all been released. I took your father home this very morning."

Fergus let out a sigh. "God be praised. Is he well?"

"Well enough. Thin and pale, but tough as a tree root. He wants only rest, fresh air, and good food."

"As to provisions, I have a contribution to make," said Fergus, patting the heavy linen bag over his shoulder.

"What is that?"

"Salt. I've just been paid off."

Tavish's eyes lit up. "A bushel of salt! That is a boon indeed."

"Aye, and the best payment I've ever received in exchange for military service."

"Your enlistment is up, then? You're free to go home?"

"I am. The city is taken, and Smith's Legion is dissolved. The recovery of Wilmington was our regiment's sole mission from the beginning. Did you see the rest of the family? Are they well?"

"Perfectly well—including some new additions. I have another son, Fergus. We've named him Archibald, but I'm calling him Archer, in honor of Mr. Franklin, who wanted to arm the troops with bows and arrows."

Fergus laughed and shook his brother-in-law's hand again. "Congratulations, Tavish!"

"Thank you. Your sister is not as strong as I could wish, but with the two of us, and Rory, returning to the farm, she'll not have to work so hard."

"Rory? Where has he been?"

"In the militia with me. He joined not long after you left to join Rutherford."

"Rory, in the militia? But he's only fourteen years old."

"And you were only seventeen when you first joined in the early days of the war."

"There's a big difference between seventeen and fourteen."

Tavish shrugged. "Needs must when the devil drives. Besides, he wanted to fight. That raid on the farm this past summer, with him helpless to defend the women or the animals...it changed him."

"I suppose it would," Fergus said heavily. "I suppose we're all of us changed, for better or worse."

"Aye, undoubtedly. And speaking of change, there is one other alteration on the farm that you ought to—"

"Forgive me, brother, but I must go. There are some matters I must attend to before I head home. Will you take charge of my bounty for me? 'Twould save me the trouble of rebalancing my saddlebags."

"Gladly," said Tavish, taking the bag of salt. "They'll be happy to see it at home, and yourself as well. But I really must tell you—"

"Nay, there's no time. As long as everyone is alive and well, and my younger sisters have not eloped, nor Rory run off to sea, I'll be content, and take the changes as I find them."

Fergus was already walking away before Tavish could reply.

"I'll see you at home, then," Tavish called, and Fergus raised an arm behind him in farewell.

Fergus walked to the horse-yard outside the Burgwin stables where he'd left Bran. The horse whuffled softly at his approach.

Combing his fingers through Bran's coarse mane, Fergus murmured, "Well, my lad, 'tis done. After ten months of British control, Wilmington is free—and so are we. What do you think of that? You're a hardened war veteran now. How will you like sleeping in a box stall again, and pulling a plow? Will you be glad to go home? Will you remember the meadow where you used to play as a foal?"

He fetched his tack, saddled Bran, and loaded his gear, then led Bran out of the yard and climbed into the saddle.

He sat a moment at the corner of Market and Third, facing northward, toward home—a place he hadn't seen in close to a year. He ought to feel glad to be going there, but all he felt was dread.

His baby brother, a soldier. His unshakable father, an invalid. All the spots where he used to go with Melina, empty of her now. Home wasn't the same, and neither was he.

His thoughts turned again to Richard Severn. It wasn't too late. Fergus could go to the bull pen and take him out. He could tell Severn he'd reconsidered his offer to hire Fergus as his bodyguard. It wouldn't be difficult to get him alone, and then—

Fergus shook his head hard. What was the matter with him? What had happened to him? Had his time as a soldier changed him past all remedy?

He had to get away. He couldn't let himself become like so many others who had used the war as a cloak for working out their personal animosities. He couldn't be on the farm, so close to Melina, wanting her the way he did, when she was married to another man.

He turned Bran around and rode away to the south.

Chapter Twenty

"**F**ather wants to see you."

Melina's hands froze partway through a purl stitch. She had brought her knitting upstairs to be out of the way of Mr. Shaw's homecoming. His family ought to have him to themselves for a while—besides which, she felt uneasy about seeing him. Now Nessa stood in the doorway, her eyes red-rimmed in a face that glowed with joy.

Melina folded her knitting away. She must face him sometime.

"Where is he?" she asked.

"In the dooryard, soaking up sunshine. Heaven knows he's seen little enough of it these past months."

Melina went down the stairway. What would Mr. Shaw say to her? He was a man of layers—grave and stern, yet humorous and kind. She expected he would deal gently with her. But would things ever be the same?

She passed through the front door. A rocking chair had been placed on the walkway flags, and in it sat Mr. Shaw, with cushions at his back and a blanket over his lap. His hair had been shorn close to his head, and hair and skin alike looked stripped of color. And he was so terribly thin. A stark tracery of bones showed through the flesh of the hand resting on the arm of the chair, and his knees made points in the blanket. Cheeks and eye sockets were hollow. He squinted, though the sunlight was not bright. He looked like an old man.

But when he spoke, his voice was as strong as ever.

"Miss Bryant, I was most heartily sorry to hear about your father. I wasna acquainted with him as well as I would like, but the short time we spent together was enough for me to consider him a friend as well as a kinsman. He was a fine man, and I ken he was a fond and affectionate father. He always spoke of ye with great love and pride."

Tears filled her eyes, blurring the lines of his face.

"Thank you, sir. I remember when he met you, that first night in the tavern in Charlestown. He was so pleased to have found a long-lost kinsman from North Carolina. He hadn't any brothers or sisters who'd lived past childhood, and I was his only surviving child, so we really had no other family. And then for you to agree to take me in after Charlestown fell—'twas very good of you, and I know it eased Papa's mind."

"He'd have done the same for me."

"Aye, he would indeed. He stayed true to his principles to the end, though it cost him his life. I only wish I'd done the same."

Mr. Shaw held out a hand to her, and she knelt beside him and took it. She could feel its bones and sinews through the papery skin, but its grip was strong.

"Dinnae reproach yourself, lass. Ye acted as ye thought best at the time, and came back to us as soon as ye found a way."

"I should never have gone. I should never have been so weak and gullible."

"Never mind. Ye're here now, and that's what matters. This war has made a lot of ugliness—old friends at enmity, brother against brother, whole households divided. Now that 'tis ended, we should mend what we can, as soon as we can, and give thanks."

She rested her cheek against his knee, still grasping his hand in hers. He laid his other hand on her head.

She supposed he was right. It was useless to waste energy on regret, especially now, when they needed all their energy, not to merely rebuild what was broken, but to found a new nation on better principles. But she couldn't help it. Every night as she lay in bed waiting to fall asleep, all her past mistakes marched before her eyes, reminding her over and over of how foolish and selfish and thoughtless she'd been. She remembered the arrogant words she'd said to Fergus her first day here about the militia. She'd accused them of cowardice under fire, only to fall guilty of the same thing, cratering under pressure and grasping at Richard's empty promises. And the militia had saved the South. They'd beaten the enemy at Cowpens and Kings Mountain when no one thought they could, and fought on in swamps with little to no shot in their guns, and kept the South from being taken, holding on in the face of a bleak prospect with next to nothing to give them hope. If they hadn't, there would have been nothing left to salvage by the time Cornwallis had surrendered at Yorktown. She wished she'd been as faithful and brave as they had been—as Fergus had been. Then she could look forward to his homecoming with an unclouded conscience.

When at last she could speak again, she said, "Thank you for looking after me, Mr. Shaw. Once my father's estate is fully untangled—"

"Nay, no more of that. Ye have a home with us for as long as ye want it. We are your family now."

She swallowed hard. "Thank you."

"Ye're very welcome, Miss Bryant."

She raised her head and peered up at him. "Mr. Shaw, you're the only one left in the family who still calls me Miss Bryant. Would you do me the honor of calling me by my Christian name?"

"Very well...Melina. After all, we are fifth cousins, once removed. And ye're welcome to call me Cousin Archibald if ye'd like, though it doesna exactly trip off the tongue."

"What if I called you Father?"

For a moment his face froze, and she feared she'd overstepped. Then his lips edged up in the slightest suggestion of a smile.

"Aye, daughter," he said. "That'll do."

TAVISH CAME HOME AGAIN late that afternoon. He'd already been there earlier in the day to escort his father-in-law, but he'd had to return. Now he was home to stay, and radiating quiet joy.

Melina kept quiet and listened to the others talk. There was much to tell—about the British withdrawal from town, the birth of baby Archer, and several months' worth of happenings large and small. To bask in the joy of the others was richness enough, or ought to be. But as the evening wore on she grew agitated. There was still one homecoming yet to take place.

"Where is Fergus?" asked Nessa at last. "What can be keeping him? Didn't you say you saw him in town, Tavish?"

"Aye. He looked perfectly well and said his enlistment term with Smith's Legion was over. I dinnae ken why he isna here."

There was nothing to do but wait and wonder. Nightfall came, but Fergus did not. Melina lay on the straw tick upstairs, open-eyed and watchful, listening for the clop of horse hooves, the jingle of harness. What would he say to her? How would he look at her? Would he be glad to see her? Did he still love her?

When morning dawned without bringing Fergus, Tavish saddled Boudicca and rode to town to make enquiries.

He returned alone.

"Smith's Legion disbanded immediately after the British withdrawal, just as I thought," he said. "Fergus was free to leave. No one seems to know where he went."

"He may have rejoined the militia forces under General Lillington," Mr. Shaw said. "No doubt there's much tidying up left to be done in the area, with Fanning and his Loyalists still at large."

"Perhaps," said Tavish. "A few people did recollect seeing a tall man on a dark horse riding south."

"That must have been Fergus," said Nessa. "But I do think he might have been allowed a day's leave to visit his family before setting off again. At the very least, he could have left word for us in town."

On the fifth day after the British departure from Wilmington, a letter came. Catalyn read it aloud to the family.

Georgetown, S. Carolina.

Honored Father,

I take up my Pen to let you know that I am in Good Health & hope these few Lines find you likewise, only I have gone to S. Carolina, where plenty of British & Tories remain & much work left for a Patriot Soldier to do, which I endeavor to undertake, may it please God to grant me Success, I have no settled Plans at present other than travel to Charlestown District & see what may offer, I may join with the militia there or fall in with some Honorable Company along the way, Bran is in Good Health also, God be praised, I will write again when I have News & Opportunity, & until then, sir, please give my Best Wishes to all my Brothers & Sisters, & be assured how much I am

Your dutiful Son,

Fergus

They all looked blankly at each other.

"This is too hard!" Nessa burst out. "Just when the British have finally gone, and we've all come safely through, off he goes into the teeth of a fresh peril elsewhere! And now we must fear for him all over again, and wait in an agony of suspense for word of him."

"'Tis my fault," Melina said miserably. "I'm to blame. He doesn't want to come home because I'm here."

"But he doesn't *know* you're here," said Catalyn. "Not unless Tavish told him."

Tavish shook his head. "I tried to tell him, but he rushed off before I could."

"Then why?" Melina asked. "Why go off so rashly, without even saying goodbye?"

No one had an answer to that.

Catalyn had laid the letter on the table. Melina picked it up. Her heart gave a peculiar throb at the sight of his familiar handwriting, clear and stark and strong. She loved every terse, disjointed, oddly punctuated line on the page.

But it was a poor substitute for the man himself.

Chapter Twenty-One

Making his way down the western banks of the Ashley River with Colonel Lee's Legion, Fergus thought of the map Melina had once made, using the contents of the Shaw dining table, of the city of Charlestown and its environs. Charlestown proper had been a triangular peninsula of mashed Jerusalem artichokes, flanked by the Ashley to the west and the Cooper to the east. James Island, south of the city, must be a very large island indeed, as Melina had used a platter of fish cutlets to represent it, whereas Sullivan's Island, far to the east beyond the Cooper, had been a mere biscuit.

He was on his way now to Johns Island, somewhere to the west of James Island. He'd heard it was large, but Melina hadn't assigned any platter to it, so he had no sense of scale. He supposed he really ought to look at an actual map.

It was surprising that there was so much fighting left to be done in a war that was essentially over. Weeks earlier, on his solitary journey from Wilmington, he'd come across some South Carolina State Troops and learned that General Greene was moving his headquarters to Round O, so he'd headed that way. The general was not at all averse to adding a capable North Carolinian mounted infantryman to his force. Fergus had been assigned to the Legion infantry, under the same Colonel Lee who'd brought news of Cornwallis's surrender to Rutherford's army a month earlier. Greene's men were ill supplied with blankets, cloaks, and—as usual—ammunition. It was the same old story—they simply didn't have the numbers to sweep the enemy out all at once.

But they were making progress. After weeks of patient Patriot finesse, the British had nothing left in South Carolina but Charlestown, the isthmus, and the Sea Islands—including Johns Island, the current destination of Lee's company. Their mission was to cut off the British troops there from Charlestown and Savannah.

As he rode, Fergus's attention wandered to the other side of the Ashley. Trailing Oaks was there. How had it fared? Was the house still standing, or had the British gutted and burned it? Had the fields been ravaged? And what of the huge, heavy-limbed trees for which it had been named? Were they still standing, or had they been lopped down?

By the end of the first day's march, Lee's force reached scenes of such luxury and delight as might almost have driven thoughts of Trailing Oaks—and Melina—from Fergus's mind, if anything could. For the past two years this region had been touched little by the war. Its lush rice plantations, gracious homes, and rich gardens were a balm to the senses.

The country only improved on further acquaintance. Its crowning glory was its young women, who seemed as pleased to see the soldiers as the soldiers could be to see them. Far from resenting the necessity of quartering Lee's men, the inhabitants showered them with hospitality. It was a new and pleasant sensation for Fergus to see beautiful young women looking at him with evident pleasure, and seeking him in conversation.

For the first time, Fergus began to get a sense of the sort of luxury in which Melina had grown up. When he'd first met her, he'd thought her terribly spoiled. Now he was amazed that she'd accepted the Shaw farm with as good a grace as she had—and even, perhaps, come to love it.

Returning from a patrol one morning around dawn, Fergus stopped at a ramshackle farmhouse to water Bran. The master of the place came out to meet him, trailed by an assortment of dogs—hounds, spaniels, terriers. One of them was so small that Fergus thought it was a puppy at first, but at second glance he saw that it was a grown dog. Some sort of spaniel, delicately formed, with a short, pointed muzzle and curling tail, and reddish in color. The long coat might once have been luxuriant but now hung in mats. There was a sharp intelligence in the dark eyes set beneath a high, rounded forehead and peaked ears.

Fergus dismounted and watched the little red dog as Bran drank. Could it be...?

"Ruby!" he called.

The little dog jumped straight into the air and gave Fergus a look that cut him to the quick. She was like an exile hearing her native tongue in a foreign land.

"Where did you get that dog?" he asked the man.

The man's face took on a guarded, considering, scheming expression. "What's it to you?" he asked.

"She belongs to a kinswoman of mine. You see that I know her name, and that she answers to it."

The man glanced at the little dog. "Lucky guess. Lots of red dogs are named Ruby."

Fergus turned back to the dog, wracking his memory, and praying he'd get the words right.

"Ruby," he said, "what does King Charles say to the Short Parliament?"

Instantly, Ruby sat on her little haunches and put her front paws in the air in an attitude of supplication. Her round dark eyes were fixed on Fergus's face.

"Ruby," said Fergus, "what does King Charles say to the Long Parliament?"

Almost before he'd finished the question, Ruby went down on her belly and covered her ears with her paws.

Fergus turned to the man. "Well?"

The man shrugged. "Take her, then, and good riddance. She's a regular puler, that one, always grieving and whining and carrying on. And her coat's a bother to look after."

Ruby certainly wasn't grieving now. She was groveling at Fergus's feet, making low groans in her throat. And judging from the state of her coat, it had been a long time since anyone had taken any trouble with it.

He picked her up and held her close. The wind had risen with the sun, and Ruby was shivering with cold as well as excitement. He tucked her into his frock coat, where she eagerly snuggled down.

And in that moment, he decided to go home.

Chapter Twenty-Two

Melina clipped a bough of meadow holly and laid it in her basket, atop the ample pile of greenery she'd already collected to adorn the Shaw house for Christmas. Besides the traditional holly and ivy, she'd picked other, distinctly American evergreens—wax myrtle, mountain laurel, Christmas fern. The long, wiry jessamine stems could be twined around candlesticks, while strands of leafless beautyberry, studded with purple berries in clusters the size of a baby's fist, could be hung in swags at the mantel.

The Shaws were tolerantly amused by Melina's fervor over Christmas. Hogmanay was their great holiday; they scarcely observed Christmas at all. But Father Shaw had given her his blessing to celebrate this one as ardently as she pleased.

In truth, her own enjoyment of the season was not the ingenuous, uncomplicated pleasure of past years. But it was warmer, deeper. She had forfeited all rational expectation of Fergus's love or even esteem, and she hadn't yet secured her property in South Carolina. But she'd learned to place greater value on an inheritance that was forever secure against theft and decay. She had lost Papa, but had been given the solace of a new family. She'd been showered with grace, which couldn't be repaid, but she could give thanks for it, and she did.

Fergus hadn't written much of substance, or much at all, since his trek southward. His letters from South Carolina were sparse, factual, unsatisfying documents, giving little information beyond the good health of his horse and himself—wholly different from the earnest, confidential ones he'd written home during the months when Lillington's militia had lurked in the countryside around Wilmington, which she still kept in her trunk upstairs.

There had been something in his latest letter about the warm welcome Lee's men had received from the residents of the region around the Ashley, planter aristocracy families who had once been Melina's friends. She got a hot, choked feeling inside when she imagined him surrounded by girls she'd grown up with, all of them vying for his attention, and flirting with him. She had no right to feel that way, but that made no difference.

She was reaching up to snip a branch of inkberry when she heard a voice say, "Melina."

She froze in place with her fingers outstretched. She knew that voice. She would have known it anywhere.

Slowly she turned and saw Fergus standing not three yards away from her.

She'd forgotten how tall he was, unless it were possible that he'd grown taller. He wore a new coat, new to him at least, plain but well made, and well suited to his height and frame. He was bareheaded, with his black hair smoothed neatly back from his wide brow, showing the strong, clean lines of cheek and chin and jaw.

The basket fell from her arm, and the forest swam before her eyes.

In an instant he was beside her, taking her arm.

"Are you all right?" he asked. "You look very pale."

"I'm perfectly well," she said, though even now, her knees were about to give way, and her heart fluttered in her chest.

The next thing she knew, she was seated on a sandstone slab with Fergus beside her and no idea how she'd gotten there. He was vivid and solid and near, with his hands holding tight to hers and his coat giving off a scent of wood smoke.

"I thought you were in South Carolina," she said.

"I was. My return was not looked for. I didn't write first. I've only just arrived."

"Your family will be so glad to see you. They've missed you so very, very much."

Her voice was shaking, but Fergus didn't seem to notice.

"Melina—Miss Bryant—nay, I beg your pardon, Mrs. Severn. Why are you here? Why are you not in town, or England, or Nova Scotia, with—with Mr. Severn?"

Her breath caught in her throat. Had he really said what she thought he'd said? Did he truly think—

"I am Miss Bryant still," she said faintly. "I ended my engagement to Mr. Severn some months ago."

Fergus's face drained of color. "You—you didn't marry Severn?"

"Nay. I broke with him in September, and your family received me again most graciously at their home."

"September? You've been here since *September*?"

"Aye. You'd only just left for General Rutherford's muster in Salisbury when I arrived."

His dark eyes burned into her. "All the time I was in South Carolina…"

"I was here," she finished. "I've been here all along, Fergus."

He released her from his gaze and stared into the middle distance.

"I remember sitting astride Bran that day, after the city was liberated and the British ships sailed down the river," he said. "My duty was discharged. I was free to go home."

"Why didn't you?"

She saw his throat contract in what looked like a painful swallow. "I saw him in town—Richard Severn. He was being taken to the bull pen. A man was beating him. I put a stop to that. And then Severn—he told me what he'd done to you, how he'd coerced you into agreeing to marry him, to protect us."

"Why did he tell you that?" Melina asked.

"He let it slip. He thought I already knew, that you must have told me. But I—I misunderstood. I thought you'd already married him. And I—Melina, I didn't trust myself. I had to get away from that man before I killed him. I couldn't bear to come home, and see all the places where I'd fallen in love with you, and not have you here. It would be like losing you all over again. I love you, Melina. I wish I could conjure up great words to tell you how much, but my heart is too full for words. And yet I think you will understand me anyway. You have always understood me."

Melina's throat closed off, and her eyes stung with tears. "I love you too," she whispered. "Oh, Fergus, I love you so much."

His face shone with joy. As he bent his head toward hers, a lock of dark hair escaped the queue in back and skimmed across her cheek, making her quiver all over.

And then he kissed her.

It was like falling backward into something exquisitely soft and sweet—falling, falling, and never reaching bottom. Her hands slid around his head and neck, and he pulled her close to him.

When at last their lips parted, she kept her eyes shut and rested her forehead against his. "All this time, you were keeping away from me because you thought I was Richard's wife," she murmured. "If only you'd come home that day! Then you'd have learned the truth, and we'd have been together."

He laughed softly. "You won't wish for that when you find out what I got for you in South Carolina."

He pulled away from her, turned his head over his shoulder, and whistled.

He had distinctive whistles for each of the horses, and one for Dougie. This was different—three short notes in quick succession, piercing and high.

Melina heard a faint rustling sound, punctuated with tiny patters like raindrops. Something small and swift was coming their way.

Then a ball of reddish fur launched itself into her arms.

Melina heard a scream and dimly knew that she had made it. She fell off the sandstone and landed on the ground. She tried to cuddle the wriggling, silky body, but Ruby wouldn't hold still. She yipped and squirmed and licked Melina's face. She was trembling with joy and whining low in her throat, while Melina sobbed without reservation or shame.

When at last Melina raised her tear-streaked face, Fergus was watching her, grinning hugely, his eyes red-rimmed and shining.

"How did you do this?" Melina asked. "Where did you find her?

"On Johns Island, near Greensborough. I thought she might be your dog, so I called her name. She jumped straight into the air and looked at me like a long-lost friend. The man who had her didn't want to hand her over at first, but I put her through her tricks, and that settled the matter."

"You remembered her tricks?" Melina's voice rose to a squeal.

"Of course I remembered—and so did she. I never saw a dog so happy to obey. We've been together ever since. Her coat was in sad shape at first, full of mats and burrs, but I managed to work them out. She was good company on the ride home."

"You brought Ruby home from Queensborough, on horseback?"

"Aye. Of course she couldn't trot so far on her wee legs, so I acquired a traveling basket for her and strapped it to the saddle."

"And all that time, you thought I was married to Richard Severn."

"Well, I did have good reason to think so! I thought you might have left town since the evacuation, but I reckoned I could get word to you somehow, and you and Ruby would be together again."

He had brought her little lost dog back to her across a hundred and seventy miles, while believing her to be married to another, because that was the sort of man he was.

She took his hand again. It was rough and hard and strong, but gentle.

"You have no idea how good and noble and upright and decent and utterly irreplaceable you are, Fergus Shaw," she said. "But I do."

FATHER SHAW CAST A suspicious eye at the sprig of mistletoe hanging from a red ribbon in the central passage of the house. "Kissing beneath a parasitic plant! I've never heard of the like. Such heathenish things were never done in my youth."

"'Tis a new British custom, Father," said Nessa.

"We've spent the past six years throwing off British tyranny, and now we're falling in with their fads?"

"Not all British ways are an evil, sir," said Tavish. "The English language is rather fine. I hope the United States will keep it. And this new custom of kissing beneath the mistletoe is a very pretty one, I think."

"Of course, American mistletoe is not the same as European mistletoe," Catalyn said. "The leaves of North American are shorter and broader, and the berry clusters are longer. It belongs to a distinct genus of the Santalaceae family."

"Aye, just as ye belong to the MacGregor genus of the Shaw family," said Tavish. "And ye must kiss me now," he added, holding over her head a tiny sprig that had fallen from the mistletoe at the ceiling.

Ruby was wearing some holly and ivy, tied around her neck with a ribbon, and scampering around the Shaw house as if she'd always lived there. Dougie wore a greenery-bedecked ribbon as well.

"What is that bit of foppery Dougie has on?" Father Shaw asked. "He looks like a debauched cavalier. He'll be wearing his fur in lovelocks next."

"Nay, Father Shaw," said Melina. "He's a most upright and sober Presbyterian dog. Dougie, what did the Covenanters do at Greyfriars Kirk?"

Dougie sat on his haunches and soberly raised his right paw as if taking an oath.

Father Shaw let out a roar of laughter. "Och, look at the pious creature, ready to swear to uphold the Reformed faith! Ye clever lass, I believe ye could reconcile me to almost anything."

The whole household had a festive air. Lachlan was in high spirits, alternately playing with the dogs, running from room to room, and launching himself at his father every few minutes as if to reassure himself that he was still there. Each time he did, Tavish scooped him up and tossed him into the air, making Lachlan scream with delight. The baby, Archer, looked around with a wide-eyed stare, beat his small fists in the air, and gave an occasional lusty shout. He'd grown apace in the past three months, but his proportions were as long and slender as ever. Catalyn wished he would put on more flesh, but he was strong enough, and Tavish said he must be in such a hurry to gain height that he couldn't yet be bothered with breadth.

Nessa was in a glow of good spirits that made her more beautiful than ever, and Morna, quiet and great-eyed, had acquired an air of womanly grace. Rory had grown gangly and awkward and didn't talk as much as he used to. Melina missed his bold, confident speeches, but he was whole and sound after his time in the militia. They all had much to be thankful for.

On Christmas Eve, Melina and Fergus took a walk in the woods arm in arm. It was a still night. Tree trunks and branches, and all the delicate filaments of pine needles, showed black against the deep blue sky. The gibbous moon glowed. The stars shone sharp and bright. The very air was bracing and sweet. A faint tracery of frost lay on the ground. The only sound was the crunch of sugar sand beneath their feet.

"I keep thinking about the reading of the banns," Melina said. "What a thrill it gave me to hear the words spoken from the pulpit yesterday! *I publish the banns of marriage between Fergus Shaw of Saint James Parish and Melina Bryant, also of Saint James Parish.* Our names linked, our engagement made public. I shiver every time I think of it. Only two more Sundays to go, and then we can be married in January."

"But are you sure you want to be married so soon, my love? The wedding will have to be very small and plain if we make such haste. We could wait, you know."

"Nay, I will brook no delay. You and I have waited quite long enough."

"What will you wear?"

"One of my old Charlestown gowns. I don't care if they're out of fashion. What do I care about gowns when I have such a splendid, handsome husband?"

He stopped and looked down at her with a grave face. "I think you do care very much for gowns and ornaments and such. And you are a beautiful woman with exquisite taste. You ought to have a new gown for your wedding day. You know you want one."

She shrugged. "The fact of the matter is that there are no dress goods in town, and that cannot change very soon. The blockade will not be lifted before a peace treaty is signed, and we cannot expect negotiations to even begin until after Christmas, so I see little chance of having a new gown made until many months have passed, perhaps a year or more."

"Precisely. So hadn't we better wait?"

She arched an eyebrow at him. "Mr. Shaw, I begin to suspect you repent of asking me to marry you, and wish yourself unattached."

He smiled tenderly at her. "Melina, I have seen for myself your former mode of living, and I know how great a step down it is for you to marry a plain planter. And if we marry in haste, there is much else that we will have to do without, at least in the short term. I can't hope to have even a small cabin ready for us to live in."

She took his face in her hands and looked up at him. "Fergus Shaw, in marrying you I will not be descending. Whatever I wear, wherever we live, you will be making me the happiest woman alive. And the sooner that day comes, the better I shall be pleased."

"FOR THE LAST TIME," said Father Shaw, "a dark-haired man is the man of choice for First Foot. The reasons are as plain as day. A fair-haired man might be a Norse invader, but a dark-haired man is sure to be a fellow countryman. So it has always been, and so it shall ever be."

"Nay, not in all parts of the country," Tavish said stubbornly. "I speak the truth: in the west of Scotland a dark-haired man augurs ill, because he might be a pirate from Portugal or Spain."

Father Shaw folded his arms over his chest. "I have never heard anyone say so but yourself."

"Just because ye've never heard it doesna mean 'tisna true. Am I not right, Catalyn? Is not that a logical fallacy of some sort, a fallacy of ignorance?"

"Nay, not in this case," replied his father-in-law. "For if there had been such a custom, I most certainly *would* have heard of it."

"Not necessarily. It could be an extremely localized custom in a very small and isolated community."

"Och! If that line of reasoning is to be permitted, ye could suppose all manner of bizarre things to take place in all sorts of unknown wee pockets of humanity."

"I heard it directly from the mouth of a Scottish earl who was visiting Mr. Nash's estate," said Tavish.

"D'ye mean to say ye're presuming to school me on the customs of Scotland based on the words of a stranger in Virginia? He probably wasna even a real earl."

"I feel compelled to remind ye, sir, that ye have never actually visited Scotland yourself."

"I've come a lot nearer to it than you have, laddie."

Melina nudged Nessa. "Didn't they have this exact same conversation last New Year's?"

Nessa smiled. "Aye, and for every New Year's before that, ever since Tavish joined the family. 'Tis a holiday tradition in its own right now."

It was close to midnight on New Year's Eve. The MacGregor boys had been allowed to stay up to ring in the New Year. Lachlan had been alternately sleeping on a soft, warm palette in front of the fire, and running around the house, while Archer watched the family's antics from his cradle.

Melina had not known about first-footing in Charlestown, nor indeed about Hogmanay in general, but in the Shaw household it was the most important celebration of the year. The house had been given a thorough cleaning, symbolizing a fresh start for the year to come, and juniper logs were burning in the parlor fireplace, making a clean, pungent aroma that was supposed to rid the house of evil spirits.

The first visitor to enter the house in the new year, called the First Foot, was perhaps the most important element of the day, as the character of that person was said to determine the fortunes of the household for the entire year to come. Ideally, the First Foot must be male, tall, and—according to Father Shaw, at least—dark of hair. Not willing to leave so vital a matter to chance, neighbors often arranged ahead of time to first-foot one another's households. But for many years, ever since he'd passed his father in height, Fergus had performed the service for his own family, and eventually for his sister's household as well. It was acceptable for the first-footer to be a resident of the house, so long as he was not actually within doors at the stroke of midnight.

"The whole notion of a year's fortune being determined by the identity of the first person to enter the house on a given day seems terribly heathenish to me," said Melina. "Doesn't it strike any of you as inconsistent to decry Christmas as a papist feast while holding to so superstitious a custom?"

Everyone exclaimed loudly against this, and Melina protested that they were burning a ritual fire at this very moment, and proposing to secure the fortune of the household for the near future by a ceremonial act. Voices rose in lively debate, and the matter was no nearer being settled when a distinct rasp came from the longcase clock. The clock always made that sound just before striking, as if taking a deep breath.

Everyone turned to the clock with a start. Both hands were pointing straight up.

In the next instant all eyes were on Fergus, and the stroke of midnight was drowned out in shouts of dismay.

Father Shaw's voice rose above the others as he turned on Fergus. "And just what d'ye think ye're doing, sir, sitting on your bahookie in the parlor, quite at your ease? Ye should be standing outside the front door, ready to knock! Now ye've missed your chance!"

"You and Tavish hadn't finished debating the matter," Fergus said serenely. "You can't expect me to loiter about in the cold waiting for the two of you to wrangle out my fate. I've been exposed to enough rough weather recently, and I will take my comfort where I can get it."

"Nay, I never had the remotest chance of winning my point," said Tavish. "You should have known as much. I'm surprised at you, brother. The new year has begun, and ye can be sure that any misfortune it may bring will be entirely owing to your own negligence."

Fergus shrugged. "I first-footed the house last year, a year that brought ill fortune enough. Is Craig's occupation of Wilmington to be laid to my account as well?"

"Ill fortune!" said Catalyn. "You surely cannot mean that, brother. Certainly the year had its trials, but the good outweighed the bad by far."

"Aye, the victory at Cowpens took place scarcely halfway through January," said Tavish. "And Guilford Courthouse not two months after that."

"Guilford Courthouse was a defeat," said Rory in his new, startlingly deep voice.

"Only from a tactical standpoint," said Tavish. "The enemy's losses were greater than ours."

"And the same year that saw the start of Craig's occupation also saw his removal," said Nessa.

"Not to mention the victory at Yorktown," said Tavish.

"And Archer's birth, and Father's safe return to us," said Catalyn.

"Aye," said Tavish. "So ye see, brother, the balance of the year was favorable, which is very much to your credit."

"To his credit?" Melina repeated. "Do you even hear yourselves? You are speaking, all of you, as if Fergus's height and hair color actually had any bearing on any of these events. I am shocked—not only by your heathenish ways, but by how hidebound you are. This is the New World, and we should make our own traditions. The truth is we aren't going to be visited by Vikings *or* Spanish pirates here on the coast of North Carolina."

"Spanish pirates are more likely," Tavish put in. "There's a precedent for that, at least."

"Three decades past," Father Shaw objected. "And they made it only as far as Brunswick."

"You're missing the point, both of you," said Melina. "This is *our* country. Forget tradition for a moment. What manner of man do we want for our representative visitor in the new year?"

Before anyone could answer, a knock sounded at the front door—firm, confident, sure.

"There," said Melina. "Someone has come to your rescue—no doubt a tall, dark-haired neighbor."

"Nay, for we've made no arrangements," said Father Shaw.

"Who could it be?" asked Nessa. "Who would turn up unannounced just past midnight on New Year's Day?"

"Only one way to find out," said Melina.

She went to the door and opened it.

Standing at the threshold was a lean, tough young man with an unmistakable nautical air. His red-gold hair hung long and loose to his shoulders, and he wore a light beard. He was a stranger to Melina, and yet there was something familiar about his face, and his look of calm competence and quiet daring.

'Tis a Viking after all, Melina thought.

Then Nessa, who had followed her into the passage, screamed, "*Liam!*"

She launched herself to him, almost knocking Melina down, and threw her arms around him. The rest of the family poured into the passage, pressing Melina to the wall. Liam was passed from sister to brother and on again, and the barking of the dogs added to the chaos.

Then Liam said, "Hello, Father."

Father Shaw stood in the parlor doorway. His face was set and stern, but the mouth trembled, and he just managed to choke out his son's name before folding him into his arms.

Silence fell. Even the dogs stopped barking. Across the passage, Melina saw Catalyn smiling through her tears.

Father Shaw released Liam at last, giving him a parting slap on the shoulder, and dabbed quickly at his eyes. Archer let out one of his yells from his cradle while Lachlan peered out at his uncle from behind a chair. He'd been too young when Liam went away to remember him now.

Then Rory said, "Liam! You're our First Foot!"

Liam frowned. "Am I? That doesn't bode well. I'm too fair for a First Foot."

"Nay, laddie," said Father Shaw. "Ye're exactly right."

"And you've even brought some first-footing gifts!" said Rory. "Look, here's a bit of evergreen caught in your cuff, and some salt crystals on your sleeve."

"Aye!" said Liam. "And I can do better still. I haven't any whisky, but I've some rum in my flask. Here's a Spanish doubloon for gold, and for bread I've got almost an entire ship's biscuit, with the weevils already plucked out."

After everyone had laughed over this, Nessa said, "Why are we all still crammed into the entry? Let's go to the parlor. Are you hungry, Liam?"

As she and Morna busied themselves getting something for Liam to eat, Fergus introduced him to Melina. She could hear the pride in his voice as he spoke of her as "my bride-to-be." Liam said he was very glad to meet her, and looked as if he meant it.

"Now that ye've been feted and fed, ye must give an account of yourself, lad," Father Shaw said sometime later. "Tell us about the naval action ye've been involved in."

"Well, sir, I began on the *King Tammany*, one of the brigs charged with protecting Ocracoke Inlet, but I soon changed to the *Bellona*, a privateer. And for these past two years I have been on the *Red Hart*, with Captain Johnstone."

"Did you take many prizes?" asked Rory.

"Not many, I'm afraid. But we captured a British merchantman and made it through the blockade with her. She's in the port right now, loaded with china and dress goods."

Fergus turned to Melina. "Did you hear that, my love? It looks as if you'll have a new gown after all."

Chapter Twenty-Three

Fergus lay on his side, propped on one arm, watching Melina sleep. Her hair lay spread over the pillow in a soft cloud of spun gold. She had her arms flung out like wings, bent at the elbows, with the curled hands and fragile wrists showing just above the sheet. Her eyes fluttered behind lids as pale and translucent as bone china, edged with their thick fringe of dark gold lashes. Every line of her face was at the same time delicate and strong—the wide brow, the impossibly graceful curve of cheekbone, the firm chin.

Melina opened her eyes. She smiled up at him sleepily, then rolled onto her side, shivering a little. Fergus pulled the bedclothes up to her chin, then draped his body around hers, cupping their curves and angles together, and covering her loose fist with his own hand. He could feel the small knob of the black pearl against his palm. A Wilmington goldsmith had made a simple setting for it.

"Better?" he whispered into her hair.

"Mmm, lovely. You're as good as a wool coverlet."

"Thank you, madam. I do my best."

Morning sunlight filtered through the thin homespun curtains, and outside, the dawn chorus of the birds had reached its peak. It was April now, and Fergus and Melina were three months wedded. The marriage had taken place as soon after the banns as either of them could wish—and she'd had a new gown, and Ruby a new ribbon, made from dress goods provided by the prize taken by Captain Johnstone's privateer. The blockade was still in effect, but the end was truly in sight, and grew clearer every day.

The House of Commons had voted at the end of February to end hostilities, and peace negotiations had begun in London. But the British still occupied Charlestown, Savannah, and New York, leaving plenty of opportunity for additional bloodshed, and the animosity between Tories and Patriots remained strong. The machinery of vengeance would not quickly cease operation.

But here, within the house, all was peaceful, though the rest of the family was beginning to stir. Floorboards creaked, and somewhere on the second floor, a door opened and shut.

"No point in lingering any longer," Fergus said. "Time to get up, and we might as well be brisk about it."

He threw back the covers, but Melina protested and pulled them back over herself, burrowing into the bedding like a chipmunk, as he'd known she would.

But she poked her head to watch him cleaning his teeth. At one point he thought he heard her giggling, but by the time he turned around her face was serious. He spat out the tooth powder, rinsed his mouth, poured some water from the pitcher to the basin, and began to wash.

While reaching for a towel he caught her watching him intently.

"And why do you observe my ablutions so keenly, madam?" he asked.

"Because they fascinate me. Do you have any idea how charmingly you brush your teeth? Every morning and night it is the same. You stand with your feet braced firmly apart, grip the washstand with one hand, and with the other scrub the tooth powder so vigorously that the washstand shakes."

"I had no idea I was an object of ridicule to my wife. From now on I will be circumspect and dignified while cleaning my teeth."

"Nay!" said Melina, bouncing on her knees. "You must go on doing it exactly the same way. You mustn't deprive me of one of my chief delights."

"One of your chief delights? Watching me clean my teeth? You cannot be serious."

"I am perfectly serious. But an even greater delight is watching you wash. I have never seen a handsomer creature than yourself, just now, with the towel carelessly tossed over your bare chest and your hair all damp around your face and clinging to your neck."

He felt his face grow warm. Three months married, and she could still make him blush.

"Well, no more of this lolling about," he said briskly. "'Tis time you got up and made some ablutions of your own."

He sprang toward her as if to haul her bodily out of bed. She shrieked and dove under the covers.

"Keep your voice down, woman! You'll shock my father."

"Impossible. Your father is shock-proof."

He dropped back onto the mattress. A bit of a tussle ensued, and for a time it seemed more likely that Fergus would stay in bed than that Melina would leave it. But after a while she was up and at the washstand herself.

"And what do you undertake to do today, sir?" she asked him.

"There's some new fence to be laid, and Tavish wants to notch the ears of the new bull calves. Who would have thought we'd be blessed with another set of healthy twin bullocks so soon?"

"No one could. 'Tis a boon from God—and a reflection of Tavish's skill as a cow midwife. What about the house? Will you work on it at any time between laying fence and notching ears?"

"Of course. I work on the house every day. That goes without saying."

"I like hearing you say it, nevertheless."

The building site had been marked off, and the lumber was cut and curing. With help from his father and brothers, Fergus had almost finished laying the cellar.

"How about you, madam?" he asked, as he pulled on his stockings. "What will you do today?"

"What else? Sew for our future household."

"And how much longer will you be about it, do you think?"

"I haven't the faintest idea. I don't see any end in sight. So much linen to be sewn! Sheets, pillowslips, towels, counterpanes, quilts, bedcurtains, tablecloths—there seems no end to the things one must have. I never knew a household required such a mountain of linen. I would be terrified without Catalyn to tell me what to do. 'Tis just as well our house is not ready yet, for apparently it would be a shameful thing to set up housekeeping without our full complement of linen."

Even once the house was ready, it would be absurdly smaller than the ones in which Melina had grown up, but it would feel wonderfully spacious compared to their current cramped accommodations. They had stayed their wedding night in Fergus's childhood bedroom, and slept there every night since. He'd expected this to feel strange, but it hadn't. He hadn't actually slept in the room for over a year, since before Camden, and Melina had done what she could, with Catalyn's help, to fit it up as a married couple's bedchambers.

Liam and Rory had moved in temporarily with Catalyn and Tavish. Two new rooms had been added to the cabin, one for its master and mistress and the other for Lachlan and Archer. The Shaw brothers slept before the fireplace.

"Even when the house is ready, 'twill not provide the style of living to which you are accustomed, with servants and finery and room upon room," Fergus said.

"Nay, you're wrong, for I've grown unaccustomed to the style in which I grew up, and I'm glad of the change. I had plenty of space as a child, but no brothers or sisters to share it with. As for the servants, they're gone, and I would not wish them back. I wish them well, wherever they may be. I love this house, crammed though it is with sisters and brothers and nephews, and a gem of a father-in-law, and two dogs. And I know I'll love our own house better still."

"The others will be glad of the change too, I daresay. Once we move out, Liam and Rory can have their old room back—though in truth I don't think Liam will stay much longer. He'll be going back to sea as soon as he can find a berth, blockade or no."

Melina laid out her stays on the bed and adjusted the lacing to make it evenly loose.

"I agree. But in the meantime, what a crowd! So many sons and brothers all around one! I wonder how Catalyn and Tavish can bear it, having so little privacy."

"They manage."

Melina gave him a curious look. "You sound very certain. How do you know?"

Fergus shrugged, suddenly shy. "There's an old corncrib in the forest, and sometimes they...go there."

He could feel her staring at him. "How do you know this? Did Tavish tell you?"

"Nay, of course not. I'm simply observant. I've known them to steal away before in the middle of the day, and one day I found the corncrib swept and tidy, and furnished with some old blankets from the house. The conclusion was not a difficult one."

"Goodness! How clever of them. Perhaps we should be on the lookout for a retreat of our own. I know of a lovely stream, perfect for bathing."

"I think I know the one you mean, madam. Another week or two, and it should be warm enough for even a delicate southern blossom like yourself."

She slipped the stays over her head and pulled them into place over her shift, and Fergus started tightening the lace, beginning at the bottom and working his way up.

"What an expert stay-lacer you've become these past few months," Melina said.

"I'm glad you're satisfied with my work, though I daresay any man of modest intellect and abilities could learn to do as well. Besides, I prefer taking them off again."

She turned her head, showing an impeccably pretty profile, and smiled archly at him over her shoulder. Then she reached behind her, gently pulled his hands aside, and started loosening the lace.

"Breakfast can wait," she whispered.

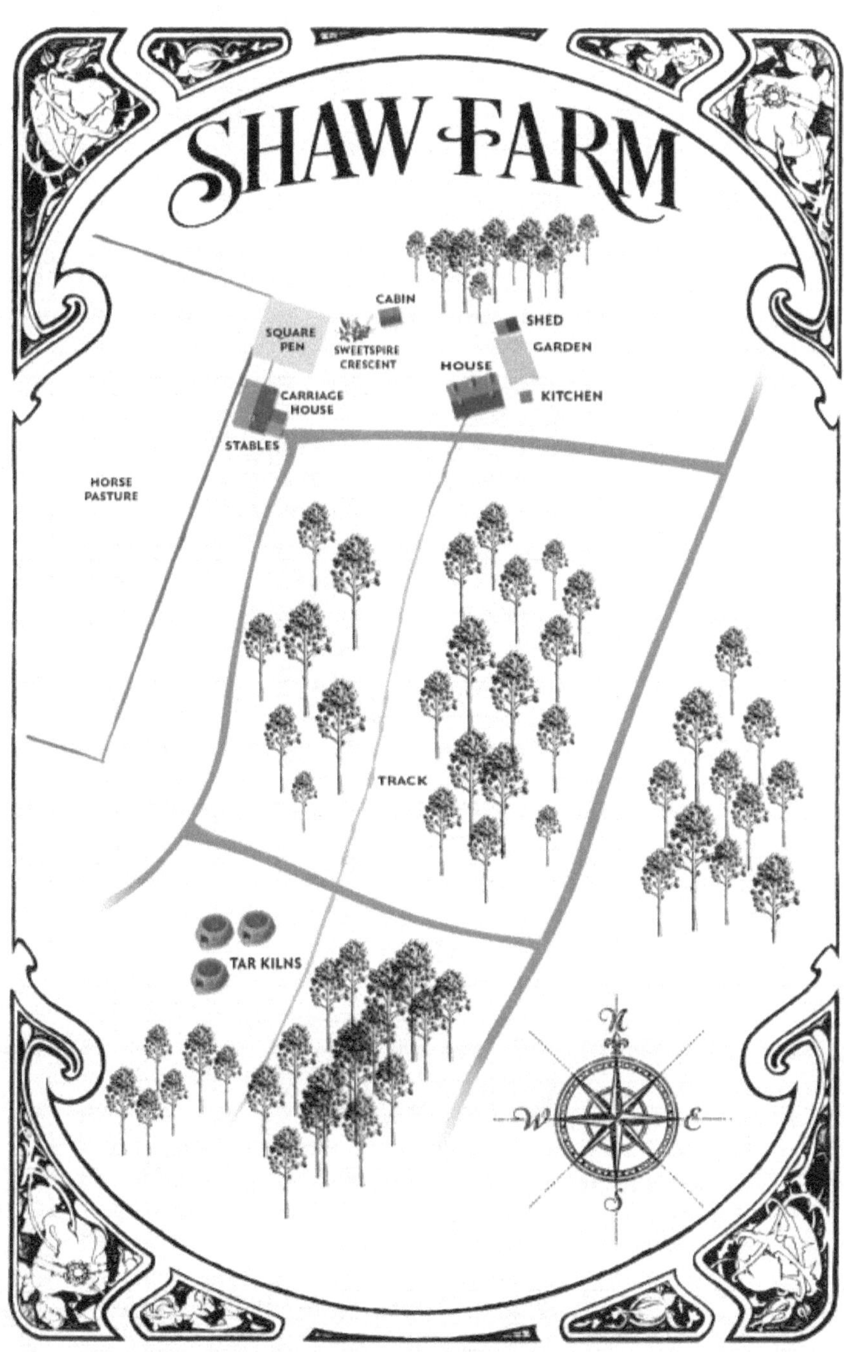

SHAW FARM
CABIN
SHED
SQUARE PEN
GARDEN
SWEETSPIRE CRESCENT
HOUSE
CARRIAGE HOUSE
KITCHEN
STABLES
HORSE PASTURE
TRACK
TAR KILNS
N
W
E
S

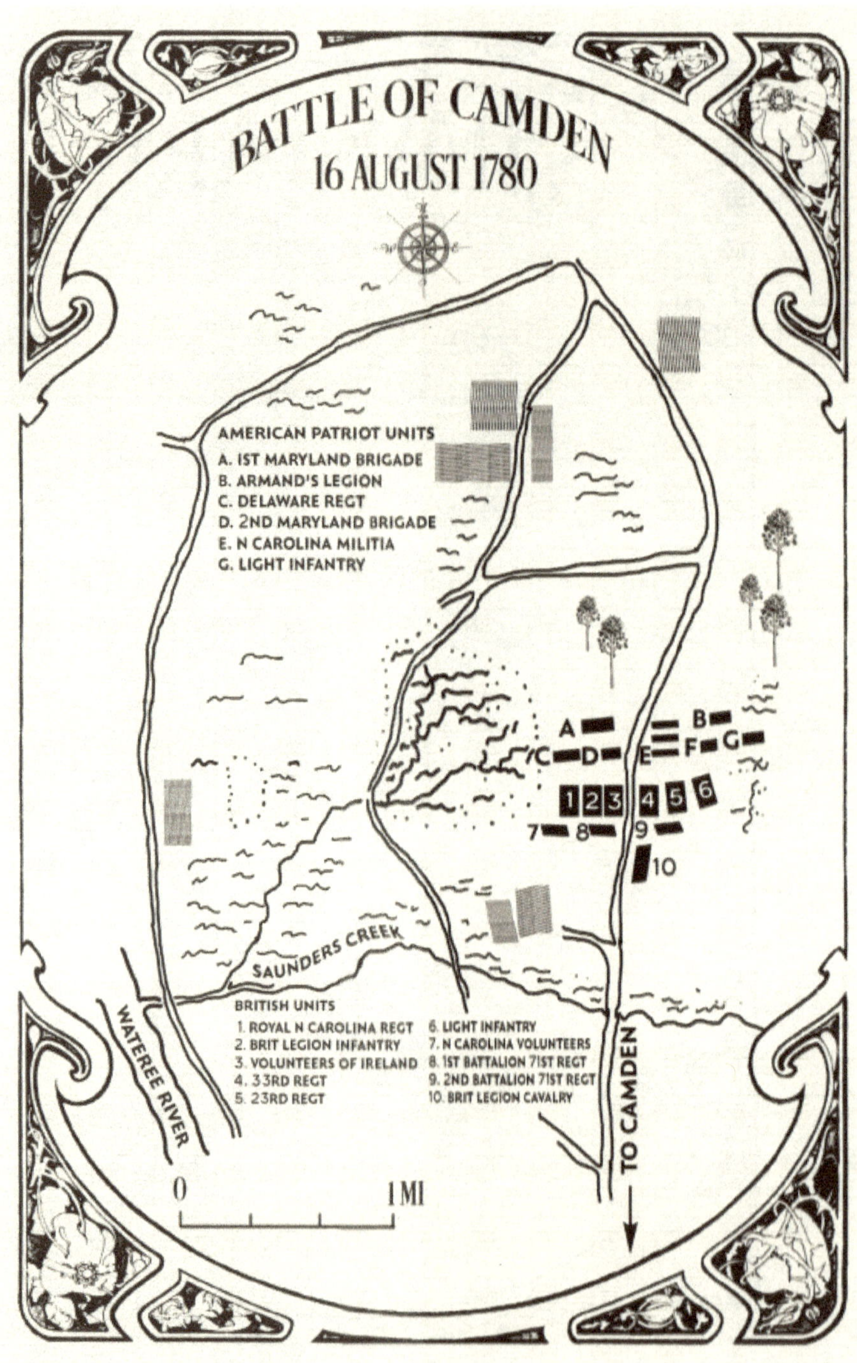
BATTLE OF CAMDEN
16 AUGUST 1780

AMERICAN PATRIOT UNITS
A. 1ST MARYLAND BRIGADE
B. ARMAND'S LEGION
C. DELAWARE REGT
D. 2ND MARYLAND BRIGADE
E. N CAROLINA MILITIA
G. LIGHT INFANTRY

A
B
C
D
E
F
G
1 2 3 4 5 6
7 8 9
10

SAUNDERS CREEK

BRITISH UNITS
1. ROYAL N CAROLINA REGT
2. BRIT LEGION INFANTRY
3. VOLUNTEERS OF IRELAND
4. 33RD REGT
5. 23RD REGT
6. LIGHT INFANTRY
7. N CAROLINA VOLUNTEERS
8. 1ST BATTALION 71ST REGT
9. 2ND BATTALION 71ST REGT
10. BRIT LEGION CAVALRY

WATEREE RIVER

TO CAMDEN

0   1 MI

Acknowledgments

Once again, I owe many thanks to my friend J.D. Lewis, this time for helping me navigate primary sources concerning the Battle of Camden and figure out what really happened between Gates, de Kalb, Caswell, Rutherford, and the rest. I was pretty relentless about this, and he showed great patience in answering email after email on the subject. His website, carolana.com, continues to be my go-to source for all things related to the Revolutionary War in the Carolinas.

I also thank my critique partners, particularly Janalyn Knight, for ruthlessly telling me what to cut; Mary Johnson, for gently reminding me what to leave in, and why; David Martin, for his unfailing eye for clarity in prose; and Cheryl Crouch, for her boundless encouragement, enthusiasm, and excellent judgment. Thanks also to each of you for your friendship.

Thanks to my editor, Sharon Oitzman, who not only is great at what she does, but also understands and shares my vision for my books. I appreciate your professionalism and your friendship. It's a pleasure working with you.

Thanks to Darleen Dixon, cover artist extraordinaire, whose beautiful work on my books makes me happy every time I pick one up and hold it in my hands.

Thanks to my assistant, Allyson Larison, for taking over a long list of tasks in the indie-publishing workload and doing them better than I could. I appreciate your hard work, creativity, and professionalism.

Many thanks to my husband, Greg Midkiff, for giving me the freedom to pursue indie publishing with the attention it deserves; my daughter Grace Midkiff, for keen insights in beta-reading; my son, Daniel Midkiff, for sharing his knowledge of weaponry and warfare; my mom, Donna Siddall, for filling my childhood with (almost) all the books I wanted; my mother-in-law, Ann Logan, for being one of my biggest promoters; and my sister, Teri

James Gillaspie, for reading every one of my books and discussing them intelligently with me afterward.

Finally, thanks to all the readers who read the first book in the series and took the time to ask for more. I can't express how precious you are to me.

Historical Notes

Slavery During the American Revolutionary War

African labor was part of the North American British colonies, including those that would later become the United States of America, from the beginning. There were workers of African origin at Jamestown and Plymouth, though it's debated whether these were permanently enslaved individuals or indentured servants who would eventually gain their freedom. Slavery was introduced early in the New England colonies but did not take hold there for a variety of reasons, including the unsuitability of slave labor to the New England style of agriculture, the growing belief among Puritans that slavery was morally wrong, and the fact that few individuals brought there from Africa survived the transition to a much colder climate.

The word "slave" derives from *Slav*, a legacy from the Middle Ages, when the forced bondage of Slavic persons was widespread in Europe and the Islamic world. Slavery was also common in India, China, and other parts of Asia; throughout the Ottoman Empire; and among indigenous people groups in the Western Hemisphere. By the time of the American Revolution, slavery had been going on around the world for millennia, though it had largely died out in northwestern Europe by 1200. (Slavery is, of course, still commonly practiced in many nations today.)

What was unique about the enslavement of African-descended persons in the American colonies was the separateness of their existence. Rather than getting absorbed into the population of their enslavers, they lived in their own quarters, married among themselves, and had children who almost always became slaves themselves. Before long, this produced a whole class of persons with a distinct physical appearance associated with enslavement. This presented a set of special problems.

The dissonance between the reality of slavery and the ideals set forth in the Declaration of Independence wasn't lost on the Founding Fathers, but the institution was already so firmly established, especially in the South, that they couldn't see a way out that wouldn't lead to social and economic chaos. It was hoped and believed that slavery would soon die out. Unfortunately, in the generations that followed the Revolution, slavery became more and more deeply entrenched in the South, along with an ideology of institutional racism that promoted slavery not as a necessary evil but as a positive good.

A reckoning was inevitable. Thomas Jefferson recognized this as early as 1785, when he wrote about the probable consequences of slavery in his *Notes on the State of Virginia*:

> ...can the liberties of a nation be thought secure when we have removed their only firm basis, a conviction in the minds of the people that these liberties are of the gift of God? That they are not to be violated but with his wrath? Indeed I tremble for my country when I reflect that God is just: that his justice cannot sleep for ever: that considering numbers, nature and natural means only, a revolution of the wheel of fortune, an exchange of situation, is among possible events: that it may become probable by supernatural interference! The Almighty has no attribute which can take side with us in such a contest.

The War of Independence in 1780

The year 1780 was a dark one for the American Patriots. After some heartening victories over the British early in the war, the Continental Army now suffered one humiliating defeat after another—including the fall of the port city of Charlestown, the then capital of South Carolina. Major General Benjamin Lincoln—an excellent officer who, like Major General Horatio Gates, had served in the hugely successful Saratoga Campaign—was in overall command of the Continental Army in the South at the time of the siege. His defense of the city was hampered by interference from city leaders and a lack of cooperation from the Continental Navy, leading ultimately to the disastrous defeat illustrated by Melina Bryant at the Shaw dinner table with biscuits, various platters, and a dish of pickled peppers.

But all was not lost. With Lincoln now a prisoner of war, General Gates stepped into his place as commander of the Southern Department and headed to North Carolina to take charge of local militia units, the remaining Continentals in the area, and additional Continentals sent from New Jersey under Major General Johann de Kalb. The Patriots' eventual goal was to oust the British from the city of Camden in South Carolina.

It's easy to criticize unsuccessful military leaders from the comfort and safety of a quiet book-lined study, decades or centuries after their failed campaigns. Much has been written about Camden, blaming or absolving General Gates for the colossal defeat the Patriots suffered under his leadership there. My own opinion is that Gates was a gifted administrator, who served admirably as Washington's Adjutant General, but was out of his depth with a field command. His victory over Burgoyne at Saratoga in 1777 owed more to Burgoyne's inexperience, and the skill of other Patriot commanders, than to Gates's generalship. But it boosted Patriot morale at a time when a boost was desperately needed, and enhanced Patriot prestige enough to convince France to openly join the cause. By 1778, many senior officers had lost confidence in Washington and wanted Gates, the Hero of Saratoga, to replace him as Commander in Chief. The cabal failed, but the murmurings hadn't entirely ceased in 1780, and in appointing Gates to his new position as head of the Southern Department, the Continental Congress went over Washington's head.

Major General Baron Johann de Kalb, one of many European veterans to take up arms in the American Patriot cause, was sent south by Washington on 16 April 1780 at the head of 1400 Continental troops. These were drawn from the famed Maryland and Delaware units, who had already performed nobly at most of the key battles of the war. Originally, de Kalb's large force was meant to reinforce the defenders at Charlestown. By the time they received word of the city's capture, they'd come as far as Granville County in North Carolina. They remained in North Carolina, eventually reaching Deep River on 6 July. On 25 July, Gates arrived to take command.

Earlier in the summer, North Carolinian Major General Richard Caswell had mustered 1200-1500 militia soldiers from the eastern part of the state. He initially joined de Kalb at Deep River on 18 July before leaving to keep an appointment with General Rutherford, who had gathered about 350 men from western North Carolinian counties, plus some Virginia militia. Rutherford and Caswell met at the Pee Dee River and progressed south on opposite sides. On 7 August, the Patriot forces united near Lynches Creek, forming what Gates called his Grand Army, before marching toward Camden to take it back from the British.

On the surface, prospects for a Patriot victory seemed good. Gates's Grand Army wasn't as grand as he supposed—he had overestimated his numbers by quite a lot—but his combined force did outnumber that of the British and included some elite troops. But Gates failed to use his superior numbers to good advantage, and deployed the various units in a way that made no strategic sense, positioning untried militia units against distinguished British foot regiments, while placing some of the best Patriot troops, the First Maryland Brigade, behind the main body, where they could do no good in the initial assault.

It's disappointing, though hardly surprising, that when faced with so intimidating a force of well-trained, hardened soldiers, large numbers of militia soldiers fled without firing a shot. It was certainly an inauspicious start to the battle—but even then, a Patriot victory was not out of the question. There were choice units and able officers among the Continental forces capable of pulling it off.

But they didn't have a Commander in Chief—at least, not for long. General Gates fled the field early in the battle and did not return. He later claimed that his horse had panicked and ran away with him, swept away in the tide of fleeing militia. But it strains credulity that a seasoned military man of Gates's experience would be powerless to control his mount. At the very least, he could have turned around and come back.

In Gates's absence, there was no one to direct the battle, and no one to order a retreat once it was clear that a retreat was needed. The Delaware and Maryland regiments were mown down without mercy. By the time the dust settled, the Continental Army in the South was destroyed.

A Long Aside About General Richard Caswell

It's common practice for leaders at the top to pin a big failure on a convenient scapegoat several rungs down the command structure, and General Caswell of the North Carolina militia made an easy target. Militia forces in general were held in low regard by Continental forces (more on this below), and Gates seems to have held them in particular disdain.

According to the narrative that soon emerged, and is still widely believed by historical writers to this day, Caswell's responsibility for the loss at Camden started months before the battle itself. It was said that Caswell deprived the Continentals of sustenance by stripping the countryside bare in advance of their coming. This is an odd accusation, considering that militia troops had to eat just as the Continentals did, and also demonstrably false in light of the routes taken by the various forces. It wasn't Caswell's responsibility to provision the Continentals. He had his own men to feed. Caswell's men did thresh a great quantity of wheat for the approaching Continentals prior to leaving Deep River, but this was apparently intercepted by the Virginia militia and never reached Gates.

It was also said that Caswell defied de Kalb's repeated orders to join his militia force to de Kalb's Continentals. But it's unclear whether de Kalb, or Gates, had the authority to order Caswell to do anything. As a state militia general, Caswell was under no obligation to take orders from the Continentals unless instructed to do so by his own governor, Abner Nash. This may seem like a minor point, but protocols exist for a reason, in military and civilian life, and we ignore them at our peril. Furthermore, Caswell and de Kalb were in fact together at Deep River for a full week before Caswell left to meet Rutherford. The only primary source I could find that supported the narrative of Caswell's insubordination to de Kalb was a letter written by Major Thomas Pinckney in 1822 in defense of General Gates. (Pinckney appears to have been responding to another letter, highly critical of Gates's conduct at and leading up to the Battle of Camden, written in 1780 by Colonel Otho Holland Williams of the Maryland Line. Apparently the Williams letter had recently been printed, reviving the subject of the defeat, and who was to blame for it.) Pinckney stated that Williams himself, who served as Adjutant General under de Kalb and then under Gates, made the same criticisms about Caswell's conduct. I could find no mention of this in the text of Williams's 1780 letter, so I searched the Otho Holland Williams Papers, the sum of which the Maryland Historical society has obligingly put online. I couldn't find a single mention of Caswell's name. On the other hand, the Colonial and State Records of North Carolina contain letters between

Caswell and de Kalb, showing that they were in active communication and apparently on good terms.

The deeper I dug, the more it appeared to me that Caswell's supposed incompetence was nothing more than a wild accusation by Gates, supported by Pinckney, who falsely cited Williams and de Kalb, both of whom were long dead and couldn't set the record straight. This version of events has been accepted without question by generations of historians ever since.

It may seem that I have spent an inordinate amount of time defending the reputation of a militia general who has no personal connection to me and who is unknown to most Americans today. But I see it as a prime example of a troubling tendency to accept and promulgate spurious and defamatory narratives without consulting primary sources. The image that emerges of Caswell—and of the militia in general—is one of insubordination, irresponsibility, and incompetence. And that's just not fair. Richard Caswell served his country with honor. He rebuffed the Loyalists at Moore's Creek Bridge in February of 1776, saving the Patriot cause in the state from an early demise. The legislature honored him by giving him the highest rank in the North Carolina Militia, that of Major General. He was the first governor of the new state of North Carolina and served the maximum three terms. He served two terms in the Continental Congress, co-authored much of the North Carolina State Constitution, and essentially wrote the new state's militia laws. He deserves to be remembered for these accomplishments.

Aftermath

The Battle of Camden is considered the worst defeat in the American Revolutionary War. It was certainly the low point in a year that had already been heavy with loss.

But 1780 wasn't finished yet.

With Gates in disgrace, Washington was allowed to choose a new commander for the Southern Department, and he chose his most trusted general, Nathanael Greene—described by Fergus Shaw as an asthmatic Quaker with a limp. Having no prior military experience, Greene got all his preliminary knowledge of warfare from books, but he was a quick study. And although his physical limitations initially kept him from being made an officer in the state militia unit that he had personally helped to establish, his outstanding abilities couldn't be ignored for long. Eventually he was put in overall command of the Rhode Island regiments, and later rose to the rank of Major General in the Continental Army.

The American Revolutionary War is sometimes portrayed as a conflict between well-trained but hidebound red-coated soldiers on one side, stupidly lining up in rows to get shot, and scrappy sharp-shooting militia soldiers on the other, cunningly taking aim from behind cover. In fact, there were regular and militia units on both sides. The regulars were full-time professional soldiers with uniforms. Militiamen were citizen soldiers who provided their own weapons and equipment. They served in rotations, ordinarily of a few months' duration. Sometimes they deserted, returning home ahead of schedule to work their trades, tend their crops, and protect their families—not unreasonable, considering the necessity of making a living and the danger of enemy raids. Often they were frustrated by inactivity at a muster when there was so much work to be done at home; as always in the military, there was a lot of "hurry up and wait."

Militia units did train and drill, but not enough. And because of the Patriots' chronic shortage of powder and shot, Patriot militiamen rarely practiced with live ammunition, which meant they had little or no experience performing the complicated loading sequence under the strain, smoke, and noise of battle. It's not surprising that when fired upon by a flesh-and-blood enemy, many of them fled.

As for British regulars standing in lines, naively presenting vivid red targets for their more circumspect Patriot foes, this is a gross oversimplification. Standard practice for the time on both sides was to form battle lines and fire away. The inaccuracy of muskets, with their round balls and unrifled barrels, meant that the only way to do any appreciable damage to the enemy was to send a solid barrage of bullets into their line, while keeping your own line together. Brightly colored uniforms helped soldiers distinguish friend from foe in the thick black smoke of battle.

There were several rifle units on the Patriot side, including the 11th Virginia Regiment, led by Daniel Morgan, and the Pennsylvania Rifle Regiment. (The British and Loyalist forces also employed rifle units, but not as many as the Patriots.) Rifles were more accurate than muskets, but took even longer

to load (the Winchester repeating rifle was still almost a century in the future). When cover was available, riflemen did make use of it, often with excellent results, as at the Charlotte Town battle that Leithan Stratten describes
to Fergus Shaw and Tavish MacGregor. (The British Army did go on deploying in lines and wearing bright uniforms for longer than was useful—as late
as the start of the Boer War.)

Throughout the American Revolutionary War, the Continental Army
disparaged the Patriot militia for laziness, unreliability, and cowardice. And
after Gates's Grand Army was destroyed at Camden, the militia forces were
the only fighters the Southern Department had left. It was at this low point
that the militia forces came into their own, and the tide of the war in the
South began to turn. In the absence of senior leadership, junior officers had
the freedom to make decisions in the field. They were operating on home
turf. They could make lightning strikes against the enemy, then melt away.
While not engaged in active campaigns, they could go home to their families
and livelihoods, then assemble again when needed. In short, the decentral-
ization that followed the debacle at Camden allowed militia units to do what
they were best at, rather than try to conform to a mold that they'd never been
trained for.

And so the dark year of 1780 ended with a huge Patriot victory at the
Battle of Kings Mountain, fought by militia troops on both sides. The start
of 1781 brought another victory at the Battle of Cowpens, followed by the
nail-biting Race to the Dan, which the Patriots won on 17 January 1781 under the leadership of Daniel Morgan. Interestingly, Morgan, who served in
both the militia and the Continental Army during the war, had fought in the
Saratoga Campaign along with Gates and Lincoln.

Time would fail me to do justice to the further exploits of Morgan, the
Old Wagoner, or of other militia officers in the South, with or without cool
nicknames—Francis Marion, the Swamp Fox; Thomas Sumter, the Carolina
Gamecock; Andrew Pickens, the Wizard Owl; Isaac Shelby, Elijah Clarke,
Francis Nash, and John Sevier.

The surrender of Cornwallis at Yorktown happens offstage in my story,
but it involves a commander previously mentioned. Cornwallis did not attend the surrender ceremony in person but sent his second-in-command,
General Charles O'Hara, to turn over Cornwallis's sword. O'Hara first of-

fered the sword not to Washington, but to Washington's French ally, the Comte de Rochambeau. (No doubt it was less galling to surrender to a French nobleman than to the American upstart.) Rochambeau directed O'Hara to give the sword to Washington himself, whereupon Washington deferred to his own second-in-command—Major General Benjamin Lincoln, whose own surrender at Melina Bryant's city in 1780 had been made so needlessly humiliating. Over a year after the Patriot troops had been marched ignominiously out of Charlestown without being given the honors of war, Lincoln accepted the sword of the overall commander of British forces in the Southern Theatre.

In the end, the War for Independence was largely a war of attrition. Passage over the Atlantic in those days took anywhere from six weeks to several months, making it impossible for the deployed British troops and the authorities back home to exchange updates and orders in a timely manner. The entrance of France on the Patriot side escalated the conflict into a global one, stretching British resources thin. The Empire was overextended, and the American Patriots had home field advantage. They had only to hold on long enough for the British to give up.

The Patriot victory at Yorktown was the beginning of the end of the American Revolutionary War, but nearly two years would pass before the peace was formally settled in the Treaty of Paris. During that time, an ultimate Patriot victory was by no means a foregone conclusion. There were battles yet to be fought, as well as Tory conspiracies that could have undone all the progress toward independence. But that's a story for another day.

Bibliography

Borick, Carl P. *A Gallant Defense: The Siege of Charleston, 1780.*

Chapelle, Howard I. *The History of American Sailing Ships.* New York: Bonanza Books, 1982.

Conser, Walter H., Jr, and Cain, Robert J. *Presbyterians in North Carolina: Race, Politics and Religious Identity in Historical Perspective.* Knoxville: The University of Tennessee Press, 2012.

Dunkerly, Robert M. *Redcoats on the Cape Fear: The Revolutionary War in Southeastern North Carolina.* Jefferson: McFarland & Company, Inc., 2012.

Fraser, Walter J., Jr. *Charleston! Charleston! The History of a Southern City.* Columbia: University of South Carolina, 1991.

Hemphill, C. Dallett. *Bowing to Necessities: A History of Manners in America, 1620-1860.* New York: Oxford University Press, Inc., 1999.

Howell, Andrew J. *A History of the First Presbyterian Church, Wilmington, North Carolina.* Wilmington: First Presbyterian Church Committee on History, 1951.

Lee, Henry (Light Horse Harry). *The American Revolution in the South.* New York: Arno Press, Inc., 1969.

Lee, Henry, Jr. *The Campaign of 1781 in the Carolinas.* Philadelphia: Quadrangle Books, Inc., 1962.

Lennon, Donald R., and Kellam, Ida Brooks, ed. *The Wilmington Town Book, 1743-1778.* Raleigh: Division of Archives and History, North Carolina Department of Cultural Resources, 1973.

McKoy, Elizabeth Francenia. *Early Wilmington Block by Block From 1733 On.*

O'Donnell, Patrick K. *Washington's Immortals: The Untold Story of an Elite Regiment Who Changed the Course of the Revolution.* New York: Atlantic Monthly Press, 2016.

Pedlow, Franda D. *The Story of Brunswick Town and Fort Anderson.* Wilmington: Dram Tree Books, 2005.

Piecuch, Jim. *The Battle of Camden: A Documentary History.* Charleston: The History Press, 2006.

Schaw, Janet. *Journal of a Lady of Quality: Being the Narrative of a Journey from Scotland to the West Indies, North Carolina, and Portugal, in the years 1774 to 1776.* Edited by Evangeline Walker Andrews and Charles McLean Andrews. Lincoln: University of Nebraska Press, 2005.

Smith, David. *Camden 1780: The Annihilation of Gates' Grand Army.* Oxford: Osprey Publishing, 2016.

Still, William N., Jr. *North Carolina's Revolutionary War Navy.* Raleigh: North Carolina Department of Cultural Resources, Division of Archives and History, 1976.

Van Doren, Mark, ed. *Travels of William Bartram.* New York: Dover Publications, Inc., 1955.

Watson, Alan D. *Society in Colonial North Carolina.* Raleigh: Office of Archives and History, North Carolina Department of Cultural Resources, 1996.

———. *Wilmington, North Carolina, to 1861.* Jefferson: McFarland & Company, Inc., 2003.

Don't miss out!

Visit the website below and you can sign up to receive emails whenever Kit Hawthorne publishes a new book. There's no charge and no obligation.

https://books2read.com/r/B-A-WVWY-IYITC

Connecting independent readers to independent writers.

Also by Kit Hawthorne

Cape Fear Legacy
Carolina Crossing
Treason Trail
Savanna Storm

Watch for more at https://kithawthorne.com/.

About the Author

A lifelong resident of the American South, Kit Hawthorne makes her home on a Texas farm that has been in her husband's family for seven generations. She spent several years as a semiprofessional musician, singing, composing, and playing Irish pennywhistle in a Celtic folk band. All those ballads and boat songs awakened in her a love for a Scottish heritage that spans both sides of the Atlantic. She's an avid reader, especially of history, biography, mystery, theology, and romance, and enjoys logging her reads (and plotting her life) in her Bullet Journal. She also enjoys drawing, sewing, quilting, knitting, and restoring old furniture to beauty and usefulness.

Read more at https://kithawthorne.com/.

www.ingramcontent.com/pod-product-compliance
Lightning Source LLC
Chambersburg PA
CBHW030428160726
47991CB00005B/1637